Praise for
LORA LEIGH
and her novels

"Leigh draws readers into her stories and takes them on a sensual roller coaster." —*Love Romances & More*

"Leigh writes wonderfully straightforward and emotional stories with characters that jump off the page."
—*The Road to Romance*

"Fraught with tension from the first page to the last . . . Will have you glued to the edge of your seat."
—*Fallen Angel Reviews*

"Blistering sexuality and eroticism . . . Bursting with passion and drama . . . Enthralls and excites from beginning to end." —*Romance Reviews Today*

"A scorcher with sex scenes that blister the pages."
—*A Romance Review*

"Explosive . . . A perfect blend of sexual tension and suspense." —*Sensual Romance Reviews*

"An emotional read." —*The Best Reviews*

"Hot sex, snappy dialogue, and kick-butt action."
—*Romantic Times* (Top Pick)

"Ms. Leigh is one of my favorite authors."
—*Erotic-Escapades*

"Electrically charged, erotic, and just a sinfully good read!" —*Joyfully Reviewed*

"Wow! This was one hot . . . romance. The lovemaking is scorching." —*Just Erotic Romance Reviews*

Nauti Nights

Lora Leigh

BERKLEY SENSATION, NEW YORK

THE BERKLEY PUBLISHING GROUP
Published by the Penguin Group
Penguin Group (USA) Inc.
375 Hudson Street, New York, New York 10014, USA

Penguin Group (Canada), 90 Eglinton Avenue East, Suite 700, Toronto, Ontario M4P 2Y3, Canada
(a division of Pearson Penguin Canada Inc.)
Penguin Books Ltd., 80 Strand, London WC2R 0RL, England
Penguin Group Ireland, 25 St. Stephen's Green, Dublin 2, Ireland (a division of Penguin Books Ltd.)
Penguin Group (Australia), 250 Camberwell Road, Camberwell, Victoria 3124, Australia
(a division of Pearson Australia Group Pty. Ltd.)
Penguin Books India Pvt. Ltd., 11 Community Centre, Panchsheel Park, New Delhi—110 017, India
Penguin Group (NZ), 67 Apollo Drive, Rosedale, North Shore 0632, New Zealand
(a division of Pearson New Zealand Ltd.)
Penguin Books (South Africa) (Pty.) Ltd., 24 Sturdee Avenue, Rosebank, Johannesburg 2196,
South Africa

Penguin Books Ltd., Registered Offices: 80 Strand, London WC2R 0RL, England

This is a work of fiction. Names, characters, places, and incidents either are the product of the author's imagination or are used fictitiously, and any resemblance to actual persons, living or dead, business establishments, events, or locales is entirely coincidental. The publisher does not have any control over and does not assume any responsibility for author or third-party websites or their content.

NAUTI NIGHTS

A Berkley Sensation Book / published by arrangement with the author

PRINTING HISTORY
Berkley Heat trade paperback edition / November 2007
Berkley Sensation trade paperback edition / August 2009
Berkley Sensation mass-market edition / December 2010

ISBN: 978-0-425-23817-2

BERKLEY® SENSATION
Berkley Sensation Books are published by The Berkley Publishing Group,
a division of Penguin Group (USA) Inc.,
375 Hudson Street, New York, New York 10014.
BERKLEY® SENSATION and the "B" design are trademarks of Penguin Group (USA) Inc.

PRINTED IN THE UNITED STATES OF AMERICA

10 9 8 7 6 5 4 3 2 1

To the proud, the brave, and the daring.
You make the rules, you break the rules,
and you forge the paths
the rest of us only dream of taking.

PROLOGUE

―

Somerset, Kentucky
Lake Cumberland

Eight Years Ago

Crista Jansen stared at the bed and the man sprawled across it in horror as she stumbled back, the knowledge of the mistake she had made the night before pounding through her head like the strike of a tambourine. Over and over again.

She covered her mouth with her hand, her eyes wide, her stomach churning in sick realization of exactly how huge this mistake was. The mistake and the man. He took up almost every inch of space on the mattress, his powerful legs sprawled, his strong arms moving restlessly as though searching—for her.

And he would be. The man was inexhaustible. A veritable sex machine with no off switch once he got started. And she should know now—she and every other woman he had ever had in his bed.

She could feel the memory of the night before on every inch of her body: her breasts, swollen and sensitive from his lips suckling at the tender tips, her lips abraded and tender from his kisses, and between her thighs—

That memory nearly brought her to her knees as her gaze slipped to his thighs, to the half-erect flesh that appeared threatening and overlarge, even though he wasn't fully erect.

Yet he had fit inside her. Stretching her wide, often in a pleasure bordering pain. He had managed to work every inch of that iron-hard flesh inside her, and he had destroyed her with it. Pounding inside her with a force that shook the bed and shook her senses, throwing her into one orgasm after another, bringing such pleasure that she had been unwilling to deny it. Unwilling to deny him anything, even at the end.

Her hand covered her mouth as tears filled her eyes. Oh God, she hadn't let him do those things to her, had she? Lifted her rear for him and begged for more as his tongue caressed forbidden flesh, then screamed in pleasure and in pain as the head of his cock began to work inside the heavily lubricated little hole.

He had marked her. He had taken her virginity, and he had taken her sanity. When he had finished marking the wet depths of her pussy, he had turned her to her stomach and marked her rear as well. With heated slaps, with diabolically talented fingers, and finally, with the deep, controlled thrusts of his cock.

He had taken her anally, and she had let him. And as she had lain beneath him, fighting for breath, he had told her how much better it could be. How three cocks would take her, move against her, pleasure her.

And with those words he had destroyed a part of her soul. She had dreamed of sweet, gentle words. Endearments. Soft kisses and maybe at least a promise to see her again. She hadn't expected him to tell her that soon, so soon, she would have his cousins as well.

They shared their women; she knew that. It wasn't just rumor, wasn't just hinted at. Alex, her brother, had warned her repeatedly that the stories didn't come close to the reality of the sexual lifestyle Dawg and his cousins lived, and she hadn't heeded that warning.

Shaking in fear, she quickly jerked her shorts and T-shirt on, not bothering to search for her panties and bra. God only knew where they were. She had to get out of there before he awoke, before he realized how incredibly stupid she had been.

He had been drunk. He might not remember. God, he'd been drunk; just getting him back to the houseboat had taken every ounce of strength she possessed. But she had understood the drunkenness. His parents had just died in a horrifying wreck; he had buried them, stood over their graves, and known they were gone from him forever. He deserved a few hours of freedom from the pain.

If only she hadn't been stupid enough to go looking for him when she learned he wasn't with Rowdy and Natches. If only she hadn't grown worried about him, borrowed her brother's car, and gone searching for him.

But she had, and she had known better. She should have sent Alex after him. She should have sent anyone after him but herself. Because she had known how it would end, and she had known where he would want it to go.

Rather than accepting that, she had fooled herself into thinking that taking her, realizing her innocence, her feelings for him, that he would show a spark of possessiveness. Just a moment's hesitancy in sharing her with other men, with seeing another man touching her, taking her.

She was crying as she eased the lock back on the glass door that led to the lower deck of the houseboat. It was still early. The mist was thick on the lake, surrounding the houseboats and creating a luminescent, otherworldly air that cut into her soul. Touching him had been like touching power itself. He was huge, so tall and broad, his body leanly muscled and graceful. His chest lightly furred, the crisp curls had raked her nipples as he thrust into her. When his lips hadn't been suckling them. But it was more than just the physical. That power had seeped inside her, filled her with emotions she had tried to hold in check, tried to protect herself from. She loved him. He made her heart clench and her soul ache. He had the power to bring her to her knees or to make her fly in ecstasy with only a glance from those odd green eyes of his.

And when he touched her . . . When he touched her, he'd had the power to make her forget that she knew exactly who and what Dawg Mackay was.

As she slipped down the docks, she kept her head down, kept her eyes on the floating walkway, and prayed no one saw her. Dawn was barely breaking over the mountains now; most of the inhabitants of the houseboats wouldn't be moving around for hours yet.

She could get lucky. She could escape, and no one would ever know she had spent the night with one of the most notorious sex gods in five counties. One of three.

She swiped at her tears. She hated crying. She had learned years ago that no good came of it. It only succeeded in making her feel worse than ever.

But she couldn't stop the tears any more than she could stop the pain. Dawg had been chasing her all summer. Those light celadon green eyes framed by the thick, inky black lashes, so pale they mesmerized her and pierced into her soul.

His smile was always slow and sexy, knowing. As though he were aware of the ache that centered between her thighs and tormented her long into the night. As though he knew how often she dreamed of feeling him against her, touching him, being touched.

The dream had turned into far more than she had expected. Part nightmare, part temptation. Forcing herself out of that bed had been next to impossible. She had wanted him to flow over her; she wanted to take his cock into her mouth again and practice what he had taught her.

She wanted to hear him moan her name again, watch his eyes darken. She wanted to run and hide and make certain she never let herself become so vulnerable to him ever again.

And it was breaking her heart. Walking away, turning her back on the only man her young heart had ever raced to was killing her. It hurt physically. It made her stomach cramp. It made her heart feel like a raw, aching wound.

She wanted to hide. She wanted to hide and nurse the pain and the fear. She was terrified. Terrified of the things she knew Dawg could make her feel and terrified of the knowledge that she would do anything, commit any act he asked of her, for just one more chance to take another hot, mind-numbing kiss from his perfect lips.

She would become no more than one of a long line of

Nauti playthings, and that would destroy her. She could never share him with another woman, and on the same coin, she could not have survived, emotionally, being shared.

As she moved quickly along the floating dock and over the bridge that stretched to the shore, the sound of a motorcycle moving into the parking lot beyond had her heart racing with dread.

She hadn't just destroyed her own dreams but perhaps a friendship as well. Dawg and her brother were close friends. When the Mackay cousins weren't busy sharing their women, Alex had invariably been in their company until he joined the military. And even now, when he returned home on leave, he spent a lot of time with Dawg and the other Mackay cousins.

This could destroy that friendship, and Alex didn't have many friends.

The implications of the past night were racing through her soul with a power that had sobs tearing from her chest. She reached the car she had borrowed at the same time her brother pulled up to the vehicle on his motorcycle.

The powerful throb of the motor eased, then went silent as Alex extended one long leg, bracing his foot on the pavement as the other propped on the foot pedal on the other side.

He wiped his hand over his face slowly before staring out at the houseboats for a long, silent moment. This was her older brother; he had all but raised her. Her parents rarely had time for anyone but the store and themselves and whatever scheme her father had for making more money. It had left Alex with the responsibility of raising the daughter they never seemed to know what to do with.

And now he had to face the fact that his sister had obviously just had sex with not just his best friend but a sexual legend in the county. And Dawg wasn't even twenty-five yet.

She stood still, silent, unable to stop crying as he stared back at her silently. His gray eyes were heavy with sadness, his regal, handsome face drawn into a weary expression.

"Did you tell him no?" he finally asked her gently.

She shook her head. She hadn't even thought to tell him no.

He turned his head, staring toward Dawg's houseboat in resignation. She could see his anger in the tight, controlled line of his lips, in the flash of dark emotion in his eyes.

His jaw bunched with it as the lean muscles in his shoulders and arms flexed warningly.

"Did you want to tell him no?"

She shook her head again, shaking beneath the knowledge in his eyes.

She couldn't have told Dawg no if her life had depended on it. Each touch, each kiss had been a fantasy come to life.

He nodded slowly. "Let's go home then. We can talk about it there. No sense in making things worse by lingering out here long enough for anyone to see you. If you want to keep this quiet, you're going to have to pretend it didn't happen." His gaze sharpened then. "Do you want to keep it quiet, Crista?"

"Yes." She bit her trembling lips as she swiped at her tears. "Oh God, Alex. I just want to get out of here."

"Do you have your keys?"

She dug them out of the pocket of her shorts and quickly unlocked the door before jerking it open.

"Crista." His voice, despite its gentleness, resonated with a dark, hidden fury. "Was he alone?"

Her hand gripped the doorframe as she met his gaze. "It was just Dawg and me, Alex. I swear." This time. She knew if it happened again, if she dared to let it ever repeat, then it wouldn't be just Dawg. And when that happened, Dawg would make an enemy of her brother for life.

"Let's go home, Crista." He breathed out roughly. "I'll follow you."

As they pulled from the driveway, she couldn't help the sob that tore from her chest again or the fear that rolled through her.

She had cried last night when he touched her the first time. Because she had dreamed of it for so long. Because he had stroked more than just her body, kissed more than her lips. He had touched that inner core of her being that she hadn't realized could be possessed. When his fingers had parted the folds between her thighs and his expression had hardened with lust, he had wet his fingers on her juices, then brought them to his lips, his lashes lowering sensually at the taste of her.

A second later he had dipped his fingers between her thighs again and brought them to her lips. And she hadn't been able to deny him. She hadn't been able to deny him a single thing in the hours they had spent touching and tasting each other.

Everything he had asked of her, she had given. God help her if he ever had her that weak again. She would never be able to deny him. Never be able to hold on to her pride or her soul. Because if he shared her, he would break her heart forever. But if he asked it of her, she knew she would never be strong enough to tell him no.

"God! You're so fucking hot. So tight. So tight, Crista. So tight that when Rowdy and Natches get their dicks inside you, you'll destroy us all . . ." She hadn't heard the rest of the statement; her mind had shut down. Her soul had withered in her chest.

She had to get away from Dawg, because if she didn't, he would own her soul. And that terrified her more than the thought of leaving her home ever had. She would never be able to defend herself. She knew his touch now, knew his kiss, and she knew beyond a shadow of a doubt that she would never love anyone as she loved Dawg Mackay.

ONE

Somerset, Kentucky

Eight Years Later

It was a nightmare.

No, it wasn't a nightmare, because she was pretty damned sure she was awake. And in nightmares, bullets weren't real. They weren't real, and they weren't exploding around the warehouse like hellish fireflies destroying everything they lodged inside.

Nightmares came with a certain understanding that it was a dream, *not real*. This was definitely real, and if something really good didn't happen very soon, then she was going to have holes in her body that were not supposed to be there.

She fought to hold back her screams as bullets whizzed over her head again, popping in the wood crates around her and sending a shower of wood chips and shattered glass from inside around her head.

This was bad. Very bad. She stared around, wide-eyed and dazed, as she scrambled around more boxes, more crates, fighting for as much protection between her and the bullets as she could find.

Crista Jansen was certain her horoscope hadn't said anything about bullets today. Something about dark knights and ill-advised trips, but there had been nothing in there about bullets.

She would have remembered.

She would have changed her plans.

Oh boy, would she have changed her plans.

Scuttling behind what she hoped was a very thickly packed crate, she covered her head with her arms as glass sprayed around her.

Those weren't just regular bullets. Those were fast bullets. Automatic? Uzi? Something. The kind that spat fire as they pelleted out dozens of rounds at a time. And she knew because the red flashes of light in the otherwise dark interior of the warehouse were a pretty good clue.

A terrified *squak*, a cross between a squeak and a squawk, fell from her lips as chips of wood exploded from the sides of the crate she found to hide behind.

They were serious out there. People were killing people, and she was caught in the crossfire and wondering how the hell she was going to get out of this one.

She knew this was a bad idea.

She knew. She had felt that sick feeling in her gut the minute she stepped into the cavernous warehouse and realized the lights didn't work. But had she, dumb ass that she was, backed out and left? Oh, hell no, she had just pulled her penlight from her purse and trudged merrily on her way, looking for that stupid box. She told the delivery company to deliver to her home, not here. Yet when she returned home from work, what had she found? An official notice that her package had been dropped off at their local distribution warehouse and why, lookie, there had been the magical key to open the damned locker it was in.

Well, guess what? There's no locker here, she told herself sarcastically. No locker, but plenty of bullets singing a macabre tune through the darkness.

So now, rather than collecting her belongings, she was just trying to stay alive. When did fate decide to bust Crista Jansen's ass? For God's sake, hadn't she had enough bad luck in the past eight years?

This was all Dawg's fault, she decided. Every bit of it. He

lived and he breathed and because of it, fate hated her. Fate was female, right? It was probably jealous. There could be no other explanation.

This was so bad.

"Where did the fucking girl go—?" a harsh, accented voice muttered roughly.

Okay she was the only girl she knew of in this stupid place. She had only heard male orders, commands, and screams since hell had erupted around her.

Crista turned, crawling on her hands and bare knees—she should have worn jeans instead of one of her few good skirts—trying her best to get as far away from the mayhem and bloodshed as possible.

She knew not to come in here, she reminded herself. Remember that sick feeling? That panicked feeling? Hadn't she learned years ago it meant bad things? Get the hell out of Dodge type things?

She had been feeling it more and more lately. And this was just another event in a long string of very odd events. Clothes that would go missing and then turn back up in her closet, freshly washed. The feeling of being watched and strangers who thought they knew her.

Hadn't she told her brother last week that something was wrong? And speaking of screwy brothers, where the hell was hers? Damn it, Alex *would* have to disappear when she needed him most.

Military mission be damned. She didn't need him across the world, unavailable; she needed him here, now, getting her ass out of trouble.

And she hadn't told him good-bye when she talked to him.

Strange that she should remember that as she wedged herself into a dark, musty corner surrounded by crates and backed by a cement support beam.

She hadn't told Alex good-bye when she talked to him last week. She had just hung up on him because he had said something totally idiotic.

Something along the lines of "Call Dawg."

Oh yeah, right. She was going to do that.

He should have known better than to make such an insane

suggestion. Where the hell had his mind gone in the past eight years? Had he forgotten how hard it had been for her to stay in Somerset that summer? Dawg had chased her with steady determination for months before the rest of her world had collapsed around her. Even though it was more than obvious that he hadn't remembered that one stolen night she had spent in his bed, he had still chased after her with a tenacity that reminded her why they called him Dawg.

Because he never let up. He never gave up.

She flinched as a projectile tore through the side of the crate that she had hoped was thick enough to protect her. She stared at the hole it made coming out mere inches from her upraised knees and gagged.

It was nearly the size of her fist.

"Get down!"

She heard the male voice screaming from a distance as another bullet ricocheted against the cement beam, inches above her head.

She went down. All the way down. And fought to get through the small crack between the support beam and the heavy crate, wondering how the hell a bullet could penetrate it when she couldn't even move it.

Clawing desperately at the side of the crate, she pressed, pushed, wedging herself into the minute amount of space and almost—almost managing to escape.

She screamed, terror racing through her, freezing her blood to ice as hard fingers grabbed her hair and pulled her back, jerking her back by the thick, dark strands and sending agonizing pain racing through her neck.

Her hands reached back, her nails clawing at the wrist behind her, fighting, struggling as she was dragged from the only means of escape in sight.

"Stupid whore! Where's my fucking money? I teach you to betray me, *puta*!"

She was jerked around, staring back in horror at the dark eyes and pitted face of what she was certain had to be a demon.

Stringy black hair fell over his narrow brow, his flat cheekbones were ruddy with rage, his dark brown eyes lit almost red with fury. And he had a gun.

Crista watched in slow motion. She had heard that expression, events passing in slow motion, and hadn't believed it until now.

Now she was watching it. Tearless. Breathless. Watching in slow motion as his arm raised. One hand pushed her against the cement support, the other was coming up. Up.

But the shot came too soon.

One minute she was watching that black weapon level up to her, the next a shower of red exploded around her as her hands flew to her face and a scream tore from her as his body jerked forward, then fell.

Right at her feet.

"Goddamn you, Crista!"

She recognized that voice.

Jerking her head up from the sight of the bloody mess her assailant's face was now, she stared back at the dark figure, Law Enforcement emblazoned across the bulletproof jacket he was jerking from his broad chest.

"Put it on, damn you!" His voice was a hard rasp, guttural, animalistic, as he jerked her around and strapped her into the vest until the black Velcro strips were holding it snugly to her chest and back.

"Let's go!" Hard gloved fingers wrapped around her arm as, with a shove, the crate she had been fighting to move was pushed back as though it were no more than a heavy box. "Move it!"

He pushed her through the opening before gripping her arm again and pulling her through the dark.

"What's going on?" She breathed out roughly. She couldn't scream, she couldn't cry. All she could do was follow Dawg.

And she knew it was Dawg. Those brilliant celadon green eyes, that dark, male, honeyed voice. No other man sounded like Dawg. No other man moved like him or smelled like him.

And besides, it was just her dumb luck. He was here. She was here. Hell was erupting around her. Fate was laughing her ass off, and it was all Dawg's fault.

"Shut up!" he snarled, not even bothering to so much as try to explain as he pushed her through the darkness. "Keep your mouth shut, keep your head down, and if God is in a good mood today, I might be able to save your ass."

Save her ass?

"But I was just here—"

"Just fucking save it." He pushed her against something cement, the dim light that spilled in from overhead windows emphasizing the enraged flames in his eyes. "I just killed a man for you, princess. A man worth a hell of a lot more alive than he was dead. Now shut your goddamned mouth and do exactly what I say. Exactly. Or I'll slap cuffs on you and haul you in so fast, you won't have time to twitch that pretty ass of yours."

Before she could process the fact that they were racing from the back of the warehouse, Dawg was lifting her into the backseat of his black four-by-four double cab pickup. He pulled the bulletproof vest from her and jerked it back on, his eyes glowing with rage as his fingers tangled in her hair. He stared down at her, remorseless, before gripping the bottom of her T-shirt and wiping it roughly over her lower face.

Blood. She shuddered at the thought. Someone else's blood stained her now. Then Dawg forced her head back a second before his lips covered hers.

Gunfire receded. Reality dimmed. The world narrowed down to his lips slanted over hers, his tongue pressing between them as hers opened. Electricity sparked, exploded, and sizzled through her head with a dazzling display of color as pleasure tore through her system.

Eight years without him. Without this. Without the hunger that consumed and burned away the ragged wound in her soul that leaving him eight years before had left inside her.

Her hands curled against the bulletproof vest, and a whimper that shocked her vibrated from her throat as he tore his lips from hers as quickly as he had taken them.

She stared up at him, wide-eyed, shocked, as he glared back at her.

"Where did you park?" he snapped out.

Her lips trembled as she fought to drag in enough air to answer him.

"The back lot," she whispered as he jerked her purse open and before she could stop him, pulled her keys from inside.

"You're damned lucky your car wasn't here when this started, Crista," he snarled. "Luckier than you'll ever know. Now, lie down. Don't move. Don't speak. Don't twitch. So help me God, if you give yourself away in here, I'll toss you into a cell so deep and so dark you won't know up or down. Do we have that clear?"

She tried to nod, just as she was trying to breathe. A second later he was pushing her to the seat, pressing her cheek into the fine black leather with a harsh order to "Stay," before the door slammed and he was gone.

And she was alone. She could still hear the gunfire, but it was distant and easing away. It was replaced with shouted orders, vehicles moving, and strident calls.

Inside the truck she shuddered, drew her knees to her chest, and tried to still the shaking in her body.

Shock. She knew she must be having some kind of shock reaction, because it was the middle of the summer. She shouldn't be freezing so much she was shaking; breathing shouldn't be hard. And God help her if she puked in Dawg's truck. He would probably shoot her himself.

She forced herself to breathe slowly, evenly, to draw in the scent of Dawg that permeated his truck and filled her senses with memories. Memories she had fought to forget for eight long years.

The feel of his thighs between hers as he parted them and lowered himself to her. Watching as one large hand gripped the shaft of his cock, nudging it against the hot, wet curls between her thighs.

"Wax your pussy," he had growled, *"so I can see your soft flesh gripping my dick."*

Her womb clenched at the memory, as clear now as it had been the morning after.

And he didn't even remember it. She still had to fight back the rage and the pain of that one. The bastard. He had seen her two days later and had looked right through her as she stood in her parents' convenience store, her heart in her throat, certain that he had come for her.

But he hadn't. He had smiled and flirted, and on his arm hung some stupid twit blond bimbo who cooed over his muscles as he paid for ice and snacks.

He had made some cheerful comment to Crista about her hair, and she glared at him. He had frowned, tried again, and she had turned her back and left Alex to take care of him. Because she couldn't look at him; she couldn't bear remembering and knowing that not so much as a glimmer of that night remained in his memory. Knowing, that if he had her again, they wouldn't be alone.

And then, weeks later, the knowledge that she hadn't escaped that night without repercussions. She had carried his child.

Her initial reaction had been one of anger, of resentment. He was partying, enjoying his life and his women and the dirty little sex games he and his cousins played, and she was pregnant.

But within days that anger had stilled. The knowledge that she would always have a part of him had consumed her young mind, her heart. The heart she had given Dawg on a sultry summer night. And that happiness had built, filling her, glowing inside her.

Until three months to the day after he had taken her. The day she had lost the child she had grown to love so deeply. She had left the clinic Alex had taken her to, packed her bags, and left for Virginia with friends who had been visiting that week.

And here she was, eight years later, her fingers curled into the leather of his truck seat, shaking, terrified as the sound of gunfire finally eased away and shouted commands filled the night instead.

Suddenly, the implications of her very precarious position slammed inside her head. She was at the scene of an obvious raid of some sort. Wasn't that what they called it? A raid? A sting? And she had been right smack-dab in the middle of it.

Which meant she was about to be right smack-dab in the middle of a whole lot of suspicion.

FUBAR. That's what this entire fucking night had turned into. Fucked up beyond all repair, and it was all his own damned fault.

He stared into the shadowed expanse of the warehouse parking lot, his brows lowered, trying to make sense of what he had done and why. The why of it more than anything else.

What had crashed through the hard core of training and beliefs in what he was doing long enough to rush Crista from the warehouse and hide her? What had made him risk his own soul this way for a woman?

Not just any woman though: Crista. The woman that had invaded his dreams for longer than he wanted to admit. The woman who had, somehow, wormed her way into his soul before she left Somerset eight years ago. And the why of that one had no explanation. Just as the dreams of her that had tormented him over the years made no sense.

"I moved her Rodeo," Natches said, sidling up to Dawg as he stood guarding the warehouse entrance. "She was parked outside the range of the cameras, and her head was down as she came through the entrance. With any luck, we can cover her identity."

Dawg glanced at his cousin and best friend from the corner of his eye. He was half tempted to blame his cousin for every second of this madness. Following the vague warning he had given, Dawg had moved to find who they assumed was the female seller who had entered the warehouse. She was the only one unaccounted for now.

Dawg had moved to intercept her ahead of the rest of the team and reacted rather than thinking. If he had given himself time to think, she would be stretched out on the warehouse floor with the rest of the bastards they had arrested in the raid.

They had the buyers, the sellers, four missing experimental missiles, and their guidance chips. It was a damned good haul for the investigation. Except for the fact that the woman who had masterminded the deal hadn't arrived.

That, or she was hiding in the backseat of Dawg's pickup truck.

"Remind me why we're covering her identity," Dawg said softly, his gaze tracking the rest of the combined ATF and Homeland Security team.

Hell, he knew why, but damned if he wanted to admit to it.

This wasn't something Crista would do. He knew it wasn't. At least, it wasn't something the Crista he had once known would do.

"Because she's not involved?" Natches hazarded a mocking guess.

"She was here," Dawg pointed out, even as he ignored the hard mental flash of denial that Crista could be involved in this in any way.

"Uh-huh." Natches nodded. "Of which I warned you. You were the one who jerked her out like a wolf protecting its mate, not me, Cousin. I just covered your six. That's my job. Remember?"

Like a wolf protecting its mate. Or a Dawg protecting a bone, he thought sarcastically.

He had taken one look at her, and something inside him had exploded in awareness. He knew damned good and well what would happen if he didn't get her out of there. If she had been caught with the others, with the description of the female suspect they had, she would have never gotten out of the arrest and subsequent imprisonment, involved or not.

And why that should matter to him, he couldn't figure out.

"She's not involved." Natches cradled his rifle in his arms like a lover as he stared back at Dawg. "That's not Crista, Dawg."

Maybe it wasn't. But then again, maybe it was, and he just couldn't see it for his own lust.

Dawg tightened his lips and stared back at the organized chaos inside the now well-lit warehouse. He was a paranoid son of a bitch. He trusted no one but the Father, the Son, and the Holy Ghost, and Crista wasn't included in the Trinity last he checked.

Yet he was risking his own reputation to protect her. Not because of Natches's warning but because his own emotions had interfered with the job for the first time in eight years. And as he stood there, watching the arrests, the recovery of the missiles and their chips, and felt the sense of triumph that the team radiated, he felt disassociated.

He was impatient. Eager to have it over with, because his mind was brewing with all the possibles filtering through it.

It was possible Crista wasn't involved. And if she wasn't, then it was possible that for the first time since her return a year ago, he had an edge on her. She couldn't just turn and run, as she was wont to do whenever he came near.

Oh no. Not anymore.

His eyes narrowed, and his lips curled with an anticipatory smile.

He had lived on instinct too damned long to discount it, and instinct was giving her the benefit of the doubt. But he was still a part of the ATF, and she was at the scene of an arms buy. She also fit the brief description of the one female in the group of thieves that had hijacked the weapons and attempted to sell them.

He was going to have to keep an eye on her. A very close eye on her.

"Oh hell, I hate that smile," Natches suddenly groaned beside him. "Dawg, what the hell are you up to?"

Dawg glanced over at him, his brow lifting in mock innocence. "I'm just considering how best to determine who's guilty and who's innocent," he drawled. "Nothing for you to worry about, Natches. Nothing whatsoever."

It was a lot for Dawg to worry about, and even more for Crista.

For Dawg, because Crista made him break his own rules, and that was something he never did, under any circumstances. And for her, because he was going to take payment for those rules out of her sweet little body.

Natches's shoulders slumped. "Hell. Why do I have a feeling now that I should have just played the knight in shining armor myself rather than giving you the opportunity to pull your head out of your ass?"

Dawg snorted at that. "Stop worrying. I have it covered."

"I'm guaranteed to worry at any time that you tell me not to worry. It's a cosmic rule."

Dawg lifted his brows and chuckled in amusement. "Trust me."

Natches stared back at him in worried disbelief. "Man, don't go pulling that kamikaze shit on me again, okay? Four years of it in the Marines were enough. You promised to take it easy once we got home. Remember?" Natches reminded him. "Think about your knee, man. You're only one good accident from being a cripple. Let's not push it, 'kay?"

Dawg let his grin widen. "Take it easy? Easy wasn't what I had in mind, but taking it sure as hell is."

Natches stared at him suspiciously. "Don't do something you're going to regret, Dawg. I don't have time to pull your ass out of any fires."

Dawg clapped him on the shoulder before moving toward the men being lifted from the cement floor and prepared for a nice little trip to the nearest jail cell. "No worries, Natches." He grinned over his shoulder. "No worries at all. Grab her car. Tell the commander we drove in separately; they won't know any better. You were just borrowing a friend's vehicle. And I'll catch ya later."

He had plans to make. Plans that included one sexy little waitress, his bed, and all kinds of wet, hot, nasty sex acts.

The next time she turned her back on him, she would at least remember what it felt like, what it meant to be owned by him. And by God, before it was over, he would own her. Heart and soul. By fair means or by foul. Dawg wasn't playing anymore.

TWO

She was still where he left her. Not that he hadn't expected her to be, but it was always comforting to know one was right about these matters.

"Stay put," he told her as he moved into the driver's seat and stuck the key in the ignition. "Wouldn't want anyone to see you as we leave, now would we?"

He flipped the music on. AC/DC rocked through the cab of the truck as he held down the button to the windows, opening them all the way, and peeled from the parking lot like a man on a mission.

He lifted his hand to the state police officers in the front lot, and not for the first time was thankful that he had parked his truck alongside one of the abandoned buildings rather than coming in with the rest of the team later.

He and Natches had been posted to watch the area through the day and give the go-ahead when the team could move in. It was the one thing that had saved Crista's ass. No one would be any wiser when Natches explained that they had come in separately and he pulled out in Crista's Rodeo. They might wonder, until the gossip hit that one Crista Jansen was currently residing with one Dawg Mackay on his infamous houseboat, the *Nauti Dawg.*

As he put distance between the truck and the scene of the arrest, he let the muscles of his neck and shoulders relax before turning down the music and glancing between the seats to the long bench seat in the back.

Something inside him clenched at the sight of her pale face and wide, dark brown eyes. Chocolate eyes. She had big, dark, chocolate eyes, and he was a man that knew how to savor that particular sweet.

"You can come up here now," he told her, turning his attention back to driving as he turned onto one of the curving country roads that wound through the county.

She moved slowly, uncurling from the backseat and moving into the empty passenger seat beside him before settling in and staring out the windshield stiffly.

"Put your seat belt on." Dawg propped his arm on the open window frame and scratched at his jaw consideringly as he drove.

Beside him, Crista clipped her seat belt, moving almost hesitantly, glancing at him every few seconds with silent wariness.

She knew she was fucked. She might not know just how well she was going to be fucked, but she was definitely fucked.

"Let's play a game," he finally drawled in amusement as he glanced over at her.

"We've been playing one for a year," she retorted. "You just keep forgetting to forward the rules to me."

He grinned at that. That was Crista. Never without a snappy little comeback.

"This is an easy game," he promised her. "A guessing game. Tell me, if you will, exactly what the hell you were doing in the goddamned warehouse."

He had to snap his teeth together as anger flamed with each word, overriding the amusement he had previously felt. Once again, he saw her, staring up at that damned terrorist, her eyes wide, her face pale, that gun rising steadily to her face.

She flinched.

"My things," she answered then, her voice haunted. "Mark had the rest of my belongings shipped from Virginia. I have a note. The delivery company said they were at the warehouse in one of the lockers. I have the key here." She was digging in her purse, her voice shaking. "See. I have the key."

She held a key out to him.

Dawg took it slowly, glanced at it, then handed it back to her. It was indeed a locker key with the initials SIY, for Store It Yourself, stamped on it.

"Where's the note?"

She didn't go digging in her purse. Her teeth were biting nervously at her lower lip instead.

"Where's the note, Crista Ann?" he asked her again.

Crista flinched. "I left it in the Rodeo, my car. Back at the warehouse."

Dawg shook his head. "Didn't stick it in your pocketbook, huh?" He glanced at her suspiciously.

"It's there. In the passenger seat." She was gripping her hands in her lap, her fingers twisting together.

She used to do that every damned time she got around him. From the time she was sixteen until just a few months before she left town a little over eight years ago.

"We'll see," he grunted.

"Is this game over now?" she asked him irritably. "I'd like to go back home."

At that point, Dawg grinned.

"Dawg, you are going to take me home, aren't you?"

He heard it in her voice. She was getting a clue.

"Not yet." He flashed her a quick grin, anticipation beginning to build along with the heated lust at the knowledge he saw in her eyes.

"Where are you taking me then?"

"Your new home."

"And that's where?" She pushed the question through gritted teeth. Dawg almost chuckled. Oh yeah, things were changing now.

"We'll play your question and answer game later," he retorted, refusing to answer her for the time being. "For now, let me ask you this: Do you have any clue what the hell was going on in that warehouse?"

She breathed out wearily, leaned her head back against the seat, and said, "Drugs?" It was said with such an air of resignation that he was inclined to believe that maybe she wasn't involved with terrorists.

With her background, it was damned difficult to believe she was. Her brother, Alex, was one of the finest Special Forces soldiers Dawg had ever known, his reputation was solid, and Dawg knew for a fact it had been Alex who had raised Crista.

"Know how much trouble you're in?"

He glanced over in time to see her lashes drift closed, feathering over her cheeks like dark shadows.

"Are you taking me to jail?"

Was he?

Hell no, he wasn't. If he was going to turn her over to the authorities, he would have done so in the warehouse. He was damned stupid was what he was. A horny fool.

"Not yet." He tightened his lips before moving his hand from her cheek and letting his forefinger brush over his lips, remembering her kiss as he watched the road thoughtfully, his elbow still propped on the window frame.

Damn if he wasn't stepping into a mess this time.

"What are you going to do, Dawg?" she asked him quietly.

The sound of her voice made him harder. Not just hard, hell, his dick had been hard since the day he glimpsed her walking down Main Street a year ago and knew she was back, even before he caught sight of her face. No, he was harder. Painfully hard.

A vision of her head lowering to his cock suddenly had his entire body clenching painfully. Wide, innocent chocolate eyes staring up at him as his cock head disappeared into her mouth almost had a groan ripping from his chest.

That vision haunted him; that one and several others. The sight of her pussy, dark curls saturated with her juices as he parted the tender folds with his thick erection. The sound of her cries as he tucked the hungry crest at her rear and took her there, hearing her shock, her pleasure. Dreams that had haunted him for years. Dreams he intended to make reality now that he had her.

"To the boat." His houseboat. The *Nauti Dawg*. His home. He heard the hard breath she took.

"No."

He glanced at her, seeing the revulsion on her face, and a flare of anger pierced his mind again. She hadn't been good enough to step foot into his home eight years ago, and she still thought she was too good for it.

"You prefer jail?" He eased up on the gas, glancing around as though looking for a place to turn around.

"I wasn't doing anything," she argued desperately then. "You know I wasn't, Dawg. It was a coincidence—"

"I don't believe in coincidence, Crista."

"A mistake then," she cried out as he began easing to the wide shoulder just ahead. "God, Dawg, you know I don't do drugs."

He pulled over and came to a stop. Draping his arms over the steering wheel, he stared back at her silently.

"You can't take me to jail, Dawg. Alex will be home soon, he'll tell you. This is all a mistake."

"Alex can't fix this one, Crista," he told her softly, meaning it. "You're stuck with me." He gave her a minute to process that. "Or jail. Your choice."

She was breathing hard, erratically. If it were only fear that he had glimpsed in her eyes, he would have let her off the hook right then. God knew Alex could definitely deal with this when he got home. But it wasn't just fear; he saw heat there, and something more. Something elusive, a knowledge, a certainty that something was getting ready to rock her little world.

She licked her lips. A quick little flick of her tongue that had his guts tightening in hunger. He wanted that tongue, and he wanted it bad enough to do something so despicable, so dirty it almost, just almost, made him cringe.

He smiled instead, because it was going to be good. So damned good.

"Do I turn around, or do we continue to the marina?" he asked her then. "Your choice, sweetheart."

And if she chose turning around, what the hell would he do then? He waited, staring back at her, his expression bland, his gaze, he knew, hot and hungry. She knew what he wanted. She knew the price he was exacting for pulling her out of this one.

Her lips trembled before she licked them again. Her gaze flickered with indecision. And he wasn't going to help her. He'd be damned if he would go back to chasing after her like a dog after a bitch in heat and being turned away every time. Not this time. This time, it was his game. His way or jail. Or at least, that was the impression he was intent on giving her.

"Don't turn around," she finally whispered, her gaze dropping, her head turning back to stare stiffly through the windshield once again.

"We go to the *Nauti Dawg*, then?" he asked her.

"If that's my only choice." Her voice was tense, angry.

Fine, let her be angry. He'd been damned mad himself eight years ago, and he could still remember the fury when he realized she had left town with another man. Realized, nothing, he had seen her in the car with the bastard as they drove out of town.

He still remembered that one. Hell, he had nightmares about that one when he least expected them.

"It's not your only choice, Crista Ann," he said softly. "You can go explain to the authorities what you were doing there. That one's real easy."

Of course, he'd have to explain why she wasn't arrested with the rest of the crew, but he was hoping she wouldn't realize that.

"Yeah. I could do that," she snapped back mockingly. "And of course, you would deny to hell and back pulling me out of there. Right?"

He grinned. God love her, he had to give her credit.

Dawg shrugged. "What can I do? I didn't check my backseat until I heard someone move around in it. I can be a bit absentminded when I'm in a hurry."

"And the reason Natches is driving my Rodeo rather than riding with you?"

Dawg widened his eyes. "You and Natches are friends, Crista. You loaned him the Rodeo."

Okay, he wasn't really that damned dirty. Hell, if she chose jail, he'd take her home and figure something else out.

But she should have known that. If she didn't know that, well, that was just her mistake, not his.

"That's dirty, Dawg," she retorted, disgust thickening her voice.

"Sure it is." He nodded in agreement. "But I have a reputation for being dirty. Don't I?" His grin was pure innocence. One of the kind that normally had Natches looking for the nearest escape route.

She rubbed her hands over her face before pushing her fingers through the hair she had pulled back tightly into a long ponytail.

Hair he was dying to loosen, to spread out behind her as he laid her back on his bed. Hair he longed to grip while he rode her hard and deep.

She shook her head before staring straight ahead once again.

"So, we head to the marina, right?"

She nodded slowly. "Fine."

Dawg let off the brake and eased back onto the road before adding speed and heading down the dark highway.

"You act like you're heading to the gallows." He grinned.

She didn't reply.

Dawg glanced at her again, watching as she rubbed at her bare arms and stared out the window, her expression bleak, disheartening.

Damn her. It wasn't as though he intended to rape her. Blackmail her a little bit, definitely. But sex would be only under certain conditions. He'd make damned sure she wanted it as badly as he did, first. He wasn't a complete bastard.

But he was a horny bastard. And a mad bastard.

Eight fucking years she had lived in his dreams, and he couldn't figure out why. She had changed him at a time when he needed to retain that edge of careless unconcern. She had pricked his emotions, filled his head, and he couldn't make sense of it.

She tormented him. It was that damned simple, and it was time the torment eased.

"Don't worry, darlin'. It won't be so bad," he assured her, reaching over to pat her knee in a totally false gesture of comfort. "We used to get along once, remember?"

Once.

Crista turned her head slowly and stared at his profile. Once, she had loved him with all the passion and innocence of a young girl who revered the town's baddest bad boy. But she wasn't a girl anymore; she was a grown woman. She was well aware of just how easily he could destroy her life again.

"I remember how stupid I was," she finally answered him with a measure of self-disgust at the memory. "And I remember learning my lesson. I don't really remember much other than that, Dawg. Perhaps you could remind me of a time that we actually got along."

He didn't remember that night. Crista knew he didn't. And she knew Alex would have never told him what happened. He had promised her.

Dawg tapped his fingers on the steering wheel. "You ran from me every chance you got," he growled back at her.

Not every chance. Not one dark night when she had found him too drunk to drive and helped him home. And then helped him break her heart.

"I was smart then," she said, feeling the regret that welled inside her. If only she had been smarter. If only she had faced the truth then, and what had happened. Maybe the past eight years would have been different. If nothing else, she might not have been tormented with so many what-ifs and the fact that she had been a coward.

Dawg grunted at that. "Too bad you weren't smart enough to stay out of dark warehouses at night. If you had, you wouldn't be here now."

Too bad she hadn't been smart enough to stay in Virginia to begin with. But no, she had to come home. She missed being home. She missed the mountains, the lake, and home. And she had known it was time to lay old ghosts to rest. She had come home to make peace with the memories and with herself. And with Dawg. She just hadn't expected to make peace with him in quite this way.

Instead, she found more demons. She found herself in the untenable position of relying on Dawg for something as imperative as her freedom. And there wasn't a doubt in her mind exactly how he intended to manipulate this one.

He had been after her ever since she had returned to Somerset a year ago. He hadn't stalked her. He was just always around. Always smiling that rakish grin of his, giving her that mocking once-over, that invitation to play. If he wasn't doing that, he was glaring at her. And he filled her dreams. Heated dreams, memories of one unforgettable night and the consequences of it.

She watched the miles pass by, feeling his hand on her knee when he wasn't shifting gears in the powerful pickup, and feeling the warmth of his touch burning through her skirt.

At least he wasn't groping her. Her body was so hyped on nerves right now that she wondered if she could bear that. If her heart could bear it.

She thought she had learned her lesson before leaving Somerset. After all, she knew what Dawg was, she knew what he intended, and she knew she could never live with it.

The Nauti Boys were legendary in Somerset and the surrounding counties. Their prowess, dedication to a woman's pleasure, and insistence on sharing those women had been well-known. Her brother, Alex, had warned her about Dawg repeatedly.

Her head had warned her about Dawg, but her heart hadn't wanted to listen. She could tame the bad boy, she had assured herself. Love would make him possessive. All she had to do was touch him, love him, and he would realize he loved her.

She snorted silently as she peeked a look at his hard profile.

What a fool she had been. Naive, impossibly innocent, incredibly foolish. And she still hadn't learned her lesson, not all the way to the soul. Because a part of her had never forgotten that one night. That sultry summer night when he had taken her with singular determination and fiery lust. When he had taught her the true depths of carnal pleasure and the ultimate despair.

"This isn't going to work." The words tore from her lips as he pulled into the small marina his uncle Ray Mackay owned.

She could feel the panic building in her chest now, the certainty that the *Nauti Dawg* was going to hold more memories and more heartache than she could bear.

"I can't do this." She was shaking as Dawg pulled the truck into the private parking slot in front of the marina.

He turned off the motor. Pulling the key from the ignition, he turned and stared at her silently.

Him or jail. She could see it in his expression.

Crista shook her head slowly before swallowing tightly.

"I'm not one of the Nauti Boys' whores," she whispered harshly. "I can't play one to stay out of jail, Dawg. I'd rather rot in prison than buy my freedom at the expense of my soul."

He stared back at her, his light green eyes icy, unemotional, as he watched her. His expression was as dark as the shadows around them and as still as death.

This wasn't the man she had known eight years ago. Charming, though brooding, James "Dawg" Mackay had had a will of iron, but he hadn't been cold. He'd been hard but not unemotional. Not as he was now.

He had joined the Marines just after she left town; she knew that. He'd spent one tour, when he had been shipped home because of a wound that shattered his kneecap. Not that she had seen any sign of an injury in the way he moved.

But right now, he was rubbing his knee almost absently as he watched her.

"We'll talk about this on the boat," he finally said warningly. "Not here."

"No, Dawg." She reached out, gripping his arm as he moved to open the door. "Not at the boat. I won't go out to that boat, and I won't spread myself for the Nauti Boys. I wouldn't do it when I was too stupid to know any better, and I sure as hell won't do it now. You're fooling yourself if you think you can convince me to do otherwise."

"And if going to that boat didn't mean spreading yourself for anyone but me, Crista?" he asked her. "Would you go then?"

THREE

Eight years ago, she had slipped from Dawg's upper-deck bedroom and stolen from the *Nauti Dawg* like a thief in the early morning mists. But she had left something behind that morning, a part of herself she had never regained.

Now Crista stepped back through the reinforced French door that led into the living room and stilled herself against the memories that threatened to overwhelm her.

He still left a low light shining on the small table that sat beside the couch. It was a maroon plush couch now, where before it had been black leather. A matching recliner sat by the side of the same table.

The television was now mounted on the wall on the side they entered, and across the room on the opposite side sat a small dining table and four chairs.

A teak bar separated the dining area from the kitchen, two captain's barstools placed under it.

The rug was a rich, thick forest green. Eight years ago it had been a dark tan. The living room and kitchen were more refined now, stating a mature taste in furnishings but still a broad male influence. Dark woods and few frills.

A picture of his Marine Corps unit sat on the table by the

couch alongside a picture of the Nauti cousins in camouflage greens and a picture of Rowdy and his fiancée, Kelly Salyers.

There were no pictures or prints on the wall. There was nothing to decorate the rooms. Beyond the kitchen was another large bedroom and small washroom as well as an extra bathroom. From where Crista stood, she could also see the curving staircase that led to the upper deck and master bed and bath, as well as the steering controls.

She flinched as the door closed and locked behind her.

"I need a beer," Dawg announced. "Want one?"

Crista shook her head as she gripped her purse and watched him move across the living room, then into the kitchen. He pulled a beer from the refrigerator before unscrewing the cap with a quick twist and tossing the cap beneath the bar, where the garbage can must have been hidden.

He moved to the sink first, pulled a dish towel from a small stack on the counter, dampened it, then tossed it to her.

"Clean your face."

She felt her stomach heave at the thought of the blood that had sprayed over her. It was on her face, her clothes. She scrubbed at her flesh quickly, harshly, hoping she managed to clean it away as he stared at her.

He tilted the bottle of beer to his lips and drank deeply, his gaze never leaving hers.

He had stripped the bulletproof vest, but he still wore the shoulder holster and weapon. His black T-shirt stretched over his wide chest and thick biceps. Black jeans rode low on his hips and outlined long, muscular legs and a more than impressive bulge.

"You're clean," he announced, holding his hand out. "Give me the towel."

Her gaze jerked from that area. It was more than obvious he was aroused, ready for her. And she hated admitting that her body had been ready for his since the moment he asked her if she was willing to spread herself for him alone.

She tossed the towel back to him, ignoring his mocking grin as he caught it and dumped it in the sink.

She was insane. She should have run from him while she had the chance.

"One night," she whispered. "That's all."

The bottle was smacked on the bar top so hard beer sloshed from the top, and Crista jumped at the sound.

"You aren't making the deal here," he informed her, his expression hardening. "You didn't catch me possibly breaking the law and consorting with criminals, Crista. I caught you, remember?"

Her fingernails dug into the leather of her purse.

"And I know what you want in exchange for my freedom," she snapped back. "Fine, you want to fuck. You want something you haven't been able to con me out of this year: my body. You can have it. For one night."

"And if I want more than one night?" The black velvet tone of his voice had a tremor quaking through her womb, clenching at the muscles of her stomach as she stared back at him in shock.

"Why would you want more than one night?" She shook her head in confusion. "How many women have you kept more than one night, Dawg?"

She still had friends she had kept in Somerset, and they liked to gossip. Dawg was as newsworthy now as he had been eight years ago.

"You aren't every other woman, Crista," he drawled. "I've never had to chase one for eight years before. It's built up a hunger. One that I doubt one night is going to sate."

She blinked back at him in shock. She had expected what he wanted, but she hadn't expected this. One night she could handle. More than one night?

"How many nights?" She kept her voice from trembling, barely.

Dawg's expression hardened further. "I haven't decided."

"You haven't decided? So I'm supposed to just be ready and available for you whenever you get a hard-on?"

Mocking consideration filled his face then. He nodded slowly. "That would work for me."

Crista clenched her teeth and calculated how long she still had to wait before Alex returned. He had been gone three months. Her last conversation with him, he had indicated that he could return within the next few weeks.

Could she handle being Dawg's lover that long? Could she walk away with her soul if she did?

"Don't think about it too damned hard," he bit out irritably. "I might change my mind."

Crista wrapped her arms over her breasts and stilled the anger beginning to rise inside her. She couldn't afford to be angry at this point; she had to think. Dawg always managed to mess up her mind. She couldn't afford to let him do it this time.

"You're being a bastard," she told him forcefully. "You know I wasn't involved in whatever you were doing there. I don't deal with drugs, I never have."

He shrugged easily as he propped himself against the bar. "I haven't seen you in eight years, Crista. People change in that time."

"Oh yeah, and people dealing in drugs work as waitresses at crappy little diners where they don't even make minimum wage, too," she snapped. "Don't play with me; I don't like it. At least admit that you're using this to force something out of me that I wasn't willing to give you."

A frown snapped between his brows, causing her stomach to clench nervously. "I wouldn't force you."

"Then what do you call it? I can fuck you or I can go to jail? Hell of a choice there, Dawg," she sneered.

Crista watched the muscle at his jaw tighten, a heavy tic rippling through it as he watched her.

"I thought I was being rather charitable," he growled. "Deny you're interested in being in my bed."

"I have. Every time I've ignored your petty little efforts at flirtation. Or didn't you notice?"

"I noticed that kiss earlier, too." Black velvet seduction. His voice raked over her nerve endings and reminded her just how good it had been. "That wasn't force, Crista. Stop fooling yourself. You loved it."

Okay, he had her there. Her stomach tightened at the memory and at the knowledge that she had no defenses against him.

"I agree to one night—"

"And I said one night isn't enough. I want the summer. All summer."

Crista froze. Three months? Summer had just begun, and he wanted the rest of it.

"Why?" She forced the word past her numb lips as she stared back at him.

"It takes time to determine guilt or innocence, Crista Ann. I want you close while I figure which one to attach to you. If you're really innocent, then at the end of the summer, you're free to go. I find out you're guilty, and your ass heads to jail. Consider it your trial period. Except instead of sitting in a jail cell, you're enjoying all the comforts I can provide you."

His smile was dangerous, sensual. It curved like a predatory smirk that had her heart racing in her chest.

And he was messing with her head again. Her mind filled with memories, the touch and the taste of him. How the slightest brush of his fingers could steal her defenses and leave her shaking in his arms.

His kiss. It was drugging, fiery. And what he could do to her heart, her emotions, should be illegal. He could tie her up in so many knots on the inside that she wondered if they would ever be untangled.

Crista swallowed tightly against the onslaught of remembered sensations and pleasures.

"You keep thinking about it." He shrugged easily. "You can take a shower, rest a bit before you decide. I'll loan you a clean shirt." He smiled again. "You won't need it for long."

"You've changed, Dawg," she whispered then. "You didn't used to be such a cold-blooded bastard."

"Sure I did," he drawled. "You were just one of the few that hadn't recognized it. Didn't you hear all about that nasty little court battle after my parents died? Hell, honey, even my parents knew I was a lost cause."

She had heard about the court battle. How his aunt had tried to take the entire estate his parents had left him based on a few letters his father had written to his aunt. Letters that were filled with disgust over his son's lifestyle and his belief that Dawg didn't deserve to share his name.

It had lasted for years. Even after he was in the Marines, he had been plagued with legal conflicts and the fight to hold on to his inheritance. It had finally ended after his return home four years ago, but he had lost tens of thousands of dollars in the fight.

"No." She shook her head. "You weren't like this before. You would have never forced this on me then."

"But I am now. You can make your choice while you're cleaning up. But when you step back into this room, you damned well better have made your mind up. You're mine for the summer, or you can belong to the federal government, it's all up to you."

Dawg didn't let out a relieved breath until Crista disappeared into the lower bathroom long minutes later, one of his T-shirts clenched tightly in her fingers, her large brown eyes watching him warily as she closed the door behind her.

Minutes later he heard the shower running and ran his fingers through his hair as he blew out another hard breath.

For a while there, he honestly thought she was going to choose the alternative. When she had finally headed for the shower, he had to force himself to hold back, to keep from assuring her that nothing in hell could convince him to turn her over to the authorities. To just let her go.

He rubbed at the back of his neck as he grimaced at the thought. Eight years he had dreamed about her. When he least expected it, when he was weak, tired. Dreams so blistering hot he would wake up pumping his own dick like an adolescent and moaning her name.

The past year had been worse. He was like a damned love-starved teenager going out of his way just to see her. Hoping to catch her smile, craving the sound of her voice.

Damn, he had missed her after she left town. Not that he had stuck around for long. He had signed up with the Marines before his parents' death, and he shipped out just months afterward. Long-distance court battles and the hell of trying to hold on to his parents' estate had consumed him, but through it, he had thought of Crista.

She had left so suddenly, before he had the chance to gather up his nerve and do more than flirt with her a little bit.

When she returned to Somerset the year before, he thought maybe, this time, he could make it work. Until she stared at him like a slug crawling out from under a rock.

Why the hell did he even care? It wasn't like she was the

only game in town. He could have his pick from dozens of women. One night, one week, one month, one whole fucking year if he wanted to keep one that long.

Instead, he was blackmailing a woman who clearly had no interest in doing a damned thing about the attraction burning between them like wildfire.

And it was there. It sparked and exploded every time they were within seeing distance of each other. He could see her response to it. The widening of her eyes, the accelerated breathing, her hard little nipples pressing beneath her clothing and a wild flush to her creamy cheeks. She wanted him almost as damned bad as he wanted her, but she was denying it, fighting it with everything inside her, and Dawg wanted to know why.

He knew women. They didn't fight something that strong without a damned good reason. Now, he just had to figure out the reason.

Breathing out roughly, he moved upstairs to his own shower and quickly stripped before stepping beneath the spray.

He showered quickly. He didn't want to give her time to run. He wanted to give her time to think, though—to consider her options as they stood.

She wanted him, that much he knew. Wanted him enough that the whole time she was arguing the deal, her nipples were pressing harder beneath her shirt and her gaze was flashing with a subtle spark of lust.

Dawg had made it a point to know women before he had any business knowing them. Too young and too dumb to even understand why, he had been drawn to their softness, their veneer of sweetness. The dark undercurrents of passion, power plays, and feminine wiles.

Women who were the exact opposite of his cold-blooded, crazy mother. Women who gave soft touches and whimpered for the pleasure he gave them. Who reached for him, who whispered his name in ecstasy rather than cursing it in hatred.

He knew how to read them, how to pleasure them.

And he knew that look of veiled hunger they gave to indicate their willingness to be pleasured.

Oh yeah, Crista wanted him, but for some reason she wasn't willing to accept the fact that he was there for the taking.

Dawg grinned at the thought as he quickly toweled dry and dressed. The cotton briefs and sweats did nothing to hide the hard-on raging beneath the soft material. Pulling on a clean T-shirt, he moved back downstairs, his gaze roving around the dimly lit room as he searched for her.

And there she was. His T-shirt draped past her thighs as she sat nervously on the couch, her long hair still a little damp. She had obviously made use of the blow-dryer he kept in the guest bathroom.

Beautiful long, thick, dark chocolate hair that fell to the middle of her back and gave her a waiflike appearance.

Damn, she was small. Barely five feet six inches tall in her bare feet, with delicate bones and a nicely rounded figure. She wasn't stick skinny, and he liked that, though he was well aware of the delicacy of her body in comparison to his.

Her face was still pale, her eyes too dark, but she looked composed. Hell, she looked like she was heading to the gallows rather than his bed.

"You aren't the best salve to my ego, fancy-face," he told her as he moved through the room, watching her with an edge of amusement.

She rose slowly to her feet.

"I wish you wouldn't call me that."

She had never liked being called fancy-face, but that was how he saw her. Her face was a little irregular, her lips pouty and winsome, her nose pert with the slightest little tilt, and high, glorious cheekbones.

She was different in a way that stood out. She wasn't beautiful in the acceptable sense of the word, rather she was eye-catching, mysterious. Unique.

"Why?" He glanced at the clock and almost winced. Damn, it was nearly two in the morning; no wonder she looked like she had been run over by a truck. She was exhausted. And so was he.

Now, if he could just convince his cock how tired he was.

"Because I hate nicknames," she retorted.

Dawg shook his head. "Look, it's damned late. I just had a killer day, and from the looks of it, yours wasn't any better. Let's sleep on this, then we'll see how things look in the morning."

She licked her lips warily. "In separate beds?"

"In your dreams," he grunted back. "Damn it, Crista, stop waffling like a damned little sissy. Either you're going to fuck me or you're not. Let's get this over with now so we can both get some sleep."

"I haven't decided yet." Crista narrowed her eyes on Dawg, considering the irritation in his expression and the flash of lust in his gaze.

She was trying to keep her eyes off the erection clearly displayed beneath his sweatpants. Okay, she had already made her decision. Sort of.

She was furious over it. It wasn't enough that she had tried to stay out of his way, that she had rebuffed every overture he had made. Now he had to take the decision away from her, force her to risk her heart to him again, knowing the outcome.

As the minutes had ticked by, she had only become angrier as she showered. It had taken her years to put him behind her enough to even date another man. And still, when the nights were the darkest, she felt the same ragged pain and loss that she had felt that summer, as clearly as she had felt it then.

He crossed his arms over his chest. "You haven't, huh? What are you waiting for?"

Crista clenched her teeth in anger. "I'll sleep with you."

His brow arched.

"But I won't just spread myself for you, Dawg. I can't just fuck you like that."

"Spread yourself?" he asked softly, his voice dark as his gaze narrowed back at her. "Like what, Crista?"

"Like one of your damned playmates," she bit out.

The more he stared at her like that, the more angry she became. Nerves, exhaustion, and the fallout from terror were crashing through her system. On top of that, she had to deal with blackmail by a man she could have never expected blackmail from.

"You are my playmate now." He grinned back at her, his expression becoming one of intense satisfaction. "And I do like to play, Crista. You should be aware of that by now."

"Aware of it!" The anger snapped through her then.

"Dawg, I was aware of it eight damned years ago when you decided you were drunk enough and horny enough to fuck me without your cousins standing by to join in. I'm not the one that forgot that fucking night; you are."

Horror slammed through her. Her hand clapped over her mouth, and the breath stilled in her throat as his expression slowly stilled from amusement, then shock, then outright fury.

She had never seen Dawg mad. Few people had ever seen Dawg really mad. Crista had only heard of it, and she had decided long ago she never wanted to see it.

"You're lying." Cold, brutal certainty filled his voice.

She was already too pissed off to take that one silently. Her hand lowered from her lips as her gaze raked over his body with heated memories and fiery anger.

"You know better," she sneered. "You were falling down drunk outside of town the night you buried your parents, Dawg. How do you think you got home? I brought you home, and you spent the night screwing me. All night," she cried out. "Before you told me exactly how those Neanderthal bastard cousins of yours were going to fuck me. Where and how, and how long."

She hated the fear and the pain and the fist-sized lump that tore at her chest every time *she* remembered. By God, if he was going to blackmail her into his bed and sneer at her attempts to protect her heart from him, then he could hear the truth.

"Don't worry, Dawg," she spoke in ragged bursts now, just trying to find the breath to sustain her through the rage. "You don't have to worry about the one that got away. Because she never got away from anything but the foursome you seemed determined to force her into."

She stepped back, fear and panic raging through her body with the same force, as eight years of pent-up anger finally flowed free.

Escape. She needed to get away from him. She needed to run, just as she had before, just as far away from him as she could get.

"Touch that fucking door, and I'll have you arrested in an hour flat." His gaze smoldered with anger now.

Oh, this wasn't the Dawg she knew. The Dawg she knew was unaffected, playful, cynical. He didn't become enraged, and he sure as hell wasn't tormented. Which was exactly how he seemed now.

He paced into the kitchen, jerking another beer from the fridge before uncapping it and tilting it to his lips. In two long draws, he emptied it. A second later it shattered as it hit the wall.

Crista flinched violently, staring at the dark paneling across the kitchen, bits of glass clinging to the dampness a small amount of the liquid had left. Dawg rubbed his hands roughly over his face before pushing them through his hair and dislodging the leather thong that held the loose ponytail at the nape of his neck.

"Did I rape you?" His voice was unemotional, but his eyes weren't. They seethed, darkening in spots, lightening in others as he stared at her from across the room.

"You didn't rape me," she gritted out. There were times when she wished she didn't have such an aversion to lying.

"What happened?" His lips were a thin, furious line, his expression rigid.

Crista shook her head wearily. "Dawg—"

"What. Happened," he bit out again, his voice harsher, icier.

"You were drunk. I brought you home. We had sex. End of story."

"How?"

"What?" She watched him warily now, her stomach knotting in tension at the tone of his voice. It was hoarse, brutal.

"How did we have sex?" he repeated, his chest moving harshly, nostrils flaring as his expression seemed to grow colder.

"The usual way?" She retreated an additional foot.

His gaze sharpened at her movement as his lips twisted in contempt. "I didn't rape you then; I won't do it now," he rasped. "Now answer me. How?"

"I answered you." Her fingers tugged nervously at the bottom of her shirt as the air filled with dangerous tension.

"You were a virgin." It didn't sound like a question.

Crista nodded slowly.

"I took you." He swallowed tightly at that point. "I took you hard."

Did he remember? He didn't appear to, yet he was right. He had taken her hard, and she had loved it.

Crista nodded again. She began to shake.

"I fucked your ass!" His lips curled back in an enraged snarl as his hands curled into fists and the muscles beneath his T-shirt rippled and bunched tensely.

She didn't shake her head, she didn't answer him. She stared at the phenomenon that she was certain no one else had ever seen.

Dawg enraged. She had only rarely heard of him appearing truly angry, let alone enraged. Even drunk, he had been playful, mocking, a little silly, but never angry.

"Answer me!" he shouted, causing her to jerk violently.

"Why should I answer you?" she snapped back. "It's obvious you've remembered it. Why pursue a piece of ass you've already had? And why the hell would you be stupid enough to blackmail me into giving you more? You didn't think much of it the first time, or you wouldn't have wanted to give it away."

She watched him cautiously, rather like watching a rabid bulldog straining at a chain.

Dawg saw the wariness in her dark eyes. He dreamed of those eyes. Dreamed of being mesmerized by the chocolatey color, drowning in them, burning in them.

And her face, a flush of arousal burning across her cheekbones, her lips swollen from his kiss, and her voice whispering across his mind. Begging for more.

It hadn't been a dream. The words crashed in his skull. The dreams that tortured him for eight long years had been insidious memories that had managed to survive the drink-induced haze his mind had been in. He had had her, and the memory of it, so dim and shadowed, had haunted him ever since.

FOUR

Dawg shut back the rage and the fear that he had somehow hurt her and she wasn't admitting it. No doubt, this changed things. Son of a bitch, he couldn't blame her for staying as far away from him as possible all these years. But that didn't mean he was willing to let her go.

He would have been inclined to doubt that he could forget a night with her, but there were too many dreams, too many indications that she was right.

He had taken her virginity. He had taken her without consideration of her innocence, her youth. He had taken an eighteen-year-old virgin to his bed and done things that even mature women would blink at being asked to do.

He cleaned up the glass from the broken bottle carefully, aware of her watching him now with quiet concern. Fuck that; he didn't need her concern. He wanted her. He wanted her hot and wild, all that hunger and passion he had glimpsed in her burning for him.

She would have loved him, he thought, to have followed him into his bed all those years ago. It made him cringe, wondering what he had done to her, how he must have hurt her to make her run before he even awakened.

And he deserved it even less now than he had eight years ago.

"This deal. It involves us only," he told her as he threw the glass in the garbage and kept his back to her. "No one else."

When she didn't speak, he turned and stared back at her.

What the hell had been wrong with him the night he had taken her? He had known that Crista wasn't the sharing kind. She was a one-man woman, just like Kelly.

"Why can't you just let me go? You owe me that, Dawg."

Yeah, he owed her. If his dreams were anything close to what had actually happened, then he owed her a hell of a lot more than he could ever repay.

"You owe me as well," he told her coolly. "All I have are fragmented dreams that drive me fucking crazy. Whatever we started eight years ago, we'll finish this summer. One way or the other."

Nothing on earth could convince him to let her out of his sight now. Possessiveness, desire, and emotions he hadn't felt in so many years he barely remembered them rose to the surface of his consciousness. Emotions he felt in those dreams. Something softer, more tender, and yet a thousand times hotter than lust alone. He wouldn't call it love; he had assured himself years ago that love didn't exist. Besides, this went deeper than anything he had heard love described as.

"Just like that." Bitterness curled at her lips. "As though the fact that I don't want to finish anything doesn't matter."

"It wouldn't be blackmail if it did." He shrugged, fighting back the guilt he could feel building in his gut. "If you wanted to pay the price, then it wouldn't be such a dirty word, would it?"

She stared at him with big dark eyes filled with hurt and made him wish he were someone other than who he was.

"Tell me something," he asked her then. "That night we had, did you at least enjoy it?"

Her gaze flickered away as sharp heat filled her face.

"That's not the point."

"If my dreams are anything to go by, you were just as hot for it as I was. Tell me I'm wrong, Crista. Tell me you hated it."

He moved toward her then, watching as her head snapped back and her eyes tracked his progress across the room.

She didn't retreat; she couldn't be frightened of him. She stared back at him defiantly, her hands clenched at her sides, her expression mutinous.

She wanted to say she hated it, but she couldn't. She hadn't been able to lie worth a damn when she was younger, and she couldn't do it now.

"It was hot, wasn't it, Crista?" He stopped within inches of her, his hand cupping her arm, smoothing down it to her wrist before he lifted her hand to his shoulder and gripped her waist. "So hot we burned down the night. That's what I dream. That you're wet and wild, screwing me with the same crazy lust I'm screwing you with."

Her face flamed brighter.

"And you slipped out on me that morning, didn't you? Just ran away, like the scared little girl you were."

Her eyes flashed with anger.

"I'm not a plaything for the Nauti Boys. Not then and not now."

"And you were too scared to stick around and fight for the singular position, too, weren't you, Crista. What happened, baby? Did it get too hot?"

"Fight for Dawg?" She widened her eyes as though mocking him. She tried to mock him, but he saw the pleasure she was fighting to hide as he drew her closer, nudging his cock against her lower belly and feeling the muscles clench. "Why fight over something every other woman in the county had already had?"

Dawg smiled. "You were scared."

"I was disinterested." She couldn't lie. He heard the tremor in her voice, saw her grimace as she acknowledged it.

He shook his head at her as he allowed the fingers of his free hand to twine into those long, silky strands of hair. Soft, fragrant hair. In his dreams it had twined around him, snaring him, binding him to her. And it had never let him go.

"Are you more interested now?" The hand at her waist bunched the material of the shirt in it.

He was going to have her. He was going to touch her, taste her, feel her come apart in his arms.

"Dawg please . . ." Her voice trembled then.

Dark eyes stared back at him almost pleadingly as the shirt cleared her thighs and rose higher.

"Please what, Crista Ann?" He lowered his head until he could inhale the scent of her. Sweet vanilla and wild roses. She always smelled of vanilla and wild roses to him.

That elusive little scent wasn't enough though. He had to taste her. His lips touched the silken flesh of her neck, his tongue tasting her flesh, and he swore he saw stars as the taste of her exploded against his tongue.

His arm came around her back, lifting her to him as primal hunger replaced the careful seduction he had intended.

He pulled her head back, covered her lips with his own, and found the fiery heat he had been searching for, for eight damn years.

And son of a bitch if it wasn't worth waiting for. She exploded in his arms. A shudder rushed through her, then her hands were twining in his hair, pulling at the thick strands, and pulling his lips harder against hers.

God, she made him feel. Made him feel things he couldn't remember ever feeling, except in his dreams. Dreams of her. Dreams of heat and primal pleasure and sensations he couldn't have imagined really existed.

But they existed here with her in his arms, her body straining toward him, her whimper of pleasure and distress filling his ears as his tongue parted her lips and delved inside.

Fiery sweetness. Spicy ice. She was every contradiction in the world, and his blood raced at the defiance, the challenge, and the sheer response he felt radiating from her.

Crista tried to tell herself she could fight the attraction, the pleasure. Before he touched her, she tried to convince herself she could hold herself aloof from him.

Until his eyes had dilated with pleasure and he had pulled her to him. Until his lips touched her neck; then that hungry moan had left his lips a second before his kiss rocked her mind.

This was a very bad thing. Starbursts of pleasure were exploding inside her bloodstream as she fought herself, fought her response to him, and failed.

Oh how she failed. She was trying to climb into his body

instead, to burn in the center of a sensation so hot, so dark and heated she was lost beneath it.

"Off!" His lips lifted from hers only long enough to whisk the shirt from her arms and over her head before she could react. Before she could stop him. Then he was bending to her, his lips moving unerringly for the tight, too-sensitive nipples lifting to his lips as though they had craved this caress for eight years.

And they had.

"Oh God. Dawg." She arched in his arms as he sucked her nipple into his mouth.

And it was as good, no, it was better than before. His lips drew on the tender tip, his thigh pressed between her legs, and within seconds she was pressing the aching flesh between her thighs into the heavy muscle of his leg and riding it almost frantically as he sucked at her.

"Yes." The word hissed from between her lips. "Oh yes. Do that. Just like that."

Just as he had that night years before. His teeth raking over her nipple before he sucked it back, hard and hot, his tongue lashing over it like a fiery whip.

She was falling. Dizzy. Off balance. And before she knew it, stretched out on the couch with Dawg's lips still ravishing her tender nipples, first one, then the other, growling with hunger and heat as his hand cupped between her thighs.

Finesse was forgotten, but it wasn't finesse she wanted. Dawg was rumored to be smooth, practiced, deliberate in every touch. But there was nothing deliberate or practiced in his touch now.

Experienced, yes. Confident and too damned experienced.

His fingers parted the curl-covered folds between her thighs, and a second later, one broad, male finger was piercing her core.

Crista froze. Heat exploded in her vagina, tore through her bloodstream and into her womb as she felt the tender muscles clenching desperately around his caressing finger.

"So hot." He was panting as his lips lifted from a reddened nipple, and his eyes, darker now but still mesmerizing, almost hypnotizing, stared into hers. "So tight and hot, Crista."

Her hips jerked as his finger pulled back, then stroked

inside her again. One long thrust that had her gasping and arching in his arms, her thighs falling farther apart, her hips lifting for a deeper, wilder penetration.

"You'll destroy me," she cried out, her fingers digging into his scalp as his tongue licked over her nipple. "Again. You'll destroy me again, Dawg."

He had to understand. He couldn't do this to her again. She could easily give herself to him, just like before.

"It's okay, Crista. I won't hurt you, baby," he groaned. "It's just us. See? No one else is here. Ever. God, I'd kill the man that tried to touch you now."

She cried out as another finger joined the first, thrust inside her, parted flesh that had never known another man's touch, never clenched, never became slick and hot and achy as it did for Dawg.

"Mine." His snarl shocked her.

His lips covering hers again fed the hungers rising sharp and deep inside her.

Her hips lifted, arched as she bucked against him, writhing beneath his larger body as his fingers fucked into her, sent a firestorm of sensation raging through her.

She had sworn she would never let this happen again. But here she was, naked, hot, wet, and begging for more.

Her lips were wild beneath his, taking kiss for kiss and returning it with another. Her fingers held him to her. Her thighs tightened on the cloth-covered leg between her knees, and she fought to hold his fingers inside her.

She was falling. Just like she had before. Losing her common sense, her heart, and her soul to this man.

Dumb. Caution was screaming through her brain.

"Now this is a pretty sight. Damn, Dawg, you started without me. I'm hurt."

Like a slap of cold water, Natches's voice tore through her head as Dawg's head lifted, and Crista swore she heard him curse.

Anger. Pain. Fear. It lashed through her as she stared up at Natches, fighting back the wave of sickness as his gaze flickered over her with amused lust. He was leaning against the bar, thankfully dressed, grinning, and the epitome of every

reason why she should have fought harder, should have remembered why she couldn't let Dawg have another part of
her soul.

"Let me go!" She slapped at his shoulders. "Get off me."

"Damn it, Crista. You're naked," he snarled the reminder.

"Get off me!" She kicked at him, jerking out of his arms
and rolling from beneath him.

"Look your fill, asshole," she told Natches as she grabbed
Dawg's shirt from the floor. "Because it will be the last damn
look you ever get the chance to take."

Clasping the material over her breasts and making certain
it covered her thighs, she tore from the room, rushed past
him, and ran for the stairs.

Fine, she was flashing her ass. Let them both look. One
last damned time.

"Natches, you're a bastard," she heard Dawg curse.

Natches was laughing, and Crista felt like crying.

Because for a few precious moments, she had believed.

She was a fool for it, she admitted to herself. A fool for
Dawg. And seconds later, staring around the opulent bedroom,
the monstrously large bed, and the drape-shrouded windows
that surrounded it, she realized what she had done.

She had run straight to his bedroom rather than the spare
room. Straight into Dawg's private lair.

Dawg stared at Crista's perky little butt as it disappeared up the stairs and sighed heavily.

"What the hell do you want, Natches?" he asked his cousin
wearily, turning to him and watching as Natches grinned back.

The other man hadn't watched the charming display of
flesh; it was the only reason he still had all his teeth in his
head.

Natches shook his head. "You and Rowdy. Man, you two
are so possessive it's enough to make a man's stomach turn.
And here I thought I could depend on you to hold out."

Dawg grunted at the comment. "You didn't answer my
question."

"I brought her Rodeo back. I thought I'd drop in and see

how you two were doing before heading to bed." His grin was pure evil. "And I thought I'd give you this. It was in the passenger seat."

Dawg took the slip of paper. Express Movers. The letterhead and address were legit. The scrawled handwriting assured Miss Jansen she could now pick up her items in Store It Yourself, and enclosed in the envelope she would find the key to the indoor warehouse locker.

"I hacked the company computers before coming over here. They don't have a record for the delivery. Someone set her up."

Dawg tucked the note carefully into the pocket of his sweats until he could lock it in the upstairs safe later.

"Looks like you were making progress, anyway," Natches smirked.

"We were doing fine until you opened your mouth. But I think you were aware of that."

Natches glanced toward the stairs then. For a second, regret sliced across his features, then his ever-present mocking smile was back on his face.

"One-man woman, huh?" he asked, though from his look, it was more a statement.

Dawg stared back at him, seeing the flash of loneliness, of knowledge that filled his cousin's dark, forest green eyes.

"She's not as agreeable to being my woman as I would wish, though." Dawg raked his fingers heavily through his hair as he glanced at the stairs again. "I blackmailed her."

He glanced back at Natches in time to see his cousin shaking his head.

"I knew you were going to do something dumb like that." He chuckled, though the sound carried little amusement. "Good luck on that one. I just stopped by to drop these off." He dropped Crista's keys on the counter. "And to tell you Cranston wants our final reports in his office by the end of the day. Oral and written. He's still a little upset over losing the woman. But he seems certain the men he captured will talk."

"They probably will." *But who would they identify?*

If Crista had been led there, then it was for a reason. The thieves would spill their guts in a heartbeat, either way.

"I don't know." Natches shrugged. "I followed them to the van when they were loading them up. All Cranston got from them were vague looks when he was questioning them. They might not know."

Dawg stared at him in complete disbelief.

"Hey, we can hope." Natches snickered, holding his hands up in surrender before straightening from the bar and heading for the door. "I came in the back, I'll leave through the front. Give the gossips something to crow about. While you're having fun, I'll see what I can find out, see who's too interested in the setup you have going on here. I don't like this a damned bit, Dawg, I'll tell you. She shouldn't have been there tonight. It's a setup."

Dawg couldn't agree with him more. "Let me know what you find out."

As Natches left, Dawg relocked the doors behind him and reset the alarms. But he didn't immediately follow Crista to the bedroom on the upper deck. He stared around the lower level instead, seeing more than the crisp, clean lines of the interior and the nice furnishings.

He'd been living on the *Nauti Dawg* for years. Only through the coldest months did he leave the marina and stay in the small apartment he had above the lumber store. He rarely stayed at the underground home his father had built before his death.

He sat down slowly on the couch, leaned back, and breathed out wearily. God, he was exhausted. Tired and horny and conflicted. It was a hell of a state to be in at three o'clock in the morning.

His silent laughter was bitter and mocking. Hell, he was turning into the bastard his father had always predicted he was. Maybe he was more like his grandfather, Nate August, than he wanted to admit. The son of a bitch had left three bastard sons and a daughter in Somerset before returning to his Texas home more than fifty years before. Of the four children, Dawg's father and his uncles and aunt, only Ray Mackay, Rowdy's father, had shown any sort of decency to his wife or his children. His aunt didn't count. She worshipped the ground her son, Johnny, walked on, but many suspected she had driven her husband, Ralph, to his grave.

Dawg rubbed at the ache in his knee, feeling every steel pin that held the joint and kneecap together. The weather was getting ready to turn damp; he could predict it within days now. And he'd been on his leg too damned long. He was riding close to twenty-four hours without sleep, and Cranston wanted him in to give his final report.

And upstairs, Crista was waiting in his bedroom. Pissed off and probably feeling just as betrayed as she had every right to feel.

He should just let her go. He owed her that much. But he couldn't do it. Everything inside him howled in protest at the thought of letting her go. He had a hold on her now, a way to keep her in his bed if nothing else. A chance to figure out why she had haunted him for eight fucking years.

She wasn't the only woman he had fucked in his life that he couldn't remember. For a few years there, there had been more than a few. But she was the only woman who had ever lingered in his head to the point that the thought of her nearly drove him insane.

Seducing her wasn't going to be easy. He didn't just want her body; he wanted more, and he was man enough to admit to it. Just fucking her would never be enough. He needed to capture the elusive sense of something more that was so much a part of her.

He rubbed his jaw as he considered that one. Hell, he had never courted a woman a day in his life, especially not one he knew he could fuck. He could walk upstairs to that bedroom and within a few hot kisses, have her ready and willing. For the moment.

But she would resent it. She would eventually hate him for it, and that wasn't what he wanted. He wanted her sweet smiles, her soft touches. He wanted her to be his lover, not just a bedmate.

He'd never really had a lover.

Dawg frowned at that. He was thirty-two years old, yet he had never had a steady lover, a woman he wanted in his bed for more than a night or two. And he couldn't figure out why.

Oh, he had considered it once. Eight fucking years ago.

When he had been trying to get Crista into his bed, he had known then that he wanted more than a few nights with her. A few weeks, a few months, maybe.

Something tightened in his chest at the thought, something akin to regret, a knowledge that even a few months might not be enough.

One step at a time, he thought tiredly. Tonight, he'd just sleep with her. Just hold her. See how that went. That was something else he had never done, just held a woman through the night and felt the warmth of her against him.

Rowdy swore that some nights, it was better than sex, just having Kelly next to him, soft and sweet.

Would it be like that with Crista?

He glanced back at the stairs, his mind filling with the memory of her sweet scent, the warmth of her delicate body. Maybe, for one fucking night in his life, he could sleep without dreaming, if he were holding her.

He pushed himself to his feet and moved through the houseboat. He checked the windows, the back deck door, and the security alarms before moving up the stairs. When he stepped into the bedroom, he stopped in surprise.

He expected her to be awake and ready to shoot him. She had been madder than hell when she flew up that metal staircase. Instead, she was curled beneath the blankets of his king-sized bed, the covers pulled up to her nose, sleeping like a baby.

And she wasn't just on the edge of the bed. She was in the middle, where he slept. A slow smile curled his lips as he stripped silently, leaving the small, dim light, which sat on the corner table on the far end of the room, turned on. He moved around the bed, slid beneath the blankets, and carefully, very cautiously, he eased in beside her.

She muttered something not so nice. A drowsy little comment about cold feet, but she settled back to sleep as his arm came over her and he drew her against him.

She didn't awaken.

His frown deepened. A woman who slept alone was always aware when a man slid into bed beside her.

Crista was used to sleeping with someone.

Had that someone held her through the night and kept dreams of Dawg at bay? The bastard. He gritted his teeth at the thought of any other man holding her like this.

She belonged here, curled against his chest, snuggled into his body, keeping him warm.

It was . . . interesting.

He was still harder than hell. Hornier than he could re-member being in years, but there was no need to hurry. No race to satisfaction so he could be alone.

His eyes closed as she muttered something again. Some-thing about Alex and the electric bill, and he grinned. Female fluff stuff that Rowdy always teased Kelly about.

Hell, this was nice.

His eyes drifted closed, his arousal pounded between his thighs, but the edge was tempered with exhaustion and a slow easing of the tight sense of cold anger that had gripped him for years.

He buried his face in Crista's hair, breathed out slowly, and let the darkness have him, for a few hours at least.

FIVE

Some days, it just didn't pay to wake up. Waking up in Dawg's bed had been bad enough, but thankfully he had been gone. She'd been able to steal a shirt and someone's smaller-sized sweatpants, call a cab, rush back to her brother's house to shower and change, and arrive to work on time.

Only to be fired.

Fired from a crappy waitress job in a diner that obviously didn't have enough help to begin with. And it had been more than clear that the owner was reluctant to fire her, which led Crista to only one conclusion. Dawg had influenced the owner.

He had her fired.

He wasn't even decent enough to stop at just blackmailing her when she knew he had to know she was innocent. But now she was out of a job so he could have his little plaything close by.

She stood by the register as the manager wrote out her final paycheck and sighed wearily.

"Thanks, Madge," she said quietly when the other woman, concerned and clearly upset with the orders to fire her, handed over the check.

"I'm sure sorry 'bout this, Crista." Madge sighed, her hazel eyes compassionate. "Owner just called and said do it. Nothing I could do."

Crista shrugged. The owner was friends with Dawg, she knew that, she knew how it happened.

Turning from the register, she tucked the check in her purse and made her way across the floor. There were few customers at this time of the morning. Some coffee drinkers, an early rising tourist, and Johnny Grace, her next-door neighbor and Dawg's cousin. Though Dawg admitted to the relationship only when he was forced.

He sat at the back table, a heavy frown on his brow as she moved toward him.

"Crista." He stopped her before she could make it to the door. "Is everything okay?"

"Fine." She gave him a stiff smile. "Cutbacks, I guess."

She liked Johnny. He ran a bakery from his house beside hers and often brought her over fresh bread and sweets on baking days, free of charge, just because, he said, they were neighbors.

His gaze flicked to the manager, the frown still darkening his amazingly clear, soft brow. Dark blond curls framed his face, giving him an almost feminine appearance.

"Is there anything I can do?"

Anything he could do? She had a feeling there wasn't a damned thing anyone could do. She shook her head, forcing a stiff smile to her face.

"I'll be fine, Johnny. I have to go now, though. I'll catch you later."

Johnny was a good neighbor, but not a confidant. Right now, she couldn't handle discussing this with anyone.

Her hand tightened on her purse as she stepped from the diner, her gaze swinging unerringly to the big black pickup across the street.

How the hell had she known he would be there? What instinct possessed her that she could feel him watching her, wanting her?

He was a dark shadow behind the tinted windows, until the passenger side window rolled smoothly down, revealing his unsmiling countenance and the dark glasses shielding his eyes.

His overlong black hair was tied back at the nape of his neck, revealing the strong line of his jaw and the arrogance that permeated his expression.

His hand lifted from where his long arm was stretched along the backseat, and his fingers beckoned her to him with regal confidence that she would come. Like a damned pet.

Her eyes narrowed on him as she turned and stalked down the sidewalk to the side of the diner where her Rodeo was parked. She had packed a suitcase that morning before heading to the job she didn't have anymore. She had actually given Dawg the benefit of the doubt that he would at least trust her to work while he was playing the high-and-mighty blackmailer from hell.

But could he do that? Hell no. He had to have it all.

She jerked her keys from her purse as she heard the powerful motor moving behind her. She threw a glare over her shoulder before striding furiously across the parking lot.

She had bills to pay, a college loan to honor, not that she was using the damned degree at present, but there was always the potential of getting a decent job. Now she was going to go job hunting again and pray there was someone willing to laugh in his face when he ordered her fired.

God, he hadn't changed. In eight years, most people managed to mature a little bit, but Dawg was still Dawg. Just a little darker, a little more dangerous, but still determined to have everything his own way.

"I don't think so." His big hand shackled her wrist as she moved to shove the key into the lock of the Rodeo.

Crista stood still, freezing as anger threatened to overwhelm her.

"I can't believe you." She tried to jerk her arm back, then stared at his fingers as he refused to release her.

They were shackled on her wrist like irons, snug enough to hold her in place, to remind her that he was bigger, stronger, harder than she was.

"What can't you believe about me?" he asked, drawing

her along with him to the truck where it sat, driver's side door still standing open, a few feet behind him.

"Let me go, Dawg! I have to go job hunting," she sneered with false sweetness. "Someone cost me this job."

Mocking disbelief filled his face. "No! Someone got you fired? Shame on them."

Wicked amusement filled his eyes, almost playful, inviting her to share in the fun when he had just taken her only means of support.

When she jerked her wrist back this time, he let her go.

"Tell me, Dawg, how do you expect me to support myself? To pay my bills? To keep my car? I don't have a job now because of you."

"You have a job." The playful amusement left his expression.

"I have a job?" she jeered bitterly. "Let me guess, you're going to pay me to play your whore?"

His expression stilled then. "Get in the truck."

She should have been nervous. She had seen that expression on her brother's face before, and it was one that was best avoided. One she would have avoided if she weren't so damned mad.

She knew what he expected, and it enraged her.

"Not on your egotistical little life!" Her hand slapped against his chest as she felt anger engulf her. "I have a job to—"

The breath rushed from her chest as he jerked her to him, her breasts flush against his broad chest, the fingers of one broad hand tangled in her hair as he pulled her head back, his gaze imprisoning hers as she stared back at him in shock.

"We made a deal." His voice rasped with something akin to anger, and yet it went deeper than anger.

Crista trembled as she stared into the light green eyes and the determination that glowed inside them.

"That deal didn't include stealing my job and my life. You had no right to do this."

"My bed, or jail. My terms. And my terms say that while you're sharing my bed, then by God you'll share when I want you there, not when you have time for me."

Shock filled her, and not for the first time. This wasn't the

Dawg she had known eight years before, but he was the man who had taken her that night so long ago.

The veneer of teasing charm had been stripped away, and in its place was a man she wasn't certain she could handle.

"You won't arrest me." Her voice trembled. "You know I wasn't doing anything wrong."

"We have a deal," he repeated. "Now get your ass in that truck. We'll discuss the terms of it back at the houseboat, but we will not discuss them here, in the middle of a goddamned parking lot."

He didn't give her time to argue. He picked her up by her waist, turned, and pushed her into the vehicle.

"My clothes . . ." She tried to scramble back out, only to come face-to-face with eyes that began to become turbulent in their color. Light greens, sparks of darker color, a swirl of chaotic shades that had her suddenly stilling.

His jaw bunched with tension, the muscle in his cheek twitching twice before he managed to control it.

The keys were plucked from her fingers.

"Don't move. So help me God, you come out of that truck, Crista, and you'll regret it. Because I'll turn you over my knee and paddle your ass here and now. Do you understand me?"

She stared back at him warily.

He stomped, literally stomped the short distance to her Rodeo, unlocked it, and dragged her suitcase from the front seat.

"My flowers." Her voice gained strength. If all she was risking was a spanking, then he could damned well get everything she had packed. "And the box in the back."

The suitcase thumped on the ground as he turned and stared back at her broodingly.

"Surely I can at least have the few things I need." She smiled back at him tightly. "Even condemned prisoners get a few personal articles, Dawg."

His eyes narrowed before he locked the driver's side door and slammed it closed. He paced to the back of the vehicle, unlocked the hatchback, and jerked it open. The box of extra clothes, makeup, and personal items was set out, then the miniature rosebush and flowering cactus that sat in the corner.

Slamming the hatchback closed again, he locked it and packed her items in the backseat of his truck.

"Move over." His voice was harsh as he stepped to the opened door once again.

"I need my car."

"I said move over."

"You can't just leave my car sitting here, Dawg, I need it." She forced herself not to scream in complete frustration. "This is going too damned far . . ."

He gripped her waist, and before Crista could fight him he had lifted her over the console and dropped her into the passenger side seat before climbing in.

Damn him. She gripped the door latch with every intention of throwing herself from the truck and reclaiming her precious Rodeo.

"Open that door, and so help me, you'll regret it."

She stilled at the sound of his voice, turning to glare at him furiously as he put the truck in gear and turned the monster vehicle around.

"I need my car."

"Natches can collect it later." One hand tightened on the steering wheel, the other on the gearshift that rose from the floor as he drove from the parking lot and turned back onto Main Street before heading for the interstate.

"That's not fair. None of this is fair, Dawg," she yelled. "You stole my job. That's the same as stealing everything I own."

And that wasn't much, admittedly. Mainly the Rodeo, but it was the thought that counted.

"I'll take care of your bills," he bit out.

"Why not just stamp *whore* on my head," she sneered.

The truck was jerked to the side of the road, rocking to a hard stop as he turned to her, the effort to control whatever rose inside him visibly apparent on his face.

"Call yourself a whore again, and I'll make sure that spanking you have yet to receive is nothing pleasant," he snarled between clenched teeth.

"What do you call it then?"

"I call it a deal you made and agreed to." He spoke with

hard deliberation as his eyes speared into hers. "And I make the rules. You don't. Now sit back, fasten your seat belt, and stop arguing the point with me before I do something guaranteed to show everyone who passes by this truck just how little I care about propriety or their fucking opinions of either of us."

Which amounted to nothing, and Crista knew it. Gritting her teeth against the furious words rising to her lips, she slammed the seat belt latch in, crossed her arms over her breasts, and stared straight ahead.

She admitted to being slightly nervous. Not exactly frightened of Dawg, but warier than she would have been even two days before. There was a glow of lust, of hunger in his gaze that had the feminine core of her shaking in trepidation. And it had her mind spinning.

Dawg had always been so fiercely controlled. He never showed anger, at least that was the rumor. He was a get-even rather than a get-mad kind of man.

It wasn't anger she saw in him now but the dark, primal core of a man who was no longer hiding who or what he was. And the savage hunger that glowed in his eyes aroused her more than the false charm ever had.

This was the Dawg she had always sensed lurking beneath the surface. The one who had held her back when she was younger, who frightened the immature sexuality she had possessed then.

It was that inner man he had let loose on her the night she had spent with him. The drunken charm had evaporated once he had her in his bed, and though he hadn't been rough, he had been determined, hungry.

"What happened that night?"

His voice had her stilling, her heart beating faster in her chest. She didn't want to talk about that night. She didn't want to relive it any more than she already had.

"We had sex. Period."

"We had sex, so you ran out of town with another man, stayed away seven years, and now you're fighting something between us that threatens to burn down the county once we get back into bed. Sorry, fancy-face, that one doesn't go over so well with me. You're lying."

She remembered, this was how he got his name. She'd heard Ray relate the tale, how even as a child he would get something in his mind and wouldn't let it go. Like a dog with a bone. Dawg. He hadn't changed much.

"What happened eight years ago doesn't matter, Dawg." She shook her head tiredly. "What's happening now does. I can't afford not to work for three months, and I won't accept money to sleep with you. I have to have a job."

"We're not talking about that right now." His voice rumbled with displeasure.

"And we're not talking about what happened eight years ago, either," she retorted. "Actually, that night is really pretty fuzzy in my head. I've all but forgotten it."

And that had to be the biggest lie she had ever told in her life.

Crista glanced over at him, satisfied and yet more nervous than ever once she saw the dark, brooding intensity of his expression.

"It just pisses me off when you lie to me, Crista Ann," he growled, glancing at her over the top edge of his dark glasses as he came to a stoplight.

The vehicle rolled to a stop as Crista stared out at the town that stretched on each side of the highway running through it. It had grown in the years she had been away from it, but it was still filled with the same qualities she had missed.

There were no high-rises here, no frantic rush of people walking down the sidewalks, fighting to get from office to office and ignoring everyone around them. She could walk into any store and see someone she knew or had known from her childhood.

She had friends here, distant relatives, and history.

She was aware of him glancing back at her as he put the truck into gear and accelerated through the green light, gathering speed and heading to the marina outside town.

"How long have you been working undercover against the drug dealers around here?" she asked him then. "I know Alex said the problem had grown, but I didn't know it was bad enough to warrant late-night raids."

"They're rare." His voice was clipped, the message clear. He didn't want to talk about it.

"It must be getting pretty bad. The guy who caught me in the warehouse looked like one of the monsters television portrays. If the Latin factions have moved into Somerset, won't it be hard to weed them out?"

His fingers tapped against the steering wheel as he glanced at her.

"Doubtful." He was determined not to discuss it with her, that was more than obvious.

"Do you know who the woman was who was supposed to be there?"

At that question, he froze. "Not yet."

Crista bit at her lower lip nervously. "You've questioned the other men though, right?"

"This morning."

"Did you find the money they were missing?"

His head swung around briefly, his gaze hidden behind the dark glasses now.

"Not yet." Clipped, dark, his voice sent a shiver down her spine. "Why?"

"He seemed to think I had it. That was what he said to me: 'Where's my money, *puta*?' Evidently, he's not the only one that considers me a—"

She swore he growled. Crista compressed her lips at the silent snarl that pulled at his lips.

"What else did he say?" he snapped out.

"He didn't have time to say anything else. You splattered his blood all over me less than a second later."

"It beat seeing your fucking blood staining that damned warehouse." Violence filled his voice before Crista watched him forcibly rein it in with a tight grimace. "Did you hear anything else? See anything else?"

She shook her head slowly, feeling the terror that had risen inside her the night before beating at her head again. Dawg had relieved the horror of the event the night before, strangely enough, with his obnoxious blackmail demand. But now it was beginning to set in. The fact that she had nearly died. That if she had just gone to Dawg before, this might not have happened.

She licked her lips nervously. "Look, this is probably totally unrelated, but before this, weird things were happening anyway. So weird that when I told Alex about them, he just about ordered me to call you."

"What things?"

She went through them briefly: missing clothes, the feeling that someone was following her, watching her.

"Do you think it had something to do with last night?" she asked as she finished.

Dawg didn't think; he knew. He could feel it burning in his gut and itching along the back of his neck. Primitive possession roiled through his mind as he glanced at Crista and realized that somehow, for some reason, someone among the crew they had rounded up last night had known to use her.

It was far-fetched; he would do better to suspect her of being involved to begin with, but his unruly dick refused to let him consider it.

But, if someone had been trying to throw her into the mix, then it was because they knew of his obsession for her. And there were very, very few people who knew that Dawg couldn't forget one Crista Ann Jansen.

He wiped his hand down his face and considered his options. They hadn't caught the one female of the group who they knew had been involved. The mediator between the buyers and sellers had been a woman; the vague description the team had of her resembled Crista. And if she was telling the truth about the buyer, Aaron Grael, then the woman had made off with half down on a two million dollar deal.

He blew out a rough breath as he glanced over at her. She was watching him worriedly, her chocolate eyes filled with indecision and a hint of fear. But there was no guilt. Over the years, hell, even before he joined the Marines, he had been able to spot most lies a mile away. He couldn't see anything in Crista's gaze but her worry and her discomfort.

"You haven't answered me." There was a snap to her voice that assured him that she wasn't frightened enough to have forgotten her earlier anger with him.

"Let me check into a few things and talk to Natches about this," he finally said, his voice rough. There was too damned much money missing to discount any of it. "But my best guess is that it's all connected. Somehow. I just have to figure out how."

"If you're undercover, as I assume you are, because I haven't heard anything about you working with the DEA, then someone would have to know the truth to know to use me," she said hesitantly.

He had to give her credit for being smart. No one had ever accused Crista of being without her own sense of intuition.

Too bad he wasn't really working with the DEA; his problems might be easier at the moment.

"Natches and I both are undercover," he finally said. "The deal we broke up last night had been in the works for over six months. We pulled in everyone except the buyer I killed and one more player. We're looking for the other person now."

She didn't say anything for long moments.

"The other player is a woman," she finally guessed, her voice trembling. "And she resembles me, doesn't she?"

Dawg made the turn into the Mackay Marina in silence before he glanced over at her again.

"The description we have of her resembles you," he admitted softly, seeing her flinch from the corner of his eye. "She's the only one missing; she has the money. There's no reason for any focus to linger on you."

"Unless one of the men you captured saw me? Or recognized me from town? Or someone associated with them sees me now?"

"Let's not borrow trouble, Crista." But they were thoughts brewing in his own mind. "You concentrate on the here and now; I'll concentrate on the rest of it."

"Just concentrate on your little blackmail scheme?" she retorted acidly.

"Make happy with my dick, and I'll be a happy little camper." He said the words for shock effect. He hated seeing the fear in her eyes, in her expression. And that took care of it nicely.

"Has anyone ever told you what a bastard you are, Dawg?" Hostility radiated from her now.

Dawg let his lips curl into a mocking grin. Oh yeah, he knew what a bastard he was. His father had made certain he had known at a very early age.

"You're telling me now." He pulled into his parking slot close to the docks, his gaze moving carefully around the area as he shut the pickup off before turning to face her. "You ready to make nice and go to the boat yet? Or do we need to sit here and have a screaming match instead?"

"I don't have screaming matches." Her expression lit with offended anger.

"You'd be the first woman then," he grunted, moving from the vehicle. "Let's go. I need a cold beer."

Summer had just started, but it was already warming up with a ferocity that sent waves of heat curling up from the asphalt.

He pulled her suitcase from the backseat as well as the box and tucked it under his arm as she rounded the front of the truck.

"I'll get the flowers." Her expression was anxious, as though she couldn't trust him to take care of two damned pots of flowers.

But hell, why should she? She couldn't even trust him to help her when Alex advised her to.

Son of a bitch. Missing items from her home, a feeling of being watched and followed. She had all the signs of a stalker at the very least, and she hadn't contacted anyone. If she had contacted the sheriff, Zeke Mayes, he would have let Dawg know.

Dawg let her gather the two oversized pots in her arms. The red miniature rosebush with its pot was nearly as tall as she was. The flowering cactus was smaller but no less bulky.

"I can have Natches come back for those," he told her doubtfully.

The glare she gave him had his lips tightening in annoyance.

"Fine." He slammed the doors closed as he turned back to her. "Let me carry one of them before you topple over."

"I have them." She peeked between the branches of the rosebush. "Just lead the way."

"If you fall in the lake because you can't see over those damned pots, then I'm going to let you drown," he warned her.

He knew better. He was so damned stupid where she was concerned, he'd save her and the fucking plants.

"I know what I'm doing." Dark brown eyes narrowed on him. "Just go on. I'll be right behind you."

"After you." He smiled tightly. "And watch where you're going, if you can. Don't walk off the side of a dock. Please."

As she moved ahead of him, Dawg stayed close to her, just in case. She was so damned stubborn she would probably kill herself rather than see a single rose damaged.

He frowned at the small roses topping their green branches. He had given her a rosebush once. He wondered what had happened to it. On her seventeenth birthday, an attempt to sweeten her toward him. He had arrived at her home, endured Alex's glare, and given her the plastic-wrapped little bush for the tiny rose garden she had behind the house. He had noticed that. How much she liked roses.

She'd probably tossed it out just like she had tossed out the memory of them together.

Memories that were still foggy to him. At twenty-four, he had drunk too much, partied too damned hard, and had no sense where women were concerned. But he had been smart enough to think Crista was different. Special.

Hell, she was special, and so different from any other woman he had ever known that it was like night and day. The leading difference being the fact that Crista had never been bowled over by the famous Mackay charm.

At least, not until he was too drunk to remember what had convinced her to sleep with him in the first place.

Now, he had to deal with a hard-on that made common sense iffy at best and the knowledge that someone had been drawing Crista into this game between the agents looking for missiles and those involved in the buying and selling of those missiles.

Damn. He knew the only missing component to this case was the woman who had escaped with a million dollars in unmarked bills. He prayed she was running far and fast and was the only person aware of Crista. Not that he could get that damned lucky, but he could hope.

Unlocking the glass door that led into the houseboat, Dawg checked the security monitor as he entered the living room before setting the suitcase and box on the couch and watching as Crista stood hesitantly in the room, looking around.

"Can I put the flowers upstairs?" she asked. "There's more sunlight there."

"Set them down. I'll take them up later." He strode across the room to the refrigerator and the cold beer inside.

Twisting the cap off the bottle, he took a healthy drink as he stared at Crista through the dark glasses he wore. Better to hide his eyes, to hide the emotions he knew he wasn't holding back very well. Even Natches had watched him in concern during the meeting with the joint ATF and Homeland Security task force that had been working the investigation.

Something about Crista made him dangerously hungry. Knowing he had had her and being unable to remember anything but the dimmest events made him crazy.

"You have a choice." He set the beer on the counter with enough force to cause her to jump.

"Do I?" She was watching him nervously.

At least it wasn't in fear.

He pulled the sunglasses from his nose and tossed them to the counter before turning his gaze back to her. Immediate. Her response came as fast as her gaze took in his.

He watched her breasts begin to rise and lower with her quicker breathing, watched the little points of her nipples tighten beneath her shirt and a softening in the defiant stance she had adopted.

His hand went to his belt, loosening it slowly as her eyes began to widen.

"Dawg." She swallowed tightly. "I'm not ready for this yet."

At least she hadn't said no outright.

The belt came loose. Moving toward her, he tore the metal button open, then rasped the zipper down. Her eyes became wider, darker, and sharp little teeth bit at her lip.

"I dreamed." The rough sound of his own voice surprised him. "I dreamed of your mouth taking me. Sucking me into a pleasure so hot I nearly died from it."

Her eyes seemed to glaze; her face flushed heatedly as he pulled her to the couch. Dragging his jeans down his thighs, he sat down, removed his boots, then kicked the material free as she watched in shock.

He was desperate. So fucking hard he was dying from the hunger crawling through his system.

"Say no, and it stops," he bit out. "Just say no."

"And go to jail?"

He clamped his lips shut. He had one advantage over her, and that was it. She very well might not be ready for the rest of it yet, but he had to have this, or he was going to die.

"Your choice."

SIX

Her choice.

Crista stared down at him, feeling every cell in her body reacting to the sight of Dawg, leaning back on the couch, his devil's black hair mussed around his face, his light green eyes darkening, and she felt her vagina flood with the response.

She was dampening her panties. Growing so sensitive that even the air from the air conditioner was a caress against flesh still covered by her clothing.

"Dawg—" She could hear the plea in her voice.

"You're so pretty, Crista," he whispered. "I dreamed of it last night. Your sweet mouth moving over my cock, driving me insane. Give me that. Just that. We can wait for the rest of it."

Wait for the rest of it?

Was this his idea of seduction? If it was, then she was weaker than she could have ever imagined, because it was working.

"Come here, baby." He gripped her wrist, drawing her to her knees as he leaned forward.

As she settled before him, his hands gripped the hem of her shirt and drew it upward, drawing it over her head, then her arms, until he tossed it away.

"Sweet God have mercy," he groaned, his eyes like brilliant pinpoints of color in his dark face as he stared at the white lace covering her breasts.

"Dawg, this is too soon." She had to force the words past her lips. "You have to let me—"

One hand cupped around her neck, tilting her head back as the other touched her lips.

"You have the memories of this," he said, his voice rough. "Give me one now. Just one memory, Crista, instead of a dream that tears my guts to ribbons with hunger."

One hand gripped her wrist as he settled against the back of the couch once again and folded her fingers partially around the width of his cock. They wouldn't surround it.

The hard flesh throbbed beneath her hand, silky and ridged with heavy veins, the bloated head darkened as a drop of pre-cum beaded at the tiny slit.

She knew what he tasted like. Like a storm coming in from the mountains. She knew what was going to happen the minute she took him into her mouth. She was going to lose herself in the sensuality he wrapped around her.

He terrified her. The knowledge of what he could do to her had her shaking before him.

"There, Crista." His hand tangled in her hair, cupping the side of her head as he drew her forward. "Just a little bit, fancy-face. Suck me just a little bit."

Just a little bit?

Crista whimpered as the thick crest touched her lips, parted them, slid inside.

She couldn't help herself. Because she did remember that night, and she knew exactly what he had taught her. She knew what he liked then, but would he like it now?

Tentatively, she swirled her tongue over the engorged head, feeling his thighs clench, hearing the ragged groan that rumbled in his chest. His hand tightened in her hair, pulling at the strands and sending a tingling heat through her scalp.

His chest was moving fiercely, rising and falling quickly

as her own breathing became labored, and she let her mouth fill with the head of his cock and the few inches beyond that she could manage.

"Sweet God. Crista. Sweetheart. Ah God yes, suck my dick, fancy-face. Hard and deep . . ."

Dawg felt his head fall back against the cushion behind him and fought to breathe. Her mouth was hot, tight, drawing over his cock head, her tongue rasping the ultrasensitive flesh beneath it. His balls drew up painfully tight as her fingers were tucked beneath them, cupping them, massaging the taut sac with such wicked caresses that he had to clench his teeth to hold back the brutal pleasure tearing through him.

He struggled to open his eyes, to stare down at her. God help him, she was gorgeous. Long hair flowed around her flushed face, her lips stretched wide around his dick, her dark eyes almost black.

Delicate fingers gripped the shaft, working it slow and easy as she drew on the pleasure-tortured crest. She sucked it, tongued it. Her cheeks hollowed and her eyes glowed, and he swore he saw the same needs in her eyes that he felt ripping through his guts.

Hunger like nothing he had ever known before.

"Ah yes." He hissed out on a hard breath of pleasure as she worked the head of his cock with strong sucks and fast, flickering lashes of her tongue. "That's good, baby. So good."

He pulled at her hair, drawing her head back, feeling her fight the tug at the strands and watching the pleasure that consumed her expression.

He pulled at her hair again, his teeth gritting as her lashes fluttered and she took his cock deeper into her mouth.

"Like that?" He was almost shaking with the pleasure.

"Hmm." She lifted her lips from his aching flesh and raised her eyes.

"Do you?" she asked him a second before her tongue took a lingering taste of the underside of his cock.

"Oh hell yes," he groaned, sending a surge of pleasure racing through her. "It's so damned good I'm about to burn alive with it."

His abdomen flexed and rippled with tension. His scrotum

was tight as she cupped and caressed it in the palm of her hand, and heat radiated from him.

Crista took him into her mouth again, holding his gaze, sucking him deep and hard as she remembered, licking the underside and feeling her own edge of ecstasy twisting inside her at the pleasure she was bringing him.

She knew better than this, better than to allow herself to be affected by his pleasure. But she couldn't help it now any more than she could have done anything to stop it eight years before.

She loved giving Dawg pleasure. She loved watching his expression tense as he fought for control, how his body tensed and a sheen of sweat slicked his muscles.

Her mouth moved on his cock, taking as much as possible, holding it deep and then retreating to suckle at the head with loving greed. She moaned at the taste of pre-cum that whispered over her taste buds and teased more to her hungry mouth as his hands tightened in her hair.

Fingers tugged at the long strands, pulled it forward, drew it over his taut abdomen, and a whispered male groan filled her ears.

"Ah, Crista. So sweet and good." His voice was low and tight with lust. "Perfect, sweet mouth."

She tongued the underside of his cock, licked and probed and gloried at the shudder that traveled through his heavily muscled body.

She wasn't as hesitant as she had been eight years ago. She knew what he liked then, what he still liked now, and she applied the lessons he had given her through the long, dark hours on an unforgettable summer night. Lessons she had dreamed of, fantasized about using on him once again.

"Crista, sweetheart." Dawg could feel the sweat building on his flesh, the heat rushing through his body.

His head fell to the back of the couch, his eyes closed, and memory slammed into him.

Innocent brown eyes staring at him from the same spot where she knelt now. She had helped him into the houseboat and then to the couch, and there he had pulled her to his lap, kissed her, caressed her, and teasingly convinced her to go down on him.

"Suck my dick, baby," he whispered now as he had whispered then. "God, your mouth is killing me."

She had been more shy then. Hesitant. A bit of fear in her wide eyes, but mixed with that fear had been immeasurable excitement.

He forced his head up, his eyes to open, and he stared at her now. Not that much had changed. She was still shy, a little afraid, but the hesitancy was gone. And the pleasure was starker, clearer.

The sight of that pleasure nearly destroyed his control. That coupled with the heat of her sucking mouth, the tempting touch of her fingers on his shaft and his balls, and her moan, and Dawg knew his control wouldn't last much longer.

"Sweet mercy," he groaned, arching, driving his cock deeper in her mouth as she began to lengthen and quicken her suckling strokes. "You're destroying me, Crista."

He hadn't expected this. He had expected a fight. Hell, he halfway wanted a fight. Anything to give him an excuse to escape the hunger that dug into his guts like a dull knife.

There was no escaping it with Crista's hot mouth wrapped around his dick, though. No escaping the pleasure or the pain. Each time he stared down at her, past and present merged. What he had believed were dreams swirled alongside reality.

His chest clenched at the sight of her, emotions held so closely in check for most of his life swirling inside him, confusing him, multiplying the pleasure until he was pulling at her hair, his hips lifting to her, his cock flexing, tensing.

"Crista. Sweetheart." He could barely breathe. Sensation tore through, wrenching at his muscles and stealing his control. "Ah God. I'm gonna come, baby."

He couldn't stand it. His balls were so tight they were torturous, the seed boiling in them, building, breaking down the walls of his restraint as easily as a hammer against sandstone.

Crista's lips, mouth, and tongue were destroying him. Giving more pleasure than he had ever known. How could it be so good? How could one woman, one sweet, shy little mouth rip his control to shreds?

"Ah, God. Crista." His voice was rasping, guttural. "I can't hold back. Ease up."

She didn't ease up. Her mouth was hungrier, her moans hotter, her fingers . . . hot, wicked fingers playing with his balls while the fingers of her other hand stroked his shaft. Her mouth sucked, her tongue licked, her teeth scraped with delicate greed, and an edge of fire ripped through his balls and tore the choice from him.

The first explosive spurt of semen had a strangled cry tearing from his throat. His body tightened to breaking point, his hands gripping her hair, holding her in place. Praying . . . "Oh hell. Tongue it. Suck it. Fuck. Yes."

His head slammed back to the cushions, and light exploded in front of his eyes as pleasure became a fiery, torturous ecstasy unlike anything he had experienced in his life.

He filled her mouth. Forced her to take his release. Held her head in place and nearly writhed with the sensations burning and twisting through his body. His hips lifted from the couch, and her hungry moans rippled over his cock until finally, blessedly, the hot fingers of electricity eased from his spine, and he slumped back to his seat, fighting just to breathe.

Dawg forced himself to release his fingers from Crista's hair, and despite the shame that raged through him, he made himself stare down at her.

Shock wound through his consciousness at the sight of her. A temptress's smile curved her plump, swollen lips as she licked down the shaft of his cock in soothing motions, easing the sharp, heavy contractions in the still-hard flesh. Her eyes were nearly black with her own arousal, her cheeks stained with a flush of lust and shyness.

"Come here." He caught her arms as she moved to distance herself, ignored the flash of hesitancy in her expression, and lifted her to him before bearing her back on the cushions.

Moving over her, Dawg didn't give her time to argue or to protest. His lips covered hers, and for once, his distaste at kissing a woman who had just consumed his seed was absent.

He needed her kiss. The sweetness of her response. Her arms twining around his shoulders and her body softening beneath his.

Her lips parted for him with a gasp, and he nipped at the swollen lower curve before sinking into another, different whirl-pool of arousal.

The past few years, sex had been rare. Even the desire for it had been rare. But now, as though fighting to make up for lost time, his body went into overdrive. His cock thickened back to full strength, and the need began to whip through his system once more.

Because of Crista. Because there was something about her that made him hungry. Hell, made him ravenous for the taste of her. For her touch, her breathy little moans and the kisses that burned through his soul.

He tore his lips from hers a second later, turned to her jaw, nipped and licked, kissing his way down the graceful arch.

"Dawg. Wait," she gasped, her voice thick with arousal.

He could hear the hunger in her tone, feel it in the heated silk of her flesh. His hand flattened on her upper stomach, slid down, his fingers gripping the metal button of her jeans.

"Wait for what?" Damn, he was nearly shaking. Every cell in his body was in a frenzy of need to mate. To fuck. If he didn't bury inside her, he was going to go crazy.

"Dawg, please." Was it a protest or need?

His hand flattened on her abdomen, beneath the loose ma-terial of her jeans, and felt the muscles there flexing, spasming.

He needed her. Sweet heaven, her womb was clenching for release; her pussy would ripple and contract around him. It would hug him like a hot little fist and welcome him more eagerly than her mouth.

His lips moved to the swollen, flushed mounds of her breasts above the lace of her bra then. Her nipples were hard and pointed beneath. With his free hand, he drew the material over the flushed mound and stared in rapt attention a second before the overriding need to taste her had his head lowering.

Dawg groaned at the feel of her nipple against his tongue, the taste. The acceptance she allowed when his lips closed over one hungrily.

She jerked as though jolted with a hard surge of electricity. Her nipple tightened further, fit perfectly against his tongue, and drew him into a heated intimacy he had never known before.

He had never known, never understood how intimate this act could be. How it could feed his arousal, feed that deep, uncharted core of emotion he kept trapped in his soul.

It wasn't trapped any longer. It spilled from inside him, filling him with blistering pleasure and acceptance. She was accepting him. Giving to him. Letting him inside her soul as he drew the tender bud farther into his mouth.

He drew on the hard, silky flesh, lashed it with his tongue, and felt his own body tighten in pleasure as her thin, sensual wail filled his ears.

Her fingers pulled at his hair, her nails kneaded his scalp, sending tiny pinpoints of fiery pleasure to erupt through his head before it exploded straight to his dick.

Dawg lifted his head, tore his T-shirt from his shoulders, and stared down at her for a long, intense moment.

As her lashes lifted, he watched the pleasure rising inside her, the hunger and needs, and keeping a rein on his own was almost impossible.

"Now," he growled. "I need you now."

Crista stared up at Dawg as his fingers hooked in the loosened waist of her jeans and began to draw them, along with the thong she wore beneath, slowly over her hips.

Naked, aroused, his eyes glowing with unsuppressed hunger and raging need, he looked like a vanquishing conqueror. All the warriors and warlords that the best romances wrote about.

But this wasn't a story. It wasn't a book, and it wasn't fiction. It was the man blackmailing her into his bed and stealing her soul with his touch.

"Dawg." Trembling fingers slid over his shoulders as she tried to force strength into her arms to push him away, to push herself away from the temptation.

"I dreamed of you, Crista." The material slid over her thighs as he drew back. "I dreamed of your kiss, your taste. I dreamed of every wicked fantasy a man could have about his woman for eight years." His voice strengthened as he tossed the jeans and panties to the floor, and his eyes sharpened with angry desire. "Eight years, damn you. One fucking night, and you didn't give me a chance to make up for it. You didn't give me a chance to prove you're fucking *mine*!"

The snarl that drew his lips back held her mesmerized. Possessive, dominant. His eyes slid over her naked body, heating her insides and sending her juices spilling between her thighs.

Crista felt her head shaking, felt the denial born of a sudden knowledge that Dawg wasn't what she expected. This wasn't going to be an affair she could walk away from. Dawg wasn't a man she could watch walk out of her life a second time and survive it.

"Yes, damn you," he cursed, calloused hands pressing her legs apart as he slid deftly between them.

His lips lowered, stealing her protest and replacing it with passion and fire, with a whipping hunger she had no defenses against. As his tongue entered her lips, she felt the blunt pressure, the heated head of his cock pressing against the swollen folds of her pussy.

Tingling fingers of sensations began to play across her flesh. She froze beneath him. She remembered this part. Clearly, so clearly.

Her eyes struggled to open as she felt Dawg lever up, looking into his absorbed expression before she followed the point where his gaze had locked.

There, between her thighs. Her legs were draped over his thighs, spread wide, her hips angled to the thick spear of flesh pressing into her.

Crista watched as the wet folds parted, separating for his cock, hugging the wide crest as he pressed closer, penetrated the tender opening, and he groaned with hoarse male pleasure.

"So sweet. So hot."

Crista whimpered as her body began to stretch to accommodate the impalement. She shook her head against the cushion she lay on, dazed by the pleasure beginning to build inside her.

No, this went beyond pleasure. It went beyond words that Crista could compare it to. It was like being the center of a flame. It was burning in rapture.

"Dawg . . . It's so good." She watched. Watched as the wide crest disappeared inside her. As aching pleasure-pain began to fill her.

"Easy." He held her as her hips twisted, as she fought for more. A deeper stroke, a hard, filling thrust. "You're too tight, Crista. We'll go slow. Easy."

"You didn't before," she whispered feeling the agonizing need clawing through her system as her gaze lifted to his. "Like before, Dawg. All of you. All over me."

His hips bucked, piercing her another inch before he controlled the impulse. She didn't want his control. She wanted his hunger. As frightening as it could be, as dominant and possessive as it was, she wanted it all.

Her hands lifted from the cushions her nails had been digging into. Lifting her arms, she arched them behind her head, stretched, lifted, then lowered them until her hands could cup her breasts, and her fingers could play erotically with her nipples.

"You were wild that night," she whispered.

She had seen his desperation to separate dream from reality, and now some wicked imp insisted that she help him remember.

"How wild?" His gaze blistered her with erotic hunger.

"You didn't hesitate." She brought a finger to her lips, dampened it, then painted her hard nipple with the moisture.

His gaze sliced to the motion before pulling back to her eyes, hotter, darker than before.

His breath was sawing in and out of his chest; moisture clung to his forehead, his shoulders.

"It might hurt," he groaned, easing back.

"It destroyed me," she assured him. "Pleasure and pain." Her breathing hitched at the memory. "And you were wild and hungry . . ."

Her head tipped back as a ragged, strangled scream left her lips at the penetration.

Halfway. He was buried halfway inside her, but he pulled back quickly, his muscles bunching as he gripped her hips and plunged inside her again.

All the way.

Crista arched to him, her hips jerked, writhed, undulated

to the fiery stretching, the pleasure-pain and ecstatic sensations whipping through her like wildfire now.

"Like that?" He spoke, but he didn't stop.

Hard hands held her beneath him, his hips thrust and churned, his erection plunged inside her, spreading the fire and sending it burning through her body. Across sensitive nerve endings, through her pleasure-dazed mind and back to the clenching, spasming muscles of her vagina as it struggled to hold him inside, to hold on to the sensations that built to cataclysmic proportions.

"Is that what you want?" he snarled, fucking her furiously now, building sensation on top of sensation.

Her hands latched onto his wrists as he held her hips, her gaze locking with his as she felt perspiration begin to roll off her body.

"Like this," she panted, shuddering beneath him, her hands sliding up his arms, reaching for his face. "All of it. Like before. Just like before."

Before, his lips had been at her nipples, his lips, teeth, and tongue ravaging the tips as his cock ravished her pussy.

And he knew. A hollow groan left his throat as he came over her, his lips covering her nipple as Crista became lost in the eroticism of being possessed by Dawg.

Hard plunging hips, the thick length of his cock, his lips suckling at her nipple, his hands latching in her hair and pulling at it sensually.

The band of tension in her womb began to tighten. Her hips flexed beneath him, arching to him as he fucked her with mindless hunger, took her with dominant strength.

She was possessed. Taken. Fingers of fire rippled and burned beneath her flesh, and within seconds the conflagration overtook her. The orgasm that tore through her had her crying out at the intensity of the pleasure that rushed through her system. It exploded through her; it ripped through the few remaining defenses around her soul as it released more than just the sexual tension.

She held onto him, her arms tight around his neck as she shuddered through each spasm of pleasure, felt his release tearing through him, and whimpered at the remembered sensation of his semen pulsing inside her.

The man was known for his paranoia with condoms, and twice he had forgotten while taking her. It was enough to terrify a woman.

As he collapsed over her, Crista let a weary breath leave her throat and felt her muscles become relaxed, slack. Weariness washed over her, and she gave in to it. Because it was better to give in to it than it was to think about exactly what had happened. Because if she had to think, then she had to remember. And if she had to remember, then fear was going to overcome her. The fear of losing her soul once again.

"Crista," he whispered her name against her ear then. "Did I make it better this time?"

"What do you mean?"

"Tell me the truth now." He kissed the shell of her ear gently. "That first time, did I hurt you?"

Silence filled the room. Memories and regrets clashed inside her, tearing at her soul.

"More than you'll ever know, Dawg. More than you'll ever know."

SEVEN

Dawg had learned years before how to read between the lines when it came to women. The survival instinct was strong, and as a boy he had learned that a soft smile and a gentle voice didn't always mean a gentle heart. Just as he had learned that there were often a dozen different definitions to any one comment that a man could garner when it came to difficult questions.

Had he hurt her? He heard the flash of remembered pain in her voice, but the memory wasn't of a physical hurt. He hadn't forced her, he hadn't taken her so roughly that he had destroyed girlish dreams of a first time. If her response to him in the living room was anything to go by, then she had hungered as much for him as he had for her over the years.

No, it hadn't been her body that he had hurt. It had been something far more delicate. He had hurt her young heart and possibly scared the hell out of her when he spoke of bringing his cousins to their bed.

As he lay in his bed the next morning and stared up at the ceiling, he would have snorted at that thought if he weren't more concerned about waking the woman now sleeping next to him.

Share her? He couldn't imagine it. Even then the thought of sharing her had sent a spike of denial tearing through his chest, despite his stubbornness to remain dedicated to the extreme, raunchy pleasure to be had in the act.

And now? Hell, he hadn't shared one of his women in years, despite Natches's obvious dissatisfaction in his cousin's recent lack of desire to participate in the games of their youth.

The truth had become obvious when Rowdy returned home from the Marines last year to claim his stepsister. Even as the sharing had begun to wane, Dawg and Natches both had been certain they had known what was coming. That when Rowdy returned, the need for the fun and games would return.

For Dawg, it hadn't returned, though. He had seen the possessiveness his cousin felt for Kelly immediately. He had been amused. More understanding than Natches had been, but privately relieved. As much as he had once desired the little vixen that Rowdy was now engaged to, he found that over the years that desire had slowly changed. Affection and protectiveness had replaced the lust.

But the need for Crista had only grown over the years. Maybe he had understood Rowdy more than Natches did because Crista had been back in town when Rowdy returned, and Dawg had been fighting the demons that came with her return: the knowledge that he was missing something with her, that something had been taken away from him. And now he knew exactly what he had lost.

A night of memories. The knowledge of how she smelled, how she tasted, the sounds of her cries and the whisper of her desire as he took her. All the things he cherished about the sex act were missing from the night he had spent with her in his bed.

All he had were the dreams. Fragmented, broken, more tease than knowledge of an event that threatened to take his head off with the pleasure.

Oh yeah, he remembered that much. In his dreams, he remembered being consumed by a fire so overwhelming it had been all he could do to survive it. The same fire had ripped through him the day before when he took her downstairs on the couch, pushing into her, possessing her.

He should have known, he told himself as he turned his head to stare at her. All these years, he should have known that something had happened that night. If not because of Crista's abrupt change, then because of her brother Alex's.

Alex Jansen had become more mocking, if possible, and even more critical of the cousins' lifestyles the same week Crista had gone from an emerging sex kitten in her flirta-tiousness with Dawg to a cold, frightened woman running from a nameless terror.

Too young and too dumb, Dawg thought now. That was what he had been.

Which made him an even bigger bastard now in her eyes. His lips twitched at the memory of her fury the previous day as soon as she realized exactly how damned sexy she had been when he took her.

He couldn't believe he had dared to blackmail her into his bed. He could still remember the shock in her eyes, the disbe-lief, the way she had watched him through the day as though expecting him to suddenly smile and declare it had all been a joke. Right up until she had opened her eyes, stared into his, and realized there was no chance to escape now that he had had her.

She was dreaming if she thought that was ever going to happen. Dawg had learned a lot of things in the four years he had been in the Marines and then the last four years training and working with the ATF. He had learned how to be hard. How to kill. He knew how to assess a situation in a single moment and make lightning-fast decisions that had saved his life on more than one occasion.

And he had known, standing outside that warehouse with Crista safely hidden in his pickup, he had known there wasn't a chance in hell she was going to come to his bed in any con-ventional manner. No, he would have to take the choice from her first, then work on making her forgive him for it.

He turned his head and looked at her now, a smile playing at his lips. It had taken hours to get her to try to sleep. She

had spent the day pacing the downstairs section of his houseboat, railing and arguing and coming up with some damned
good arguments as to why he was a class-A bastard and a
disgrace to the human race.

Her last argument still had him holding back a chuckle.

"Alex is so going to kick your ass!" she had raged as he
finally grew tired of the arguments, picked her up, and carried her to his bed. "He'll have your balls for this, Dawg."

As though she would tell Alex.

Alex most likely knew about the night they had spent together, but he didn't know enough to want to kill Dawg. Eight
years ago he could have done it. It would be a little harder
job now, however.

She was in his bed, though. Still wearing her T-shirt and
panties, but minus the jeans that had covered her slender legs
when he pulled her up here. She might have been too angry
to give him another taste of the heated arousal he knew she
felt, but the knowledge that she felt it was still there.

He drew the sheet from her legs slowly, ignoring her mumbled little protest as she shifted on her back, one leg bending
at the knee, the other stretched out along the bed.

A soft cotton thong covered her pussy, the material shaping itself over her mound and revealing the soft curls beneath.
Dawg rarely liked that silky growth on a woman's mound. It
hampered his dining pleasure when he was going down on a
woman. He wanted to taste her flesh, feel the responsiveness
of each soft fold that hid the treasure beyond.

Those curls would have to go. Binding Crista to him
wasn't going to be easy. She was stubborn as hell, and she
had already made up her mind that Dawg and his sex games
were too far out of her league.

Because she was scared. He had seen that flash of fear in
her eyes. That feminine knowledge that she had come up
against something or someone that she wasn't certain how to
handle.

She would learn how to handle it, how to handle him, because the bottom line came down to the fact that he couldn't
risk letting her go.

The information they had on the female within the group
of thieves that had stolen that arms shipment en route to the

U.S. Army garrison in Fort Knox was too similar to Crista's description. There were no photographs yet, no one had managed to identify her, and Dawg was going to make damned sure that Crista didn't get identified in the criminal's stead.

He didn't like the pinch in his gut that warned him that some bad shit was coming down the road. He could feel it, like a premonition. An instinctual warning that danger was moving in on his position like a bird of prey gliding over the valley searching for food. And Crista was sitting smack-dab in the middle of that valley, a tasty little morsel just waiting to be plucked into the jaws of whoever or whatever was moving in.

It had to do with these missiles; he could feel it. It wasn't a coincidence that she had been there, but he couldn't convince himself she was involved, either. He had found something else in the small house her parents had left her and Alex, though.

The freshly swept carpet had shown signs of traffic. He knew Crista; like most women she did things in a certain way, and he remembered Alex bitching years ago about how she always swept the floors before they left the house. She would sweep back to the front door, storing the sweeper in the hall closet before they left and leaving the carpet pristine and devoid of tracks.

Crista's carpet had tracks in it. Tracks just slightly too large to be hers. Or so he tried to convince himself. They were subtle; he gave credit to whoever had made them, someone had tried to wipe them out, but they hadn't completely managed it.

The tracks had started in the living room, just off the small foyer. They had walked through the living room, gone up the steps, and moved into her bedroom to her dresser, then to her closet. While there, Dawg had found the address to the warehouse tucked into a dark bronze blazer that had been hung haphazardly in the closet. There had been nothing else. Not a scrap of paper, not a stash of money, nothing to tie her to the theft of the weapons, other than that address. There had been just enough of a disturbance to allay his conscience in lying to his superiors.

Not that he needed to excuse that very often. He had a very high respect for the chain of command, there was no doubt; he was, after all, a Marine. But he knew that sometimes, some things needed a little closer investigation before he reported them. Crista was one of those instances.

Soft, warm, hotter than hell, and fighting him tooth and nail. But she was back in his bed and sleeping next to him.

How many times had he awakened over the years, certain he would find her next to him, knowing that the dream that had haunted his sleep had to be more than a dream. And each time he had awakened alone, until now.

Hell no, he wasn't letting her out of this one. He would blackmail her a thousand times over if that was what it took to get her into his bed and to keep her there.

He watched her carefully, reaching out with his hand, his fingertips only touching the silky flesh of her thigh.

Damn, she was soft. Like the finest silk. The most expensive satin. Warm and sweet.

She shifted again, a muttered little moan slipping past her lips as he let more of his fingers experience that heated sensation, caressing the rounded flesh gently.

She whispered a sigh, her thighs falling farther apart, giving him a clear view of the sweet flesh covered in cotton.

Was she wet?

His fingers paused on her thigh, only inches from what was paradise.

"Does this deal include molesting me in my sleep?" Her half-drowsy exclamation of contempt was punctuated by a quick jerk at the sheet to draw it back over her thighs.

He grinned. Damn, she was going to be a challenge, maybe more than he anticipated.

"I think I should start a list," he murmured lazily, drawing the sheet back toward him. "Keeping your little butt off the firing line could get complicated. I'll need compensation."

She didn't let go of the covering. Her fingers tightened on it, her chocolate eyes glared back at him.

"Now, Crista," he chided her gently, though his gaze was anything but gentle as it met hers. "Let go of the sheet. Let me see what I'm lying for today."

"You wouldn't turn me in."

He could see the bravado in her gaze now. She was well-rested and feeling more confident, better able to handle him. Let's see if she could.

He pushed back desire, need, temptation, and gave her the steely eyed look he had perfected in the Marines. The one that assured those both above and lower in rank that he was someone to be reckoned with.

Her eyes flickered with indecision.

"It's like this, fancy-face." He smirked. "When Alex returns, he won't be able to do a damned thing about what's happened here, right now. If my superiors connect you to this case, then you're gone."

"Over drugs?" She snorted. "I don't think so, Dawg. Drug dealers are not terrorists."

"Unless terrorists are dealing in drugs." He shrugged, omitting the fact that his case didn't have a damned thing to do with drugs.

She blinked back at him silently again. Damn, that little mind was quick. He could see it working in her expression, the play of emotions that crossed her face finally settling into lines of resentment and anger.

"Stop doing this," she finally pushed out between clenched teeth.

"Why?" If she had a good reason, he might relent. For this morning.

"Because I don't want it." He could feel her tensing as he drew the sheet fully away, his gaze going to the mounds of her breasts beneath her shirt.

Didn't want it, his ass. He restrained a knowing smile. He knew women, and he knew body language, and if he wasn't totally wrong, she wanted it just as bad, maybe worse, than he did. Though he couldn't imagine her wanting it worse. He swore his cock would rupture with the need to burrow into the tight, heated confines of her pussy.

"Your nipples are hard." And he was going to taste them soon. "Is your pussy wet? Sorry, baby, but if you didn't want it, then you did a damned good imitation of it on my couch yesterday."

Shock, arousal, it filled her face as surely as the blush that began to work up along her neck and into her face. And it was damned enchanting. He hadn't seen a woman blush in years.

But she wasn't ready for another round yet, and Dawg could sense the uncertainty in her. If he weren't careful, she could choose prison over him. Crista could be incredibly stubborn as he well knew. She wasn't above cutting off her own nose to spite her face.

"No answer, huh?" He let an amused grin quirk his lips.

Hell, Crista was fun. Even with her back up and her mad on, she was fun.

She licked her lips, and his gut clenched. He wanted that tongue on his dick again. If she didn't decide on his course of action pretty damned soon, then he was going to have to play another very delicate card in the hand he had dealt himself.

Yep, blackmail was a very dirty word, and a man had to have some way of backing up his threat.

"I have to meet with my team this afternoon." He rolled away from her, stretching lazily as she seemed to freeze beside him. "We have bad guys—and girls—to catch." He threw her a careless smile as he untangled his legs from the sheet and rose from the bed.

Her eyes were narrowed on him, but her fingers had a death grip on the sheet as she held it over her.

She was thinking, though. He could always tell when she was rolling something around in her head. He remembered before she left, catching that look on her face and wanting to be so deep inside her that she couldn't hide anything from him. That need had only grown. Right now, he would give his eyeteeth to be buried so deep inside her that even their cells would bond.

"So what am I supposed to do now that you've had me fired from my job?" she snapped back at him irately. "I'm going to assume that during this game you're playing, I'm not allowed to work."

Dawg scratched at his chest, feeling a surge of satisfaction as her gaze licked over him. He was naked, aroused, and he would be damned if he was going to try to hide it from her.

"You have a job," he assured her, turning to the low chest of drawers on the other side of the room and pulling out clean clothes.

"What kind of a job?" The low, wrathful tone had his lips twitching again.

"Fucking me. I'm fairly high maintenance, Crista. You won't need another job."

Then he ducked to avoid the alarm clock that came sailing at his head, then to avoid the picture frame that held a picture of his Harley. But he felt a swell of joy rise inside him as he jumped for her, gripping her wrist as she reached for the lamp, pulling her under him and holding her to the mattress as she bucked and writhed and cursed with all the exuberance of a damned sailor.

Crista couldn't remember ever being so furious. A haze of red distorted her view, and a mix of murderous, adrenaline-crazed fury pumped through her veins.

"You bastard!" She tried to scream past the tightening in her chest, her throat. "Do I have *whore* written on my fore-head? Do I look like one of your sex-starved little bimbos?"

She cringed from his body lying atop hers now, from the heavy, naked thighs pushing between her own and the pow-erful arms that held his body just far enough above her to allow her to breathe.

She wasn't unaffected. Arousal pumped side by side with the fury, bringing angry tears to her eyes as she collapsed beneath him, exhausted, panting as she glared up at him.

"I hate you," she hissed, feeling the first tear fall from her eye and track down her cheek. "I can't believe what a bastard you've turned into."

His gaze lightened, then became shadowed as he held her wrists in one hand and the other came up to touch the tear on her face.

"You cried then, too." His voice was soft, brooding. "Didn't you? When I kissed you, you cried."

Oh yeah, she was going to answer that one for him. Not. Not in a million years would she ever tell him what he did to her then, and now.

"You told me you dreamed of me." His jaw tensed as a flash of lust lit up his eyes like lightning.

"I wouldn't dream of you if you were the last man on earth," she scoffed, panting at the effort to force him to release her. "Get off me. I don't want you anywhere near me."

She didn't want the blood pumping to her nipples and her clit with a force that had them straining, tight and engorged, against the material of her clothing as he covered her.

She didn't want her skin so sensitive she could feel the hairs on his chest, even through her shirt. And she didn't want the pleasure that was building, burning through her as he held her beneath him, restrained. Helpless.

"I thought of that all night as you slept," he said guardedly. "Taking you again, having you beneath me. It was better than the dreams, Crista. They didn't even compare."

His voice dropped to a guttural whisper as his gaze flared with carnal heat. It was mesmerizing, watching his gaze flare, then lighten with sexual need.

"Get off me, Dawg." It was all she could do to push the words past her lips. "I won't let you turn me into a whore for your own amusement."

"Say that word again, and I'll make you regret it, Crista." The order was clipped and filled with menace. "I haven't called you a whore, and I never believed you were one."

"Don't you? Evidently you do, if you think my only job is fucking you." She strained against him again, only to still as she felt the broad head of his cock butt against the crotch of her thin panties. Too thin, because she could feel the heat of his thick flesh pressing against her.

"Until I figure out what the hell is going on, that's exactly what your job is. Because, make no mistake, fancy-face, I'm not a very charitable person anymore. Just because you're not guilty doesn't mean you don't look guilty. You need me so you can stay out of jail. And you know the price for my help."

Was he serious? And did it really matter at this point if he was or not? Her senses were suddenly rioting at the feel of his cock head pressing against her, causing her to grow wetter, her flesh more sensitive.

She didn't want this.

Crista shook her head as she felt Dawg's lips at her cheek, rough velvet, sliding over her flesh as her breath hitched in her throat.

"Nothing matters to me but fucking you." Self-disgust filled his voice. "Being so deep inside you that this hunger that's eaten at my gut for eight years dissolves." His head lifted as he glowered down at her from between sensually narrowed eyes. "Make no mistake, Crista, you will spread those pretty legs for me again, and you'll give me what I want. Because it's the only way I can keep your ass out of jail. Walk away from me, and I won't lift a finger to help you when they slap the cuffs on your wrists and you disappear. Because, baby, it will so be out of my hands then that I couldn't help you if I wanted to."

"But you can if I'm sleeping with you?" Disillusionment, disappointment, he heard it all in her voice.

Quite simply, as he said, unless he relented, she had no choice.

"Of course." His smile was tight and hard. "I'll know where you are. I'll know if you're playing dirty or playing nice, and then putting my neck on the line won't feel like a fool's fucking errand to me. Now make your choice."

Crista stared back at him, finally admitting that the man she had dreamed of for eight years was gone, in more ways than she had imagined.

"It's the same as rape," she whispered, then bit back a moan as his free hand reached down, pulling her panties aside and allowing the heavy crest of his cock to slide through the juices gathering there.

"Do you enjoy lying to yourself, Crista?"

Dawg was breathing harder now, and Crista found it nearly impossible to draw in enough oxygen herself. The air was ripe with steamy carnality, her body so sensitive now, her clit so swollen, she wondered if she could survive if he didn't fuck her.

"Damn," he suddenly groaned, his hand gripping her hip as he let his cock slide through the heavy moisture until the feel of it rasping over her clit had her jerking in his hold and whimpering in heat.

"Your pussy's so hot I'll burn to ash," he muttered, lowering his head again, his lips brushing over hers, though he ignored the parting of her lips to move to her jaw. "Like hot silk, molten silk. Let me have you again, Crista. I'll take you so easy this time." His lips caressed the shell of her ear now. "I'll slide inside you slow and sweet, darlin'. And I promise, I'll make you scream again with pleasure."

As he had the first time and again yesterday. But then, he had pounded inside her both times, rocked her. Impaled her. He had taken her with a force that had left her shaken, not just from his possession, but from her response to it.

As he spoke, his free hand slid beneath her T-shirt. Broad and calloused, it rasped over her sensitive flesh, sending brilliant spears of pleasure exploding through her system.

"Dawg, don't you think—"

"I never think around you," he muttered as his lips moved back along her jaw. "All I do is feel." His hips moved, dragging his erection down, the thick head sliding through saturated folds, then with wicked effectiveness, pressed into the clutching entrance of her vagina.

Crista stilled. She stared up at Dawg as his head lifted, his eyes nearly colorless, the green so light that the pupils of his eyes were stark in the center.

"Are you protected?" His voice was tortured.

"Fine time to ask that question." Her fists clenched, her wrists straining against his hold.

Of course she was protected. She had learned her lesson. She stayed protected.

It was too much pleasure. She could feel it rising forcefully inside her, tearing at her senses, dissolving her objections. Just as he had the first time, he was ripping her from the moorings of her own common sense.

"Answer me!" His lips were tight, his body straining.

"Yes—" The cry that tore from her was a mixture of pleasurable agony and bitter realization.

The heavy, hard thrust that sent him tunneling through unused muscles and slick, heated flesh was almost as painful as it had been the first time. And it was definitely more pleasurable than it should have been.

Crista stared up at him in shock and surprise, uncertain,

confused. This wasn't supposed to happen. Not like this. Not this fast. Not at all, if she hadn't been so weak, so wet.

"Dawg." She would wince at the beseeching tone of her voice later. For now, all she could do was lie there, feeling the muscles of her pussy ripple, clench, and struggle to accept the flesh impaling it.

Little darts of sensation were racing over her body, detonating with trembling force in erogenous zones that she didn't know were erogenous zones.

"Do you know"—a heavy grimace contorted his expression as his hips flexed against her, causing the head of his cock to stroke the deepest part of her vagina in a way that had her breath catching violently—"know how tight and hot your pussy is? How you feel wrapped around me?"

She shook her head. She couldn't do this again. Hear his voice, his words causing her to grow wetter, hotter. She couldn't let him steal her mind or her heart again. But he was, stealing it all as the pleasure began to tear through her senses.

"Here. Come here, darlin'."

She nearly wailed at the feeling of his cock shifting, stretching her farther as he lifted her enough, just enough, to pull her shirt free of her body, baring the lacy bra she wore beneath. A bra that did nothing to hide the straining nubs of her nipples.

"This is so—so not a good idea," she panted as the front clip of the bra released, and her breasts spilled out to his waiting palms.

"Did I suck these pretty nipples that first time?" he asked then, his voice a hard, rough rasp. "I dreamed I did. I dreamed I dined on them. Fed from them."

Her head tossed on the mattress as her hands gripped his wrists. To hold on or to protest his fingers caressing the swollen mounds, his thumbs brushing over her tight nipples, she wasn't certain.

"Dawg, think—" She needed to think.

"Don't think." He pulled the bra free before tossing it away. "You think too much, Crista."

A second later her panties were ripped from her hips, the

scraps tossed to the floor as she stared down her body. Straight to where they were joined.

Dark brown curls glistened with moisture and pressed against his pelvis. Her legs were spread wide to accommodate his powerful thighs, her knees bent and hugging the outside of his legs.

"See how good we look together." His voice was an insidious murmur of heated lust and pleasure as he flexed inside her again. "Let me show you, sweetheart. Look at this."

EIGHT

"Let me show you . . ."

Crista couldn't help but watch. Dazed, mesmerized, even more than she had been yesterday. She watched as Dawg shifted his hips back slowly, his erection pulling free of her inner grip as a whimper of denial left her lips.

The thick, hard flesh was flushed a ruddy red, his cock head purpled and throbbing and wide enough to make her swallow tightly at the sight of it.

It glistened with her juices, shimmered in the afternoon sunlight spearing into the high, narrow windows over the bed.

It was powerful, iron hard, and hot, and within seconds easing inside her again. Crista watched that, too. She couldn't help it. It was so sexy, erotic. Inch by inch, it disappeared inside her until once again his pubic hair was tangling with hers as a low groan fell from his lips.

"I've dreamed of this," he rasped. "Watching my dick fill you slow and easy. Watching you take me."

She was caught in a whirlwind, sensations piling atop each other, pleasure ripping through her as the stiff length of his cock stretched her, sending a burning ecstasy roiling through her system.

How was she supposed to deny him now? How the hell was she supposed to survive again once it was over and Dawg went on to the next conquest? Because this—oh Lord—this could become addictive.

Her gaze moved from where he was buried inside her, lifting over the flat, rippling planes of his abdomen to his fiercely set expression. Light green eyes glowed in the dark expanse of his face; long, sooty lashes were lowered to half-mast; and a flush of erotic pleasure stained his cheekbones.

He was a warrior, a conqueror, and he was stealing her soul.

"You like this." He shifted, moved, drawing free of her body slowly before pushing heavily inside her once again.

Mercy. It was too good. Her back bowed as she arched to it, driving him inside her as she felt the muscles of her pussy stretch again. Burning, searing pleasure.

"Tell me you like this, Crista." His voice was filled with wicked knowledge as he began a slow, heavy rhythm, fucking her as though he had all the time in the world when she knew that if she didn't orgasm soon, she was going to die.

"Come on, honey," he urged, his voice insistent, almost gentle. "Tell me you missed feeling me inside you, fucking you slow and easy, making you burn for me."

Her head shook desperately. She couldn't miss what she hadn't had, could she? He had taken her hard, fast, in a variety of ways and positions, but he hadn't taken her like this. Like the act mattered. Like she mattered.

"Look at me, Crista. Come on, open your eyes, honey."

His voice was too gentle, too rough with passion. Her eyes opened, and she felt the first tear fall. A stupid tear, because he was taking her too deep, stealing too much of her.

Dawg almost stopped at the sight of that single tear easing down her cheek. And he would have, if he hadn't seen much more than that in her eyes. Shimmering damply, they were filled with such tormented need, a hunger that he recognized, one he knew went clear to the soul.

It was a hunger he recognized because it was the same

hunger that had tormented him for too long. So many years dreaming of her, and she was better than the dream. Sweeter than passion, hotter than lust.

Silky wet with the juices gathering inside her, coating his dick with syrupy heat and lubricating each heavy thrust inside her.

Delicate muscles clamped on his cock, stroked over him with a tight-fisted grip, and nearly destroyed his determination to go slow. To take her easy. To relish every fucking minute inside her when he wanted nothing more than to pound into her pussy with greedy, harsh strokes.

He was a hard lover. He had always known that. Sometimes, he hated that part of his sensuality, because going slow and easy had always taken thought. He had to think his way through each thrust to keep his head. Until Crista. Taking her slow and easy was—damn, it was easy. He wasn't thinking, he was relishing, enjoying, burning alive in her heat.

"I shouldn't have taken you so hard yesterday," he crooned, suddenly wondering if he had been too rough with her after all, if he had hurt her.

She was delicate, tender. Not like the other women he had been with, women who knew and anticipated that hardened side of his sexuality.

"Dawg." She was panting. Those stiff little nipples were pushing closer to his face as her lips parted to drag in more air. "Please . . ." Her head tossed on the pillow. "Not like this."

Not like this?

He pushed inside her, deep, forcing himself to stop, to make her *feel* as his dick throbbed inside her.

"You're wrapped around me like a fist," he gritted out. "Feel it, Crista. I can. Your pussy is working over my dick like a hot little mouth starving for satisfaction. Deny you want this. Just like this."

He flexed inside her again, feeling the head of his cock stroking her, the crown positioned just right to notch the flared, stiffened edge into her G-spot. He stroked her internally, watching her eyes darken, her face flush a delicate pink as the pleasure began to build higher, hotter.

Damn, she was making him high just from the feel of her. The blood was pounding in his head, adrenaline and lust clouding his vision as he shook his head and breathed in roughly.

Just a few more minutes. God, he had to feel her just a few more minutes. He couldn't come yet, not yet, not until those little ripples around his dick began to clench and spasm in release.

Crista felt her legs lifting, felt her body melting, and she whimpered at the surrender that rushed through her mind. She couldn't fight this. He was buried inside her, fiery hot and thick, pulsing and stroking internal muscles that even after all this time hadn't forgotten the pleasure he could give her.

She bit her lip as she stared up at him. Her wild man. That was what he was, a wild man. Maybe not hers, but here, buried inside her, for this moment in time, he was hers. And he was every inch a primal, sexual male.

His eyes were so light now they seemed to glow within his face, his lips tight with the fight for control. She didn't want his control. She wanted what she had before. Wild, primitive. Maybe, just maybe she could survive the fallout later.

As she watched, a smile tugged at the taut line of his lips, and he began to move again. That slow, destructive rhythm that forced her to feel every blazing inch of his cock.

Oh, that was good. Her breath hitched; a hard, jerking shudder tore through her body as her hips jerked upward to hold him inside her as long as possible.

"Oh yeah, you like that," he muttered, his voice becoming thicker, rough. "I like it, Crista. I like it a lot."

Of course he liked it. He was winning. Triumph glittered in his gaze as her hands tightened on the wrists beside her head.

"Let's see if you like this."

The rhythm stayed the same, but his head lowered, his lips surrounding a hard, sensitive nipple and drawing it into his mouth.

"Oh, God. Dawg, please, don't . . ." Don't make her feel this. Don't make her lose her senses to him.

Her head twisted against the mattress, though she arched closer, pushing the peak deeper into his mouth.

His lips, teeth, tongue. They all played with the hot nerve

center of her nipple. Licking, nipping, suckling with male greed as he continued to thrust inside her slow and easy.

Her pussy was clenching around the length of his erection, spasming with brutal need and desperate lust. Her hands moved from his wrists to his head, trembling fingers sinking into his long hair, holding him closer as her hips moved beneath him.

"Harder." The cry shocked her. It came from her in a voice strangled with furious need. "Fuck me, Dawg. Please. Please, like before."

The desperation rose inside her. The need for more, the need for racing bolts of electric ecstasy tearing through her rather than zipping teasingly around her.

"How was it before, baby?" he whispered, his voice a guttural rasp now. "Tell me what I missed, Crista. Tell me how I took you."

"Hard." She was panting, shaking. Sweat dampened both their flesh now as her juices built along her thighs, easing from around Dawg's cock with each movement inside her.

She was so wet, so hot, and becoming violently sensitive to each touch of his mouth against her nipples, each stroke inside her.

"How hard?" He nipped the sensitive curve of her breast before stroking his stubbled cheek against it.

Crista felt the breath tear from her throat.

"So hard. Please, Dawg."

"Did I pound inside you?" Tortured, hungry, his tone stroked her senses just as his cock stroked inside the burning center of her body.

"Yes," she hissed, writhing beneath him.

Crista could feel her response blazing out of control now. Her senses were overwhelming her common sense. She knew it; she couldn't stop it. She couldn't force it back inside her now that Dawg had released it.

"Do it!" She jerked beneath him, her legs rising, her ankles clasping at his hips as she shoved upward, then cried out at the feeling of him delving deeper, stretching her farther.

A hard male groan tore from his chest then. Hard hands pulled her legs free, pushed them back as he rose to his knees in front of her and gave her what she demanded.

Just as he had the first time.

He rose over her like a sex god come to life. Hard hands held her behind her knees, forcing them to bend, forcing her legs back as his hips began to move.

A bed pounder. The headboard would have been striking the wall behind them if it weren't attached. The mattress shook, and Crista felt the tender tissue of her sex quaking in rapture as he began to fuck her with hard, driving strokes.

Burning strokes.

Pleasure and pain that combined inside her and had starlight bursting in front of her vision as she exploded beneath him.

Lightning tore through her veins. It licked over her nipples, her clitoris, then ruptured forcefully inside her womb as she felt the wet, hot force of her orgasm frothing inside her, around Dawg's pounding erection.

Within seconds, it was joined by his release. His teeth clenched, his lips pulling back as his gaze caught hers, held it, and the feel of his semen spurting inside her triggered another forceful, screaming, sheet-clawing orgasm inside her.

"Fuck yes!" he snarled. "Come for me, Crista. Like that—fuck yes, milk me with that sweet pussy. Take it. Take it all." He jerked spasmodically inside her before his head tilted back on his shoulders, and a harsh tremor shook his hard body.

He released her legs slowly. They melted back to the bed as he came over her, still buried inside her, his cock jerking weakly now as he covered her.

"I came like that inside you the first time," he panted at her ear. "I remember that, Crista. Over and over again I came inside you."

He had. Her lashes lifted to stare at the ceiling, to force back the bitter memories.

"Tell me." His voice was insidious, low, dangerous. "Were you pregnant when you left Somerset? And don't bother lying to me." His head raised, his gaze spearing into hers. "Did you have my baby?"

She stared back at him, the bitterness rising inside her like a cancer she couldn't rid herself of.

"There's no baby," she whispered harshly, wondering why the hell she even bothered. "I didn't have your child."

His eyes narrowed as fury began to light the depths.

"Did you abort my baby, Crista?"

God help her if she had. Crista could see the murderous rage lurking in the depths now.

Her lips twisted mockingly. "There was nothing to abort, Dawg. And if you can ask me that question, then you have no business coming inside me. Tell me something now. How many of your bimbos have you double-fucked with your cousins and not worn a condom? Maybe I should be checked for STDs rather than a pregnancy."

A snarling smile pulled at his lips now as he leaned close, nearly nose to nose, his gaze flaring, heating, lightening, then darkening again.

"I marked your pussy eight years ago, and I marked it today. And trust me, sweetheart, no other has taken my seed. I've made damned sure of it."

Her eyes widened in a parody of joy that didn't hint at the anger running through her. "Oh wow. Dawg gave me his seed three times now." She fluttered her lashes. "How lucky am I? Well, just let me up right now so I can jump for joy and tell the world my accomplishments. I have finally arrived in life."

A grin quirked his lips. Bastard that he was, he was amused.

"There you go, sugar, you're getting the idea," he murmured as a slight grimace twisted his features as he pulled free of her.

And her stupid, traitorous body tried to hold on to him. Clenching around his flesh, her hips jerking upward as though to relish that final stroke of heat and pleasure.

She flung the sheet over her as he rolled from the bed, pushing his fingers through his hair as he glanced back at her.

"You're a smart-ass," he grunted.

"Just figuring that one out? And here I thought I was being less than subtle for the past year."

Twelve months of trying to keep him at arm's length, of trying to hold back the bitterness and the memories that tormented her, and what had she done? She'd twisted and mewled beneath him like a bitch in heat. Apt, considering his nickname, she told herself cruelly.

She was setting herself up for heartbreak again, and Alex wasn't here to save her. Mark wasn't here to comfort her, and his lover wasn't here to make her laugh and help her rebuild herself once Dawg was finished with her.

For the first time in her life, Crista could feel how very alone she was.

"At least you were smart enough to use protection that first time." He sighed, though she fooled herself into thinking she heard an edge of regret in his tone.

Fooling herself. Just as she had fooled herself those months before he took her to his bed that first time. Fooled herself into thinking he cared about her, that she mattered.

"Yeah, that's me, intelligent to a fault," she bit out as she wrapped the sheet around her and moved from the bed. She needed to find her clothes. She needed to shower and wash the smell of Dawg from her body. The scent of sunrise and a storm. Wild and hot. He should bottle it. He would be a millionaire. Hell, she should bottle it, but she would be too stupid to sell it. She would hoard it all for herself.

That was her. Greedy as hell when it came to Dawg.

Too greedy, she imagined, for the lifestyle he had chosen years before.

"I need a shower," she told him, furious with herself and her emotions.

It had been eight years since she had left Somerset. Eight long, exhausting, completely unproductive years, because all she thought about was coming home, returning to the mountains she loved and the man she couldn't forget.

And he had forgotten her so easily.

"Go ahead. I'll hop downstairs and shower. The two bathrooms have separate hot water heaters. You'll have plenty enough for a bath or a shower."

The *Nauti Dawg* had all the comforts of home, she remembered. Including a sinfully deep tub large enough to hold even Dawg.

The thought of soaking in that tub, easing the aches and pains from her still-bruised body, was almost irresistible. Almost. Unfortunately, she had things to do. Things like finding a newspaper to begin job hunting. Again.

It was Friday, so actually hunting up a job wasn't going

to happen today. But she needed to return to the house and get organized.

The waitressing job had been okay for a while. It kept her going while she finished the tests for her business degree, but she had no intentions of staying there, anyway. She had been marking time since completing her advanced degree three months before. Something she had put off when she had landed the office manager job in Virginia.

It had been a good job. Until her boss married, and the wife decided she could save her husband's money by doing the job herself. Crista had received two weeks' notice and a very small severance package, and then good-bye.

"I need a ride back to the restaurant to pick up my car," she told him as she gathered her clothes from the floor and headed to the bathroom.

"I'll drive you back," he said behind her. "Then we can go to the house and collect the rest of your things. Did you have any furniture you have to bring back with you?"

Crista froze at the bathroom doorway before turning back to him slowly.

"Why would I need to bring my furniture? You just said until the end of summer." She kept her voice calm. When dealing with Dawg, one had to learn to stay calm, or he would drive one insane.

He pulled a pair of shorts over his naked hips before straightening without answering.

His gaze pierced hers. His arms crossed over his chest in a stance of pure power, and he looked straight down that arrogant nose of his as though he were lord of all he surveyed.

Her calm slipped, just a little bit, as she stared back at him incredulously, her fingers fisting in the sheet she held around her. "Have you lost your mind?"

"Do you have furniture that needs to be moved?"

"No, I don't," she replied with sugary sweetness. "Because I'm not moving in here with you indefinitely. As soon as I can, I'm returning to the house."

The house she shared with Alex was small and located farther outside of town than she liked, but it was nice. It was home.

It was nothing like the nice apartment she had shared with

her roommate Mark and his lover, Ty: the two-bedroom, ultramodern, brightly lit apartment with a balcony that overlooked the beach. It hadn't been home, though. Somerset was home.

"Tell me, Crista, do you *want* to die?" he asked her then. "Because you will. Those men at that warehouse weren't playing games with those bullets, fancy-face. They were serious. And now, someone else could possibly believe you have their money. How long do you think it will take them to find you and slit your throat in your sleep?"

Crista felt the color leech from her face.

"But I didn't have anything to do with that," she argued weakly, feeling the stupidity in her response even as it came out of her lips.

"You were there."

"Accidentally." She shook her head at the futility of her own argument. "Money's involved, right? They won't just kill me."

"No. They'll torture you first." He nodded with mock sobriety. "They'll tie you down, cut you a little, let you bleed some. Rape you, most likely." His gaze flickered over her with a flare of inner rage. "And when they realize you don't know anything, they'll really start having fun. You'll pray to die before they finish. Is that what you want?"

She was shaking by the time he finished, knowing he was right, knowing her life had just taken a very serious turn for the worse.

She breathed out wearily. "I don't have furniture. Just some clothes." And not a lot, at that. Most of her stuff she was still waiting for. Mark and Ty had been good enough to hold it for her until she had a place for it. She just hadn't found a place yet.

The same furniture and small items that she thought had been waiting for her at that warehouse. They hadn't been there. Her earlier call to Mark had confirmed that he hadn't sent anything.

A year.

Had a year really gone by since she left Virginia?

A year that she had been steeped in the memories she had deliberately pushed behind her when she left home. Memories that had the power to break her if she didn't get a handle on them. Getting a handle on them hadn't been easy.

He nodded abruptly. "Get your shower and get dressed. We'll pack the rest of your stuff and bring it here. You can keep your car in the private marina parking that Uncle Ray lets us use."

"I still need a job." Her chin lifted defiantly.

"I can put you to work at the lumber store." He shrugged. "I hear you're pretty slick in the office."

Crista's eyes narrowed. "I applied there months ago. There were no openings."

"I'm the boss; I'll make an opening," he gritted out.

"And you couldn't make one before I had to take that job at the diner?"

He grinned, devilry glittering in his gaze then. "I didn't have enough incentive then. Maybe I do now."

If she had something to throw at him, she would have given a pitch worthy of a baseball player at that moment, just to wipe the smirk off his face.

"You're a real ass, Dawg," she sneered instead.

"So I keep hearing, fancy-face. So I keep hearing."

NINE

Aaron Grael was dead, and no one else was talking. As far as the thieves and the buyers were concerned, there was no one missing from either little group. And that was bullshit. They already knew that, a million of the two million dollar price tag on the missiles had been paid to a middleman, or woman as the case may be. And Dawg knew Grael had been convinced Crista was that woman two seconds before Dawg killed him.

Dawg's report was turned in. He had seen Grael firing at the team; he had wounded several of them. Dawg had made the shot and taken him out. It wasn't exactly a lie, of course, but it wasn't the truth, either.

Now they had to figure out where the missing middle person was, where the money was, and how it affected the case.

The four experimental, newly designed Sidewinders could be launched from greater distances and carried an explosive weight nearly double their predecessors. And they could be nuclear-armed.

They were built with detonation chips, a safeguard that disabled the missiles entirely and effectively halted any chance of detonation or guidance of the weapon without them. They were to have been transported to Fort Knox without those chips before heading to another base. But, somehow, the Army fucked up. The missiles were shipped with their safety chips, and the shipment was hijacked.

Fortunately for the task force, it seemed the hijacking was done by a group with little or no experience in the stealing and selling of the Sidewinder missiles.

A Swedish mercenary had negotiated the buy for a Middle Eastern terrorist with fingers in damned near every conflict in the world. The Swede, alias Akron Svengaurrd, had contacted Aaron Grael for the exchange of half the money down and two of the safety and guidance chips. The rest of the money would come once the chips were authenticated—and the Army had made certain they were authenticated—and the missiles were in place for the Swede's team to pick up.

The operation the combined ATF and Homeland Security task force were working netted not just the thieves but the Swede as well. And it was the Swede they had wanted most. Him and the missiles.

The thieves might not have had much experience in the stealing and selling of weapons, but they were damned smart. And they had the contacts imperative in such a sell. It had also made them harder to catch. They were paranoid, and they were damned careful. And the only man they had a chance of getting any information out of was dead.

Because Dawg had a hard-on for Crista.

"The woman was there." Timothy Cranston wiped his hand over his balding crown in a sign of disgust as he handed out the reports to be passed around. "No one identified her; no one saw where she went."

"Do you think she killed Grael?" Greta Dane, a grimly determined agent at Dawg's right, spoke up.

"Why would she kill him?" Natches snorted. "That's her moneyman. She would want him alive."

"He could identify her," Greta pointed out with a snide look in Natches's direction. "And he would have known there would be plenty of his guys left alive when the smoke cleared. Someone could have talked."

"She didn't kill our man," Timothy assured them all, glancing at Dawg. "Shot came from the back of the head and from Dawg's weapon. Autopsy confirmed it this morning. The camera's put our lady in front of him. After she disappeared behind those crates closest to the wall, she disappeared from sight completely. All we have on the outside cameras is some erratic shadowing too large to be a woman."

Dawg sat back in his chair and kept his mouth carefully shut. He didn't give a damn that Grael was dead, but he knew Cranston was pissed. Ultimately, it would work for them rather than against them. The Swede was a major player in several conflicts; just catching him had been an incredible coup.

Which was pretty much Cranston's opinion. But it also left the team with a contact they had been lusting after, a potential double agent.

And that was too bad. That contact was a dead end, and Dawg's lust had come first. He had dibs on it.

"I want to know who that woman was," Timothy barked in irritation. "Come on, boys and girls. All we have is brown hair, brown eyes, slender, and pretty. That's a third of the fucking women in this state or any other. If we get her, we get the money and hopefully break the silence among the thieves. This is the weak link, or they wouldn't be so nervous they're pacing their cells. She's our weak link. I can feel it."

Dawg almost grinned. Timothy's fat little hands were rubbing together in glee.

He was the most unlikely looking OHS agent that Dawg had ever seen. Portly, grandfatherly, the crown of his head shining, and the short gray hair around it standing out in spikes, he looked more like an accountant or overworked executive than one of the sharpest minds in Homeland Security.

"Dawg, have you or Natches heard anything new?" Timothy barked then.

The lumberyard and Natches's garage were two of the gossip points in the county. Information on the theft had come to Dawg's lumberyard before news of it had made the agency channels. Considering the fact that so far, news of it hadn't hit the television or radio stations, they were fairly certain it had to have leaked from the thieves themselves.

"Johnny's come up clear on involvement." Dawg grimaced at the thought of his estranged cousin, who raked on his nerves worse than nails over a chalkboard. The news of the hijacking had first come from Johnny when he stopped by the lumber store to buy shelving materials for the bakery goods store he owned outside of town. "We can't place him anywhere with our buyers or sellers, and according to the agent that questioned him, he overheard it at the store. But he gets a lot of customers, especially out-of-towners and soldiers from Fort Knox, so that makes sense. He could have just heard about the hijacking. And he likes to gossip about everything he hears."

Asking Johnny where he heard it hadn't worked out, and Dawg and Natches both knew better than to push it. The snaky little bastard would immediately see a weakness and strike.

"Would you know it if you even heard anything?" Greta suggested snidely, her honey-colored eyes gleaming with bitterness in her pale, freckled face.

It was rumored that she had lost family to a terrorist attack, and Dawg had always tried to temper his sarcasm toward her, for that fact alone, but her own bitterness was beginning to create a sense of tension in the team whenever she was around.

"Meaning?" He arched his brows mockingly.

"Meaning these are your people." She waved her hand to the files and reports. "Whoever stole the missiles knows this area like a native. Which means the woman is probably a native. You wouldn't suspect a friend or an ex-lover."

He heard Natches snort mockingly at that statement.

"Sweetheart, I live for paranoia. I suspect everyone but the Father, the Son, and the Holy Ghost." He gave her a toothy grin and watched as irritation thickened in her expression. "Are you in that group?"

"Dawg." Timothy's voice was a warning little snarl. He was always snarling when he wasn't rubbing his hands in glee.

Dawg turned back to him, his brow lifting in question as Natches smirked behind him.

"Don't you two get on my nerves." He pointed his finger back at them demandingly. "I won't be nice."

Bald and portly he might be, but he could put a hurtin' on the ego if a man wasn't careful.

"Go over that information, and we'll meet back here tomorrow afternoon," Timothy finally ordered with an edge of frustration. "Keep your eyes and ears open and hope we get something before the week is out, or my boss is going to rip all our asses. Boys, we don't want that."

Dawg flipped open the file, his gaze running over the pages in a slow scan. He was more concerned about finding any incriminating evidence that could have come up against Crista than he was information he had already read. If she was guilty, now was the best time to know. If she wasn't, then she would gain the benefit of the doubt until he saw otherwise. But not a lack of suspicion.

They were lucky. Crista had been in the shadows the entire time she had been there when the agents moving into the warehouse had assumed she was with the buyers. They had swarmed the back end of the cavernous building and worked their way forward.

Dawg had gone after Grael when the other man had sprinted for the shadowed, crated area in the front of the warehouse. Grael had gone after the woman he believed had betrayed him. If Dawg had been a second later, Crista would have died.

No one could possibly know Dawg was involved in this investigation. Other than the task force members, no one else could have known. And they were die-hard agents. It would shock him to his back teeth to find out one of them was a traitor.

But hell, he had been wrong before. And as he said, trust wasn't one of his virtues. If he even had a virtue. He was a vices type of guy; virtues weren't his strong point.

The file was empty of any incriminating evidence against Crista, which meant he didn't have to tell Cranston she was involved. At least, not just yet.

Slapping the file closed on the desk, Dawg rose to his feet and glanced at Natches. His cousin was rising from his own chair and snagged the dark glasses he had left lying on the table.

"Ready to roll?" Natches smirked, his dark, forest green eyes gleaming with amusement.

He knew Crista was waiting for them at the lumber store, safely ensconced in Dawg's office and going over his paperwork. Her eyes had gleamed in joy the minute she saw the mess his personal office had become over the past year. A man would think she was staring at diamonds rather than the paperwork from hell.

And Natches, being Natches, had found no end of amusement in the sight of Crista's curvy little ass plopping in Dawg's oversized chair as she told him, none too politely, to just get the hell out of her way while she organized his mess.

"Do you think I have an office to return to?" Dawg sighed the question in resignation.

"Think smelly candles and vases of flowers." Natches lifted his head, his nostrils flaring as though testing the air for a sweet scent. "I'm betting vanilla and roses," he said then, looking back at Dawg.

Hell, if all it took was the scent of vanilla and roses to keep her tight ass out of trouble, then he was all for it. He was to the point that he was ready to pull his hair out. He hadn't had her in his life forty-eight hours yet, and she already had him on such a tight edge that explosion was imminent.

Explosion of the sexual sort. He was so damned hard he was about to rupture his jeans with his erection. Or choke said erection with the confinement.

He hadn't had enough of her that morning. Hell, he had a feeling he could take her for hours and still not have enough of her.

As they left the small downstairs office Cranston had taken in the London, Kentucky, courthouse, Dawg stayed carefully on guard for watching eyes. Exiting the lower level, they were able to stay out of the main portion of the courthouse. The other agents used other exits, other hallways.

Paranoia. It had been bred into him by his coldly suspicious parents long before he ever joined the Marines and then the ATF. Even as a kid, too damned young to know what the word meant, he had begun to develop a suspicious nature.

Of course, with two cold, selfish egomaniacs as parents, how could he help it? His mother saw shadows in shadows, and everyone was out to get her. Emotions were her worst enemy, and she had fought against them tirelessly. And his father. Hell, his father had been as much a bastard as Natches's father was. Sometimes Dawg wondered how Rowdy had hit it so lucky. His father, Ray, had been tough but caring. And Rowdy had never suffered a beating in his life.

Until Dawg was old enough and big enough to fight back, his father had taken great delight in making his son cower.

Dawg hadn't inherited his father's habit of striking first, but his mother's insidious paranoia was a part of him.

So much so that he couldn't get out of his head the look in Crista's eyes when he asked her about a pregnancy. For a second, pain and fear and sorrow had flashed in the chocolate orbs. It had been so quick he couldn't even be certain it had been there. Paranoia or fact?

He shook his head as he and Natches moved toward their Harleys. Dawg pulled his dark glasses from his shirt pocket and placed them on his nose as he stared around the sunlit courthouse parking lot.

"Stop worrying so much," Natches murmured as they straddled the bikes. "We have any number of reasons for being here."

Dawg glanced over at him before turning the key and starting the cycle. The rough, dangerous rumble of the motor ignited beneath him. The relaxing sense of freedom it normally gave him was absent now.

He had found a new freedom. A new peace. That of being buried so deep inside Crista that he could feel her heartbeat.

Agonizing arousal clenched his cock and balls at the thought of taking her. The shock and surprise that had at first filled her eyes had been followed closely by desperation, desire, and emotions he didn't want to even think about. But she had burned him alive.

There had been more pleasure in her arms than he'd had in a lifetime of sexual acts, and that was damned scary.

Because he wasn't a fool. He knew what they were facing. One little slipup, one agent remembering the wrong thing, and he would be revealed; Crista would be betrayed. And, hell, that would suck. Because there wasn't a chance he was going to let Homeland Security get their hands on her.

If he was paranoid, then Homeland Security was over the limit. Even Cranston, as much as Dawg liked the special agent in charge of the investigation, was more paranoid than anyone Dawg had known before or since. He would jerk Crista out of Somerset and send her straight to a detention center out of the country. And once there, she would be buried in so much fucking red tape and shadows that he would never find her again.

Once they were far enough from London to find a relatively secure spot to pull into, Dawg and Natches turned their Harleys onto a secluded lane and pulled into the small, deserted clearing hidden from the road.

Cutting the motor, Dawg bit off a curse and stared around the clearing before turning his gaze to Natches.

"What did you find out?"

Natches had talked to the agents last night, subtly questioning them and covering Crista's ass.

"No one saw anything but me," he drawled. "I reported that you came in before me, and I borrowed your girlfriend's car to drive in. I was point, remember? No one can question me, because no one else knows any different."

Natches had indeed had point outside the front of the warehouse, communicating with the rest of the team that had been in place as the interested parties drove in. He'd announced the arrival of the woman, and in his voice Dawg had heard something the others hadn't. A warning.

"Watch the front, Dawg," Natches had drawled. Not because Dawg had been closest, as Cranston had reminded him sharply.

"My mistake," Natches had murmured into the communications link.

Dawg had known then. Natches didn't make mistakes, not like that. Whoever the woman was, something was wrong, and Dawg had moved to intercept her.

The agents assigned to this case were wild-eyed and bitter, paranoid and determined. And it didn't help one damned bit that Crista so closely resembled the superficial description they had of the woman acting as a contact point between the buyers and sellers.

"If someone set her up, then we need to know why." If

someone set her up. Son of a bitch, he was aching so bad to fuck her that he was trying to find excuses where he knew he should be finding handcuffs instead.

"Someone's setting *you* up," Natches grunted as he stared at Dawg over the rim of his glasses. "And that's not a good thing. Who could know you're on the team?"

Dawg shook his head. "Better yet, who would know to use Crista if they did?"

Natches gave him a long, mocking look then. "Dawg, Cuz, who *doesn't know* that Crista Jansen is your weakness? You've been dogging her ass like a stray mutt for months now." Natches smirked at his own puns.

"Ha-ha," Dawg sneered.

Then he rubbed the back of his neck. Hell, had he been that transparent?

"Even Johnny noticed." Natches was gleefully snickering now. "And he just can't understand the attraction, doncha know?"

Dawg grimaced. Johnny Grace. He was a lousy damned excuse for a cousin. When Dawg's parents had been killed in an auto accident, Johnny's mother, Dawg's aunt, had decided to attempt to claim part of the estate Dawg's parents had left him. Dawg had spent a year protecting the inheritance that amounted to the only damned thing his parents had ever willingly given him.

And there had been Johnny, standing in a court of law, reciting his father's complaints against Dawg and swearing that his parents had meant to leave the better portion of their estate to his mother.

And through it all, Johnny had sneered and snidely reminded Dawg over and again that his relationship with Dawg's father had been much deeper than that of his son's.

Because Johnny was an ass-kissing little bastard that played up to Dawg's father's opinion of himself.

"Old man Thompson was by the garage this morning," Natches said then. "He was bitching about the lights moving back along the mountain last night behind his house. We could check it out again."

Again. That about summed it the hell up.

Dawg rubbed his hand over his stubbled cheeks before

making a mental note to shave before rubbing on Crista again. She had razor burn on her neck that morning after her shower.

"Someone knows something, Dawg," Natches said softly. "They know enough to throw Crista at you to distract you. Give you someone to suspect."

Dawg shook his head. "I know better than to be distracted that easily. Besides, we have everything but the money and the woman. How am I a threat to either, as things stand now?"

"This is someone who doesn't know you heed your common sense when it's important," Natches pointed out. "This is someone who only knows the fact that Dawg distrusts everyone but the Father, the Son, and the Holy Ghost. Which could be just about everyone you've met in this country and a dozen others. And it could be someone who is afraid one of the men we captured will talk. If he talks, who says they won't name Crista?"

Dawg wasn't known for his trusting nature.

"We'll let them think they've succeeded then." He smiled slowly, watching as Natches grimaced. "And Crista has an alibi. You were using her Rodeo; she was at home."

"Man, I hate that smile." Natches sighed, resignation glittering in his gaze. "What are you going to do?"

Dawg leaned forward, rested his forearms on the handlebars of the motorcycle, and let his grin widen.

"I'm going to let Crista distract me, of course. Why fight it? And while she's distracting, I'm going to see who's watching and what happens later. If she was thrown into my path to catch me off guard, then they threw her in for a reason. Let's see what they intend to do with it now that they have her there. And why it's so damned important that she be there. They couldn't have expected the raid. So their plans are going to be off balance."

"They expected her to be arrested, shipped off, and you running at her heels," Natches bit out. "Be careful they don't catch you in that little net, and you and Crista get shipped off together."

Yeah, that one had occurred to him around midnight.

"I guess I'll just have to take my chances. Hell, I've already broken more laws than I want to think about just getting her out of there. They told us to use initiative, but I don't think that's exactly what they were talking about."

"Sure it was," Natches drawled. "We knew she wasn't involved, so we evened the playing field with no fuss and no muss. It's redneck code. That's what we'll tell 'em." The laid-back country-boy drawl wouldn't fool anyone who happened to know Natches. There was pure bloodthirsty redneck bloodletting in that tone, and it was something Dawg knew he could count on. Natches would watch his back.

His and Crista's.

And that thought opened a whole other can of worms. One he wasn't ready to empty right now. He knew Natches hadn't taken Rowdy's defection from the ménages very well. He had waited, anticipated Rowdy's return and the slow seduction of his fiancée, Kelly. When Rowdy had put the skids on that idea, Natches had been downright pissed.

Hell, the sharing had been a part of their lives since their first sexual encounter as teenagers.

The widow Barnes. She had been soft and sweet, older, more experienced, and lonely enough to take three young boys to her bed.

At the time, no one knew she was also hiding from her psychotic husband, a man who had been watching the teenage Mackay cousins slip into her house, and through the window he had watched the sexual antics they had gotten up to.

That first foray into the dark sexuality of a ménage had come back to haunt them last year when the lady's son, warped beyond belief by his father's molestation of him and the beatings he had endured, had begun raping the girls he claimed as his own.

Then he had targeted Rowdy's stepsister and the woman that held Rowdy's heart, Kelly Salyers. The bastard had nearly killed them all before they stopped him.

And now, Natches was in the cold again, and Dawg knew that was how he had to be feeling. And he was withdrawing. Dawg had been feeling it for a while now. Natches was drifting away from them; the connection that had held him with his cousins all these years was gone now. The ménages, the emotional bond they created, Natches didn't have that anymore.

"Come on, Dawg, stop wrestling over it," Natches advised

somberly. "Let's play this out and see what the hell happens. I have an SOS out to her brother, Alex. The minute his head pops out of whatever hole the government sent him to, then he'll come running with backup."

"We'll play it out." Dawg breathed out roughly before pushing his sunglasses back up his nose.

There wasn't much more they could do. Someone else, someone who knew too much, had dealt Crista into a very deadly game. To save her now, Dawg was going to have to risk everything and pray to God they caught the thieves before the Swede pulled in friends or the task force learned she was at the warehouse. If that happened, all shit was going to hit the fan.

"Look, man, we're backup mostly. The majority of the investigation is being handled by those HS tightwads. They won't call us until something gets ready to go down anyway. We just lie back and keep watch on Miss Crista's tight little rear, and we'll do fine."

Dawg's gaze sharpened on his cousin. "*I'll* watch her rear."

It came out harsher than he had meant, a snapping reply he would have never intended.

Natches's lips quirked mockingly, but Dawg saw the knowledge in his eyes. He also saw a vague edge of distance settle over the other man's face as he nodded slowly.

"You watch her ass. I'll just watch. Whatever." He turned the switch and kicked the Harley's motor in gear before pulling out without saying anything more and leaving Dawg to follow.

Damn it to hell. Dawg hit the ignition and gunned the motor, feeling an edge of anger beginning to burn inside him. It wasn't supposed to be like this, was it? He, Rowdy, and Natches had been closer than brothers all their lives. They had fucked the same women, loved the same women, until Kelly, and now Crista.

Dawg wasn't a fool. He might not love Crista, but that edge of possessiveness had been there, even eight years before. Growing up was hell. Maturing was even worse. Three men who had been as close as ticks to a hound dog eight years ago were fading apart and, Dawg admitted, sometimes it sucked. And sometimes, like now, there was an edge of relief.

But a part of him knew that Natches was being affected worst by the maturity of his two older cousins. For Natches, the sharing had never been a game; it had just taken Rowdy and Dawg longer to see it. For Natches, it was a part of who he was, and losing that connection was starting to affect the other man in ways Dawg hadn't anticipated.

Damn, he would have ripped his own arm out to have kept this from happening. He and Rowdy had always gone out of their way to protect Natches, even as a kid. And maybe as an adult, too.

Somewhere along the way, they had all grown up, though. Even Natches. To the point that the other man had become even harder, darker, than Dawg or Rowdy. Which explained how Natches had stepped into the role of an assassin that last year he had been in the Marines. An assassin the military had been loath to lose when Natches had taken a bullet in the shoulder during a skirmish in Iraq on his off time.

Natches had stepped out of the Marines darker, harder, and more dangerous than he had been when he, Dawg, and Rowdy had stepped into basic training.

Yeah, they had all grown up. But sometimes Dawg wondered if they had grown up for the better.

TEN

She was making headway. Crista stared at the top of the surprisingly nice desk. Walnut, if she wasn't mistaken, and rather old with deep drawers on each side. The middle drawer had been removed; in its place was a keyboard shelf where the computer keyboard rested.

She hadn't powered up the computer; she had to clean it first. There was so much dust gathered around the tower that she had been half afraid to turn it on.

It didn't make sense. The houseboat was spotless. She hadn't seen so much as a dish or an article of clothing out of place. But the office was a war zone. Scattered files and papers, miscellaneous receipts—receipts for God's sake; how the hell did he pay his taxes?—and a variety of other papers, files, and memos that she knew had to be important.

Those scattered on the desk were now neatly filed. Of course, that was after she had spent hours straightening out his filing system. Not that she was finished with that chore. Last year's files were mixed with this year's files, and the aging metal file cabinet was about to give its last groan of effort and collapse into the floor.

She glanced to the glass door, looking onto the floor from

the view the office commanded. She had sent two of the stock boys for the nice wooden file cabinets she knew sat in the office supply section of the lumber store.

Dawg was smart. He had taken ideas from several smaller chains and incorporated them into Mackay's Lumber, Building and Supplies, the business his father had left him.

There was every manner of appliance, office needs, paints, and hobby supplies as well as a mix of seasonal items that added to the sales from the lumberyard.

It was a thriving business if the customers below were anything to go by. Yet, from what she had seen in this office, Dawg rarely made the effort it took to keep everything together.

She knew a manager had overseen the business while he was in the Marines. A man Dawg had promptly fired when he returned home to learn the manager had been systematically embezzling from him.

According to the floor manager, Dawg had nearly gone bankrupt that first year after his return, despite the steady business that came through the large double doors.

There was no danger of bankruptcy now. An audit, maybe. Terminal mismanagement of his office for certain. But not bankruptcy, because despite the "hellhole," as she had called it, there had been a very weird sort of system that Dawg had going on. Just not a system that anyone else could have worked with.

Shaking her head, she moved from the now-cleaned desk to the stack of files, folders, papers, books, and every manner of receipt awaiting her stacked on the other side of the room in front of the large, overstuffed couch.

Evidently Dawg also liked his creature comforts. The couch was long enough and most likely wide enough for him to sleep on. There was a plasma television off to the side, a microwave, and mini refrigerator stocked with beer. Just beer.

It was too bad he didn't like a neat office to go with his creature comforts. But, to be on the fair side, the seating area was ridiculously neat until Crista began stacking the slush inside the area.

She wiped her palms down her jeans and glanced at her

watch before breathing out a weary sigh. Dawg was supposed to have picked her up thirty minutes ago to collect her car and her clothes.

He had stashed her in his office with a firm warning to stay put, then headed out with no more information than the approximate time he would be back.

And while he had been gone, she had been thinking.

What happened at the warehouse made absolutely no sense whatsoever to her. The fact that the note from the delivery company was missing from her car made even less sense. About as much sense as the other items that had come up missing over the last few months, just to turn back up days later. She had meant to look for the note. It must have slipped onto the floor or between the seats, but Dawg hadn't given her a chance to search for it.

She propped her elbow on her knee and cupped her fingers in her hand, a frown tightening her brow as she tapped her lips with her fingers.

Why would she be deliberately drawn to the warehouse?

Unless someone wanted to mess up something Dawg was doing. It wouldn't take a rocket scientist to figure out he had been chasing her ever since he had learned of her return to Somerset.

And in doing it, they had given him the perfect opportunity to blackmail her.

Would he really turn her over to the authorities? Damn, he had looked serious, sounded serious. And he warned her in no uncertain terms not to discuss the other night with anyone.

She jerked to her feet and paced to the wide door with its tinted window to stare at the busy floor below. She was in trouble, and she knew it. She had known it even before she bumbled into the warehouse; she just hadn't wanted to admit it. Even Alex had had enough sense to know something was wrong. He would have never told her to call Dawg otherwise. Because he must have known that Dawg was some kind of agent. Alex would have known that Dawg would have the means to find out what was going on.

But Alex couldn't have known the fee Dawg would require: her body.

She shivered at the memory.

He had caught her off guard, she assured herself; otherwise, she would have never given in to him. He had been inside her before she could assimilate the change from anger to passion, even within her own body.

And her body had betrayed her. She had been so slick, so wet, that even now her face flamed in mortification. Even as she grew wetter.

She was going to have to buy more panties at this rate.

She glanced at her watch again. Nearly an hour late. If she didn't pick up her car, it was going to be towed.

What would it have hurt to let her go ahead and pick up the rest of her stuff and then meet him here? It was broad daylight. She didn't exactly live in the boondocks, and she had neighbors.

Besides, other than Dawg, Natches, and that insane person who tried to shoot her, no one knew she was at the warehouse. Except whoever sent her to the warehouse to begin with.

She shoved her hands in the pockets of her jeans and continued to stare into the sales floor. She would give him a few more minutes. If he wasn't back in a few minutes, then she would catch a ride from here to the diner where her Rodeo was still parked. It was no more than a half dozen blocks. Broad daylight. She could have her car back and her meager belongings packed and waiting in the front of the store before he returned.

It wasn't like there was much to pack.

As the thought zipped through her mind, her gaze landed on the short, leanly built man moving through the register counter below.

A smile lit her face.

Johnny Grace owned the little bakery store on the land next to her and Alex's house. The scent of the delicacies wafting through the air nearly drove her crazy on her off days.

He was obviously ringing up his purchases, flashing a smile to the checkout boy and flirting easily. Johnny wasn't deterred when it came to his sexual lifestyle. He enjoyed men more than he did women, and he saw no reason to hide it.

She glanced at her watch. She could be back before Dawg ever knew she was gone.

She grabbed her purse from the table next to her, opened the door, and hurried out before locking it as Johnny headed for the automatic doors.

"Crista." He stopped and blinked quickly as she moved around the registers and called out his name. "What are you doing here?"

She flicked her fingers to the upstairs office. "New job." *Or something.* "Look, I left my car at the diner. Could you give me a ride?"

He was maybe a quarter inch taller than she was, but she wasn't betting on it. He glanced to the door, then smiled again. "Are you sure you want me to give you a ride? Dawg and I aren't on the best of terms. If you two have something going here, then he's liable to be a tad upset if you go anywhere with me."

She flicked a glance to the doors. Nope, no Dawg in sight.

"Dawg is always upset over something." She swallowed back her own trepidation at the thought. "And I promise, I won't tell him who offered me a lift."

She smiled back at him with an edge of desperation.

Johnny chuckled in amusement, shaking his head at her, his dark blond curls tumbling about his face. He really should have been born a woman, she thought. He had a soft, feminine air about him, an almost gentle demeanor. And he was nice. He shared his baked delights with her on her off days when the store below was closed and he was alone putting together the next week's confections. And it wasn't as though Dawg could be jealous.

"Come on then." He nodded toward the doors. "I'll give you a lift. Are you coming back here or heading home?"

"I'm going home." She neglected to mention why she was going home. That was a subject she didn't want to get into just now.

Following Johnny through the doors, she glanced around quickly, expecting any minute to see Dawg bearing down on her like some avenging angel.

Yes, he had told her to stay put, but he was late, and the precautions made no sense. By his own report, the man who saw her was dead, and the other suspects had been arrested or were dead. No one else but Dawg and Natches could know she was there. No one was going to step out from behind a vehicle or a building and start shooting anyway.

Were they?

"When did you start working for Dawg?" Johnny drew her attention away from her morbid paranoia as he glanced behind his shoulder to show her a warm smile.

"Just today." She drew level with him, gazing around in front of her. "How far away did you park?"

Johnny laughed. "The far end. This is how I work off all those calories I add into my body on baking days."

The other side of the parking lot was no joke.

The early June heat was bearing down on them, causing a fine film of perspiration to break out on Crista's face as they reached the late-model Taurus Johnny drove.

He unlocked her door with a flourish. "Roll down the window," he advised. "The air conditioner went out last week, and I haven't had a chance to get it fixed yet."

She rolled down the window before closing the door and snapped her seat belt in place.

Still no Dawg.

She was tired of waiting for Dawg. The danger he kept harping on couldn't be too high, or he wouldn't have left her alone for hours at the lumber store.

She was really rethinking this whole danger and blackmailing business. She was starting to wonder if the danger wasn't more in Dawg's mind than in her life, and was just a ready means of getting her into his bed. After all, they had arrested those guys at the warehouse. And whoever got away with the money was probably spending it right now in the Bahamas or something.

And why hadn't she thought of that one before now? she asked herself as Johnny moved into the driver's seat.

"Where were you the other night?" he asked, startling her out of her thoughts. "I was at the store until late, and you still weren't home."

She glanced at him, surprised he had noticed. "I was, uhh, with Dawg."

And Dawg was making her paranoid, because suddenly she felt nervous, uncertain. Why would Johnny care where she was? Why would he check to see that she wasn't home?

Johnny faced forward as he started the car and brushed back a curl from his cheek.

"With Dawg, huh?" he asked curiously.

Technically. For a little while. "Yes," she answered carefully.

His lips turned up into a grin as he glanced over her and put the car in gear. Driving from the parking lot, he turned onto the interstate that led back to the main street of Somerset before flicking her another look.

"Be careful, Crista." He finally sighed. "You know, we call him Dawg for a reason, right?"

The gentleness in his voice had her hackles rising. She could feel the judgment in his tone and she didn't like it. She wasn't a child anymore, and she had endured enough lectures eight years before. She didn't need any more.

"Because he's stubborn?" she batted at him sweetly. "Come on, Johnny, I'm a big girl here. I can handle Dawg."

She heard lightning struck in cases of whopper lies like that one. She looked up at the clear blue sky. Not a cloud in sight, thank God.

Johnny only chuckled. "So, did he bring along the rest of the team, or was he solo?"

She nearly gaped back at him. "That's a rude question, Johnny." And it made her more nervous, more uncertain, and even more aware of the enmity that existed between Johnny and Dawg. Leaving with Johnny hadn't been a good idea.

"And entirely qualified." Johnny rolled his eyes. "Darling, despite Kelly's determination to hold out, it's more than obvious those three have been working her for years. They saved her for Rowdy, and he will share her eventually. It's a delicate little seduction technique they use. How delicate the seduction determines how serious they are about the prey."

"Oh Lord, you make them sound like wolves."

"Very well-bred wolves, I'm certain." Johnny laughed. "And you didn't answer my question."

"Dawg was traveling alone that night," she assured him.

"Otherwise, I wouldn't have been with him." Was that a cloud overhead? A rumble of thunder maybe?

Okay, no thunder. But there were two Harleys behind them, the smooth rumble of their motors reminding her of Alex.

"Interesting," Johnny murmured as he flicked on the turn signal and pulled into the turn lane to head into the smaller road that led into the old center of the city.

"Just interesting?" She smothered a yawn, wishing he would hurry.

"Dawg never seemed the possessive sort to me." Johnny shrugged. "But as I said, it's usually a seduction technique. He has any number of interesting games he's played over the years. He does give the family plenty to gossip over."

Suddenly, being here just didn't feel right. It was obvious that despite their familial connection that Johnny liked Dawg even less than he claimed Dawg liked him. Not that she figured the whole family feud thing was any of her business, but right now, it paid to be just a little wary of Dawg.

"And we're definitely in trouble," Johnny suddenly claimed morosely, his lips pursing into a pout as he glanced at the rearview mirror.

Crista twisted around in the seat, her eyes widened, then she flopped forward again and crossed her arms over her breasts.

Dawg and Natches were riding behind the car like denim-clad motorized warriors. Their expressions were stony, and the smile Dawg had flashed her was anything but friendly. It reminded her of a shark.

"Just drop me off in front of the diner, Johnny." She sighed. "I'll be okay there."

"Are you sure?" A delicate frown formed between his brows. "I feel a little funny just leaving you with him like this. Dawg isn't always predictable."

She snorted. That was an understatement if she ever heard one.

"I can handle Dawg." She hoped.

She waited as Johnny pulled to the curb several minutes later and stopped the car. She didn't give him time to say anything. She stepped quickly from the car, slammed the door, and then turned her back on all of them and moved for the narrow alley that led to the back lot.

Dawg was right behind her, and so was Natches. Opening her purse, she pulled her keys free, refusing to glance around. He had no right to intimidate her. And if she let him keep doing it, then it would never stop.

As she reached her car and unlocked it, she turned back then, lifting her brows at the two men watching her with equally fierce expressions from the motorcycles that pulled in behind her little red Rodeo.

Déjà vu. She wondered if she would end up leaving with her car this time.

The engines were cut, leaving the parking lot strangely silent, as though even the breeze itself were wondering what they would do now.

"I see you've been out having fun." She flicked a glance to the motorcycles.

"Get on." Dawg jerked his head to the side, indicating the back of the motorcycle.

"I don't think so," she said brightly. "I'm going to go home, pack the rest of my stuff, and I'll meet you back at the boat later. Why don't you and Natches there go take the edge off your tempers somewhere? I'm not in the mood to deal with it."

He swung his leg over the seat of the motorcycle as he rose; clad in faded jeans and a white, short-sleeved, buttoned shirt, he looked like the ultimate bad boy. A ravisher, a modern-day warrior.

The sight of his black hair blowing in the breeze and his light green eyes glittering in his dark face had a rush of damp warmth spilling from her vagina.

As though she hadn't been wet enough to begin with.

"Dawg." She sighed. "Don't start trying to intimidate me, okay? We both know damned good and well no one but you and whoever left that notice knew I was there last night. You're trying to control me, and a good blackmailer sticks to the main object; he doesn't blackmail for the air a person breathes. Okay?"

His eyes narrowed. "You have it all worked out, don't you, fancy-face?"

"Stop calling me that." She hated the nickname he had given her as a teenager. It had caused her no end of teasing for years. "Now, you can follow me to the house and help me finish packing, or you can go back where you came from. Your choice."

She lifted herself into the driver's seat, closed the door, and shoved the key into the ignition. She gave it a quick turn, and nothing happened. The starter clicked hollowly, but the motor didn't turn over. Frowning, she released it, then moved to turn it again.

Before she could complete the motion, the door jerked open, and she barely had time to gasp before Dawg was pulling her free of the vehicle, his expression fierce as he all but lifted her off her feet and rushed away from the vehicle.

"What the hell are you doing?" She tugged at the arm latched around her waist and stared back at her Rodeo. It was sitting there, door open, deserted, as Dawg pushed her to the motorcycle and turned back to the vehicle.

"Dawg. I'm tired. I'm dusty. And I need the rest of my clothes. If you don't have a really, really good reason—"

A loud, wrenching pop jerked her gaze back to the Rodeo. A Rodeo whose little red hood was tossed into the air like a Frisbee. The front of the vehicle suddenly shot up in flames.

Lots of flames. So fast and so hot that within a second the interior was a red, furious blaze as she stood in shock, trying to comprehend exactly what had happened.

The hood landed on the other side of the parking lot, the crash of metal to asphalt barely registering as she watched Dawg and Natches tearing toward the vehicle, the fire extinguishers they carried in the saddle packs of their motorcycles gripped in their hands.

Diners came running from the back door. The cook lugged out a larger extinguisher, and someone yelled that the fire department was on their way. And all Crista could do was stare at the driver's seat, engulfed in flames, and feel the ice moving through her body.

It appeared that Dawg had been right after all.

ELEVEN

"I hope the three of you have some damned good explanations, because I'm not really happy with you right now."

Sheriff Ezekiel Mayes, Zeke to his friends, didn't bother glancing at Crista or Kelly Salyers, who had arrived at the diner with her fiancé within half an hour of the initial explosion. He trained his light brown eyes on the three cousins instead, a hard frown pulling at his forehead.

"Don't look at me, Zeke." Rowdy shook his head, his short black hair gleaming beneath the bright overhead lights. "I just came by to make sure they were still alive." He nodded toward his cousins, a friendly smile on his lips, though his gaze was cool and warning.

The three cousins sat at the large, round table in the back of the dining room. Kelly was placed between Rowdy and Natches, and Crista between Dawg and Natches. The scene couldn't have been more incriminating, considering the Mackay cousins' reputations.

"Zeke, you keep forgetting they've grown up." Kelly leaned forward, propping her chin on her hand as she braced her elbow on the table and grinned back at the sheriff with a winning smile.

"And you used to be such a sweet, honest little thing." The sheriff clucked in disapproval. "Lying for these boys only gets everyone in trouble, Kelly. Remember?"

Kelly grimaced. "They caught him."

She was obviously talking about the stalker who had nearly killed her and the three cousins last summer.

"I could have caught him faster if these three yahoos had told me what the hell they were doing," he grunted, eying the yahoos in question. "Am I going to get any better answers this time?" His gaze finally moved to Crista. "Alex asked me to watch after you before he left, Crista. Are you going to help me out?"

She tried to smile, but her face felt frozen. "Zeke, if I knew anything, I promise I'd tell you. I don't know myself what happened."

Zeke grunted at that. "You have a homemade detonation device set in your vehicle that created enough heat to burn your flesh off your bones, and you don't know why?"

Crista's stomach rolled threateningly.

"Hell, Zeke, go a little easier on her," Dawg bit out. "She doesn't know what the hell is going on, and neither do we. I heard the ignition click and jerked her out of the vehicle in time. It was that simple. I do have a bit of experience with these things, you know."

Zeke's gaze lingered a little too long on Dawg before he turned back to Crista. "I'm going to have to start warning the women around here about getting mixed up with these boys. Bad things seem to follow them nowadays." He took the remaining chair, straddling it with an easy motion and leaning his darkly tanned forearms on the table as he stared back at Crista. "Why does someone want to kill you, Crista Ann?"

She felt the color leech from her face as Dawg's arm suddenly came around her shoulders, his chair moving in closer to hers.

"For God's sake, Zeke," he snarled. "Have a little compassion here."

Zeke didn't take his eyes off her. "Crista, you're a smart

girl," he said softly. "Alex raised you to think on your feet. Let me help you."

She shook her head. She had already ignored Dawg once by leaving the store and coming out on her own. She had almost died because of it. She was too stunned now, too frightened, to consider ignoring him again.

"I don't know why." Her lips felt numb, her body cold.

"Any strange goin' ons?" Zeke's gaze sharpened as Dawg's hand tightened warningly on her shoulder.

She could feel his heat surrounding her, but it wasn't touching the core of ice that seemed to solidify inside her chest.

She shook her head. Lying. She was lying through her teeth to friends now, covering up something that Zeke should know about.

"If nothing's going on, then why did Alex call me last week and ask me to keep an extra eye on you?" he asked her then. "He said you had mentioned some strange things then, Crista." His voice was gentle but firm. He knew she was lying.

"I'm not used to living alone," she whispered. "I was a little freaked out when I talked to him. The house sounds funny sometimes."

And it did. Sometimes, she could have sworn someone was moving around the house at night, though she had never been able to find any proof of it. That wasn't a lie, but it felt like one, because she wasn't telling Zeke the whole truth.

He sighed then. "Anyone from Virginia that you think might want to hurt you? What about that guy Alex said you were living with? Mark?"

"Mark Lessing." The tension around the table was suddenly thick enough to cut with a knife. Dawg tightened subtly, his body seeming to shift with dangerous force.

She looked at him in confusion, seeing the glitter of an inner flame in his eyes that had the blood suddenly rushing through her body with dizzying force. She swallowed tightly before forcing her gaze back to Zeke.

"Mark wouldn't hurt me. He has no reason to want to hurt me."

"So your relationship with him ended amicably?" Zeke

asked curiously. "That's a little unusual. Relationships don't just end with no anger on either side."

"Nothing ended." She shrugged. "I came home. Mark agreed it was time. End of story."

Zeke glanced at Dawg. "You believe that?"

"What kind of game are you playing, Zeke?" Dawg asked then.

Zeke blinked with a look of studied male mockery. "Just trying to figure out the rules of the game you're playing, Dawg. Leave me in the dark, and that's what I tend to do."

"He's not playing any games." Crista clenched her fists in her lap as she fought to control the shaking of her limbs. "Nothing has been going on. Mark wouldn't hurt me, and neither would anyone else I know. I don't know what happened out there or why anyone would want to hurt me."

And she was a lousy liar.

Zeke breathed out wearily as he leaned back in his chair and regarded them all cynically. "When you think you can tell me the truth, Crista, you know how to get hold of me," he finally said, then stared back at Dawg. "You know what Alex will do if she gets hurt, right? He'll come down on the three of you like a wrecking ball. It won't be pretty."

"Come on, Zeke, threats don't work." Dawg rose from his seat before gripping Crista's arm and drawing her up with him. "If you have any more questions, she'll be on the boat with me or working in my office."

Zeke's gaze flicked to the hold Dawg had on her before his eyes lifted back to hers.

"If she's not in trouble, then why isn't she staying at her place?"

"Because she moved in with me yesterday," Dawg answered coolly. "We were heading to her house to pack her stuff when this happened."

Crista was suddenly aware of the other diners packed into the restaurant, their curious gazes following them, even though the table had been moved far enough away to give the sheriff the privacy he needed to question them.

And those curious diners couldn't have helped but overhear Dawg's little announcement.

"Well, I know where to find her then, that's all that matters." Zeke moved smoothly to his feet, his leanly muscled body flexing in frustration as he glanced around the table again. "Natches, Rowdy, next time I have proof you're pulling ops behind my back, I'm going to arrest every damned one of you. I'm giving you fair warning now."

Ops. Operations. Crista knew that word, she had heard Alex use it often enough.

"Save it, Zeke." Natches followed Rowdy and Kelly as they rose from their seats as well. "We're not running ops on you. And if we were, we would know how to cover our asses."

Zeke breathed out in exasperation. "Unfortunately, that's too true." He stood as well, his gaze coming back to Crista. "Have you talked to Alex yet?"

She shook her head. "He's out of the country."

Zeke nodded. "I put out a call to his CO, and he told me the same thing. Any idea when he'll be back?"

"When he gets back."

Zeke's questions were beginning to grate on her nerves, especially when it was more than obvious that he knew the answers before he did the asking.

Zeke nodded again, his gaze going over the five of them before it landed on Kelly once more. "You're letting them get you in trouble again, Kel. Not a good idea."

At that, Kelly's laughter whispered around the table. "Zeke, they are trouble, remember? But in this case, I promise you, I'm innocent as a babe."

His lips twitched at that, and an edge of amusement filled his gaze. "Course you are, Kel." He chuckled. "And it's more than obvious that fiancé of yours is a damned bad influence. Not that I expected anything less. You, my girl, are a little too easily taken in by that rogue's smile of his."

"Ease up, Zeke." Though his voice was amused, there was an edge of steel in Rowdy's voice. "We need to get Crista back to the marina and let Dawg get her settled. Her nerves are raw, and so are ours. Like you said, you know where to find her if you have any more questions."

Crista let Dawg lead her from the diner then, aware that the sheriff watched them leave, suspicion shadowing his gaze. Not that he didn't have a damned good reason to be suspicious. She knew Zeke, and knew, from the conversations she had with her brother in the past, how seriously he took his job and the protection of the county. And suspicion meant a challenge to Zeke. He wasn't going to just let this go.

"Just hang on." Dawg's voice was a whisper of sound as he led her from the diner. "We're almost clear." He turned to Rowdy. "Did you bring the pickup?"

"Dad drove yours in," Rowdy answered softly as they moved toward the parking lot. "He's waiting to take your Harley back to the marina. We sure as hell didn't want to leave it here."

Crista wrapped her arms across herself as Dawg led her to the big black pickup truck that she had ridden in the day before.

Her life had definitely gone beyond Mercury in retrograde. Car bombs were major catastrophes, not fate fucking with you.

"We'll meet you back at your place," Rowdy told him as they neared the pickup, and Ray Mackay opened the door and stepped from it.

Rowdy's tan pickup sat beside it, and Dawg's and Natches's cycles on the other side. Ray lifted the rifle he carried from the seat, unloaded it, and calmly reached in to hang it on the gun rack that stretched across the back window.

"Few curiosity seekers and that rabid little twit Johnny," he grunted as they neared him. "Little bastard. His daddy would roll over in his grave if he knew how that boy turned out."

Crista stared at Ray in surprise. "Johnny Grace?"

"Grace my ass," he muttered. "That bitch that spawned him had to have gotten the sperm donor from someone other than Ralph. Ralph was a fine man. Ain't none of him in that boy."

"Easy, Dad." Rowdy's voice was clearly warning. "Johnny probably just wanted to check on Crista. They're neighbors. Kind of."

Ray's eyes speared into her then. "Don't tell me you befriended that little shit?"

"Johnny's always been kind to me, Mr. Mackay," she said, wishing she didn't sound so weak, so tired. "He wouldn't have meant any harm."

She was aware of the gazes now trained on her in disbelief. Her chin lifted. She didn't base her opinions or her friendships on others' opinions, and she wasn't going to start now. "Fine. For some reason you don't like Johnny, and from what he said earlier, there's not a lot of love lost. That's none of my business, and it has nothing to do with me." And she was too tired right now to make sense of any of it.

She respected Ray Mackay, trusted him. The fact that he so intensely disliked his own nephew was telling. But until Crista understood why, she wasn't going to automatically dislike him herself. She would definitely be wary, but she would reserve judgment.

Ray turned his gaze from her to Dawg as he rubbed his hand over his face in agitation before he and Dawg seemed to share some private communication. Crista hated private communications between men. She wasn't a male mind reader, so she didn't consider it fair in her presence.

"I'll take care of her, Ray," Dawg finally murmured.

"You know, you could get on my nerves fairly quickly," she told them with no small amount of her own irritation. "If you want to take care of me so damned bad, take me to get my clothes, and then leave me alone to shower and sleep."

"We'll stop on the way to the marina and buy you a few more things," Dawg told her firmly, causing her to freeze and stare back at him in disbelief.

"You said we could pick up my stuff from the house. Damn it, Dawg, I can't just go out and buy more clothes."

"And that was before someone decided to turn you into a piece of charcoal," he snapped back. "I'm not even attempting that house with you along. I'll go check it out myself in the morning and get your stuff. Until then, we can stop on the way home and buy you a few extra things."

She was aware of the interested gazes on them. The men were watching with expressions varying between amusement and wariness, and Kelly shook her head back at Crista warningly from Dawg's side.

The men she could have ignored, but there was something in Kelly's eyes that warned Crista that now wasn't the time to push Dawg. And that sucked. Because she wanted her own clothes; she didn't want to have to spend the small amount of savings she had on clothes she didn't need.

"I'll just use your damned washer tonight," she finally retorted. She wasn't about to end up more in debt to him than it already appeared she was going to be.

"Just get in the truck." He didn't wait for her to follow the harshly worded order. Dawg gripped her waist and lifted her in before crowding in beside her and forcing her to climb over the console to the passenger seat.

As she faced forward and stared through the windshield, she was faced with her poor little burned Rodeo. She had loved that little SUV.

The engine flared to life. As it did, Crista glanced over to see Dawg's hands wrapped around the steering wheel with a white-knuckled, furious grip.

"Is Lessing who you left here with?" His voice was cold, furious.

"Yes." She kept her voice soft, kept it calm.

Mark and Ty had come from Virginia that week eight years ago to inform Alex, their former Special Forces commander, why they were discharged from the Army. She had left with them when they returned home. It was supposed to have been a temporary thing. Instead, they had all become friends, family in a strange kind of way, and she hadn't moved out until returning home the year before.

"You left me for another man?"

She stayed silent, despite the shaking in the pit of her stomach. She could lie to the sheriff but not to Dawg, not about this. The words would choke her to death.

"Crista, so help me God, you better answer me now." His voice was a graveled, curt sound that had her flinching imperceptibly.

"I didn't leave you for another man," she finally answered evenly.

She had left him because of two other men, the men he had been intent on sharing her with. Then she had left town because she couldn't bear the hollow pain that burned inside her months later.

"But you went with another man?" His voice was harsher, if possible.

"I left Somerset with Mark. I moved in with Mark. I lived with him for seven years. Is that what you want to know?"

He turned his head toward her, his eyes glittering back at her with burning male lust and anger.

"No. What I want to know is, did you sleep with the son of a bitch?"

She drew in a slow, deep breath. "I slept with him often."

Three hours later, Dawg pulled Crista inside the dimly lit houseboat where Natches waited silently, jerked the door closed, and locked it before tossing the handful of plastic shopping bags filled with clothes to the couch.

His fingers were latched around her wrist, where he had learned fast to keep them as he forced her through the store and chose the clothing himself.

There were some panties in there that had his dick throbbing at the thought of pulling them from her body. Lacy little push-up bras, skimpy little pj's, some low-rise jeans and high-rise shirts that were guaranteed to make his blood boil if he caught another man staring at her.

As he released her, Natches uncurled his body from the deep shadows in the corner of the room, rising from the recliner and watching them expectantly.

"What is he doing here?" She flicked Natches an irritated glare.

She was irritated, and he was still so damned mad he was wearing his back teeth down.

"He," Natches drawled, "is being a Good Samaritan. I brought the rest of your thirsty plants." He indicated the freshly watered greenery sitting on the dining table. "And your personal stuff." He grinned as though proud of himself. "I knew Dawg was buying you new clothes, so I didn't bother with those."

Dawg watched Crista carefully. He could see the mad washing over her expression, the light flush that stained her cheeks, and the glitter of it in her eyes.

"Of course you didn't bother," she muttered through her teeth. At least Dawg wasn't the only one gritting his molars. "Wouldn't it just suck to spoil Dawg's fun?"

"Hell yeah." Natches breathed as though relieved that she understood some complicated dilemma. "We're real careful not to spoil Dawg's fun. That could get bloody."

As Crista swung around, Dawg ducked his head, hiding a grin that tugged involuntarily at his lips. Natches could play the fool better than anyone Dawg knew. He could be playful, teasing, almost innocent. As long as one didn't make the mistake of staring into the cold depths of his frozen green eyes.

As Dawg glanced down, he got a generous view of her well-rounded breasts heaving beneath her T-shirt and her fists clenching at her side.

"You have your clothes." He jerked his head to the bags. "You can take a shower now and change. I'll order something to eat."

"Shove it," she snapped.

"Don't tempt me, sugar girl." Tension fairly snapped through him, he was so damned on edge, so horny and pissed off that he didn't know if he could trust himself to keep his hands off her or not. "Because shoving it is something I could do real easy right now."

He watched her eyes widen in shock and surprise before the glitter of anger increased.

"You are not intimidating me, Dawg," she retorted.

And she looked serious.

Dawg grinned. A slow, easy curve of his lips as he let his hands move to his belt, jerking the slack through his belt loops and pulling at the buckle. Her eyes widened. Her lips parted. Dawg watched as her gaze jerked to Natches before she grabbed the bags and ran like a rabbit that just caught sight of the wicked wolf.

Natches was chuckling as she sprinted up the curving stairs, never pausing to look back.

"Man, she should have gotten a clue with the smile," Natches snorted as he turned back, his gaze smug as Dawg readjusted his belt.

Amusement lingered in Natches's expression, but there was regret lurking in his eyes.

Dawg knew where the regret stemmed from. He wouldn't be sharing in this relationship between Crista and Dawg. As fiery, as problematic and irritating as it was shaping up to be, he would be on the outside looking in. And that was a helluva place to be.

Dawg shook his head. "What did you see after we left?"

Natches pushed his fingers through his shoulder length, straight black hair as a grimace contorted his rough-hewn features.

"I saw Johnny. He was watching you and Crista like a beady-eyed little snake from the corner as you drove off. You could see his brain just calculating ways to use this. The little twit. Other than that, all I saw were the customers from the diner. There were no unknowns."

No unknowns. No one unfamiliar.

"Where could they have hidden?" Dawg wondered curiously, mentally laying out the area in his head.

"Too many places." Natches shrugged, mirroring his own thoughts. "Sheriff Mayes is having the Rodeo impounded, though. He's *investigating* the crime."

Dawg grimaced.

"Uh-huh," his cousin breathed out sharply. "My opinion of it as well."

Dawg tightened his lips as he strode over to the fridge and jerked out two bottles of beer. After handing one to Natches, he twisted the cap off his own and took a long, fortifying drink.

"This is turning into a fucking mess," he bit out. "How the hell did she manage to get herself mixed up in this?"

Natches twisted the cap off his own beer as he shook his head and paced over to the glass sliding doors.

"That's not all I found out." Natches turned back to him slowly, his gaze brooding, hooded. "When Crista left here eight years ago, she didn't just leave with Mark Lessing. Following them was Tyrell Grayson. Both men were once a part of Alex's spec op team, though they were discharged a month or so before for medical reasons. They all moved into Lessing's apartment on her arrival there, and she lived with them the whole time she was there. Rumor has it, both men were her lovers."

TWELVE

Dawg froze at that information. He remembered Tyrell Grayson, though he had never met Mark Lessing. Tyrell had been a medic in the small Special Forces team Alex fought with at one time. Leanly muscled, blond-haired, and charming as hell.

"She had two lovers," he said quietly.

"That's the rumor." Natches shrugged. "I called a friend of mine who lived in Virginia Beach, not too far from where she lived with the two men. He did a little poking around yesterday. Lessing comes from money, and his position in his father's law firm obviously pays well. The penthouse apartment he still owns is supposed to be sweet. Lots of windows and space with a view of the beach. Lessing and Grayson still share the apartment, but a few of the neighbors say she broke their hearts when she left. My contact there believes differently. He talked to Lessing, posing as a potential employer who had heard about Crista's references and her lack of a job. Both men sang her praises and seemed fairly upbeat about her move."

She had two lovers. Two men. Ex–Special Forces. Hard

men. And yet she had run from him and the fear that he wanted to share her with his cousins?

It didn't make sense.

"Any rumors of drugs or illegal activities?" Dawg asked.

"She's clean as a whistle there." Natches shook his head.

"But she could have made the right contacts to learn about the missiles and possible movements, as well as those needed to sell them." Dawg didn't want to believe that. He could feel everything inside him rejecting the idea that Crista could have possibly been involved in that.

"Initial reports say no." Natches shrugged. "Lessing and Grayson didn't associate with the military or former friends. But my contact is checking into it further."

Dawg felt his jaw tightening with fury.

"See what else you can find out," he ordered harshly. "And while you're at it, find out why she left town to begin with. Somehow, I doubt it had anything to do with avoiding a relationship with me."

Why should it have? She hadn't worried about moving in with two other men. Why run from him?

"What about the explosive device in that Rodeo, Dawg?" Natches said then. "We have the buyers and sellers, and not one of them has mentioned her name. Who struck at her, and why?"

Dawg shook his head. That question was still eating away at his brain.

"Whoever made away with the money set her up as well as the buyers and sellers for the missiles. Whoever the woman was, she knew we'd be there. She knew how to get Crista there. Why would she want to kill her now? She obviously set Crista up. Why wait till now to get rid of her?"

"Are we certain we got all the players?" Natches asked. "The buyers could have had a man on the outside. That's what I would have done."

"Why try to kill her without trying to find the money first?" Dawg asked. "Better yet, what's the point in killing her until they get the money?"

Natches stared back at Dawg silently, his expression still, calm.

"I'll watch things from the *Wet Dreams*," he finally said

softly, referring to his own houseboat, the *Nauti Wet Dreams*. "The Rodeo, I think, was more of a warning. Otherwise, it would have gone up with the first turn of the key. Someone wants the money, and they're warning her that they're not letting it go. We need to go to Cranston, pull him in on this. Show her picture to the players and see how they react."

"I don't trust Cranston that far," Dawg muttered.

"You don't trust anyone that far, but Cranston has a good grasp of how things work. We don't tell him Crista was at the warehouse. We explain about the Rodeo, our suspicions that Crista might resemble the money-girl, and go from there."

"And if they identify Crista?" Dawg asked dangerously. "Cranston could decide to go with what he can arrest and forget the rest."

Natches shook his head. "He's too good for that, Dawg. He'll want to use it, and we can use the team this way. Let's see how it works. What do we have to lose? We're her alibi, remember? Who can fight it?"

The shower shut off upstairs. Dawg turned his head and gave the stairs a long, hard look.

"Talk to Cranston," he said. "We'll see where it goes."

He was walking a damned tightrope, and he knew it. If the players arrested at the warehouse the other night identified Crista as their go-between, then all the suspicion would fall on Crista.

"Cranston's smarter than to believe it would be this easy," Natches assured him as he headed for the door. "I'll head in first thing in the morning to talk to him. I'll flash the pictures to our boys in the cells and see what we get. We could get lucky, and they won't recognize her."

Dawg grunted at that. "Don't bet on it."

He let Natches out of the houseboat and locked the door behind him before resetting the alarms and heading for the stairs.

Crista was up there. Showered, soft, and warm. And he hoped ready to give him the answers he needed. Because the thought of her living with one man had rage eating into his soul. Surprisingly, the thought of her living with two men, sharing in a relationship that his women had always shared with him and his cousins, was like an acid to his soul.

Because Dawg couldn't imagine sharing her, not eight years ago and definitely not now.

He headed to the stairs, moving up them with slow anticipation as his body tightened with the thought of her wearing the clothes he had bought her, the lacy panties he had picked out or the brief pajamas he had imagined seeing her in. The image was tightening through him with the same force as the knowledge of her lovers.

Her lovers.

God help him if that was what she needed now. Once, the thought of sharing her with his cousins would have had his cock pounding in glee. Now, he had to shake back the jealousy, fight to hold back his outrage that she would leave him for not just one man but two.

She had taken from others what she had refused to consider taking from him? He had always thought she had run because of his reputation, because of her fear of the ménages. To find out she had run straight into another one had his temper riding a thin, sharp line.

When he entered the upper-level bedroom, he came to a hard stop.

She was sitting on the bed, wearing one of his large shirts rather than her new pj's, slowly spreading some kind of lotion over her legs, which looked silky, rounded, and too damned tempting to believe.

For a moment, memory flashed through his head. Those silky legs spread, his mouth buried between them. His senses erupted with the remembered taste of silky, sweet feminine cream and hot, rich, satiny flesh. He could remember being as drunk on her as he was on the whiskey, as her fingers clenched in his hair and she whispered. His teeth clenched. She was a vocal lover. Begging, pleading, urging him on.

She set aside the lotion, her hands gripping the shirt where it covered her abdomen and glancing down at it as she rose nervously to her feet.

Oh, baby, it would pay for you to be nervous, he thought with a mix of lust and anger. Because there were so many wild, wicked things he intended to do with that hot little body.

"You have lousy taste in pajamas." She finally glared up

at him. "There's not enough material to them to cover a post-age stamp, let alone me."

He glanced over at the chair where some of the articles lay. The snug boy short panties and camisole tops would have covered more flesh than he liked, actually.

It wasn't the pajamas he wanted to discuss, though.

"Tell me something, Crista." He began unbuttoning his shirt. "When did you intend to tell me that you didn't have just one lover but two? Lessing and his friend Ty Grayson?"

Her gaze flickered, her eyes narrowing back at him as the buttons released from his shirt and his flesh sensitized with the need to touch her.

Then, a slender brow arched tauntingly. "Why would I tell you anything, Dawg? It was none of your business. And that's beside the fact that they weren't my lovers. I simply lived with them."

"You slept with them," he snarled. "You admitted to sleeping with Lessing."

She shrugged. "I slept with them occasionally."

"Both of them?"

Her arms crossed over her breasts then. "Both of them," she agreed.

"At the same fucking time?"

Her lips thinned, irritation sparkling in her eyes then. "At the same time."

Crista had never considered herself to be the type of woman who walked heedlessly into danger, but she admitted to herself that right now, that was exactly what she was doing.

She would have thought that suspecting she had two lovers would have pleased him. She had expected him to suggest blackmailing her to sleep with Natches as well. Instead, he seemed angry.

"You ran away from me, by your own words, because I said I wanted to share you with Rowdy and Natches, yet you leave my bed and move in with two other men?" Incredulity filled his voice, causing it to rise as she stared back at him in surprise.

"What I did after I left you is none of your business." She stepped back as he threw his shirt to the side of the room.

He looked enraged. Dark brows were lowered heavily over brilliant, light green eyes that seemed to glow in his dark face. His lips were a flat, thin line, his shoulders bunched with tension.

He wasn't frightening; he was sexy. He should have been frightening. Instead, she could feel a sense of overwhelming eroticism, anticipation. She should have been enraged, at least as angry as he was. But she was seeing so much emotion in his face, something besides the mocking amusement or cynical awareness he normally displayed.

He was—jealous.

Dawg, jealous?

She felt her breasts become more sensitive, her nipples beading impossibly harder against the material of the T-shirt that she wore, and it made no sense. He had no reason to be jealous; she didn't want him to be jealous. But he was.

Dawg had never been jealous about another woman. Never possessive. That possessiveness had every cell in her body hypersensitive and screaming for his touch.

Her clit was swollen, the folds surrounding it heated and wet. She stared at him, mesmerized, watching as his hand went to the wide leather belt cinching his waist, seeing as though in slow motion the loosening of the leather, the way he left it hanging to jerk the snap of his jeans free.

"What are you doing?" The words rose unbidden. He was furious with her; she could see it. Furious and aroused and so possessive she could see the emotions blazing in his eyes.

"You agreed." His lips twisted, lost their flat, furious line, only to appear fuller, almost swollen, hungry.

The metamorphosis was hypnotizing. Watching anger fall beneath hunger, suspicion beneath possessiveness, and need overtaking his expression.

"You agreed," he repeated as he toed his boots off and tossed them aside, "to sleep with me. To fuck with me."

She flinched at the sound of his voice, not his words. It was rough, guttural, filled with lust. And it struck a chord inside her own sensuality that had her womb clenching violently.

"That's my shirt," he rasped when she continued to stare back at him. "Take it off!"

Crista shook her head slowly, watching as he advanced on

her, as muscles rippled across his chest and shoulders, along his tight abs.

Below, pressing hard and tight against his jeans, his rampant erection demanded freedom.

She knew what Dawg was like when hunger beat him. She had seen him drunk and aroused but never sober and hungry. Not like this. Powerful, intent, focused only on the lust burning inside him. Burning inside her.

Even before, the one night she had spent in his bed, she hadn't known the powerful draw he could be. Tanned and hard, strong and dominant. The determination glowing in his eyes was like chains, holding her still, silent, as he advanced on her.

Her head tilted back as he came within inches of her, her gaze locked with his as his hand lifted, thumb and forefinger gripping the material between her breasts.

"Eight years it's tormented me," he murmured, his voice a dark velvet rasp over her senses. "Dreaming of it. Aching for it to the point that some nights, I couldn't even touch another woman because I ached for you to the point of pain."

He couldn't have ached more than she had. Couldn't have known the brutality of remembering a touch that ruined her for any other.

"But you still took them," she whispered hoarsely, trying to fight past the thickening eroticism building between them. "Alone. And with your cousins."

"And you went to another man." His lips drew back from his teeth in a hard snarl. "Two men."

He moved closer, pressing her against the dresser behind her as she caught her breath at the savage lust rising between them now. "Did they hold you? Did my name scream in your head each time they touched you, as yours screamed in mine?"

"Don't." Show no weakness. She had learned that so many years ago. Show no weakness, never let him see the hunger or the need that ripped through her.

And yet she was showing exactly that.

Her hands gripped the edge of the dresser behind her as she strained away from him, knowing she couldn't fight the hunger if he didn't stop touching her.

And he wouldn't stop. His hands gripped her waist, lifted

her to the top of the dresser, then slid to her knees to draw them slowly apart.

"Dawg. Dawg, you don't want to do this." She was panting, certain she couldn't breathe through this. He was stealing the oxygen between them, making it thick and heavy with lust.

"I don't want to do it?" He drew the shirt up her waist, pulling it over her breasts, then forcing her arms up to tug it free of her body.

The cool air of the air conditioner washed over her nipples, sending a talon of sensation raking down her spine.

When he tossed the shirt aside, he didn't release her wrists. They were bound in one large hand, stretched above her head, lifting her breasts high as he stared at her.

"I should have tied you to my bed that night," he whispered hoarsely. "I would have kept you with me, rather than allowing you to escape."

His other arm wrapped around her waist as he moved between her thighs, forcing them to part as he jerked her to him. A hard, quick motion that buried her nipples against his chest.

Sensation tore through her nerve endings. Crista felt her back arch, a shuddering breath ripping from her lungs as fire and ice seared her nipples, then tore a ragged, ecstatic path to her womb and the hungry depths of her pussy.

Before she could gather her breath to protest, before she could form the protest, his head lowered, his lips stole hers, and for the first time in eight years, Crista relived that first fiery kiss, that first trembling knowledge that every part of her, heart and soul, belonged to Dawg.

THIRTEEN

Crista wasn't aware of when he released her wrists; she was only aware that the second his lips parted from hers, the velvety texture and flaming heat were gone.

Her hands tightened in his hair, she lifted closer, a keening cry leaving her throat as her nipples raked over his chest, and the denim-covered heat of his erection pressed against the saturated flesh of her pussy.

"You like that, don't you, Crista?" He shifted against her, raking his chest over the sensitive tips, watching her face as she fought to hold back another cry.

"I like that," she admitted, shivering violently as his calloused palms rasped down her naked back. "I always loved your hands, Dawg. Always loved your touch."

She arched, her head falling back against the mirror behind her as his hands lifted her closer, his lips moving to her neck, his tongue licking her flesh before his teeth rasped over tender nerve endings.

"I dreamed of this." Her breathing faltered as her eyes drifted closed. "So long. I dreamed of this."

And she had. During those first pain-ridden months away from Somerset, through the loneliness of the years she had spent away from home, she had dreamed of him and his touch.

"Did you dream of this, sweetheart?" Rasping, rough, his voice was but a breath ahead of the silken rasp of the beginnings of a beard along his cheeks and jaw.

"I dreamed of this." Her thighs lifted along his hips, clutching at him as her arms moved from his shoulders, moving between them, searching for the zipper of his jeans, for the fierce, thick flesh beneath.

His chuckle was a low breath of arousal and denial.

His hands caught her wrists, dragging them back up his body. "This time, I get to savor you."

"No. Dawg." She shook her head, moaning at the thought of what she knew he intended. What he had done that first time before taking her.

"Yes. Crista," he growled.

Then he was drawing back from her, lifting her before turning and stepping to the bed, tossing her to it before he followed.

He didn't give her time to protest what she knew he wanted, what she wanted. His hands immediately spread her thighs, pushing her knees up as his head bent to the wet flesh aching for his touch.

"Oh God. Dawg." She arched, she moaned, as his tongue licked slowly through the saturated folds. "Yes. Oh yes, I need this."

She needed. She hungered for it.

He growled against the swollen curves, licked, his tongue moving with velvet roughness around her swollen clit as she stretched beneath him, arched to his mouth and did nothing to hold back her cries.

"You taste like fucking summer." His voice sounded angry. Harsh. But she knew that voice, it wasn't anger that drove him, it was a surfeit of lust that poured from every cell of his body.

Dawg couldn't believe how sweet and hot she tasted. Smoother than whiskey, yet more potent. Sweeter than candy and more addictive than drugs.

He buried his tongue in the sweetness, licked and sucked

at it, tried to draw enough of the creamy syrup into him to sate himself on the taste of her.

If he could ever sate himself. With each lick, each taste, he only burned for more.

"Dawg." She twisted beneath him as he drew the fragile bud of her clit into his mouth in a long, firm kiss. A tiny suck, a flick of his tongue before he released it.

"More," she whispered breathlessly. "I like that. Oh I like that so much."

"How much do you like that, sweetheart?" He was dying for more of her. He smoothed his fingers along the saturated curls, feeling her syrup cling to them, tasting the sweetness of her against his tongue as he licked around the swollen little bud of her clit once again.

"I love it," she whimpered. "Oh God, Dawg. I love it."

Her clit throbbed against his tongue, almost as fiercely as his cock was throbbing in his jeans. He was wild for her, driven by a hunger that made no sense to him, that had his senses consumed by her, his muscles tight with the need to taste her, touch her, fuck her.

She belonged to him.

And where that thought came from he had no idea.

But it was there, suddenly so much a part of him that it sent a hard shudder racing through his body.

"I can't breathe," she panted, arching, writhing beneath him as his hands held her still. Her voice was soft, light, echoing with her own hunger.

Dawg lapped at her; his tongue slid through the soft folds, ached for bare, creamy flesh all around. She would be visiting the spa soon, he assured himself. He needed her soft pussy bare to his lips, so sensitive that his breath washing over it would send her to the brink of climax.

As he moved lower, the snug little opening that drew him clenched and fluttered against his tongue. Sliding his hands under her hips, he lifted her higher, closer, then sent his tongue burrowing into the sweetest flesh he had ever known.

Crista knew she was losing her mind beneath his touch. Stars exploded against the backdrop of her closed eyes and sent her arching closer, desperate for more. She fought the hands holding her, the broad shoulders that held her legs wide, and pleaded for more.

"Damn, you're sweet," he muttered as his head lifted just enough to allow his tongue to lick back to her clit. Not that it brought her any semblance of control, because his fingers were moving in to replace his tongue, sliding inside her, first one, then two, stretching her with exquisite heat as she undulated beneath him.

"I could eat you for hours." His voice was a rumbled vibration against her clit. "So creamy and sweet."

His voice stroked over her senses, drawing her farther into the maelstrom of sensation tearing through her body. She was helpless against it, helpless against him.

His fingers moved inside her, fucking her with long, smooth strokes as she tightened around him and begged for release.

"Your pussy's so tight, Crista." He lodged his fingers inside her. Just his fingertips, rasping inside her, bringing to life nerve endings she couldn't have possibly known existed.

"Stop teasing me," she gasped, shaking in his hold, her hips lifting to his hot mouth as he licked around her clit with gentle strokes. "Please Dawg. Let me come. I need to come."

"Just a little longer." His breathing was harsh, the strokes of his fingers inside her pussy were deeper now, stronger.

Crista felt her pussy clenching, felt the wash of her juices and his tongue licking, stroking her.

"I want your pussy waxed," he groaned. "All sweet and soft and sensitive. I want to lick your juices from every sweet inch of this hot little pussy."

Her fingers tightened in his hair as a shaft of white-hot heat seared her womb. Perspiration gathered on her flesh, ran in rivulets across her chest and breasts. The air became heated despite the air conditioning, and Crista could feel her own body unraveling as Dawg's lips surrounded her clit, suckled, licked, and gave her release.

She wondered if he gave her death along with it.

She was barely aware of her own screams, hoarse and broken, as he fucked her with hard thrusts of his fingers and sucked at her clit with deep, hungry draws of his mouth.

She twisted beneath him, fought the explosions of rapture, and finally fell beneath the force of pleasure overtaking her. Beneath the force of Dawg's hungry touch.

There was no chance to gather herself for the next attack against her soul. How he had managed to shed his jeans so quickly she would never be certain, but before the last tidal wave of ecstasy had dissolved, he was on his knees, fitting his cock between the swollen folds of her pussy and pushing inside her.

Crista stilled, froze. Her eyes jerked open to stare in his piercing gaze as he rested on his knees, his eyes lowered to where he was slowly, oh God so slowly, penetrating her.

Inch by torturously pleasurable inch. Burning because the fit was so tight, because the width of his cock stretched her to the point of pleasured pain as it stroked inside her.

"This is what I've dreamed of." His breath was sawing, his voice guttural. "Watching you take me, hug me. Feeling your pussy tighten around me like a fiery fist."

Her hips jerked upward, and between one broken breath and the next, his erection plunged forcefully inside her, and with the surge of sensation came a surge of primal ferocity she hadn't known she possessed.

Her legs lifted, wrapping possessively around him, angling her hips up to him, taking all of him, deeper than before, harder than before.

Her nails raked over his hair-spattered chest, combing through the sweat-dampened black curls before skimming along his abdomen and back again. Just to touch him, to feel the shudders racing through his body.

Then she was moving beneath him, fighting for dominance as she watched his eyes narrow a second before he gave her what she wanted.

Surprisingly. He moved, going to his back as he lifted her above him, never dislodging from her, thrusting deeper as she settled astride him and began to move.

The feel of his cock moving inside her was exquisite. The way he stretched her, burned her. The throb of blood pounding into the shaft and rippling against her sensitive inner walls drove her crazy with need. She wanted more sensation, harder strokes, a deeper burn.

"Slow down." His hands gripped her hips as she began to impale herself on him.

"No." Crista shook her head wildly. "Not yet. Let me—"

"You're not coming yet, Crista." His voice was forceful. Dominant. As dominant as the hands that restrained her hips and kept her from riding him as she needed to.

"I need to come again, Dawg." She would be embarrassed over the whimper in her voice later. "Just one more time. Just now."

She flexed above him, straining as his cock stroked her internally.

"Soon, sweetheart." He grimaced. "Soon . . . Ah fuck!"

She lowered her upper body, her lips moving to a flat, hard nipple that she nipped at gently, then licked, tasting the salty male taste of his flesh and the heat of his lust.

His hips jerked beneath her, his cock plunging heatedly inside her, just once. Just once when she needed so much more.

"Easy, fancy-face," he groaned, allowing her to move by the smallest degree, to work herself on the thick, stiff flesh impaling her with the smallest strokes.

"Dawg, please. I need—" She wasn't certain what she needed. Wild. Hard. God yes, she needed hard. "Hard. Fuck me hard. I can't stand this."

His hips jerked at her shattered plea. Dawg could feel his balls drawing tight, his dick flexing, jerking inside her with the need to come. And a part of him needed to savor. To hold her back, to draw out the exquisite torment to the point that when the explosion came, she would know, to the depths of her soul, exactly who she belonged to.

One hand moved from her hip as the other restrained her, forcing her to the slower pace he wanted. To the long, gentle thrusts that forced her to feel every inch of his cock taking her, possessing her.

Just for a moment longer.

His free hand snagged in her hair, pulling her head up as he moved into position for her kiss.

"Come here, Crista," he whispered. "Kiss me, darlin'. Show me how you need me."

She didn't hesitate. Passion and hunger darkened her chocolate eyes and flushed her cheeks. Her head lowered, her lips meeting his eagerly as he rolled her to her back, moving between her thighs, feeling her pussy tighten on him as he retreated, then clench again with need as he thrust inside her once more.

Sweat slicked both their bodies as her legs twined around his hips and his tongue sought the heated depths of her mouth.

He was lost inside her.

Dawg groaned, growled, slanted his lips over hers and gave his cock the freedom to take her as he needed to. Deep. Hard. He began rocking inside her, fighting for the control to hold back, fighting to torment them both just a little while longer.

But the pleasure was too deep, too hard. Within seconds he was fucking her with a primal hunger that should have made him wary. As though he had never fucked before, never known a woman's touch before.

Crista could feel herself screaming into his kiss. Her hands stroked over his shoulders, his upper back. Her nails scraped and raked, her palms begging for the touch of his skin.

His kiss was like wildfire.

The feel of his cock shafting hard and deep inside her added to the surfeit of sensation. Each plunging stroke, each forceful thrust threw her higher, drew her deeper into the vortex sweeping through her.

Until finally, her senses exploded beneath the impact.

Her orgasm tore through her, swept through her mind and left chaos in its wake, detonated through her flesh and spasmed through her womb until her broken screams were joined by Dawg's hard, male cry of release.

She felt the fiery blasts of his semen filling her, sparking another explosion, another wash of ecstasy. It lasted forever; it didn't last long enough.

She collapsed beneath him, fighting for breath, certain she could never draw in enough air, when he began moving again.

"Dawg." Her voice was small, not really a protest, perhaps a question of sanity.

He was still hard, still hungry, and within seconds, she could feel her own pleasure building again. This time, when he rolled to his back and drew her above him, she didn't have the strength to fight the slow, languorous thrusts he demanded. She needed hard and fast, but her muscles were lax, too worn and drained to draw the energy for it.

She lifted herself above him, her hands braced on his chest, feeling his palms stroking over her back, her hips, and moved on him with building pleasure.

"How pretty." His voice was tight, hungry. "That's the way, sweetheart. Ride my cock. Ride it like you love it."

Like she loved it? She had loved him all her life, and he hadn't known it. He couldn't know it. And her body ached for him. Lonely nights curled into a ball because the ache was so bad. Dreams and fantasies had sustained her. Until now.

Her back arched as she lifted, her hands gripped his powerful arms now, using them to steady herself as she began to raise and lower herself, feeling him sink into her, rasping delicate nerve endings, stretching tender tissue until the world was spinning around her, and she knew nothing but his touch, but the feel of him invading her body. Her soul.

Her vagina pulsed around him, tighter for the orgasm that had filled it minutes before, swelling the muscles that surrounded his shuttling flesh and sending an agony of pleasure to wash through her system.

The release that overtook her long, long minutes later was lazier, slower, but no less intense.

And after that, long into the night, each release slammed harder inside her soul. This wasn't like the first time. He had been drunk, a little clumsier, and had taken her with haste rather than finesse.

Dawg didn't have that problem tonight. There was no hesitancy, no clumsiness; there was only hunger, intensity, and strength. Eroticism filled each touch, and his voice, guttural and rasping, explicit and dominant, filled her head.

By the time he collapsed beside her and dragged her against his chest, she was soaked with sweat, immersed in the scent of their lust, and on the verge of complete exhaustion.

His hand curled around a breast as his chest heaved for breath behind her.

"Mine," he reminded her, his voice hoarse, exhausted. "Remember that, Crista. You're mine."

Mine. Not theirs. Not one of the Nauti playmates. Just Dawg's.

FOURTEEN

"So tell me about your lovers?"

Crista's gaze jerked from the last of the full breakfast she had made while Dawg was in the shower the next morning to his icy light green gaze. She had really hoped he was going to forget about that.

"I didn't say they were my lovers. You did," she pointed out as she laid her fork on the plate and finished the last of her coffee.

He didn't deserve explanations, and Mark and Ty's relationship was their own. She wasn't going to make him feel better or ease his little mind by giving him explanations he should never be asking for.

"You slept with them. You admitted it." He scowled back at her.

"So?" She rose from the table, collected their plates and cups, and paced to the sink. "Do I ask you about your past lovers, Dawg? How many you shared? How many you didn't? Have I asked you to explain those choices to me?"

She turned back to face him, bracing her back against the counter and watching as his jaw bunched with angry tension.

"I didn't walk away from you because of the sharing," he said harshly. "You did."

"Mark and Ty never, at any time brought another woman to their bed, or another man. Would Rowdy and Natches have loved me enough to give up other women? I don't think so."

Mark and Ty had never been her lovers. They were each other's lovers. Sometimes though, when the nights were too dark and the pain followed too closely, they would draw her to their bed much as parents would a child. There, they sheltered her between them and gave her the warmth she needed to hold on to at the time.

His eyes narrowed as his expression turned stony.

"I'm not going to argue with you over this." She finally shook her head as she glanced at her watch. "The lumber store will be open in half an hour. We should go."

"I never open." He shrugged.

"Which is a lousy way to promote a locally owned business," she informed him. "And I know you know better than that, Dawg. You're more of a businessman than this. Besides, I have work to do, and I do my best work in the morning."

"My business." His smile was tight and hard. "Not yours."

"As long as I'm getting paid to organize and manage that hellhole of an office, then I have a vested interest in your business," she told him sweetly. "And holding me hostage here because you don't like my answers is not going to get you what you want."

He uncoiled from the table. Despite his size and the obvious power in his body, he moved silently, gracefully. Like a panther on the prowl, his predatory green eyes narrowed and glittering behind pitch-black lashes, his body tense but prepared. As though she would attempt to run from him.

Crista stood her ground instead, her arms crossing over her breasts as she stared back at him guardedly.

"That store could burn down around its foundations for all I give a fuck," he sneered, shocking her with the latent fury in his voice. "I keep it to piss off the holier-than-thou relatives who tried so damned hard to take it away from me, period. Its success is due to nothing more than luck."

And she didn't believe that. She knew better. He wanted

to pretend he hated it, but the stories related to her the day before by the employees showed something totally different.

Dawg did care about that business, but for some reason he refused to admit it.

"It was your father's business." She tested the waters gently. "I know your relationship with him wasn't close, but surely you don't hate him enough to let the store suffer."

"I bet he's spinning in his grave." Dawg's smile was tight and vicious. "I've hired people from the families he hated the most, and I've made certain people he would never give credit to, have it. The fact that that damned place makes money never fails to amaze me." He shook his head as though he truly couldn't make sense of it.

Yet, when he had fired the manager that had been cheating him, the current floor manager had told Crista that Dawg practically lived in his office until he had the books and the store straightened out.

He had an instinct for what people needed and what they wanted, and he hired people who could provide it. And every employee hired had been hired by him personally.

"Well, I need your help anyway," she told him firmly. "Your manager, Layla Matcher, has a pretty good handle on things, but I was going through some of the more recent catalogs gathering dust in the office and noticed you hadn't ordered for the Christmas season yet. You need to get that in."

"It's in." His lip curled in disgust, self-disgust. She could tell by his expression that admitting it didn't sit well with him.

"Then I need the order log." She turned and rinsed their dishes. "We also need to get a stack of files taller than I am filed. The stock boy I sent for the file cabinets yesterday hadn't arrived by the time I left."

"They're waiting in the office." If his voice could have become shorter, it did.

Crista hid her smile as she stacked the dishes in the dishwasher.

"Good; then you check the problem Layla told me was building in the lumberyard behind the store. For some reason, orders were missed with surprising regularity last week. Several of your best contractors have threatened to use the chain lumberyard rather than Mackay's because of the mess-up."

She turned in time to catch the narrowing of his eyes.

"Why didn't Layla report this when it began?" His lips flattened in irritation.

"Check your cell phone messages." She shrugged. "She left several texts."

A heavy grimace tightened his expression then. "I had a problem with the phone last week."

"There you go then." She moved across the kitchen where her purse sat on the far counter.

Before she could make it halfway across the room, Dawg caught her arm and turned her firmly back to face him.

"Don't start trying to run my life, Crista. You're the one being blackmailed here, not me. There's only so much I'll let you get away with."

She restrained her smile; gloating wasn't the best way to handle Dawg.

"Keep telling yourself that," she told him instead. "And while you're at it, ask yourself the same question I had to answer sometime last night when I was still trying to catch my breath. You wouldn't blackmail someone you believed was a criminal, Dawg, and we both know it. No more than you would see an innocent person imprisoned. No matter the cost. So what are you doing in this relationship?"

"Getting the fuck of my life," he snarled.

Her lips did twitch then. "So you are," she agreed, pulling her arm from his grip before moving back to her purse, then turning and glancing at him over her shoulder. "Now, the question is, what do you really intend to do with it? Or me, as the case may be. Because we're both smart enough to know that the thing you're not going to do is turn me over to Homeland Security. Fuck me to death maybe, but you wouldn't turn me in."

"Are you betting your life on it?"

"Yeah." She nodded slowly. "I'm betting my life on it."

It was a damned good thing her brother had raised her, Crista thought later as they pulled into the parking lot behind the lumber store marked Employees Only. Because Dawg was snarling and growling and being a general pain in the butt just for the hell of it. From her experience with Alex, she could tell the male irritability factor was in full swing here.

But he hadn't called his agent-in-charge, and she was fairly certain there were no agents en route to slap restraints on her. She might get lucky, and the worst she would have to deal with was a snarling Dawg.

Not that answering her own question in the middle of the night had been easy. Because Crista had known from that first night that Dawg wouldn't arrest her, and he wouldn't see her arrested. He knew she wasn't involved.

So why was she letting him blackmail her?

She had to fight to keep from laying her palm against her abdomen as they drove from the houseboat to the store. That was why she was letting him blackmail her. Because nothing had been finished when she had left Somerset eight years before. But everything had been lost.

Her dreams. The man she had loved for what seemed most of her life. And the child she had carried from that night.

The miscarriage had destroyed something inside her, something she hadn't been able to recapture after leaving town. And she had never forgotten Dawg: his touch, his kiss, or the pleasure that had filled every cell of her body.

"You're making me look bad," he snapped as he jerked the vehicle into park and turned his head to stare at her over the top of the dark glasses he wore. "I never open."

"You never hire one of your lovers to work here, either." She shrugged.

"For a woman who was supposed to stay locked in the office, you managed to filter through a lot of gossip."

"I'm good at that." She nodded benignly as she opened the truck door and stepped out of the vehicle, leaving him to snarl and curse behind her as she slammed the door closed.

She was moving around the edge of the building when he finally drew up beside her.

"You're working on a spanking," he warned her.

Unfortunately, the idea of that shouldn't have been titillating.

"Am I?" she asked sweetly. "I hear you're particularly good at that little disciplinary act. Before I left Somerset, all the girls were talking about it."

She had to force those words past her lips. Just as she'd had to force back the jealousy at the time.

He grunted. An irritated sound of male displeasure.

Crista shrugged. "You and your cousins aren't exactly good at hiding your lights under a barrel, so to speak," she told him, casting him a disapproving glare. "Really, Dawg, it's a little late to worry about gossip."

She should have known better than to dare him. She really should have.

Before she could do more than gasp, he had pushed her against the chain-link fence and stole her lips in a kiss that had her system rioting with conflicting emotions.

They weren't on the houseboat, in his bed. They were in full view, and she was very well aware of what he was doing. Marking her as his. As another woman in the very long line of women who had shared his bed.

"Stop, Dawg." She tore her lips from his, panting with the effort it cost her.

His hands were on her back, holding her against him, the length of his erection pressing into her lower stomach, as his big body seemed to surround her.

"Don't push me, Crista." He stared down at her, his light green eyes practically glowing with an anger held closely in check. "I've never given a damn about gossip or others' opinions of me, and I won't care about it now. Remember that when you're twitching that tight little ass around me and trying to convince yourself what a good guy I might really be underneath it all. I'm a son of a bitch, darlin', and one you really don't want to cross."

No, he was one she wanted to soothe, because she could see the pain in his eyes, in the mockery of his expression. She could see it in the anger he was holding back, despite his words.

"Are you going to hurt me, Dawg?" she asked him then, reaching up to touch his jaw before he jerked away from her.

"Get your ass in the store, goddamn it," he cursed, stepping back and gripping her arm to lead her to the front doors where Layla was unlocking the employees' entrance.

She cast them a curious glance, her dark hazel eyes concerned as Dawg approached.

"Good morning, Mr. Mackay. Crista," she greeted them with an attempt at brightness, despite Dawg's heavy scowl.

"If you can call me Mr. Mackay, then you can call her Miss Jansen," Dawg told the manager brusquely as Crista sighed behind him.

"Call him Dawg, Layla. Maybe he'll stop snarling at us because he had to come in so soon." Crista tugged at his grip. "And he's really not dragging me along behind him like a recalcitrant child. I get off on dominance."

Layla coughed as she turned her back on them quickly, and Dawg stopped and stared back at her in surprise.

She lifted one brow curiously. "What? I wasn't supposed to tell?"

They both knew she hated being dragged around like a favorite puppy, and she was certain that was exactly why he made a habit of doing it.

Spanked. He mouthed back at her before turning back to Layla.

Crista smiled serenely back at the other woman as she finished unlocking the door.

"Layla, follow us to the office, I want to know what the hell is going on with the lumberyard. I thought Bedsford had a handle on that?"

"He was working out great, Mr. . . . uhh Dawg," she stuttered as she relocked the door, then followed behind them. "He's been with us ever since he was discharged from the service. I don't know what happened."

Crista glanced behind her at the manager, winking as Dawg continued to drag her behind him as he mounted the steps to the office.

"When did it start?"

"Last week." They paused as Dawg dug the key to the office out of his jeans pocket, still holding on to Crista, and inserted it into the lock, turned it, then stopped.

"Dawg?" Crista tried to stare around him. "What's wrong?"

"You didn't lock up last night." His voice was carefully restrained.

"Of course I locked the office before I left." Crista frowned. "I know I did."

"I also checked it before I left Mr., umm, Dawg." Layla cleared her throat again. "I always check the office doors before I close up at night."

Dawg stepped back, his keys still hanging in the lock.

"Crista, I want you and Layla to go back out front. Use your cell phone and call Natches. I programmed his and Rowdy's numbers in last night."

"Why?" Crista could feel the dread rising inside her now.

"Layla, does anyone know you check the offices at night?" Dawg asked then.

"I don't know, Dawg." There was an edge of fear in her voice. "Jamie and the boys always go through the store with me at night when they pick me up, just to make sure everything is okay. I check all the office doors then."

"Get out front and call Natches, Crista." Dawg turned back to her, his expression closed, dangerous. "Now."

"Not without you." Her hands gripped his arm, tugging at him. "You can call him yourself. He'll come faster if you call him."

Surprise tightened his features. "I know what I'm doing, Crista."

"I don't care." She wasn't leaving him here alone. Only God knew what was behind that door. "You can come with us."

"Mr. Mackay, we should all go out front. What if whoever was in the store, if anyone was, is waiting outside?"

That had murderous fury lighting in his eyes. Dawg's gaze sliced to the tall, wide windows of the front of the store as his expression became cold, dangerous.

"Come on." Thankfully, he turned, moving them down the metal steps and headed for the entrance as he pulled his cell phone from his pocket.

Punching in Natches's number, Dawg stalked away from the women.

"It's early, Dawg," Natches mumbled into the line.

"Get to the store. Someone was in the office last night. I'm calling the sheriff to dust for prints, but I need someone to watch Crista while I'm taking care of Mayes's questions. After last night, this could get ugly."

"Shit!" He could hear Natches moving. "Bastards moved fast."

"Makes me wonder if the car going up in flames wasn't more of a distraction than an attempt. Just hurry. I'm calling Sheriff Mayes now. And you know Layla, her husband and sons are going to come down here like a pack of ravening wolves intent on protecting her. I'm going to need help here."

Natches snickered.

Jamie Matcher and his brood of overgrown sons had come to the store and stayed with Layla every day for the first damned year she had worked for Dawg. And Jamie, all six feet five inches of him, had towered over Dawg and warned him what would happen if his little Layla got smeared with gossip because of games Dawg might want to play in the privacy of his office.

As if he played games in his office. Damn it, he liked a bed for games. The office was work. Paperwork. Something he didn't handle well, despite Crista's certainty.

"Just get your ass down here." Dawg closed his eyes and rubbed at his forehead, anticipating the headache he knew was well on its way.

As he flipped the phone closed and turned back to the two women, he sighed again. Layla was looking decidedly nervous. Crista was defiant and suspicious.

"Layla, call Jamie and the boys," he told her. "I have to call Sheriff Mayes, and once the call goes out on the radio, Jamie will blow a fuse."

"He worries, Dawg." But she was pulling the phone from the case she wore on the slim leather belt that cinched her crisp tan slacks.

"He worries," Dawg muttered. "I worry." Then he turned to Crista.

She was leaning against the block wall like she didn't have a damned care in the world. Concerned but amused. She was amused at him, and that one was biting his ass. He was blackmailing her, but damned if he didn't suddenly feel like she had the upper hand.

"Layla, why don't you and Crista go to the lounge and get some coffee on. The employees will be showing up about the same time the sheriff and the state boys do. If they have their coffee, they might not make too much of a mess investigating this."

He could hope. But he wasn't betting the houseboat on it. By the time he got off the phone with Sheriff Mayes, he could feel the headache beginning in his temples.

Good old Ezekiel Mayes. The son of a bitch. Dawg swore he was going to vote against him each election, but he always managed to vote for him. Better the devil you knew . . .

He stood and stared around the store. It was just as huge now as it was each time he found himself doing this. The first year out of the Marines he had nearly gutted the place. His knee had ached like a son of a bitch that year, but he had nearly tripled the size and added to the layout. Not that he cared one way or the other about the business, he reminded himself. He had been bored.

Fuck that. Even Crista knew better. And he was kidding himself. He had been kidding himself for eight years. The estate his parents had left him was riddled with so much guilt, resentment, and bitterness that sometimes he wished he'd sold it all that first year after their death, while he was in the Marines and worrying his ass off over it.

The house especially. Where he had never lived. His father had finished it after Dawg had bought the *Nauti Dawg* from an inheritance left to him by his mother's mother. He had never spent a night in that house until after their deaths.

His father had hated the lumber store, too. But he had kept it anyway. He had always said it was the only thing Dawg was smart enough to actually make a living with. And maybe the old bastard had been right.

He had a knack for it, unlike his knack for warfare. He tended to get his knees blown off there. The ATF assignment wasn't a bad one, but the restrictions pissed him off. Answering to other people wasn't his strong suit.

Unfortunately, Sheriff Mayes liked a lot of answers to his questions.

"What the hell are you involved in, Dawg?" Zeke kept his voice low as they stood back from the state police unit now inspecting his office.

There were no prints, no hint of anything disturbed, though it was impossible for Dawg to tell if anything was missing.

He glared at Crista where she stood in the open door of the lounge beneath the office. He hadn't even recognized his damned office.

And she smiled.

That smile lit a fire inside him he didn't even want to understand. A fire-charged electrical arousal and a brooding anger, in equal intensity through his body.

Because he knew she was holding back. Some part of her didn't yet belong to him; whether it was her honesty or something deeper, he didn't want to delve into at the moment. But she was holding back. And that just flat pissed him off.

"What the hell is she involved in, then?" Zeke asked.

Dawg glanced at the sheriff before leaning against the floor-to-ceiling shelving that ran the length of the aisle they were in front of.

"Nada," he answered shortly.

"Your *nada*s are getting on my nerves," Zeke warned him.

"It's going to get on your nerves worse when I campaign for your opponent next election," Dawg pointed out irritably. "Leave it alone, Zeke."

"You're going to get her killed, Dawg," Zeke said quietly. "Whatever you're doing, it's going to backfire on her."

"Then you'll have bloodshed to clean up, Zeke." Dawg's smile, he knew, was a shark's glare. "Anyone even thinks about hurting her, and they'll die. Expect that. Count on that. Now get the hell out of my way. I have a business to run."

Unfortunately, Zeke was right. Whatever the hell was going on, someone was intent on not just drawing Crista into it, but of striking out at her.

As Zeke headed back toward the small crowd of investigators and officers, Natches moved up to him.

His cousin's dark green eyes were like flinty ice in a stone-cold expression.

Dawg crossed his arms over his chest and stared around the crowd intently, making certain no one came close.

"The investigators want to think she deliberately left the door unlocked," Natches muttered. "The scrapes on the lock are being brushed aside because there are no prints. Someone wants you to think she's incompetent at the least, using you at the worst."

Dawg nodded slowly.

"They struck after you were seen arguing with her. After the Rodeo went up in flames. None of it makes any sense or ties in. Threaten her, and you're only going to cover her closer. So why attempt to search your office?"

"Unless the point was to plant something against her," Natches said softly. "Thankfully, I was able to get in there with the first investigators. There was a map of the warehouse, the address, and a detailed list of the missiles and their chips, along with about twenty-five thousand in cash in an envelope tucked into the file cabinet. Someone's setting you up with her."

"Did you get the envelope?"

Natches nodded slowly. "Taken care of. Security tapes were fuzzed, bad. Both the outside and inside monitors were affected. There was so much static on them there's no way to tell who it was or what they were doing."

"They know my system." His was state-of-the-art with a few additional devices that should have made it impossible for the average thief to bypass.

"They know you," Natches pointed out. "I'm going to head to town, spread a little trash, and see what happens."

"What kind of trash?" Dawg stared at his cousin suspiciously.

"Well, you hired a new manager, and look what happened." Natches nodded to the officers and agents milling around. "What if, after they leave, I overhear you and Crista arguing about it? Maybe she's called her good friend Mark, and she's heading back to Virginia. Whoever's involved with this is trying to lay the money at her feet to keep suspicion off them. If she's arrested, Dawg, with the pictures they have of the woman resembling her, then any testimony the thieves give that she wasn't involved won't matter. She'll take the rap, and someone else gets away with the money."

"Do the thieves know for certain it's not Crista?" Dawg asked then, remembering the interrogation of the men they had arrested. "If they knew, why not take the deal Cranston offered them for the woman? From all reports, she was the mastermind behind this."

"Maybe they don't know who she is," Natches suggested.

"They were a few good ole boys contacted because of their knowledge of the military and their ability to pull this deal together. Someone else was the brains."

"Someone who knows my security system," Dawg mused.

"Close the store down for the rest of the day. I'll hang around until everyone has left, check things out, then head to the diner with Rowdy and Kelly. We can get the information that Crista is heading to Virginia where I think it needs to go. Whatever's going on, that diner seems to be the center of it."

"Or someone who hangs out there too much." Dawg nodded.

"Wait till after dark to leave, and when you do, take the back roads to the marina. Stay in the houseboat tomorrow; keep the windows and doors closed and Crista hidden. Let's give them time to take the bait."

Dawg nodded. It could work. At the moment, it was the best chance they had at flushing out the culprit.

"Keep me up-to-date," Dawg ordered. "And watch Cranston. He's making me nervous."

The agent was watching Crista too closely at the moment. Standing back, his head tilted to the side and his eyes narrowed on her as she and Layla kept the officers supplied with coffee.

Natches nodded sharply. "I'll be around the houseboat later tonight and let you know how things are going."

Dawg nodded again as he watched the crowd. One of his employees had to be involved; there was no doubt. But which one? And why?

He watched them milling around, gossiping, chatting, filled with curiosity. One of them had betrayed him and threatened Crista. Which meant one of them had a death wish.

FIFTEEN

Eight years before, Crista had lived for the moments she could bask in Dawg's smile. His flirting had turned her heart over, filled her with a wild, reckless joy, and made her dream of being in his arms.

She had ached for him even before she knew what the ache was. His charm, his lazy humor, and that shadow of pain that haunted his eyes drew her. And in her deepest fantasies she eased that shadow away and saw his odd, light green eyes fill with joy.

When she had first realized she was pregnant, she had been furious, resentful. Then the knowledge of that life she held stilled the anger. His child would never know loneliness, never lack for love. She would never see that shadow of hurt in their baby's eyes. She would love it, protect it. Their baby.

The day she had lost that child something inside her had died, only to be reborn when she returned and realized that that silent draw between her and Dawg was still there.

She had fought it. She had thought she could protect her heart and live on the periphery of his attention, warmed yet protected from the heat she knew could destroy her.

What a fool she had been.

Crista watched Dawg as they finished the office arrangement, going through files, searching for a reason why his office had been breached.

He was silent, angry. Determination sharpened the lines and angles of his face, giving him a warrior's appearance, a savage aura that turned her on more than it had a right to. He made quick work of hefting the furniture and sliding it into place as Crista cleaned. He helped go through files, helped pack them to the new cabinets and load them, his celadon eyes sharp and intent as he went over every inch of the office to track anything that had been bothered or searched.

As he moved, the sunlight spearing through the wide office windows on the other side of the room worshipped his raven black hair and sun-kissed flesh. It slid over his broad shoulders and emphasized his muscular arms as the short sleeves of his black T-shirt stretched over them.

Jeans molded to his powerful hips and thighs, and those boots he wore made his legs even sexier. Not to mention how the denim of his jeans lovingly cupped his muscular ass.

He was enough to steal a girl's breath, and Crista admitted to having a lot of breathless moments. And perhaps she had been wrong before when she thought he hadn't matured from the self-centered determination he had possessed in those days.

Dawg had changed over the years after all. He was harder. Still just as sexy, but more dangerous than he had been before he joined the Marines and definitely more mature.

He had proven that today. Crista had watched as he moved through the office after the sheriff's men had finished dusting for prints, and the state police had finished their questions.

They could find nothing moved, nothing bothered. The only proof there was that there might have been a break-in was the suspected tampering with the security cameras and the lock on the office door.

And Crista felt sorry for the culprit, because Dawg looked mad enough to draw blood hours later. He had sent the employees home after the police left and locked up behind Layla before leading Crista back into the office.

She stared at him from the other end of the large room as she straightened the lamp on the table by the couch and he stored the last of the files. His eyes were narrowed, his expression brooding as he turned to her.

"Do you realize you just destroyed years of deliberate chaos?" Dawg asked as the last of the files were stored away and she gave the furniture a final buffing with the polish she used. Everything gleamed, even the hardwood floor beneath their feet.

She turned and looked around, realizing how large the office was. There was plenty of room for the other file cabinets she wanted as well as the extra desk Dawg had ordered one of the stock floor boys to put together for her in the morning. A nice miniature version of the huge walnut desk he was using himself.

Deliberate chaos he called it. A slap at the father that would have taken even this from him, if he could have managed to do it without looking like the monster he had been.

"Chaos doesn't beat success." She shrugged. "Organization can raise productivity and profits. The way it is, the chain lumber stores are still running ahead of you in profits and customers. We want to pull those customers to Mackay's."

He leaned against the file cabinet and regarded her quizzically. "It makes enough money. Even with the court battle Johnny and his mother waged against me those first years, I came out of it a very rich man, Crista."

"And that's enough for you?" She knew Dawg better than that.

"It's more than most have." That irritable frown was on his face again, the one that encouraged the person he was talking to, to go straight to hell.

Crista shook her head. "It's not enough for you, Dawg."

"Says who?" He threw himself in the large leather chair behind his desk and stared back at her broodingly.

Crista rolled her eyes as she stored the polish and rag in the bottom drawer of one of the file cabinets before straightening to face him.

The look on his face was sexy and scary at the same time. Intent, brooding, dominant, and aroused.

"Stop being an ass," she chided him. "You know you love this store. You pretend you don't. You want people to think you don't. But I know better."

He folded his fingers together over his tight abs as he leaned back and let his gaze rake over her.

"And how do you know so much about me?" he drawled with a hint of anger. "It's not like you try to get close to me."

And there he was wrong. Even in the past year, Crista had soaked up every hint of gossip she could about him. She had watched him, let others talk about him, and found herself looking for excuses to be in places where she knew he would be.

She knew the lawsuit that his aunt had brought against him just after he joined the Marines had ignited a fury of controversy through the town at the time.

All the cousins—Rowdy, Natches, and Dawg—had been in the service, leaving no one in Somerset to protect his interests other than his uncle Ray. Ray Mackay had held that front line like a bulldog holding on to a bone, though.

He had hired the best lawyers, paid them himself, and kept Dawg apprised of each step of the battle. He had managed to get court dates delayed until Dawg had leave, and had stood beside his nephew, against his sister, and shed a tear on the stand as he related the times he had been forced to protect Dawg as a young boy from the father who would have abused him.

Dawg's bitterness went clear to his childhood, and it had created a man who, even at twenty-four, had been hard and shadowed with distrust. Four years in the Marines and four years working for whatever government agency he was a part of hadn't helped.

"Getting close to you would have been hard, Dawg," she finally answered him. "Your groupies stood layers deep and jealously hoarded that hard body of yours."

It wasn't far from the truth.

"Or you were just too scared to take what I was offering." He leaned forward, bracing his arms on the desk as he stared back tauntingly.

And maybe he was right there, too.

Crista shrugged. "I was young. Ages younger than you in experience."

"But not anymore, are you, Crista? Seven years in bed with two lovers at the same time? Your experience definitely matches mine now, wouldn't you say?"

Crista felt her heart pause, then race viciously in her chest. She didn't want this conversation with him now.

"My life after I left Somerset is none of your business, Dawg," she finally said, aware of the defensive sound of her own voice. "I've already explained the distinction to you."

She didn't want to explain Mark and Ty; they were none of his business. And he hadn't begun this relationship with her because of an overwhelming need or rousing love. She was the one that got away. She was smart enough to admit that to herself.

"So, if the three of us had been willing to be faithful to you, you would have considered it?"

She didn't like the look on his face as he posed that question. It was suggestive, dark, and warning.

"No. I wouldn't have." She tucked a lock of hair behind her ear before crossing her arms over her breasts and staring back at him candidly. "Come on, Dawg, it was eight years ago. You weren't in love with me. I was a nice little one-night stand that you were too drunk to remember, that's all. Now, I'm just the woman you're blackmailing. Let's not start dragging the past into it."

"Just the woman I'm blackmailing," he murmured then, his voice deepening, becoming harsher, hungry. "My own little sex toy, right?"

Crista didn't let her lips twitch or her amusement show in her eyes. She had a feeling he wouldn't appreciate it in the least.

She shrugged her shoulders negligently instead. "Do you have a better description?"

He rose from the desk abruptly, startling her enough to cause her to jump a step backward. Smiling in satisfaction, he moved to the tinted windows that looked out over the floor of the lumber store.

Layla had closed up nearly an hour ago and left with her husband and sons, leaving the floor eerily quiet below them. Still, Dawg jerked the shades closed and locked the office door.

Crista licked her lips nervously, feeling the ever-ready

heat that lingered beneath her flesh building then. As though every cell of her body was so attuned to him that it knew the moment he decided it was time to begin playing again.

"Fine, I feel like playing then. Take your clothes off."

Instantly the air was redolent with arousal and hard, male domination.

Crista had already decided that rather than fighting the sensuality and Dawg, she would instead allow herself to enjoy. To revel in the carnal intensity that was so much a part of him and to allow herself this one moment in time to enjoy his taste, his touch.

There was no other man like Dawg, and there never would be.

She couldn't fight him today. Not right now. She needed his touch as much as he evidently wanted to give it.

She toed her sandals from her feet as her fingers went to the narrow leather belt that cinched her jeans. Her heart was racing in her chest as she flicked the metal button loose and rasped the zipper down. His gaze never left her hands, following each movement as she skimmed the material over her thighs and pushed it down her legs. Stepping out of the jeans, she tossed them to the leather visitor's chair that sat in front of his desk.

She was left in the snug, narrow-strapped camisole top, lacy white bra, and matching thong she wore. Dawg's eyes darkened, dilated, as he moved slowly back around the desk and lowered the shade behind it.

His expression was pure lust. Dark, overwhelming, tight with hunger, and blazing with arousal. It sent a shaft of fiery sensation streaking to her womb, clenching it violently before snapping to her vagina and spasming through the tender muscles there. Silky wet heat spilled from her as the outer folds became swollen and heavy, so sensitive she had to bite her lip against the whimper that would have escaped her throat.

Dawg disposed of his T-shirt before bending and pulling his boots from his masculine feet. Stripping his white socks off next, his head lifted, his eyes spearing into her.

"You're not naked," he reminded her gutturally. "Take the clothes off, or I'll rip them off you."

"This is your office." She was breathless, teasing him even though she knew better.

His lips tightened in a feral smile. "And you're my sex toy. Office hours are over, and I'm ready to play, Crista."

Oh Lord, was he ready to play. The T-shirt was tossed in the corner of the room; the muscles of his chest and abs rippled with power and tensed with determination.

"Take the shirt off."

She gripped the hem of the shirt and pulled it off slowly, her thighs weakening at the sound of his harsh, indrawn breath. Tossing it to the chair with her jeans, she faced him with nothing but a few scraps of lace and a hunger she knew was as naked as his.

"Fucking beautiful," he growled, his hands loosening his belt slowly. "Now the bra. I want to see those pretty tits. Your sweet, hard nipples."

Her hands were shaking as she gripped the clasp between her breasts and loosened it. Drawing it from her shoulders, she allowed it to drop, forgotten, to the floor at her feet.

Dawg's jaw clenched. He pushed his fingers through his long black hair, pulling the thick, silky strands from his face.

He looked like a savage. Tall, hard, intent on claiming what he believed was his, for now.

Her hands went to the band of her panties.

"Leave them," he rasped. "Come over here. Right here." He patted the top of the desk in front of his chair.

Crista felt a shudder work over her body as she moved to him slowly. Wariness had her watching him closely. This wasn't a hunger that burned hot and fast. She could see that. It was simmering just beneath the surface, a banked, furious blaze that he ruthlessly controlled now.

"Absolutely beautiful," he crooned in that husky, dark voice as she moved around the corner of the desk.

Sliding in front of the chair, she began to lift herself to the walnut top when he stopped her.

"Not like that." He gripped her hip with one hand. "Turn around and lean over it."

She fought to breathe. Turning, she flattened her hands on

the desktop and, with his hand on her back, let him guide her into position.

Her breasts flattened against the dark wood, her nipples tightening against the cool desktop as she felt him move behind her.

She remembered, so clearly, just how much he enjoyed playing with that particular portion of her anatomy.

"The prettiest ass in the state." His hand smoothed over the rounded globes revealed by the thong.

His hand, calloused and warm, stroked with subtle destruction, his fingers lifting the small scrap of material that slid between the cheeks before replacing it gently.

"Did I spank you that night, Crista?" He leaned close, his lips at her shoulder as he posed the suggestive question.

"No." She was panting for air now.

There hadn't been so much as a second of foreplay, and already she could feel her juices dampening her panties.

"I fucked this pretty ass and didn't spank it?" His hand clenched on one curve as his lips began to trail down her spine. "How neglectful of me. I should rectify that, don't you think?"

She did whimper then. She had cleaned his office; she knew damned good and well that his desk held exactly what he needed to take her in any way he pleased. The new tube of lubrication he had placed there earlier hadn't gone unnoticed. And she had found the packaged sex toys herself the day before. Toys that he had opened as he grinned wickedly and washed in the attached bathroom.

He was fully prepared for any sex games he may want to play in his office. And she was no more experienced now than she had been eight years ago.

Feminine fear and nerves raced through her mind, her body. She shuddered beneath him as his lips tracked each vertebra of her spine until he reached the narrow band of the thong she wore.

"I noticed how pretty your ass was at a time when I should have been whipped for noticing." He drew the band over her thighs, his lips tracking down the side of her buttock as he disposed of the lacy material. "So soft and silky looking, and delightfully curved."

Crista fought back her cry as his teeth raked over the flesh.

She felt him move, heard the creak of the leather behind her, and knew he had sat back down in his chair. The scrape of the chair wheels over the wooden floor had her flinching as his knees bracketed her legs.

"Perfect position." Both hands gripped her rear then, spreading the cheeks gently as she felt a soft puff of air against the hidden entrance there.

"Don't do this," she suddenly begged, her nails scraping against the top of the desk as her nerves got the best of her. "I can't stand it, Dawg. Don't tease me. Just do it."

She couldn't bear it. He had already stolen too much of her. Recovering from this episode of her life would take years. What he was doing now she might never recover from.

"You're the toy, remember?" His voice was harsh with lust now. "My toy. Mine to play with, to touch and to taste." His voice sounded tortured. "Sweet heaven, Crista, how I've dreamed of this. Just like this." He parted her farther a second before his teeth gripped the side of the inner flesh and his tongue flickered over it heatedly.

She tried to jerk upright, to escape the lash of sensation that exploded through her body.

"Stay put," he ordered forcefully, one hand pressing into the small of her back a second before his tongue swiped through the narrow cleft.

Crista lifted to her tiptoes. The sheer eroticism of what he was doing would brand her soul forever. His tongue flickered along the narrow valley, found the tiny, forbidden entrance, and lashed against the nerve-ridden flesh with destructive strokes.

"Damn you, Crista, you make me wild for you," he snarled behind her as his head lifted.

His head lifted, and his hand landed on one rounded cheek in a forceful caress that sent a bolt of pleasure ripping through her nerve endings.

She jerked, shuddered, and tried again to lift from the top of the desk.

"Don't move. You owe me this. Eight fucking years of dreams, and you owe me this." His hand landed on the opposite side of her rear, sending heat blazing through her in a pleasure-pain that bordered orgasm.

Crista heard her own moan of surrender then. Her rear lifted to him, and a cry escaped her lips as his hand landed again. And again. Sweet God.

"Again." She heard herself cry out the word, knew she was bucking, pressing back, begging for more of the sweet pleasure-pain. And he gave her more.

"Do you like that, Crista Ann?" He groaned behind her, his hand smoothing over her rear before another heated caress landed on her flesh. Never the same place often enough to draw her from the sensual haze he was building in her mind. Never hard enough to bring her down from the erotic high whipping through her veins.

"Yes," she cried out.

And she did. Too much. A distant part of her brain connected the dots. She knew what each touch was doing, what each fiery slap against her ass was creating. It was drawing her deeper into the web he was weaving around her soul. Making certain she belonged to him forever. That her soul always followed him, whether his followed hers or not.

Dawg watched as Crista's ass turned a pretty, heated pink. It mesmerized him. Seeing her body accept each delicately placed, heavy caress. Never too hard. Always just enough to heat rather than burn.

And it was heating her. Not just her flesh, either. Her legs parted farther, mindlessly following the direction of his hand beneath her knee as he lifted her small foot to the desk drawer he had pulled free. He propped it on the edge, watching as her rear parted, as the soft curl-laden folds between her thighs were revealed.

Dew glistened on those folds. Sweet, soft little droplets that had his mouth watering to taste, to lick. He parted the soft swells of her rear once again and leaned forward, groaning as his tongue found the heated core of her pussy and the hot syrup filling it.

Crista flinched, cried out his name, and pressed back, giving him more, begging for a deeper caress.

Not yet. Hell no, not yet. When he finished, he wanted to be certain that not so much as a hint of her former lovers remained in her dreams. He intended to brand her body and her mind with his touch, his possession. When the summer was over, leaving him would be like tearing out her own soul. He'd make certain of it. He had to make certain of it, because he couldn't imagine losing her.

He nearly paused at the thought. Dawg, getting possessive. It was damned unheard of, but he was. So possessive that he growled, nipped at her smooth rear, then stiffened his tongue and drove inside the liquid hot depths of her pussy as he slid from his chair to his knees behind her.

Sliding the sweet, slick juices from her pussy back to her ass, he lubricated the little hole enough to take the tip of his finger. She flinched, cried out, then drove back, burying the digit to the first knuckle as he fucked his tongue hot and deep inside her.

She was like a fire, burning in his arms. Each time he took her, more memories from that long-ago night coalesced inside his head. They twisted and formed and raced through his mind with a force that left him breathless.

She had taken him then as she was taking him now: eagerly, heatedly, calling out his name in that broken little voice filled with need.

Pulling back, he turned her, ignoring her frantic little mewls of denial, and lifted her to the desk.

"Lie back." His own voice bordered on demented. "Lie back, Crista. Give me what I need. Now."

She fell back, her hair fanning out around her sweat-dampened head as her hands reached back and gripped the edge of the desk.

Dawg spread her legs slowly as he lifted them, arranging her feet at the lower edge of the desk and staring at the swollen, wet folds awaiting him.

He bent forward, his eyes closing as his tongue took a slow, greedy lick through the narrow slit.

Crista jerked beneath him, her hips lifting, a low wail leaving her lips. The sounds coming from her throat were making him crazy.

"The sweetest pussy in the world," he told her gently as he leaned back, smoothed his fingers over the wet curls and stared up her. "Will you have it waxed for me, Crista? Will you have all those pretty curls removed so I can taste your skin, lick all your juices, and show you how sweet and hot it can be when nothing hides you from me? Will you do that for me, sweetheart?"

He pulled the tube of lubrication from the opened bottom drawer as he let the fingers of his other hand smooth over the drenched curves.

"Dawg." There was an edge of hesitancy and feminine distress in her tone. But her hips lifted to him, her body unconsciously seeking more.

Moving slowly, Dawg spread an application of the lubricating gel on his fingers, let it warm, then lowered his lips to the succulent flesh before him, while his slickened fingers moved to the sweet portal lower.

She cried out his name again as he pressed against the entrance to her anus. Her hips jerked, lifted, and a ragged cry filled the air as he pierced the narrow channel.

His tongue flicked around her clit, then he drew it inside his mouth as the second finger penetrated her tight rear.

God, she was fucking hot. She twisted beneath him, her juices spilling from her. His cock was aching like an open wound, and his balls were drawn so tight against his body that they were in agony.

"Answer me, fancy-face," he groaned, lifting his lips from her sweet pussy and staring up at her as he worked his fingers inside the tender back hole. "Will you do that for me? Have your pussy waxed. Make it all slick and soft for me."

He reached back to the drawer and drew out the small butt plug he had taken from the package earlier. She liked that edge of pain. She liked the burning pleasure that seared her nerve endings and made the need for orgasm an erotic agony.

"Yes," she hissed. "Anything. Anything you want."

He drew his fingers from her rear.

"No. Don't stop," she pleaded raggedly. "Not yet, don't stop."

"Shh, baby. I'm not stopping. I'm going to make it better." He lubricated the tapered toy. "So much better."

He straightened, lifted her legs, and drew them together before pressing them back.

Her eyes snapped open. Nearly black in arousal now, they watched him warily, knowingly. She knew what was coming. She had seen the toys, knew he wouldn't wait long before using one of them.

He pressed the narrow tip against the tiny puckered opening.

"No," she whispered. "Not the toy. I want you there."

His cock jerked as a grimace tightened his face.

"I'll be there later, sweetheart," he promised. "I want you to know what this is like. Filled from one end to the other. So hot and tight that you won't know where pleasure ends and pain begins, because it's all going to be so damned good that you can't stop coming."

The toy eased inside her, stretching her, causing her to arch and whimper with sensation as he watched the pleasure contort her face.

Dawg worked the toy inside her, easing it in, watching as the little hole spread to accommodate the toy and finally tightened around the narrower base. He watched as the muscles of her rear tightened and flexed as she fought to adjust to the stretching. Heard her muttered moans as he picked up the little remote that would activate the vibration inside it.

Placing her feet back on the edge of the desk, he pressed the switch and growled as she jerked, bucked. Her hips began to move, swaying and jerking as the plug began to not just vibrate but also flex inside her.

Her eyes flew open. Between her thighs, her juices began to build on the soft folds and silky curls. Her body flushed, her nipples tightened.

"Oh God, Dawg." She arched to him as he stepped closer, his dick gripped in his hand, the heavy crest tucking against the flexing opening. "Oh God. Fuck me. Fuck me, Dawg. Before it kills me . . ."

Dawg had to fight for control. The feel of silky wet heat on the crest of his dick had his teeth grinding together as he fought for control. Just a little more control. Just another minute to relish her surrender, her pleasure.

But she was so fucking hot. And he knew how tight she was, how hungry her pussy was when she was aroused. And he needed. God help him, just for a little while, he needed . . .

What had he done to her? Crista could feel the insidious

vibration in her rear, the slow flex, an easing, then a stretching that began to make her insane for more.

Her eyes slitted open; she couldn't manage to lift the lids
fully, sensuality made her gaze heavy, made her body weak
and melting. But she was able to watch Dawg.

His broad hands held her legs up beneath the knees. His
eyes were centered between her thighs, to the spot where the
head of his cock was tucked at the opening to her vagina.

She could feel him, a heavy presence at the entrance, hot
and thick and ready to fill her.

"Dawg," she whispered his name, a sigh of pleasure, a
questioning breath as he paused.

Thick black hair fell along the sides of his face, straight
and raven black, framing his savage features.

"Taking you is like losing myself," he groaned roughly.
"I feel you clasping my dick, Crista, but I feel you pouring
into my soul."

Celadon green eyes, so light they were like pale green ice,
burned now. They flickered with a darker edge, gleamed
with carnal knowledge.

Crista whimpered at the words as well as the look.

"Don't do this," she whispered tearfully, seeing the dark
longing on his face, not the need to share, but the need to
possess more than just her body.

He shook his head roughly, his lips pulling back from his
teeth in a silent snarl as his hips moved, the broad head of his
erection working inside her, stretching her, burning her.

"Did you walk away—" A hard breath hissed between
his teeth. "Did you leave without looking back?"

She shook her head. She couldn't do this. She could let
him have all of her.

"Answer me." He paused, the head of his cock filling her,
teasing her. Daring her. "Did you look back?"

"Please, Dawg . . ."

"Tell me."

Another inch. The movement he made didn't ease his
cock inside her, that additional inch was taken with a hard
flex of his hips and a destructive flame along the tender nerve
endings it stroked.

"Yes," she cried out. The words falling unbidden from her lips. "I've always looked back."

His hands clenched on her legs.

"You didn't forget." His voice softened then, his cock shifted and moved inside her, stroking her, taking her by the smallest degrees with each movement.

She couldn't hide from him. She wanted to. She needed to.

"I never forgot." A tear fell from the corner of her eye. "I never forgot you, Dawg."

Her heart never forgot. Her soul never released the memory of his touch, his hard voice whispering at her ear, his hunger, or her need for him. Her love. The soul-deep, unquenchable agony of loving him.

"Don't cry, fancy-face." His voice was graveled now, thick and rough as she felt the agonizing pleasure beginning to engulf her. "I'll take care of you."

Each inch of his erection inside her was like a brand laid to the tender muscles. A brand of fiery sensation and exquisite pleasure.

Crista arched, driving him deeper inside her, feeling the piercing, burning sensation of being doubly penetrated, exquisitely stretched.

"There, sweetheart." He wrapped her legs around his hips as he leaned closer, his head lowering to her nipples, adding to the ecstatic pleasure already gripping her by drawing one tight bud into his hot mouth and suckling it deeply.

His hips were moving, his cock thrusting slowly, working into her with each thrust as the overwhelming sensations of heat, stretching, and brutal pleasure began to build inside her.

It was always like this with Dawg. The world centered to two beings, time stopped, nothing mattered but this, with him, the feel of him fucking her, owning her.

He owned her.

He thrust inside her, and she arched to take him deeper.

His lips, teeth, and tongue consumed her nipples, one then the other, and her hands threaded into his hair to hold him closer.

"So good," he whispered. "So sweet and tight."

Her body reflexively tightened further around him, muscles contracting, her soul glorying in the harsh male groan that whispered around the nipple his mouth returned to.

"Beautiful." He buried his head between her breasts, the rhythm of his hips increasing, and she spurred him on with her cries and her pleas for more.

"Mine!" he snarled, and she exploded around him.

Her orgasm tore through her as his thrusts became harder, deeper. He pounded into her, shafting her with surging strokes and fucking into her with an ever-growing greed.

"Damn you." He bit her shoulder, his hands gripped her hips, and as the climax began to ease, she felt the powerful first spurt of his semen blasting into her.

She arched violently through the second release. Tightening on him to the point she could feel every throb, every pulse, every ripple of Dawg's release inside her. And she felt another part of her emotional defenses collapse.

Dawg once again held her heart.

SIXTEEN

Two days later, Dawg admitted what he should have known eight years ago. Crista Ann had managed to wrap herself around his heart in a way that he knew he would never manage to escape. He could feel the bonds tightening as he pulled the pickup into the parking slot directly in front of the small, exclusive spa that had moved into downtown Somerset.

Beside the truck, Rowdy pulled up on his Harley and helped the little wildcat he was engaged to from the back. Beside Rowdy, Natches pulled his Harley in and waited.

"This is insane," Crista muttered in the passenger seat as she stared mutinously at the front door of the spa. "It's going to hurt."

"I'll kiss it all better tonight." He turned to her, letting her see just how much he was anticipating kissing the delicate flesh between her thighs and easing the memory of any discomfort she would feel with the waxing he had had Kelly schedule for her.

Her arms crossed over her breasts defensively.

"How did I let you talk me into this?" she snapped, only half-angry. The other half was uncertainty, perhaps a little embarrassment.

"Because I'm persuasive?" he asked with a waggle of his brows.

He had done his best to be persuasive. For hours. Licking, kissing, tempting her with the knowledge of how much better it could be, making her so hot, so damned desperate, she would have agreed to anything.

Her lips twitched then, a sensual smile of remembrance tugging at the lush curves as a faint blush stole over her cheeks. And his chest clenched. Right there in the front seat of his pickup, Dawg felt his heart swell with an emotion so unfamiliar he knew it was fucking love. It was strong enough, hard enough that he reached up and rubbed at the center of his chest to ease the constriction.

"You were very persuasive." She sighed, staring back at the spa morosely. "And you know I'm going to be very put out when I'm finished."

A goofy smile tugged at his lips, and his heart raced.

"I'll take you someplace special when you're finished," he told her then. "Someplace you'll enjoy."

She glanced at him from the corner of her eyes.

"How special?"

"So special I've never taken another woman there," he promised, watching her gaze jerk away, that hint of hesitancy that tensed her slender frame.

She was scared of whatever he made her feel, and he couldn't blame her. He had blackmailed her, and he would keep blackmailing her until he knew she belonged to him.

She cleared her throat delicately. "Fine. But it better be worth this." She gathered her purse from where it sat behind his seat and stared him fully in the eyes as she turned back to him. "And it better not hurt too bad."

"You'll love it," he promised her. "Just imagine me doing it."

She looked scandalized. "Oh Lord, don't go there, Dawg. This is going to be hard enough." She pulled at the door latch quickly, escaping before he could say anything that would deepen that blush along her cheeks or give her eyes more of that confused, uncertain look.

He had a feeling Crista had once believed that she knew

him. That she could predict him. He could have told her that wasn't going to happen.

He moved from the truck as she and Kelly headed into the spa, meeting Natches and Rowdy at the front of his truck and staring around the street curiously.

"We picked up a tail," Natches said quietly, his dark green eyes glancing to the gray sedan that had pulled in farther up the street. "She pulled in behind you after you hit the city limits."

Dawg glanced up the street, his gaze narrowing on Greta Dane. Normally when a woman looked at a man with an expression as cold and hard as flint as Greta was giving him, it tended to make the balls draw up in fear.

Thankfully, Dawg wasn't prone to allow such things to affect his private parts.

"Something's up," he murmured, turning back to the other men. "Have you heard from Cranston?"

"Nothing." Natches shook his head as he crossed his arms over his chest and tucked his hands by his sides. "We picked the bulldog up there just inside the city limits, and she didn't bother to try to hide it."

Dawg rubbed his hand over his chin. "Stay here. Let's see what I can find out."

He stepped to the sidewalk and strode quickly to the little sedan Greta was driving. As he neared, the window rolled down, and Greta's pinched expression increased. She was also nervous. She tucked a cigarette between her lips and lit up as he neared the car.

"What's up, Greta?" Dawg leaned against the pickup next to her and stared back at her quizzically.

"Cranston's orders," she informed him waspishly. "Unlike some people, I'm a team player."

Dawg tilted his head and smiled slowly. "Are you implying I don't play well with others, Greta?"

She drew on the cigarette again before flicking the ashes to the portable ashtray in the middle console.

"I'm not implying anything, Mackay. I'm stating a fact."

The stare she leveled back at him was suspicious, chilling in its complete lack of emotion.

"So you were ordered to watch me?" he asked her.

"No, I was ordered to follow your girlfriend." Her own smile was nothing short of relish. "I didn't ask why."

Bullshit.

Dawg stared back at her, his gaze narrowed, his body prepared. Somehow, Cranston had focused on Crista. This wouldn't be a good thing.

"Have fun keeping up with us," he told her then, returning the smile with interest. "I'd make sure I wasn't easily shocked, though. After we leave here, we're heading into the mountains. I have a blanket in the truck, and we're stopping for a light little picnic lunch that my favorite restaurant is currently putting together for us.

Then, since it *is* private property, I thought I might introduce my girlfriend to a little fresh-air lovin'. Now, I don't mind a little exhibitionism every now and then, but you should be prepared. It could get rather hard-core."

He watched her face flush. The hardened agent could kill a man without a thought, but the subject of sex seemed to make her jumpy as hell.

"I'm sure I'll survive," she gritted out.

Dawg nodded slowly and smiled again. "I'm sure you will, sugar. Just to be on the safe side though, I think I'll have Natches go with us and sit with you for a while. Some things just shouldn't be done alone, ya know? And Natches, he makes damned good company in such situations."

Her gaze flickered over to Natches and Rowdy as Dawg turned as well. Natches grinned slow and easy. He might not know what the hell they were talking about, but even from there, Natches would have seen the hard flush on Greta's face.

"You sic that perverted bastard in my direction, and I'll shoot him," Greta warned him then.

Dawg shrugged. "He'll survive. You're not allowed to kill him, and a little bloodshed between friends . . ." He smiled again. "Could get interesting." He straightened and dropped the smile. "You talk to Cranston, tell him I'm waiting to hear from him, sugar. Soon."

He didn't give her time to reply, but he was guessing she

was on her cell phone even as he strode back to where Rowdy and Natches were waiting on the sidewalk in front of his truck.

"She's watching Crista," he told Natches softly as Rowdy listened in interest.

"Bad news." Natches grimaced as he lowered his head as though to check the tips of his cowboy boots.

"How long does this female stuff take, anyway?" Dawg glanced at the doors to the spa, knowing damned good and well he wasn't waiting inside the building for Crista to finish. No way, nohow; all that estrogen could be fatal.

"Wax, trim, and style," Rowdy mused. "You're looking at three hours."

Dawg leaned against the truck. "You two can just stand here and wait it out with me," he decided.

Natches grunted. "I had things to do, Dawg."

"Get over it. God only knows what Cranston has up his sleeve, and I'm not standing outside this place by myself."

"Hell. I'm getting the shit jobs and none of the pleasure," Natches cursed. "This growing-up crap you two seem so intent on is starting to piss me off. I think I'll go talk to Agent Dane for a while instead. She's always good for a smirk or two, if nothing else."

Casting Rowdy and Dawg both an irate look, Natches ambled from his slouch against the hood of the truck and headed for Agent Dane's vehicle.

The agent in question lit up again as she watched Natches warily.

"Do you think he's really pissed?" Rowdy drawled as Natches neared the woman's car.

"With Natches, who the hell knows anymore." Dawg shook his head wearily. "That boy didn't come out of Afghanistan easy. He was going to stay with the bum shoulder despite his CO's advice until the Marines booted his ass out."

Natches, already an excellent shot when he went into the Marines and an instinctive hunter, had been quickly inducted into training as a sniper/assassin. Dawg suspected his cousin had more kills to his record than he was admitting to, and secrets that only Dawg could guess at.

"You two didn't do anything easy," Rowdy said then. "I thought the agreement was that we'd go in, do our duty, and come home without changing who or what we were."

Dawg had a feeling Rowdy wasn't talking about the lack of need in sharing his pretty fiancée.

"Hey, you started it," he said anyway. "Getting all possessive and snarly over Kelly the way you did."

Rowdy snorted at that. "Don't play dense, Dawg, it doesn't suit you."

Dawg grimaced. "We were more suited to some things than you were, Rowdy. You just didn't want to see it."

"Killing?" Rowdy asked. "You were never suited to that. You or Natches."

"You just didn't want to see it." Dawg stared his cousin in the eye then. "Killing wasn't the draw, though. It was taking out the monsters. And that was something Natches and I both were ready to do before we were out of our teens."

Dawg's and Natches's fathers were bastards. But most of the men out of that family were bastards. Literally. Good ole Grandpa August had sired sons from one end of the nation to the other. He had paused in Somerset long enough to fake a marriage to Ellen Mackay and give her a daughter and three sons. Then he had nicely informed her that the marriage was illegal because he was already married, and then he had disappeared.

Ellen Mackay had taken the August name from her sons and given them hers instead. Four kids that she had raised herself with little help, and she had died knowing that out of all those kids, only one of them had a sense of decency. Ray Mackay had been solid as the earth. The rest? Hell, the rest of them were as black-hearted and mean as the old man himself.

As Dawg understood it, his cousins in Texas hadn't fared any better. Their father, Joe August, the legitimate issue of old Nate August, had been pure evil. The hell he had visited on his sons had nearly destroyed them. It was only by a miracle that they had survived both during and after the torture they had endured.

"I saw Johnny's mother and Natches's dad with their heads together outside the courthouse yesterday when Kelly and I were driving through. They looked like they were brewing up trouble."

Nadine Mackay Grace and Dayle Mackay were vipers apart; when together, the destruction they could cause had destroyed more than one life.

"Hell," Dawg cursed. "Dayle's already disowned Natches. What more could he do to him?"

"I just wish I knew for sure it was Natches they were targeting." Rowdy sighed. "I don't know what the hell's up, Dawg, but it's not feeling good."

Hell, no, it wasn't. Dawg could feel his teeth clenching and his neck itching. Those two things were a surefire warning that shit was coming down.

"Fallback position?" Dawg murmured.

"I have you covered," Rowdy answered.

Dawg had explained Crista's presence at the warehouse as well as the risk that Crista could be identified as part of the group attempting to sell the missiles.

Their fallback position was clear: Rowdy and Natches would hold the line, while Dawg pulled Crista into the mountains to an old, hidden hunter's cabin they had found years before as teenagers. No one knew about the cabin but the three cousins, and it would be the ideal place to hide Crista until they figured out the best way to protect her. Or until Alex and his group returned from wherever the hell they were.

"I'm going to put out a call to Alex's contact," Dawg muttered then, hating the need for that. He had hoped to be able to avoid contacting Alex. "We need to let him know Crista could be in trouble before it's too late."

Rowdy nodded, then glanced back to where Natches leaned against the sedan farther down the street, obviously arguing with Agent Dane.

"When was the last time you saw Natches argue with anyone?" Rowdy asked.

Dawg glanced at his cousin and grinned. "The last time Greta spoke to him."

"Interesting."

"Damn interesting," Dawg agreed as he pulled his cell phone from the holder at his belt and flipped it open. It took only a second to hit the speed dial number that connected with Alex's contact.

"Leave a message." The voice was cold, hard.

Dawg said one word. "Crista." Then disconnected the call. Within hours Alex would know things had the potential to go from sugar to shit with his sister in a very short time.

And then he propped himself against the hood of the truck and glanced at the front door of the spa. Crista was inside, possibly getting the intimate waxing he had spent so long that morning talking her into.

His body tensed, lust rose sharp and painful inside him, hardening his dick in an instant.

God help Cranston if he messed with Dawg's fun later that evening. He had waited years, hell, Dawg felt as though he had waited all his life for this. The man or woman who dared to mess with it would pay. Painfully.

Being intimately bald was a curiously disconcerting feeling, Crista thought as she rode beside Dawg several hours later toward the surprise he had promised her.

In the backseat, a covered wicker basket emitted the succulent scent of fresh fried chicken from beneath the large checkered tablecloth secured over the top of the lid.

There was also a new addition to the back of the truck. On the rack hanging on the window stretched a rifle. It hadn't been there when she had gone into the spa, but it was there now.

And Dawg was testy. He kept checking the rearview mirror, taking turns, and using back roads she hadn't known existed.

"Are we being followed?" Not for the first time, she turned and looked behind them.

"Yep." Taciturn and too soft for comfort, his tone did little for the nerves beginning to build in her stomach.

"I don't see anyone."

"They're staying far enough back to stay out of sight," he said as he took another turn. "I'm just getting far enough ahead of them to pull over and trash their tracker." A grin stretched his lips. A dangerous grin. "I want to get them good and lost first."

"There's a tracker on the truck?" Her voice shook, but hell, it wasn't every day she realized she was being tracked. Being followed would be bad enough.

"Hang on," he warned. And not a moment too soon. The truck came to a rocking stop.

Jumping out, Dawg strode quickly behind the truck, bent from sight, and seconds later straightened and ran back to the driver's side. Jumping in, he threw the truck in gear, flashed her a smile that was less dangerous and more filled with fun, before tossing an electronic disc out the window and speeding away.

Crista stared around the area they were in. They were deep in the mountains, and evening was coming on. Even she couldn't find her way back to town from here.

"You're going to let someone get trapped in these mountains in the dark?" she asked carefully. "Who is it?"

"A friend." He chuckled.

"You're going to get a friend lost in these mountains?" she asked in disbelief. "Dawg, your friends don't get lost that easily," she pointed out.

"Most don't." He nodded on another low laugh. The playful grin on his face reminded her of a little boy into mischief. "This friend is city, though. Don't worry, Natches is riding close to her ass, and he'll take care of her."

"Natches?" She wouldn't trust Natches in a well-lit room filled with saints, let alone on a dark mountain. "You're leaving some poor, unsuspecting woman stuck here with Natches? What did she do to make you angry?"

That canceled out any bad-guy types.

"She's spying on me." The flash of his teeth against his sun-darkened skin was playful and sexy. "For some reason, the special agent in charge of the arrests last week has a tail on you, sweetheart. Usually, I wouldn't care, but I have plans today. Plans that don't include watching eyes."

His brows waggled over the top of his dark sunglasses.

Plans that didn't include watching eyes? Crista felt her heart race faster than it was already after he mentioned that she was being followed rather than him.

"Why is she interested in me?" She could feel the fear clogging her throat.

"I don't know yet." He shook his head briefly before turning back onto one of the wider country roads and accelerating along the blacktop. "I tried to call her boss, but he's not taking his calls right now. He'll let me know eventually."

"He knows I was there," she whispered. "Are they going to arrest me?"

"No one is going to arrest you, Crista," he growled. "I have another call out to Alex. A contact number I doubt you had. He should be calling us soon. Until then, we're just waiting to see what's happening and playing with the fools sent to watch you."

"Your boss doesn't trust you anymore then," she said worriedly. "They could arrest you, too, Dawg."

"Stop worrying."

Stop worrying?

"One of us should worry here," she gritted out. "Dawg, if he's got someone watching me, then he thinks I was involved."

"If he had proof, he would have had you arrested at the spa. He wouldn't have someone watching you. Not to say that he's not suspicious. But Cranston doesn't make a move without proof. He doesn't have proof."

Crista bit her lip, chewing at it worriedly as she watched the road ahead of her.

"You sound certain." She needed him to be certain.

"I know Cranston. But I am interested in what is going on. Natches should be able to figure that one out; then we'll figure out where we go from here."

"The note was in the Rodeo," she whispered. "I left it there. I know it was in there. I was going to look for it, but you kept dragging me away from it." And then it had blown up.

"Don't worry about it." His voice became more clipped as he turned up another road, a graveled road rather than dirt.

Pristine white fences ran along the side of the road. A few dozen cattle meandered in thickly grassed pastures, their heads lifting curiously as the truck sped down the road.

"I do worry about it. That was the only proof I had."

Dawg knew that. Just as he knew that proof was safely locked away in his safe.

It was hidden. Just in case. But damn, telling Crista he had it all along was going to piss her clean off. That wasn't what he wanted today.

He would tell her tomorrow. He wasn't letting anything interfere in his appreciation of her slick, honeyed flesh when the time came.

Just a few more hours. Six hours at the most, and the sensitivity of the delicate flesh that had been waxed should be back to normal. The spa, Kelly swore, had the best technicians in the business, and the emollients they used after the waxing soothed the irritated flesh immediately.

He would tell her about the note tomorrow. The letterhead of the delivery company, the date, and note would help. Unfortunately, it hadn't been signed by the delivery person. At least the handwriting on the note definitely wasn't Crista's.

That added to the fact that even with Natches's contacts, computer abilities, and general sneakiness, he couldn't find so much as a spare penny in Crista's name in the house she shared with Alex or anywhere related to her. And he had spent the better part of the past days searching for it.

Crista wasn't the money girl, the lone female that had taken the buyers' million dollars, supposedly in the thieves' interest.

The men in custody hadn't named her, but Dawg hadn't been able to interrogate them, either. And he was damned sure it wasn't Crista.

Where had that trust come from? That question rolled through him as he passed the cattle guard in the road that led to the property he had been working on for years now.

The land, over two hundred acres of woodland and pastures, was bordered by an arm of Lake Cumberland. The sprawling two-story log cabin he had begun building the summer before sat on the rise overlooking the lake, surrounded on three sides by fir, oak, and maple trees. The ranch yard was surrounded by the same white fences that stretched along the road. Stables sat a quarter mile to the left, and the barn and tractor sheds to the right. All the buildings were placed so that they were protected on three sides by the dense woods that surrounded the area.

The little coves of cleared land that had been created inside the tree line gave the land a natural, peaceful appearance. It also pleased his need for space and privacy.

This was Dawg's. Bought by the money he saved while in the Marines and then the ATF, along with part of the profits from the lumber store in the past four years. It wasn't bought from his father's inheritance, and it wasn't tied to memories of his parents.

It was his. Just his. Just as Crista was.

"Stop worrying." He glanced at her and saw the frown on her face. "No one knows we're here. Hell, no one in Somerset but Natches, Rowdy, and Kelly even knows about this place."

"Where are we, anyway?"

"Jabez. We're still in Pulaski County. You can see the lake from the back, but it's a small distance to it."

Dawg stepped from the truck before opening the back side door and dragging out the picnic basket.

"You coming?" He looked over the top of the sunglasses, and that look sizzled. "There's a nice little clearing out back where we can picnic. I'll show you the house first, though."

Crista stepped from the truck and stared at the house. The dark logs helped it blend into the trees around it, as did the dark brown color of the tin roof. A porch surrounded it, as did a balcony on the top floor.

"I'm having a hot tub installed on the balcony outside the master bedroom on the back." He swept his hand toward the house as he met her at the front of the truck. "When the inside is finished, I'll probably bring the *Nauti Dawg* out and tie her up to the dock where I managed to buy permission to build on the shoreline."

"Are you trying to become domesticated, Dawg?" she asked as he opened the wood gate and ushered her into the ranch yard.

He could still hear the nerves in her voice, her fear. The knowledge that Cranston now suspected her had thrown her. But there was no guilt in her eyes or her expression. Confusion, fear, yes. But it wasn't blazing; it was subdued. Whether Crista wanted to admit it or not, she trusted him.

"Come on into the house." He unlocked the front door, pushed it open slowly, and checked out the open, airy rooms before leading the way inside.

The walls were unpainted. The floors were unfinished. The stairwell wasn't banistered, and the upstairs wasn't much better. It was, as he liked to tell Rowdy and Natches, a work in progress.

Kind of like Crista. He looked at her as she stared around the entryway nervously and smiled. That same smile that seemed to worry Natches so much. Possessing her heart might not be easy, but he was damned determined to do just that.

SEVENTEEN

Dawg's house was incredible. The large entryway held a curving staircase to the second floor and an open hall that looked out over the unfinished balustrades. There were no doors on the five entrances on the second floor, but sunlight spilled from the windows on the front section and bathed the hall as well as the foyer in myriad sunbeams from the tall windows that looked out on the graveled road.

To her right, a large, open entrance led into what she assumed would be a living room with another entrance to the far end into another room. On her left, farther along the foyer, was another wide entrance into a dining room. Crista moved forward hesitantly, staring into the room and seeing the two sets of French doors that led onto the wide porch wrapping around the house. At the end of that room was another entrance that led into what was clearly a kitchen.

"Come on, I'll show you around." Dawg led the way into the dining room, then into the kitchen. "The foyer opens up to a back hall." He pointed out another door as they entered a large kitchen. "There's a pantry, a washroom, and a small spare bedroom along the hall as well as an office that opens into the living room."

Nothing was finished. By the look of the drywall and the dust along the floors, it hadn't been long since it had been installed.

"I'm surprised," she said as he gave her a quick tour of the house, upstairs and downstairs. "You've managed this without a hint of gossip."

He flashed a grin as they stepped from the stairway back into the foyer. "That wasn't easy, either. I bought the land about three years ago through a third party, and I've had the work done in stages, through the same people. Once it's complete, we'll file the proper deeds, etc., through the county. But it's mine, regardless."

"So why hide it?" she asked as they moved back into the kitchen.

Dawg moved to the roughly framed center island where the picnic basket sat on the strip of plywood covering the top frame. He braced his hip against the side of it and looked around silently for long moments.

"Pure spite, probably." He sighed, shaking his head ruefully. "The relatives seem to delight in knowing every damned move I make, so it's become a game to do things they don't know about and rub their noses in it."

"What about the house your parents left you?" Crista had seen the outside of that property several times. The front of the house was all that showed at the bottom of the mountain it had been built into. Dawg's father had been said to be one of the premier architects in the country for such buildings.

"The place makes me damned claustrophobic." He grimaced. "I'll probably sell it eventually."

"Once you've milked your relatives of all the satisfaction you can squeeze from them?" She smiled in turn.

A wry smile curled his lips as he stared back at her.

"We're not exactly a close family," he admitted. "Nadine Grace and Dayle Mackay are thorns in my side, not to mention Natches's and Rowdy's. If they could destroy Uncle Ray, they'd do it in a heartbeat. Unfortunately for them, Ray figured out how to protect himself early from them. They were snake mean even as kids, from what I understand."

"Except Ray." Crista had heard that herself. Of all the older Mackays, Ray was the only one spoken of kindly.

"Except Uncle Ray." Dawg nodded, his expression flickering with affection. "Ray raised Rowdy right, and Rowdy helped raise Natches and me until Ray could get his hooks into us. Neither one of them gave up on us. Rowdy held us together."

"Even to the point of drawing you into the sharing?" she asked.

A bark of laughter left his throat then. "Come on, we'll talk while we walk."

Dawg held his hand out to her, waiting, watching as she gazed at it a second before lifting her smaller, more delicate hand to his. Dawg twined his fingers with hers, watching as her paler, softer hand meshed with his.

It looked right. It felt damned right. Damn her. She had his guts and his heart twisted in so many knots he knew he would never be free of her.

As he led her from the house and into the tree-shaded backyard, Dawg found himself feeling emotions he hadn't expected. Aside from the protectiveness he felt, there was a well of heated hunger, fierce possessiveness, and a gentleness he had never felt toward another woman.

"You and Alex are pretty close," he said as he let her spread the tablecloth on the thick, well-cut grass at the edge of the small clearing that looked out onto a private natural cove the land created for the lake.

"We had to be," she said as she tucked a thick strand of hair behind her ear and smoothed out the tablecloth.

Dawg set the basket in the center before lowering himself on the cloth and leaning back. Crista seemed more hesitant, sitting rather than stretching out, but at least she sat close enough to him to assure him that she wasn't running from him.

"Your parents were pretty distant around people," he said as she set out the small covered platter of still-warm chicken and began unpacking the side dishes.

"They were like that with Alex and me as well." A little frown pulled at her forehead as she spoke. "They planned Alex's birth, but I was kind of a surprise." The curve of her lips was tipped with an expression of subtle bitterness. "They didn't want me. They gave me to Alex to raise pretty much.

Mom was only concerned with pleasing Dad, and he was only concerned with her and his moneymaking schemes."

Chester Jansen had always been certain a fortune awaited him just around the corner. He had searched for gold, for artifacts. He had nearly destroyed his small business playing the stock market, and he had constantly been taken in with fly-by-night moneymaking schemes.

"Alex did a good job raising you," he pointed out.

"He did. Alex was already ten when I was born. He had learned to take care of himself, and he applied it to taking care of me." She nodded as she arranged the chicken and side dishes before setting two china plates between them and pulling out the glass carafe of sweet iced tea and unscrewing the lid that covered it before pouring the dark liquid into drinking glasses.

"Neither one of you turned out too bad." He accepted the glass she handed him, then watched as she began opening the food and placing the serving spoons into it.

"We survived." She shrugged, glancing at him warily again. "He warned me about you when I was sixteen, you know."

"Really?" Dawg drawled. "I'll have to discuss that with him. What warning did he give you?"

"To stay away from the Mackay cousins." She flashed him a teasing smile. "He said the lot of you were bad news to any girl who wanted love rather than nasty games."

"And you didn't want nasty games?" He smiled back at her wickedly. He had a feeling that some of those games she would have taken to like a natural once she had gotten older. She sure as hell took to them now.

She ducked her head for a long second before lifting it slowly and staring back at him in determination. "I didn't want to be one of the Nauti Boys' Toys. That's what your women were called."

"But you wanted to be my woman?" He needed to know. He needed to hear her say it.

Crista dragged her gaze away from Dawg's and stared across the clearing to the serenity of the small cove they faced. Water lapped against the rocky shore with a soothing rhythm.

She *had* wanted to be Dawg's woman. Even then, ten years before, at a time when she had no concept what it meant to be anyone's woman. Her fascination for him had been soul-deep, and it had culminated in one heated night that had threatened to destroy her soul.

"I wanted to be your woman," she admitted on a sigh. She hadn't lied to him to this point. Lying was something she hated. She had hated it as a child, and as an adult, she hated it even more.

"What changed that, Crista?" he asked her then, his voice insidiously soft, gentle. "We had one night together, and instead of slapping me with a frying pan the next morning, you ran."

She shook her head. Over the past few days she had figured that one out for herself.

"I was too young for you, Dawg," she finally admitted as she turned back to him. "We both knew I was too young for you. I couldn't handle what I felt for you along with what I thought you wanted from me. It was too much."

"And now?"

"And now you're blackmailing me." And she loved him more now than she had then.

"If I hadn't blackmailed you?"

There was something in his voice that pulled at her then. Something she was certain she would see in his eyes if she pulled the dark glasses from his nose.

She reached out and did just that. Slid them from his face as he watched her, met his darkened gaze and felt her heart trip in her chest.

He was staring at her like no other man ever had. Equal parts hunger and pain.

If he hadn't blackmailed her?

"I would have caved eventually," she whispered, caught, held by that look in his eyes. "One of those nights that I was driving around the marina just to see if you were there, I would have weakened. I would have walked out to your houseboat, and if you had been alone, I would have come to you."

She had been weakening, and she knew it. Tempted by his

smiles, his teasing, his determined irritation each time she rebuffed him.

"You came to the marina just to see me?" He reached out, his fingertips smoothing over her collarbone and sending heated spirals of need crashing through her system.

Crista licked her lips, and for once, she didn't fight the need welling inside her. She didn't fight the love she knew no other man would ever possess.

"Often." She fought to overcome the breathlessness, the racing of her heart. "And I'd stop and see the lights on in the *Nauti Dawg*, and I'd have to make myself stay in my car. I'd have to fight the need to go to you."

"You should have come to me." His hand cupped the back of her head, and he pulled her to him. "You should have let me love you, Crista."

Crista's senses exploded when his lips touched hers. It wasn't the fiery, hungry kisses she was used to. It was a slow, tender exploration. It was letting her get used to the feel of his tongue against her lips before he slipped inside. It was sharing the taste of himself even as he drew hers in. It was heated, sensitizing, it was a kiss that drove the breath from her lungs and left her moaning with the need for more.

Her hands braced on the cloth beneath them as her hair enveloped them, hiding their faces, their kiss, shielding them in a veil of intimacy as his lips pulled back just enough to cause her eyes to open as a whimper of denial left her lips.

"I would have pulled you inside," he whispered, his lips brushing hers as he spoke. "I would have locked out the world and drawn you to my bed. I would have made certain you never wanted to leave it again."

"I don't want to leave it now." She couldn't hold the words in.

A distant part of her brain cursed her foolishness, cursed her weak heart and the part of her soul that had never released the memory of his kiss, his touch.

She watched as Dawg's eyes dilated, darkened, then he was stealing her kiss. He ravished her lips, ate at them, and grew greedy on the taste of her. His tongue licked, his head slanted, and the kiss deepened as fireworks exploded through her body. Brilliant heat. Flames licked over her flesh and seared her nerve endings.

When he drew back, all the way back, they were both breathing hard and fast and fighting for control.

"Not yet." His voice was a graveled sound of need. "Too fucking soon. You have a few hours before you can take it yet."

"There are other ways." She leaned forward, touching her lips with his again, and saw the surprise in his eyes. She whispered wickedly, "Come on, Dawg. Show me how nasty you can get."

Show her how nasty he could get? Oh, she had no idea the fantasies he had of getting nasty with her.

"What about lunch?" He glanced down at the food she had laid out.

"Fried chicken tastes better cold," she reminded him, and Dawg watched in eager anticipation at the slow little lick her tongue made at her lips. "We can always eat later."

Repacking the food was a simple matter of snapping the lids back on the containers and resetting them in the basket. The basket itself was set to the side. Dawg found himself moving, forcing her down to her back as he came over her.

"I won't be nice," he warned her. "You might want to reconsider that little dare you just made."

Letting loose his fantasies could have disastrous results. Because he had a lot of fantasies.

"It could get worse than a spanking and a butt plug that vibrates and ripples?" She stared up at him in amused disbelief, even as her hands pulled his shirt free of his jeans.

She was wild, wanton. Dawg could see it in her eyes now, and he wondered if he hadn't somehow sensed that wildness inside her years before.

He held back, feeling her slender fingers pulling at the buttons of his shirt, releasing them one by one as she stared up at him with a challenge in her eyes.

He wondered how far she would go. How wild she would let herself get before she pulled back. And maybe a part of him had to know. He had no desire to share her, but that didn't mean his sexuality had dimmed in any way. He liked his sex lengthy, hard, and nasty. Crista couldn't have a clue exactly how hard and nasty he could get with her. But he could show her. He could show her, and try like hell not to scare her off while he was doing so.

Because scaring her was definitely something he didn't want to do. But he wanted her. All of her, in ways that had his cock pounding in agony at the thought of it.

"I could definitely make it compete with the butt plug," he assured her with a smile as her fingers smoothed the shirt back from his shoulders.

Dawg shrugged the material away, feeling the summer breeze as it whispered through the trees and caressed his naked flesh. It was nowhere as sensual as the feel of Crista's fingers working at his belt, drawing the leather free of the buckle before pulling at the metal button that held the band secure.

"You steal a girl's breath with your wicked ways, Mr. Mackay," she drawled teasingly, that hint of Southern belle deliberately thickened as his zipper rasped lower.

Dawg felt helpless above her. He stared into her chocolate eyes, certain he should be doing something himself. Kissing her soft lips, drawing her clothes from her body, but it was all he could do instead to maintain the strength in his arms to hold himself above her.

His jeans were loose now; her silken hands gripped the waistband and began drawing it from his body.

"That's only going to go so far," he warned her with a grimace. "We still have to get rid of the boots, sweetheart."

She smiled, a reckless, heated smile that had his balls drawing tight in anticipation.

"Lie down," she ordered softly, her palms pressing into his abdomen. "Lie down, Dawg, and we'll see if we can't get rid of them."

He lay down.

Giving a woman control had never been his strong suit, but he gave it to Crista. Because watching her, feeling her touch, was like being warmed in the winter. It wrapped around him and eased him into the sensuality rather than allowing him to throw his partner into it.

She cast him a heated look from beneath her lashes as she moved to his feet and removed his boots, then his socks. Then, like the wanton he dreamed of, she gripped the waistband of his jeans and began to drag them and his briefs down his legs.

It was agonizing, watching her undress him, seeing the pleasure in her eyes and knowing how hot it made her. As she tossed his jeans to the bottom of the red checked cloth he was lying on, his brow arched.

"You're still dressed, Crista."

She looked around as though gauging the privacy of where they were. As he started to speak, her hands gripped the hem of the little shirt she wore, and she drew it over her head.

She wore nothing but a thin lace bra beneath it. One that framed her perky breasts and almost revealed her tight, hard nipples.

Watching him with slumberous, sexy eyes, she rose slowly to her feet and dropped the cotton capris as she pushed her sandals off her feet.

"Leave the panties on." His voice was harsh as her fingers hooked into the little elastic band of the thong she wore.

Her lips tilted again. Knowing, sexual.

"What about the bra?"

"Lord have mercy." He sighed. "Take it off."

She released the clip between her breasts slowly and let the cups fall away from the hard-tipped mounds before shrugging it from her shoulders.

And there was no mercy to be found. There was sunlight spilling through the trees overhead and washing her creamy flesh in golden rays of heat.

When she came to him, Dawg couldn't help but suck in his breath at the complete sensuality of her flowing movements. She wasn't embarrassed. She wasn't playing coy. She was hungry, and she was going to feed on the sexual, sensual intensity blazing between them.

Her lips came to his. Her hands gripped his wrists, holding them at his head as her breasts brushed over his chest. Her nipples were like fiery brands, her lips as they sipped at his, nipped, laved them with lust, were extensions of the hunger raging between them.

Dawg's cock was so hard, so fully engorged it was painful. Each brush of her nipples against his chest had him flexing, his body raging to take control of the sex play and to bury his dick as deep inside her as he could get.

"You're riding the line, fancy-face," he growled as her lips pulled back, the curtain of her hair embracing them in an intimate world all their own.

Crista felt Dawg's wrists flex beneath her hand and glimpsed the powerful muscles of his biceps as they rippled.

"I'm not riding anything yet, Dawg," she reminded him teasingly, her head lowering so her tongue could lick at the powerful cords of his neck.

Her hands smoothed along his arms as she braced herself on her knees on each side of a powerful thigh. His cock pressed against her hip, his hard chest stroked her nipples with each breath. And beneath the lace of her panties her pussy was creaming furiously.

"Keep it up, and you're going to be riding more than you should be handling for another few hours," he warned her tightly, his hips flexing beneath her, pushing his cock more firmly against her hip.

The heavy male thigh she straddled shifted as well, bringing a gasp to her lips and a surge of sensation to the swollen clit it pressed against.

"Other ways," she whimpered. There were ways she was dying to try. Long-dreamed-of acts she needed to experience with him.

"Other ways." His voice was filled with challenge. "Better get started on those 'other ways,' fancy-face. I'm a dying man here."

He was sexy as hell, too. Stretched out on the overlarge picnic blanket, his eerie green eyes gleamed back at her from behind lowered lashes.

Crista lowered her head again, her lips and tongue finding a flat, hard, male nipple and working it in her mouth. A muted groan came from his chest. His arms moved as though to reach for her.

"Stay for me." She pressed his arms back to the checked cloth. "Just a little longer, Dawg. Let me have this."

She needed it. Needed him. Needed to taste and explore and fill her senses with him.

"Crista, sweetheart, you're killing me here." He was breathing rough and heavy, but his arms stayed in place as her lips moved to the opposite nipple and tormented the pebble-hard flesh.

Giving it a final lick, she moved lower. Her hands stroked his heavy thighs, inside and out. Her lips kissed, her tongue licked a sensual, meandering path down his chest and firm abdomen.

Hard muscles flexed beneath her lips. His thighs bunched; the thickly crested head of his cock gleamed with moisture as her fingers finally gripped the stiff shaft.

Crista knelt between his thighs and stared up at his body, tracking the damp flesh and finally meeting his narrowed gaze.

"I get to have dessert first," she said with a slow smile.

Her head lowered, her tongue licked over the straining crest, curling over it as a low, hungry growl rumbled in his throat.

"Sweet Crista," he groaned. "That sweet little tongue is like fire."

Dawg's hands knotted in the cloth beneath him. He was dying. Stretched out on a rack of sensation that had sweat building along his body and his balls tight with anticipation.

He watched as she smiled again. A drowsy, sexy little smile a second before her lips opened and she took the pounding head of his dick into her tight mouth, sucking it slow and easy. Her fingers caressed and stroked, tortured and tempted, until his hips were thrusting into her grip, fucking her lips as the heat built around them.

"Come here." He reached for her. He'd be damned if he would take the torment alone. "Turn around here, darlin'."

Her lips never left his cock. But her body turned and sweet, lace-covered flesh came closer to his hungry lips. For the first time in his sexual life, Dawg found himself without patience, without careful deliberation.

One hand gripped her leg, lifting it over his head before both hands gripped her hips. Fingers gripped the lace and drew it slowly from the newly waxed flesh between her thighs. Dawg stared up at the bare folds, luscious pink and gleaming with her juices. Sweet, soft little droplets hugged her flesh and had him licking his lips in anticipation.

"Oh yeah." He sighed, pulling her closer. "Come here, baby, let me show you how good it can be now."

It was one of the sexiest things she had ever envisioned.

Crista caught her breath as Dawg licked over the saturated folds between her thighs. The protective curls that had once covered her there were gone, and the sensations were enough to make a woman insane.

There was nothing now to insulate her from the rasp of his tongue or the soft licks he bestowed upon her. His caresses only made her hotter, only made the need rising inside her bloom to desperation. To greed.

He licked and sucked with gentle movements, never abrading the sensitive folds but soothing them, whispering over them, consuming them as her mouth sucked greedily at the head of his cock. She was determined to make him just as desperate for satisfaction as she was becoming.

She swore the breeze whipping around them was spiked with fire now. Dawg held her hips easily, controlling her frantic need for movement against his mouth. His tongue burrowed through her slit, licked and moved to curl around her clit.

He stroked, sucked, and lashed at the fiery little nubbin with hungry licks and greedy suckling lips until the inferno inside her began to blaze out of control.

Strong fingers separated her rear cheeks and caressed the narrow cleft there.

Breathing was impulse; the cries that tore from her throat as she sucked Dawg's cock were involuntary. All she knew was the heat racing through her veins, the flames licking over her flesh, and the ache building with each lick of his tongue between her thighs.

The taste of male passion and heated flesh filled her senses. The feel of his tongue rasping, thrusting, and licking overwhelmed her.

Nothing mattered now but the pleasure. Her pleasure. His pleasure. The race to release and the need for completion. It was like a fever in her blood, that need that consumed and overwhelmed everything else.

Her fingers stroked and pumped the stiff flesh of his cock. She sucked at the throbbing head. Her tongue lashed and stroked and tasted the heated male passion, while his tongue drove her to distraction. Stroking and thrusting and fucking inside her as his fingers caressed and pressed against the tender opening between her rear cheeks.

She was swamped with pleasure. Taken by it. Her hips writhed above him as he held her to him, thrusting against his tongue and driving it deeper into the aching core he possessed.

Her cries and his groans filled the clearing.

His fingers pierced her ass and her pussy simultaneously. His lips surrounded her clit, drew it in and sucked it with wicked force.

Crista cupped the fingers of one hand around his balls, fondled and caressed as the other hand stroked the steel-hard shaft and her mouth sucked the head with hungry greed.

His fingers pumped inside her, fucking her with strokes that, combined with the heated suckling of his mouth around her clit, threw her into an orgasm that would have had her screaming, should have had her screaming. But Dawg's release had him arching, pressing his cock deeper into her mouth and filling it with the creamy essence of his semen.

They collapsed long seconds later, Crista's head pillowed on Dawg's thigh as he turned to her, his lips pressing into the inside of her knee as they fought for breath.

"I won't let you go," he finally told her, his voice dangerously calm, stunning her as the words reached her ears. "No matter what you do, Crista, I'll never let you go again."

EIGHTEEN

He remembered.

As he felt Crista's orgasm shaking her body, the memories washed over him like a wave of crashing emotion. How she had found him in that damned ditch, the truck he had been driving then so damned stuck his liquored mind couldn't figure out how to get it free.

Her voice had been soft, filled with pain, and it had soothed the ragged edges of fury tearing at his mind. He had let her lead him from the truck to Alex's car, and as she drove them to the marina, the scent of her had wrapped around him like sunlight.

He had made her laugh.

He leaned close to her and said something about Alex letting her out to play with the big boys, and she had laughed at that.

Once they got to the marina, she had kept him from falling from the docks into the dark water below. Leading him to the *Nauti Dawg*, she kept up a steady, whispered conversation. Teasing, her voice urged him on and made his dick so damned hard he had been amazed. He'd thought he'd drunk enough whiskey that night to keep from getting a hard-on for days.

But he had been hard for Crista.

And once he got her into the houseboat, getting her into his bed hadn't been that hard. She had wanted to make certain he was safe. That he was comfortable.

He had fallen back on the couch, and she eased his boots and shirt off. As he struggled with his pants, she helped there, too, even as she blushed to her virgin roots. And as she began to move away from him, he had cupped his hand around her head and had drawn her lips to his.

From that moment she had been his. His in a way that no other woman had been. She had taken to his touch as though she had been created for him alone. And perhaps, in a way, she had been.

Now, eight years later and nearly two hours after the memory had seared his mind, he walked behind her, back to the houseboat, the still-full picnic basket in his hand and Crista's stiff shoulders in front of him.

She had clammed up the minute he had made his declaration.

"We need to talk," she had stated as she rose from beside him and began looking for her clothes.

"So talk." Dawg had sat up, draped his arm over his upraised knee, and watched her struggle into her clothes.

She had shaken her head angrily. "Not here. I can't do this here."

And now, he was more than interested in whatever the hell had her so damned mad.

He had fucked up eight years ago; he admitted it. But not to the extent she thought he had. Half-formed thoughts had slipped past his lips, unfinished. The possessiveness he had felt rising inside him then had shocked him, left him reeling and off balance.

Now, eight years later, he was reasonably more mature, but he still felt like he was in over his head with Crista Ann Jansen.

As they stepped onto the deck of the *Nauti Dawg*, Dawg unlocked the door and ushered her in as he lifted his brow at her continued silence.

She had barely spoken in the truck. The closer they had come to the marina, the quieter she had become.

"Here we are." He placed the basket on the table and turned to face her, crossing his arms over his chest and tilting his head.

Her gaze flickered around the room before coming to rest on him. Her lips parted, and at the same second, a hard knock sounded on the glass door behind her.

Crista jumped as though a gunshot had sounded rather than the sound of knuckles against glass.

"Who is it?" he barked out.

"Dawg, I have Cranston with me. Open the damned door." Natches's voice was anything but happy.

Pressing his lips together, Dawg stalked to the door and whipped the panels to the blinds back to see Cranston's stocky form standing behind Natches.

Grimacing, he opened the door again, watching from the corner of his eye as Crista turned to the visitors with an edge of curiosity.

Timothy Cranston stepped into the room, his briefcase clenched in his hand, his gaze going straight to Crista. Dawg closed the door, watching as the special agent watched her with an intensity that had a frown pulling at his brow and Crista's.

"What's going on, Natches?" Dawg didn't bother to soften the suspicious tone of his voice.

"You're not going to believe this, Dawg." Natches's smile was cynical, cold. "I've had a few hours to digest it, and I still don't believe it."

"Cranston?"

The special agent was still watching Crista, his gaze narrowed on her as she stared right back at him, a challenge glittering in her brown eyes.

"She's about the right height. Right eye color, right hair. But I'll be damned if you're not right about the differences."

Dawg felt his body tense as Cranston walked slowly around Crista then.

"Did you turn your boat into a auction block, Dawg?" Crista snapped irritably as the agent tracked every curve and hollow in her body.

"There's a difference in the curves. You were right there, too," he muttered.

"Natches," Dawg bit out warningly. "What the hell is going on?"

Dawg could feel the warning tingle in his gut, the itching at the back of his neck. The way Cranston was watching Crista was getting his hackles up and pissing him off. And it wasn't doing much for her, either. She flashed him a hard look, a warning to do something about the bulldoggish little man who kept watching her like a strange little puzzle he was trying to figure out.

"You're not going to believe it." Natches shook his head. "I'm still not certain I believe it."

"Why not explain it and give us the chance to believe it, Natches," Crista retorted with mocking sweetness as she edged away from Cranston and moved closer to Dawg.

It was the first move she had made toward him since their time in the clearing. Crossing the last few feet to her, Dawg wrapped his arm around her waist and pulled her to him, ignoring Cranston's sardonic look and Natches's quiet reflection.

He could feel Crista's fear in the face of Cranston, though. She knew who he was; she knew the danger he could represent to her. A danger Dawg swore he was never going to let touch her.

"Does this have anything to do with Agent Dane attempting to follow us earlier?" Dawg asked.

"Plenty." Cranston's bright brown eyes gleamed merrily as he ran his fingers over his short gray hair and flashed them a victorious smile.

Victorious. As though a battle had just been won.

"You going to explain it to us anytime soon?" Evidently, there wasn't a pending arrest in the works. Cranston wouldn't have made the mistake of trying to bring in Dawg's woman without help.

Timothy grinned cheerfully. "You know, my wife, Angie, she's always telling me I need to get to the point faster. But sometimes . . ." He stared back at them with a scary sort of playfulness. "Sometimes, you just have to have fun getting there, don't you Dawg?"

Dawg glanced at Natches. His cousin had lowered his head and was shaking it pitifully at Cranston's theatrics.

"Dawg, who is this person?" Crista finally asked.

She should have stayed quiet, he thought with a silent groan.

"That's right." Timothy stepped forward, his palm outstretched. "We haven't met, have we, Miss Jansen. I'm Timothy Cranston, Special Agent Timothy Cranston, with the Office of Homeland Security. I'm Mr. Mackay's boss."

"Homeland Security?" She looked up at Dawg, moving slightly away from him. "I thought you were with the DEA."

Cranston chuckled at that. "Oh, my, no. Your friend Dawg is with the ATF, though attached temporarily to OHS. He didn't tell you that?"

Crista let Timothy shake her hand, but she was watching Dawg, her expression tightening in anger.

"He didn't mention that."

"That's Dawg for you." Timothy nodded as he stepped back. "He's good at keeping secrets, aren't you, Dawg?"

Dawg sighed. "Get to the point, Timothy."

Cranston rubbed his hands together in anticipation once again.

"Now, what Dawg probably didn't tell you as well was that the night he broke several federal laws and dragged your pretty butt out of that warehouse, we were in the process of arresting a small team of former military assholes who thought they could hijack several experimental missiles while en route to Fort Knox before continuing on their way to a storage site. We managed to round up the thieves as well as one very sly little mercenary middleman who was buying those missiles for a high-level terrorist." He looked at Crista with sudden sharp curiosity. "He didn't tell you that, did he?"

"He didn't." Crista moved farther away from Dawg.

Timothy nodded in satisfaction as he flashed Dawg an approving look. "I'm disappointed in you, son, but glad to see you still know how to keep your mouth shut."

"Timothy." Dawg wasn't happy, and he wasn't pretending.

Crista had put several feet between them and was now watching Dawg and Timothy as though they had sprouted horns and fangs.

"Okay, here we go then." Dawg watched as Timothy tossed his briefcase to the table and rubbed his hands in that gleeful manner he had. The man was positively bubbling with satisfaction. It was enough to send a chill racing down Dawg's spine.

Timothy was no one's vision of a special agent in charge of any investigation, but that was exactly what he was, and he was damned good at his job.

"Yesterday afternoon, after your good friend and cousin here was regaling the customers in that little diner in town about how your girlfriend stalked out on you, and possibly was on her way to Virginia, she supposedly walked into the detention center where our hijackers are being held and requested a visit with the leader of our merry little bunch of thieves, Camden Cole. Our boy Camden lives just outside Fort Knox. Someone checking in as Miss Jansen here met with Mr. Cole, discussed friends and family for a few minutes, gave Mr. Cole her love, then left."

Timothy opened the briefcase and began pulling photos free.

"Meet Camden Cole."

Crista moved closer to the table, her eyes locked on the picture of the stern older man. Hazel eyes stared back with cool detachment in a face as unemotional as a robot.

"I know him." She was shocked that she did know him. "He worked for the electric company. He was at the house just after my parents died. Alex had requested a new meter be installed."

"Bingo." Special Agent Cranston beamed at her as though she had answered a particularly difficult question. "That was just a few years ago, wasn't it?"

Crista nodded slowly as Dawg stared at her in surprise. He had been unaware that she had been in town at that time, she had made certain of it.

"Alex asked me to come in and take care of a few things while he was out of the country."

"So, yesterday, while Miss Jansen was supposedly on her way to Virginia, she shows up at the detention center." Another picture slapped down in front of her, causing Crista to freeze in shock.

"That's not me!" But it looked like her. The hair, the profile, even the clothes.

"So Natches spent a considerable amount of time informing me after Dawg got my agent lost in the mountains this
afternoon."

Crista stared back at him as she felt fear beginning to
build inside her. "I was with Dawg yesterday. All day."

"And Natches was in town spreading tales of your deser-
tion." He shook his head sadly and cast Natches a chiding
look filled with mockery.

"Sometimes you have to tell a few lies to get to the truth."
Natches's smile lacked any humor.

"We were in the office after we found the attempted
break-in," Dawg reported. "I kept her up there until well after
closing."

"Yeah, Natches was telling the customers about that
one, too." Cranston nodded. "He hinted you blamed her for
the break-in?"

Dawg grunted as Crista stepped back and stared at the three
men.

"Who is in the picture?" she asked.

"Looks like you." Cranston gazed back at her blandly.

The patently false look of innocence would have been
amusing at any other time.

"Crista, look closely at the rest of the photos," Natches
said softly.

Crista moved back to the table as Cranston laid out half a
dozen glossy color and black-and-white photos. There were
none that showed the woman's face clearly. Most were in
profile, and all looked remarkably like her.

"I have clothes just like these," she whispered shakily, feeling Dawg move closer to her, his hand settling comfortingly
at her back.

The neat, almost businesslike outfits were identical to
those hanging in her bedroom closet.

"Agent Dane checked your home and confirmed that
these same clothes were hanging in your closet." Cranston
nodded.

"You were in my home?" She stared back at him in shock.
"Without a warrant?"

"Honey, it's a criminal investigation; of course we searched the house with warrant in hand. The clothes are now in custody and on their way to the lab for tests."

"What kind of tests?" Shock filled her voice now, not just her mind.

"DNA tests, little girl." Cranston frowned. "We're looking for DNA other than yours. Criminals don't always think about the many ways DNA can be found. A stray hair, sweat, sometimes blood from something as innocent as a scratch. We're hoping our boy here left something."

"Boy?" Dawg latched onto that word before Crista could make sense of it.

"Natches caught it." Timothy shook his head. "Right here."

He pulled one of the pictures free and handed it to Dawg.

Crista stared at the picture. It was a full frontal shot, though whoever was posing as her had turned their head to the side, allowing hair identical to Crista's to cover their face.

It took a minute, but she saw it. She blinked, certain she wasn't seeing clearly. The breasts were covered in the soft, chocolate brown silk of the blouse the other woman was wearing, draped over the mounds that were approximately the size of Crista's. But with one difference. In this picture the soft material of the blouse had gaped where a button had come undone and revealed a very hairy portion of flesh beneath the breast.

Crista blinked and looked again. Male chest hair?

"We went over the other pictures once Natches caught that," Cranston said. "And he found a few other anomalies. Such as this."

The next picture had a red-marked circle around a dark spot on a smooth, creamy, hairless arm that appeared female.

"This picture was taken by another agent in France, where our young person here met with Akron Svengaurrd, the mercenary that brokered the deal on the missiles."

Once again, there were no facial features, but Crista focused on the red circle that pointed out a blemish of some sort.

"I'll be damned," Dawg muttered, his voice suddenly heavy, bitter. "I can't believe it."

"He disappeared just after the missiles were stolen," Natches said then. "Remember? We wondered where the hell he had gone? He also knew Cole, he worked for Cole's father for a while on their farm near Frankfort. We cleared him on the investigation here because the connections were all superficial. Hell, Cole had a lot of acquaintances here in Somerset."

Crista stared hard at the picture, certain she was missing something. Then she saw it, remembered it. A small blemish, more a birthmark, on a friend's wrist.

"Johnny," she whispered, seeing the familiarity in the curve of his face then, in the way he stood, even dressed as he was in her clothes. "It's Johnny Grace."

"He visited the detention center deliberately," Natches said then. "To implicate Crista. Every move he's made has been made to implicate her, to distract Dawg, and possibly me as well. He had to cover himself, and this was the best way to do it. He thought you and Crista had argued, and she was heading to Virginia. The detention center is on the way, a short little detour that she could have reasonably made. Bam, she's arrested, bad guys think she has the money, good guys crucify her. And Johnny was damned good; those fucking mercenaries really thought he was a she. They would have killed Crista first chance they had to arrange it."

Behind her, Dawg was dangerously silent. Crista swore she could feel the fury whipping through the room now, from Dawg as well as Natches.

"He made friends with Crista first thing when she returned, because he knew her history with Dawg, and he knew Dawg's fascination with her. He was one of the few people that could have known what happened when she left eight years ago," Natches bit out.

"Yeah. He worked at the clinic when Crista had the miscarriage. An orderly or something," Cranston added.

Crista felt her world crash around her then.

The silence in the room suddenly became heavy, tense, and filled with danger. She didn't dare look at Dawg; she couldn't. She could barely breathe, could barely form a thought.

"Cranston, I'm going to murder you." Natches sighed then. "We had an agreement."

Cranston's gaze was going between Dawg and Crista then.

"Agreements are for men I can trust, Natches," he said mockingly. "You two broke trust with me in your attempts to hide Miss Jansen's presence at that warehouse. Consider this your slap on the wrist."

NINETEEN

Something was breaking apart inside Dawg. He could feel it. He fought it, he tried to force the pieces of his soul back into shape, but they continued to break away, piece by piece, destroying him in the process.

Cranston was a smart man. Once he glimpsed Dawg's expression, he excused himself and left. Quickly. It would have been laughable if it weren't for the fact that everything inside Dawg was silently howling.

And she hadn't said a word. Not a word. Even after Natches left, she stared at the carpet and avoided his gaze.

Dawg wasn't a man prone to tears. He hadn't cried since he was five, but at this moment, he wished he hadn't forgotten how to shed tears.

Because he wanted to shed tears. For his child, for what had been lost before it had even been born. For the woman who had fled the pain, and the man who hadn't had a clue the pain he had inflicted in one night of pleasure.

It had been a son. She had been carrying his son, and for some reason, some quirk of nature, it had been taken from her. Sweet God! Had been taken from them both.

The file held the facts on more than the miscarriage. It was her life for eight fucking years.

Every move she had made in the past eight years was there, as well as her living arrangements with the two men in Virginia and their sexual orientation.

They were homosexual. The two men were lovers, and Crista, from all accounts, rather than being a third to the little love nest, had been treated more as a little sister. A sister that needed protecting, to be cared for.

Neighbors had been questioned regarding Crista, as had her former boss. Everyone had given her glowing recommendations and stressed how dependable, reliable, and kind she was.

One elderly lady had told the agent, posing as a prospective employer, that Crista Jansen was a wounded little bird when she first arrived with Mark Lessing and moved into his apartment. Cranston had related that piece of information with curious satisfaction.

As he read, grief swelled in his chest with each word and the implications of what he had done to her. Agony pierced his heart, his soul, and ripped through his mind.

Crista had run from him, lost their child, then left town, barely healed from the miscarriage. She had immediately enrolled in business school. She had dated rarely, never seriously, and photos of those men were included in the file. An accountant, a banker, the vice president of a manufacturing firm. All three men were suave, sophisticated, and about as dangerous or sexual as a neutered house cat.

Crista had worked hard, played rarely. She had volunteered several weekends a month at a local hospital in the pediatrics ward, and everyone loved her.

And she had been alone. She had left Somerset after losing his baby. After he had taken her with drunken lust and committed the unbearable sin of having forgotten that night. Except in his dreams. Dreams where she had tempted him, tormented him. Loved him.

No wonder he hadn't forgotten about her. No wonder he had dreamed of her for eight long years and with her return had focused on her with something bordering on obsession.

And it was no wonder she had refused every advance. No wonder she had avoided him every chance she had. She should have shot him. He was amazed Alex hadn't done the job for her.

"Did you want the baby?" His baby. His child. Grief nearly ripped his guts from his body at the thought of that child that had never drawn breath.

"More than my own life." Her voice was harsh, thick with unshed tears as his own throat closed against the pain.

"You could have told me." He would have claimed her, claimed their baby. He would have held her, protected her, shared her grief.

"I was too young for you." Pain haunted her voice and his soul. "I didn't run because of the miscarriage, or because of the threat of Rowdy and Natches. I could have handled informing you that wasn't going to happen. But I couldn't handle what you made me feel that night."

Dawg lifted his eyes from the folder, and he wanted to howl at the pain he saw in her eyes.

"You loved me, even then." He knew it, knew it in his soul, and that knowledge was killing him. She had loved him, endured this alone, and he hadn't even remembered the night that had created their child.

"I loved you," she whispered. "I've always loved you, Dawg. But what happened between us . . ." Her hand lifted, then dropped helplessly. "What you made me feel. I couldn't handle it. I craved it. I cried for you for months after I left, but I couldn't come back."

"Why?" His voice was stark, chilling.

"I told myself it was because of Rowdy and Natches. I told myself I couldn't handle having my heart broken when you refused to give up that lifestyle, but when I returned last year and saw you the first time, I knew better. I couldn't come back because I knew you would end up owning my soul. And if that happened, I wouldn't be able to just walk away. I'd hate it. I'd end up destroying myself over it, but if you had pressed, I knew I couldn't have refused anything you wanted."

Facing that fact had been the hardest part of the last few days, and Crista knew it. Knowing that in her heart she had wasted eight years of her own life running from herself hadn't been easy.

"Were you relieved you had the miscarriage, Crista?" he asked, his voice bleak, shattered.

She hadn't expected that question from him. She had expected recriminations, a suspicion that she had deliberately gotten pregnant, but she hadn't expected this.

"I nearly died, Dawg," she cried hoarsely. "I wanted to die."

His head lifted from the file, his expression so stark, so furiously intent, that she felt her chest tighten with pain.

"Why did you want that baby so bad, Crista?" he asked her then.

Suspicion. She heard it in his voice, but all she saw in his face was the same expression she had seen the night she found him drunk, his truck in a ditch and his drunken bitterness pouring from his voice as he cursed his parents.

"Because it was our baby," she answered simply, tearfully. "A part of you and a part of everything I felt for you. And it was innocent, Dawg. No matter how frightened I was, or what you wanted, it wasn't our baby's fault."

Sweet God, his eyes were wet, so dark now, haunted and rife with agony as he stared back at her.

"Would you have told me about our baby?"

How to answer that one? She felt like a criminal on trial now, and Dawg was her judge and jury. The way he watched her terrified her.

"No." She wasn't going to lie to him, not now. "But Alex would have. He was already set to tell you when I miscarried. I was—" She bit her lip as she glanced away for long seconds. "I was too scared, Dawg. I don't know if I could have survived your denial of our child. You didn't even remember the night we spent together. I knew you didn't. You would have never believed I was carrying your baby."

He stared down at the file, closing it slowly and pushing it away. The heaviness in his expression broke her heart. His brows were lowered, his features tight with the grief she had felt the minute she realized she was losing his child.

"I would have believed you," he finally said, his voice rough, harsh, as he lifted his head and stared back at her, his green eyes dark with sorrow. "Don't you know, Crista? I would have used any excuse to claim you."

She had to turn away from him. Her hand pressed to her

lips as pain tore through her chest. She couldn't breathe, she couldn't stop the tears that flooded her eyes. She had to hide from what she saw in his eyes then. The shutters were removed, the distance he always forced on himself was stripped away, and the loneliness and the pain glittered in the light green orbs.

And she couldn't face it. She couldn't face the fact that she had added to it.

A second later his arms were wrapping around her, pulling her against his chest, surrounding her with a warmth that she had only known when she was in his arms.

"I would have destroyed us both," she whispered tearfully, her hands gripping his hard forearms as her head lowered. "I would have made us miserable."

"Shh. Don't, Crista," he whispered against her ear. "Don't blame yourself. We both grew up, baby. But the thought of you going through that alone. Carrying my child, losing it." One hand lifted to her face as he turned her, his opposite arm wrapping around her and holding her to him as he wiped the tears from beneath one eye. "It tears me apart."

Crista tried to shake her head.

"Don't." He stopped her, sighing heavily as his forehead rested against hers. "You've been scared to even tell me, Crista. You've held back, you've let yourself hurt and not even considered telling me, haven't you?"

"I was going to tell you when we got back here." She swallowed tightly. "I couldn't hold back any longer, Dawg. Loving you terrified me, until I awoke in your arms and realized I've always loved you. And I've been dying inside without you all these years. Never knowing, always wondering what if. The wondering was killing me. Being without you was breaking my heart more every year."

She stared into his eyes, and they broke her heart. His expression was twisted into lines of grief, his brows heavy with the internal pain she could glimpse in his eyes.

"I won't let you go, Crista," he whispered then. "Not now, not ever. We're going to get through this investigation, find out what the hell Johnny is pulling, and then we're going to figure this relationship out. Just you and me."

"I should have told you." She reached up, cupped his

cheek, and ached at the pain in his face. "I shouldn't have run from you, Dawg."

She admitted that now, though it was something she had known, even then. Running away from him hadn't been the answer. Running away from herself had, in ways, been even worse.

"No more running," he told her softly, gently, his lips lowering to hers, taking them in a kiss that had her breath hitching in her chest.

The sheer gentleness rocked her mind. The way his head tilted, the lingering emotion and banked passion seemed to sink into her soul and leave her fighting for breath in a way that the raw lust never had.

When he pulled back, grief creased his expression and sheened his eyes as well as lust. Lust and hunger and need so powerful now it stole her breath.

"If I start now, we won't stop. Let's see about our lunch, sweetheart, figure some of this out, and later . . ." His eyes were heartbreaking. Filled with pain and need. "Later, we'll pick this up."

Crista inhaled roughly and tried to pull her thoughts back into some semblance of order. She tried to give him the time he needed, and she knew he needed time. She could see it in his face, in his bleak gaze.

"I can't believe Johnny is involved in this." She shook her head, wondering how many more times Dawg could handle the betrayals from the family that should have stood by him.

He had Rowdy and Natches and Rowdy's father, Ray, but Crista had seen how alone he was other than those three. He had few friends; he trusted no one but the cousins he had grown up with and the one uncle who had stood by him.

And no one held him.

"Oh, I could believe just about anything out of Johnny," Dawg bit out, slowly drawing away from her and heading back to the table where the picnic basket still sat. "He's definitely his mother's son."

Dawg's heart was breaking for the things they had both lost because of his ignorance—for his child, for the woman he loved before he knew what love was. He wasn't that same immature man any longer. He had been too damned rock dumb to go after what he wanted, even though he had sensed what Crista would mean to his future. He wasn't dumb anymore.

"Why would he do this, though?" Crista set the basket on the far end of the bar before moving into the kitchen and pulling ice from the freezer for the tea that had been packed with the food. "He's your cousin. When I left Somerset, Johnny followed after the three of you like a shadow."

Dawg shook his head. "Johnny followed us like a shadow to see how much trouble he could brew up. We knew he was gay even then, and he was terrified we'd tell on him. Not that we cared either way; it was his damned troublemaking we couldn't stand. His and his mother's."

Crista frowned heavily as she filled the glasses with ice.

"I always remember how nice Johnny was." She bit her lip as she lifted her gaze to him, and Dawg wondered if he had ever seen that look in anyone else's eyes. It wasn't pity; it was compassion and anger for him. She was angry on his behalf, because she loved him. Even now, after everything he had done to her.

His chest clenched at the thought. She had even said the words, and this time, it wasn't just a hazy memory. She loved him, and he'd be damned if he was going to spend precious time distrusting her.

No, she wasn't part of the Trinity, but she was a gift from God himself. The days he had spent with her, despite the problems that had arisen, had been freer, happier than any he might have known in his life.

"Johnny's a deceptive little bastard. He likes to draw you in, and every second that he's playing the concerned buddy and dear friend, he's looking for ways to slash your throat. He learned the art at his mother's knee, and after the death of his father, she had free rein to reinforce the lessons."

"His father, Ralph, was one of my dad's few friends." Crista's lips tilted sadly. "Mom hated Nadine, though. She hated to even see her come into the store."

Dawg nodded in response. "Everyone liked Ralph. If he had lived, he would have divorced Nadine eventually, but maybe Johnny would have had a chance."

"How do you think he got mixed up in this thing with the

missiles?" She frowned then. "And don't think you're not going to pay for lying to me about drugs."

"I never said it was drugs, Crista Ann; you assumed." He sighed.

"You could have corrected my assumption."

His grin was still tinted with the grief that lingered in his gaze, but at least a measure of amusement tipped it now, Crista thought.

"Johnny makes a habit of making friends with military types," he told her. "They feel sorry for him at first, until they realize it's lust and not hero worship he's displaying. Somehow, he finally hooked up with someone dumb enough to get pulled into one of his schemes or let out the information, and he used it. Either way, as soon as Natches and Cranston have the information together and a warrant, he'll no longer be a threat."

She paused, staring back at him as disbelief slammed inside her head.

"What are you talking about? Aren't they arresting him now?"

"Not without enough proof. We don't have enough yet." Dawg set plates on the table as she continued to stare at him in horror.

"But it was him. We all recognized him, Dawg."

He shook his head, his expression weary, bitter. "Doesn't matter, Crista. Any decent defense lawyer would have him out of jail within an hour and a lawsuit against the arresting agents not long afterward. We need proof, not the testimony of two cousins who have every reason in the world to want to crucify him."

The bitterness in his voice wasn't one of hatred but one of disillusionment.

"I'm sorry." She fought to rein back her anger. "Family should stick together, not try to destroy each other."

She couldn't have survived childhood without Alex. Her brother had been her rock, her anchor, and later, her best friend. She couldn't imagine having him hate her enough to try to destroy her or anyone she loved.

"Yeah well, that's in a perfect world, sweetheart." He shook his head as though shaking away his own regrets, then flashed her a smile that was at once teasing and filled with hunger. "Let's eat our lunch. We're hanging around the marina for the rest of the day, until Natches gets back to us. Once we've decided what to do, things will move fast enough. Let's enjoy the quiet time we have for a while."

As he said that, a knock sounded at the door.

Crista's lips twitched as she glimpsed three shadows, two taller, the other petite and delicate.

"Hell!" Dawg pushed his fingers through his hair and stalked to the door.

Ray Mackay, Rowdy, and Kelly were waiting on the other side. Kelly was concerned, but Ray and Rowdy were pissed off.

"God bless Ralph Grace's soul." Ray shook his head as Dawg closed the door behind him. "He's turning over in his grave."

"Easy, Uncle Ray. We'll get things worked out."

Crista heard the tone Dawg used and wondered at it. He was comforting his uncle rather than accepting any comfort.

"I'll work it out," Ray snapped. "With the business end of my rifle. You think you're the only Mackay who knows how to shoot a gun?"

"Dad." Rowdy glanced at Dawg, and Crista saw the worry in his eyes. "Let's see what we can do to help rather than shed blood here."

"Seems like shedding blood would be the best help." Ray grimaced, though he moved to his nephew, slapped his shoulder in that gesture of male camaraderie, and shook his head in disgust. "Dawg, son, one of these days, you're going to have to learn: give those damned people an inch, and they take a mile. I can't even convince Natches of that, not all the way down. You thought they'd back off when you let that land go. I told you Johnny would never stop."

Bitterness pierced Ray Mackay's voice as well, and Crista began to glimpse the family dynamics that were rife with pain and anger.

"I'll get the land back when they arrest Johnny, Uncle Ray. My lawyer will make certain of it."

Crista watched, confused, as Kelly walked over to her and leaned against the bar beside her.

"Johnny's mother managed to win over half the property in Dawg's father's estate," she told Crista softly, obviously seeing the confusion in her face. "It was a prime piece of property and borders the land Dawg bought to build the house on. She and Johnny have gloated over it ever since. Just as Dawg gloats over the fact that he owns the rest of that valley and they have no idea who bought it out from under them."

"This is insane," Crista muttered. "How could they steal his inheritance? Didn't his parents have a will?"

"A will Nadine protested based on several letters Dawg's father sent to her stating that Dawg didn't deserve it, and how he wished Johnny had been his son as well. They read those letters in the courtroom. I was there when it happened. I swear, Crista, you could see something break inside of Dawg then. For years, there was so little softness inside him that he would have terrified you."

It terrified her now. It would have destroyed most men.

"Johnny's a dead man walking," Kelly said then, her voice steady, saddened. "Rowdy, Ray, or Dawg won't touch him, but Natches . . ." She turned and looked Crista in the eye, her own gaze heavy with remorse and fear. "Natches will kill him. He's closer to Dawg than he is to anyone else. He won't let this go."

And that would destroy Dawg.

Crista stared at the three men as they moved into the kitchen, and she could hear the worry in Ray's voice as he asked about Natches.

"He'll be fine, Uncle Ray." Dawg was assuring his uncle, but Crista could hear the worry in his voice, too.

"You know he didn't start building that house until you moved back to Somerset, don't you, Crista?" Kelly asked then.

Crista stared back at her in surprise.

The other woman's face was reflective, her gaze assessing.

"I hope you love him as much as I think you do, and that doesn't even compare to how much I know Dawg loves you. Don't betray him." Kelly's voice hardened then. "Betray him, and you'll make some very bad enemies."

It was a warning, and one Crista took no offense to. She shook her head as a smile tipped her lips.

"Kelly, I'd die first," she said softly. "I didn't wait eight years to grow up and come back to him, just to betray him. You can forget the warnings, because they're not needed."

A bright smile tipped Kelly's lips then, and a hint of teasing laughter filled her eyes.

"We're going to be great friends then," the other woman declared. "After all, we need each other to talk trash on them. Trust me, you'll have days you'll swear you should have shot him rather than loved him, but it all balances out good. Rowdy and Dawg are too much alike. There are days I swear I'm going to shoot Rowdy, but I know I could never live without him, so I resign myself to dealing with it."

Crista let her gaze linger on Dawg again. He stood with Rowdy and Ray at the other end of the kitchen. They were talking in low voices as they fortified themselves with the beers Dawg had taken from the refrigerator.

His eyes met hers, and the corners of his lips tipped into an encouraging smile as he nodded at something Ray said.

"Dawg's different with you, Crista," Kelly said then. "Calmer. Not as prone to stand distant and apart from the others. He was doing that before you returned. Slowly drawing away from Rowdy. It was breaking Rowdy's heart."

As she watched Dawg, she could understand why he would have been drawing away. Rowdy had a father who loved him, a family, and a woman to fill his heart. Dawg understood what he was lacking in his own life, just as Crista had always known what was lacking in hers.

"Rowdy was loved," Crista murmured then. "He had something Dawg knew he needed as well."

Kelly glanced at Dawg, then back to Crista as she nodded slowly.

"The change didn't come after he blackmailed you. It came with your return. Dawg knew what he was missing, and he thought he'd never find it. When you came back, the part of him that knew how to love reawakened, Crista. Don't doubt that. And don't doubt for one minute that he would give his soul to protect you."

As she would give hers. No. She amended that. She no longer had a soul separate from Dawg's. It was melded with his and had been for over eight years.

"Let's get more plates and get them fed," Crista said then, calculating the amount of food sitting on the table and how far it would go. It should just stretch.

"Good idea. Food usually settles Rowdy's bloodthirsty instincts." Kelly sighed. "He's ready to help Ray kill Johnny."

He wasn't the only one.

As they gathered around the table, Crista continued to watch the three men, drawing in impressions and letting the final pieces of the puzzle that represented Dawg fall into place.

His bond with Rowdy and Ray extended to Kelly, but there was no lust, no hint of desire, when he looked at the other woman. Crista saw friendship, affection, but nothing more. As she watched, she realized that one of her greatest fears had been that of seeing Dawg stare at Kelly with arousal.

She knew the games he had played in the past with his cousins and found it hard to believe they could step away from it so easily. Even for love.

But it appeared that at least Dawg and Rowdy had done just that. Crista wasn't uncomfortable when Rowdy looked at her; she saw no interest other than the casual interest that would have been expected.

Dawg teased Kelly, laughed with her, but he didn't desire her.

Watching the interplay made her realize exactly what she had missed in the years she had been away, but they weren't years she would regret. She had matured, grown up, learned something of herself and of the world around her. Enough to know where home was and who her heart belonged to.

Dawg belonged to her. She felt it, where she had feared it before. Just as she belonged to him.

"What do you think, Crista?" Dawg's voice drew her back from her thoughts and had her staring back at him. She blinked and refocused to see the heat stirring in his light green eyes and the heavy interest in his expression as he watched her.

"About what?" she asked.

"About taking tomorrow morning to head into town for some fresh baked goods. After all, as far as Johnny knows, none of us know what the hell he's up to. How do you feel about shaking him up a little bit?"

She stared at the three men and one woman watching her expectantly and felt shock rise inside her.

"I think you've lost your minds," she retorted in disbelief. "Don't you think that once he realizes I never left Somerset that he's going to get suspicious? That he'll figure out that you're onto him?"

The smile Dawg gave her was frankly terrifying. It was filled with expectation, anticipation, and a gleam of dangerous determination.

"That, fancy-face, is exactly what we're counting on."

TWENTY

"I don't like it!" Crista exclaimed again, hours later, after the houseboat had cleared out and she followed Dawg upstairs, where he carefully pulled a panel from the bedroom wall and displayed more weapons than she wanted to think about.

Lord, the man was an armory by himself.

"It's perfectly safe, sweetheart." He was using that conciliatory tone that he had used downstairs.

She hated it then, and she definitely hated it now. It smacked of patronization, and that was something she had never tolerated well.

"Don't you sweetheart me," she told him fiercely. "And don't bother patronizing me now that you can't blackmail me any longer, Dawg. That's only going to piss me off."

"And blackmailing you didn't piss you off?" His eyes crinkled with amusement, amusement overlying pain, as he glanced around the opened panel and pulled free several handguns and clips.

Crista stared askance at the weapons. She recognized the Glock handguns; Alex had several similar ones. That didn't mean she liked them or the necessity of having them.

"At least I understood the blackmail," she snorted. "I would have done it myself if I had the chance."

He paused, his brows arching, as he laid the two handguns on the dresser and reclosed and locked the panel as he stared back at her in interest.

"You would have?" His gaze heated, filled with arousal, as she watched his body tense in preparation.

Crista frowned back at him fiercely. "Don't go there, Dawg. We're going to talk about this."

"Of course we are," he assured her smoothly as he sat down on the bed and patted his knee. "Come here, fancy-face, and tell me what you would have done if you could have blackmailed me."

Her lips pressed together firmly, controlling the amusement that would have slipped free.

"I wasn't talking about blackmailing you." She crossed her arms over her breasts and glared back at him. "Dawg, Johnny can't be completely sane—"

A bitter bark of laughter left Dawg's throat. "Crista, sweetheart, Johnny isn't insane. He's highly intelligent; he graduated only one point below valedictorian. Just under Natches, who claimed that honor during their high school graduation. He's not crazy; he's a highly intelligent menace who will cut your throat if you turn your back on him. Just like he did the driver of the military transport carrying those missiles."

Crista stared back at him in horror. "They killed him?"

"The lone female of the group sliced his throat open. We suspect, based on the video and voice box in the cab of the transport, that he knew her. Or him, as the case may be. We know Johnny has portrayed himself as female through this whole deal. As you."

"He set the explosive in my Rodeo then?" she whispered.

Dawg nodded heavily. "He's the only one with a motive, Crista. Killing you would have made it look like a hit by the mercenaries and placed all guilt on you. He would have gotten away with the money, and the mercenaries would have been in prison scratching their heads."

"What about friends of the men you arrested?"

He shook his head as he reached out and drew her to him, pulling her onto his lap.

Crista leaned into him, her head resting on his shoulder as her arms looped around his neck.

He kissed the top of her head before he answered her. "The mercenary and his team didn't have a name for the woman, only a description, which they gave. No name, and the physical features of the face, though similar, weren't yours. The buyers aren't talking yet. Cole knew your name, but only after Johnny visited in the detention center. In the small talk, Johnny told him to get fucked, pretending to be you. He had the money and he was free; Cole wasn't. That would have drawn those mercenaries right to your door. They learned different during the interrogation Cranston and Natches led after Johnny's visit. We suspect even they weren't certain exactly who they were dealing with. Johnny's slick like that, Crista. He always was. I'm just surprised that he could actually kill in cold blood. I didn't expect that out of him."

Neither had Crista. But she had a feeling Johnny had disappointed Dawg as well. For all Johnny's faults and his mother's influence, Crista had the feeling that Dawg had managed to hold out a measure of hope for his other cousin.

"He was the one who told Natches's father about the sharing, when we were teenagers," Dawg said then. "I thought Dayle had killed him when we got to the house with Uncle Ray. Natches's mother had called, calm as hell, and told Ray he needed to come for Natches before Dayle killed him. There was blood everywhere, and his father was still trying to beat the hell out of him. He was in the hospital for a week and refused to admit his father had done it. He still has scars on his back. And Johnny cried when we confronted him. Blubbered like a baby and swore he hadn't meant for it to happen. That he had been playing, poking at Dayle because he was always so critical of him."

Dawg's voice echoed with that past horror.

"He meant to do it?"

"I don't know," Dawg mused. "To this day, I still don't know. But I suspect he knew what would happen. We all knew not to push Dayle where Natches was concerned. He took great pleasure in beating the hell out of him whenever he could justify it."

Crista blinked back her tears.

"And your father?" She already knew part of Dawg's history, had known it even before that first night she had spent with him.

"He wasn't as violent as Dayle." He shrugged negligently. "And I knew how to fight back. Natches never fought back, and I never understood why."

"Because of Janey." Crista lifted her head and stared up at Dawg, suddenly suspecting why Natches had never fought back.

"Janey?" he asked.

"Natches's sister."

"I know who Janey is, but what does she have to do with this?"

"Maybe he didn't fight back because he was afraid Dayle would turn his aggression on Janey. Maybe he was trying to wait until she was old enough to run if she had to."

Janey was a lot younger than Natches, at least ten years younger. She would have been ten or eleven when Natches was publicly disowned so long ago.

"Maybe," Dawg said thoughtfully before sighing heavily. "God help the bastard if he ever hit her, though. Natches would murder him."

"Do we really have to do this, Dawg?" she finally asked on a sigh. "Push Johnny like that? It could be dangerous."

"Only for Johnny." His voice darkened, sending a shiver up her spine at the danger that filled it. "Mark my words, Crista, I won't let him get away with this. He knew what he was doing when he decided to frame you. And he should have known what would happen if I ever figured out what was going on."

She parted her lips to argue further but found herself instead flat on her back on the bed and staring up at Dawg in surprise.

"Enough about Johnny," he growled. "And I've waited long enough to collect on that little tease by the lake earlier."

"Tease?" she gasped in mocking offense. "That was no tease, Dawg Mackay. You weren't exactly groaning because you didn't get to come, you know."

"It was a tease, pure and simple." His hand pushed the

hem of her camisole top up over her stomach. "All I got to do was lick that sweet pussy while you drove me insane with your mouth. I need more. Sweet heaven, Crista. I need so much more of you."

Her shirt was pulled slowly from her and tossed to the floor.

"Keep your arms there." He pressed them against the mattress, above her head, as she had done with him earlier beneath the wind and the sky. "Let me unwrap you, Crista. My own special present. I must have been a very good boy at some point to deserve this."

Her throat tightened at the emotion in his voice, at the tenderness in his touch, as he released the catch of her bra and drew it from her as well.

His hands cupped her swollen breasts, his thumbs raking over her nipples as his gaze darkened at the sight of the flushed tips.

"Would you have nursed our child?" he asked her, his voice incredibly deep, filled with regret and hunger, pain and longing.

"Yes." Crista arched into his touch, feeling her nipples tighten further as his finger and thumb gripped the pebble-hard tip.

"Would you have let me watch?" His head lowered, his lips feathering over her collarbone as Crista arched to the heated caress.

"Yes." She moaned the word.

His fingers were tormenting her nipples, making her wild for the touch of his lips, lips that were moving slowly over one flushed mound, his tongue licking at her flesh as it came closer to the aching tip.

"I love your breasts. How they feel, how they taste. How hard and hot your little nipples get for me." His hands cupped the mounds again, plumping them, lifting one closer to his lips as his tongue arrowed on the stiff peak.

When his mouth covered it, Crista was on the verge of begging. Once the heat of his suckling mouth and the lash of his tongue took possession of it, she was begging.

"Dawg. Please." Her hands fisted in the blanket beneath her. "More. Harder."

His touch was light, tender. She needed hard and hot. She needed the hunger she could feel barely leashed inside him. A hunger that was tearing through her, clenching in her pussy, spasming her womb.

"Harder, darlin'?" He licked over her nipple. "I don't want to rush this. I want to build the burn inside you. I want you ready for anything, for everything I can give you."

And she remembered exactly what he could give her when he touched her slow and easy. When each deliberate caress built the fire inside her to the point that pleasure bordered pain, and pain became a sensation so erotic that even the most wicked acts were the ones that brought the greatest pleasure. The most sensation.

"We'll both remember this, Crista. Forever," he swore. "Neither of us will forget."

Because they were both aware, connected now in a way they hadn't been before.

Crista stretched before him, her hips lifting from the bed as he gripped the band of her soft capris and drew them from her legs. His palms smoothed back up her legs, over the narrow band of her panties, and drew those from her as well.

Her eyes opened, her sight dazed as she stared down at him, watching as he spread her thighs slowly. His gaze became heavy lidded, drowsy with sensuality.

"Such a pretty pussy," he groaned, his thumbs moving into the indention between her thighs and the tender folds of her sex. "Soft and pink. Your juices glistening on it."

And they were. Already the silky wash of her arousal was gleaming on her flesh.

He didn't stop to touch or to taste though. Instead, he pulled himself on the bed beside her, leaned over her, and kissed her with all the pent-up lust she saw glowing in his gaze.

One large hand gripped her wrists as she tried to lift her hands to touch him. He anchored them to the bed above her head and ravished her lips. His tongue twined with hers, tasted her mouth, and caressed her lips. His free hand caressed her breasts, her belly, her thighs. His fingers plumped her nipples, gripped and teased them, and fanned the flames glowing from them.

Crista writhed beneath the caresses. His calloused palms

stroked over nerve endings that grew hypersensitive. His nails raked over her belly. And all she could do was endure it.

He held her easily beneath him, his hands and larger body controlling her writhing undulations. She was losing thought, losing control. The need for his touch overrode everything else.

Finally, as his lips lifted from hers, his hand strayed lower than her belly. Crista's eyes drifted open again, meeting his a second before his hand delivered a heavy caress between her thighs.

"Oh my God. Dawg." She jerked beneath him, her hips arching sharply at the small, heavy pat that landed on the swell of flesh on each side of her clit.

"Not too hard," he growled. "Your flesh is so sensitive. So silken and unused to being bare."

Another pat, kissing cousin to a gentle little slap, was delivered to the flesh again. A little lower, rocking sensation through the damp folds and vibrating inside her pussy.

Her clit swelled tighter with each heavy caress, the fierce throb becoming nearly painful as her sharp moans filled the air.

"So sweet," he crooned, his voice a black velvet rasp as her thighs fell farther apart, opening for his touch. His fingers slid through the slick cleft, parting the plump, swollen folds before circling her aching clit.

"Dawg, please," she cried out softly. "Don't torture me."

"No torture, sweetheart, just pleasure," he promised, his fingers glancing over her clit before leaving the wet flesh and moving once again to her breasts.

He moved lower along her body. His lips slid over her neck, her collarbone. He caught a hard nipple in his mouth. He sucked it deep into his mouth, his tongue lashing at it, his teeth scraping it as Crista's hands tore loose from his hold.

Her hands twined into his hair. Crista arched closer, her head falling back in pleasure while his hands twined into the long strands of her hair and pulled at them firmly. She pulled at his in turn, the action instinctive, the driving need for orgasm rising inside her.

Dawg was determined in his pace. His caresses were slow and easy, building the flames burning in her womb with deliberate strokes and heated caresses.

He didn't give her a chance to catch her breath between levels. There was no chance for thought, no chance to regain control.

Before Crista realized where the caresses were leading, she was already ensnared. As his lips began to kiss a careful path down her torso and over her stomach, her thighs were parting farther, her knees bending, making room for his broad shoulders between them.

Release would come now, she was certain.

He could do to her what nothing or no one else could. Pleasure ricocheted through her body and ensnared her in a web of love and lust so intense she knew she would never break free.

His tongue licked over the newly bared flesh, and she knew why he wanted her to experience this pleasure. It was incredible. His tongue touched nerve endings she never knew existed. Each sip, each delicate rasp of his teeth and suckling kiss had her burning hotter, brighter. She could feel her juices flowing from her, moving from her pussy, easing into the narrow cleft of her rear as his fingers began to follow the path they made.

Minutes later, as his tongue finally delved into the narrow slit of her pussy, she felt the cool, slick lubrication on his fingers as they pressed against her rear entrance.

She knew that feeling. It was more than what he had done in the office; she could feel it. No toys were going to take her body this time.

The control, each deliberate kiss and caress, had been for one purpose. To one end. To claim every part of her.

"So sweet." His voice rumbled against the ultrasensitive flesh he was caressing with lips and tongue. "Like sweet, warm syrup."

His tongue pierced the snug opening as his two fingers penetrated her rear entrance and sent pleasure tearing through her system.

"Oh God. Dawg!" She screamed his name as the dual caresses had her trying to writhe, trying to escape the incredible sensations rocking through her body.

Heat and lightning, fiery flames licked over her flesh and burned beneath the skin. It was incredible. The pleasure was like being stretched upon a rack of impending ecstasy and tortured with the knowledge that rapture awaited.

Breathing was nearly impossible as she reached for it. Her legs strained with the effort to get closer. To drive his fingers deeper, then his tongue deeper. To make him, force him to give her what she needed to release her from the almost painful pleasure searing her body.

She tried to tighten her legs, to close them just enough to tighten the sensation on her clit, to give that final pressure she was certain she needed to find her orgasm.

Below her, Dawg chuckled, a rough rasp of arousal and pleasure vibrating through her as his tongue licked with wicked strokes into the snug entrance to her pussy.

His fingers moved farther back. Stroked. Thrust.

"You're killing me!" Her fingers dug into the mattress, her hips lifted, fighting to get closer, only to have him ease the pressure she so desperately needed.

A ragged cry tore from her throat as a rumbled sound of pleasure whispered over her pussy.

"It's okay, fancy-face," he assured her erotically before his tongue licked around her clit again and his fingers flexed in her rear. "I'll take care of you."

His lips covered her clit. He drew it into the heat of his mouth and suckled her, drew on her until she was screaming for relief. His tongue rasped over it, and she begged. As release built in her womb, he eased off, his head lowering, his tongue licking through her juices once again and denying her the relief she was begging for.

"Damn you! Stop teasing me." She reached for him, her fingers locking in his hair and clenching as another heated thrust filled her rear.

"I want your ass, Crista," he groaned, his lips pressing against her thigh before his teeth scraped over the flesh there.

She trembled, remembering the act, knowing what it would do to her, knowing how it would bind her to him. The ultimate submission. He had muttered those words as he took her there the first time. His.

Crista stared back at him as he moved, rising to his knees, spreading her thighs farther apart as his fingers slid from her rear.

"Dawg?" Crista shuddered, watching as he pulled her hips closer and pushed her legs back.

She watched, shocked, torn between feminine fear and erotic thrill as she saw him spread a heavy layer of lubrication over his cock.

It glistened, thick and powerful. Heavy veins pulsed beneath the flesh as the engorged crest visibly throbbed. Crista swallowed tightly. It looked huge, too large, too hard to breach the narrow opening it was tucking against.

"Dawg." She lifted her eyes back to his, mesmerized by the eroticism in his expression and the darkening of his light green eyes.

"Are you mine, Crista?" he asked, his voice rasping in the back of his throat as his cock pressed against her, into her.

"Always." She couldn't deny what her soul had always known.

A whimpering cry left her lips as he shifted his hold on her and let her legs fall to his chest while one hand gripped her hip, the other gripped the shaft of his cock.

Crista felt the invasion, slowly, a penetration that sent sensation shattering through the tender nerve endings. Her anal entrance began to stretch, to open beneath the blunt force of his erection.

"Oh God! Dawg, I can't stand this." Her body undulated involuntarily as her hands fisted into the blanket beneath her.

Flames were licking around her rear as the flesh parted. Pleasure and pain, submission and seduction. It was ownership. Not of her mind or really of her body. Ownership of her sensuality, of her pleasure. The intimacy was one so binding that even eight years after he had first given it, she had never recovered from the effects of it on her soul.

He was branding himself onto her soul and into her body.

Her lips opened on a soundless scream as the thickly flared head cleared the entrance, then forged inside once again. He buried his cock head inside the clenching tissue, groaning as she cried out his name in shocked pleasure.

Dawg paused then, his breathing rough, rapid, as sweat trickled down his chest and his eyes lowered to the tender opening he was taking.

"So hot and tight," he groaned, moving again, slow, shallow

thrusts that worked his cock deeper inside her by small degrees. "It's like being held by flames, Crista."

Or taken by flames.

Her head thrashed on the bed as his cock moved deeper inside her ass, stretching her, revealing nerve endings so sensitive that the slam of sensation echoed into her clit. She was surrounded by a pleasure so intense, so forceful, she wondered if she could survive it.

"You're burning me alive." The hoarse snarl of his voice as the final inches of his erection burrowed into her anus had her womb contracting with an impending orgasm.

It was so wickedly erotic. It was the most forbidden, most submissive act Crista could envision, and it was overriding her sanity.

Control was a thing of the past. Dawg held the control. He held her. He shifted and moved, pulling nearly free before surging forward again. He stroked and caressed and set aflame nerve endings that hadn't flared to life in eight years.

Crista arched to him, her hips twisting in his grip as the need began to spiral out of control. She needed it hard and deep. She needed him to . . .

"Fuck me." She didn't recognize her own voice as the shattered plea filled the air. "Please, Dawg. Harder. Fuck me harder."

Her lashes lifted, her gaze hazy as she tried to focus on his face. A hard grimace twisted it, pleasure racking his features as he shook his head, sweat beading and dripping down his forehead as his hands clenched on her hips and his cock throbbed inside her ass.

"Harder," she whispered again, tempting him with a flex of those inner muscles, tightening on his flesh and feeling the pleasure spasm through her as well.

"Fuck. Crista," he groaned, panting with the pleasure, just as she was.

"I need you." She swallowed tightly. "All of you. Fuck me harder, Dawg. Give me what I need."

His hips jerked, dragging his erection back before pushing it inside her with a longer, harder stroke. As he did, one hand moved from her hip to tuck between her thighs.

Broad male fingers slid through the slick essence that gathered there, found the weeping center, and two digits thrust inside heavily.

He moved then. Thrusting hard and heavy as Crista's eyes widened, her gaze dimming as ecstasy began to wash over her.

Her orgasm came fast and hard. With his fingers stroking strong and sure inside her pussy, his cock burying repeatedly inside her ass, there was no holding back. The dark eroticism and extreme pleasure was too much.

Crista heard her own cries with a distant wonder. They sounded shattered, agonized. Beneath that sound was Dawg's. His harsh male groan as he buried deep inside her rear, his seed spurting heavily inside her, would always follow her.

His broken "I love you, Crista. God help me, I love you" threw her orgasm higher, shattering her soul with the ragged edge of hope and pain she heard in his voice.

He jerked against her, spilling his semen into her rear before giving a final groan and easing slowly from the tight clasp she had on him.

Crista whimpered at the added sensation. The feel of him slowly leaving her, his cock easing from her, his fingers caressing away from her pussy were nearly painful now in their intensity.

They were both sweat-soaked as he eased on the bed beside her and pulled her to his chest. His lips pressed against the top of her head in a kiss that had her chest clenching in emotion.

Beneath her cheek his heart raced, just as hers was racing, and his lungs heaved for breath.

It was like this, every time. It wasn't just the exertion of the sex but the intense emotions that tore through them and left them weak and shaken.

"I love you, Dawg," she whispered when she could finally find her breath and her senses. "I've always loved you."

TWENTY-ONE

Graceful Sweets and Bakery sat just off North Main Street outside the old town center. The house Johnny Grace had bought sat on the plot of land beside the house that Crista had inherited from her parents.

The two-story brick home sat amid a perfectly manicured and landscaped lawn. Summer blooms grew in abundance around the property, wooden archways held trailing vines and climbing roses, and the front porch was home to cement urns filled with sweetly scented flowers.

Crista walked to the wide front door. The sign hanging on the door claimed, Open to Fulfill Your Sweetest Needs.

"This is a very bad idea," she muttered, not for the first time, as Dawg gripped the door latch and opened the door.

Instantly, a profusion of scents wrapped around them. Baking breads, sweet icings, and tempting delights. Crista inhaled unconsciously and felt her sweet tooth awaken with a vengeance.

Johnny had always kept her supplied with sweets. For the past year, she hadn't had to buy so much as a loaf of bread because of his generosity. Payment for betraying her? A guilty conscience? Betrayal and anger began to burn brighter inside her. It made her chest ache with the knowledge that Dawg had dealt with this most of his life.

"Crista." Johnny's voice greeted her with an edge of concern as she stepped into what had once been an open living room and dining room. It now held display cases of profuse sweets and breads.

There were other customers. Johnny had a steady clientele that kept him busy through the day.

He stepped away from the register cabinet, a frown pulling at his brow, as he glanced at Dawg behind her.

"Natches said you had left town." His gaze was filled with concern. "Is everything okay?"

He gripped her hands before kissing her cheek. Reacting normally was the hardest thing Crista had ever done. She wanted to rage; she wanted to cry. For all his problems with the Mackay family, she had always enjoyed Johnny's company.

"Everything's fine, Johnny. Natches misunderstood a slight argument Dawg and I had. Nothing to be worried about. But I have been missing my banana nut bread. Do you have any made?"

Johnny glanced over her shoulder once again, his gaze flickering with indecision.

Crista glanced back. Dawg hadn't taken off his dark glasses, and he looked mean enough to bite nails in half. She butted her elbow into his tight abs with a warning look.

Customers were watching the scene curiously, a spate of whispers breaking out as Dawg looked down at her and rubbed at his hard stomach almost absently.

"I always have your bread, Crista." Johnny's voice could have held nerves, anger, or fear. It was hard to tell.

He turned and moved back to the main display case. Lifting the hinged glass door to the long case, Johnny grabbed a wax liner, lifted a small loaf of banana nut bread from the case, and pushed it quickly into a white wax bag he used for the breads.

"Here you go," he said, moving to the register, his expression emotionless, his gaze flickering between Crista and Dawg. "Anything else?" His gaze lingered on Dawg, and Crista swore she saw hatred glittering in the depths then.

"I tried to tell her she could get the bread somewhere else." Dawg spoke up then, his tone taunting. "It's a nice place you have here, Johnny. Real nice. I'm glad to see your little court battle paid off."

The money and land they had won during the estate battle with Dawg had evidently paid for the store.

"Dawg," Crista chided, hating the need to maintain a semblance of compassion toward Johnny. She could feel the animosity that began to thicken between the two men. She pulled some money quickly from her purse to pay for the bread, wanting only to get out of there, to breathe without the stench of Johnny's betrayal choking her.

Johnny held his hand up, forestalling the payment, his gaze hardening as he stared back at her. "For old times." He smiled tightly. "But please, call before coming back. I'll make certain I have my assistant working that day. I don't need Dawg in my shop, if you don't mind."

Behind her, Dawg clicked his tongue mockingly. "Johnny, we're family, man. Surely I'm allowed in the store after paying for it? I can't believe you'd be so coldhearted."

This was Dawg at his most taunting. This, Crista had seen before. He was pushing Johnny, trying to make him angry, trying to make him strike out.

Johnny stared back at her instead. "Call first, Crista," he reminded her. "I'm sure you understand the reasons why."

The customers milling around the store were watching in interest now, the gossip mill gearing up for a spate of talk that would go on for months.

"I understand, Johnny." She kept her voice soft, but inside, she ached. And she felt her anger beginning to build.

This store Johnny took such pride in. The big house his mother had built, their airs and certainty of their place in society had been bought with the pain of Dawg's childhood. They had added to his father's cruelty to Dawg and exacerbated memories that haunted Dawg even now.

Crista stared at the loaf of bread in her hand, then back at Johnny. Her expression tightened as she laid it back on the counter.

"On second thought, Johnny, I think I don't need this after all."

Surprise filled his gaze as he looked at the sheathed loaf of bread, then back at Crista.

"Are you sure, Crista?" It could be paranoia, but she was certain she heard a warning in his tone. She was choosing Dawg's side rather than staying neutral, or far better, choosing Johnny's side.

Crista's lips thinned as she stared back at him, seeing now how easily he could have portrayed her. They were the same height, close to the same build. It wouldn't have been hard for Johnny to fake the curves that her body held, dress in her clothes, and pretend to be her.

Getting her clothes and putting them back wouldn't have been hard. Her house sat right beside his, and he could have copied her key the few times she had left it with him, times such as when the cable repairman had been expected and she had to work.

"I'm sure, Johnny." She stepped back from the counter before turning and glancing at Dawg. "I'm ready to go now."

She didn't wait for him. She turned on her heel and moved purposely for the door, feeling Dawg moving protectively behind her. It was the oddest feeling, knowing he was there without even looking, feeling his warmth surrounding her even when he wasn't touching her.

He reached around her as she neared the door and opened it quickly. Standing back to let her through the exit, Dawg glanced back at Johnny. He should have smirked. He could have antagonized the little bastard further, he thought.

But as he stared at Johnny, all he felt was pity. He was too much like his mother, too easily influenced by his need for petty power and his drive to have more than he worked for.

Dawg saw the hatred in Johnny's eyes. He saw the resentment and years of pent-up aggression caused by the fact that only once in his life had he ever gained the upper hand on Dawg. That once being the court battle Dawg had nearly lost.

Rather than saying anything more, he merely shook his head, sighed at the weariness of the fight that had waged between him and Johnny since childhood, and left the small store Johnny had purchased from the ill-gotten gains of betraying blood.

Leaving the building, Dawg followed Crista to the truck,

feeling the heaviness in his chest and regrets that he knew were better left forgotten.

He knew, to the bottom of his soul, that his own father would have preferred to have left his estate to Johnny and his mother. But it was Dawg's mother who had foiled those plans.

For all her paranoia and suspicious tendencies and cold, emotionless demeanor, Brenda Mackay had understood family loyalty. She might not have been able to keep her husband from beating the hell out of her son when he was younger, but she had counseled Dawg on the best ways to avoid Chandler's temper, and she had made certain that in the event of their deaths that Dawg's inheritance would be preserved. Had it not been for her careful wording of their wills and her wishes clearly stated, then Dawg would have lost everything.

He helped Crista into the truck, seeing the anger building in her eyes and the flush on her face as he closed the passenger side door and moved to the driver's side.

As he pulled himself into the truck and started the vehicle, he glanced over at Crista again and found himself uncertain what to say.

He had accepted the animosity between Johnny and him years ago. He found himself rarely surprised by his cousin until he learned he had actually killed. He had also refused to explain or make excuses for his own behavior where the other man was concerned.

Now he found himself wishing he could find the words to explain it to Crista. She was hurt and angry. Johnny had been her friend.

For the first time in his life, he was involved in a situation that couldn't be won, no matter what he did. He couldn't influence Crista's decision. This wasn't a war that he could win with a gun, his fists, or his money.

When he was younger, his fists had protected him. Once he joined the Marines and entered the shadowed world of an assassin, he had learned his gun could handle the monsters of the world. Monsters that killed and maimed. But the job had taken a toll on his conscience. In ways, Dawg often thought the bullet he had taken to the knee had been a blessing.

When he returned home, he returned to enough money to

ensure that lawyers could fight his battles and the things he needed would be taken care of.

Fists, guns, or lawyers weren't going to change what Crista was feeling now: the betrayal, the anger, the knowledge that she had trusted someone who had been using her.

He drove to the lumber store, silent, glancing at her, wishing now that he hadn't made the decision to confront Johnny in such a way. He didn't want Crista as hard or as cynical as he had become.

It would be over soon. Cranston would pick Johnny up by evening on terrorism and selling military weapons charges. After that, maybe he could breathe easy. She wouldn't be safe until then. Johnny knew she hadn't left town, knew he was trapped; Dawg had seen it in his eyes. The agents watching him would follow him, but until he was behind bars, Dawg wouldn't, couldn't breathe easy.

"I'm sorry," he finally breathed out roughly as he pulled into the side parking lot of the store. "I shouldn't have made you do that."

She surprised him with an unladylike snort and a flash of defiance in her eyes.

"If that mousy little bastard thought a loaf of bread was going to make up for impersonating me, then he has another thing coming. Just as you do if you think I need you apologizing for your cousin's stupidity."

His brows lifted in surprise as he pushed his glasses down his nose and stared over the lenses at her.

Her lips tightened as she glanced away, then back to him.

"I always thought maybe the problems between Johnny and you, Rowdy, and Natches were because of his sexual preferences. I felt sorry for him. He was so much smaller than the rest of you and always seemed so upset because he wasn't a part of the fun." She shrugged uncomfortably. "I knew about the court battle, how he and his mother tried to steal your inheritance, but I thought it was an attempt to get attention more than anything else."

Regret flickered behind the anger in her gaze.

"It may have started that way," Dawg allowed. "When we were much younger. The problem with letting Johnny in on the fun was that he tended to carry tales. Rowdy was pretty safe from it; Uncle Ray didn't have a heavy hand. Natches and I paid enough times for Johnny's inability to keep those secrets, though. So we kept our distance from him."

She grimaced painfully. "Fathers should be understanding," she whispered. "A heavy hand only breeds resentment."

"Or hatred," Dawg pointed out cynically before shaking his head and staring through the windshield to the metal side of the lumber store. "It's not worth discussing at this point. I'm just sorry you were dragged into it, Crista."

"He did it to hurt you," she said, drawing his gaze back to her. "He impersonated me, drew me to the warehouse, and then walked into that detention center dressed as me to ensure my arrest. He did it just to hurt you."

Dawg had already figured that one out, but he found himself hurting because she had realized it. His chest tightened, and his heart actually ached.

Reaching out, he let the backs of his fingers caress her jawline, feeling the warmth of her flesh, seeing the acceptance in her gaze.

"I wouldn't have had you arrested," he finally said softly. "If you had walked out the night I blackmailed you, I would have let you leave, Crista. I had the note you left in your car. I knew you were innocent."

"Do you think I don't know that?" She caught his hand and held it to her cheek. "I always knew that, Dawg. Maybe I just needed the excuse to step out of the past and reach for what I wanted."

He pulled the glasses from his nose and laid them on the dash, all the while staring at her, memorizing her features and the emotions that filled her gaze.

It was love. He could see the love. It was the same look Kelly gave Rowdy, the way Maria stared at her husband Ray. Inviting, dark, filled with acceptance and with some emotion that defied description.

Love was such a tame word for what he felt and for what he saw in her eyes.

Dawg swallowed convulsively, suddenly uncertain, thrown off balance by her. Hell, she had always managed to do that to him, even eight years before. Made him feel like an inexperienced kid who didn't know how to get a girl.

"I want to give you another baby." He grimaced as the words tore past his lips, and her eyes widened in surprise. "No, listen." His fingers covered her lips as they parted. "I know you're not ready right now. I want to marry you, Crista. I want my ring on your finger. I want you by my side. But I want to give you another baby, too. I—" He broke off, his lips tightening at his own inability to put his feelings into words.

Hell, he wanted to bind her to him; it was that damned simple. He wanted to make certain she could never walk away from him again, that she never wanted to walk away from him again.

"Dawg," she whispered, her hand reaching out to him, lying along his cheek at he stared back at her, desperate for all the things he had lost after she left town. "I won't leave you again. Ever."

Something inside him loosened at her words. As though a coil of dread had been tightening in his chest, her words released it, lifting a part of his soul that he had never known was restrained inside him. Heat rushed through him. Not just arousal and lust, but emotions that swamped him, that dazed him.

He was harder than he had ever been in his life, and yet inside, the hard core of anger, cynicism, and regret was melting.

There was nothing he could say. There was only one way to combat the unfamiliar morass of emotions tearing through him now.

He reached for her. His arms surrounded her, pulling her across the console until her rear rested in his lap, her head at his shoulder, and his lips were covering hers.

An inferno of hunger exploded in his veins. His flesh prickled with heat, and his kiss grew ravenous. He couldn't get deep enough, couldn't taste her or touch her enough.

Her lips parted for him, took him, as his fingers threaded through her hair and cupped the back of her head to hold her in place. Not that she was fighting the kiss. Hell no. Her hands were in his hair, tugging and pulling, as her tongue met his, licked and stroked and drove him crazy with the fierce, passionate battle they were waging.

She was summer lightning, striking hot and swift to the

center of his soul. She was a hot summer day and a cool, easing breeze all at once.

"God, you make me crazy for you," he groaned, his lips moving over her jaw to her neck. "I forget where the hell I'm at and don't give a damn who's watching."

And he didn't. The employees' parking lot was fairly sheltered, but it was in no possible way private. Dawg was a desperate man, though. The emotions welled inside him, the hunger for Crista that he knew would never be sated, and his hands couldn't touch her enough.

His head lifted, his gaze lowering as he pushed his hand beneath the hem of yet another of those damned snug tank top things she wore. The ones that smoothed over her breasts and skimmed over her belly just a little too snug to make grown men comfortable.

He watched as the rough, dark flesh of his hand touched her smooth, creamy belly above the low-rise jeans she wore. Crista wasn't bone skinny, rather nicely rounded, and those curves made him crazy.

His hand moved up her belly, pushing her shirt farther up until he could cup one lace-covered mound of her breast.

"Cameras," she suddenly moaned, shuddering as his fingers gripped a hard nipple and tugged at it slowly.

"Huh?" His attention was riveted on that hard little nipple, his mouth watering to taste it.

"Dawg!" Laughter and arousal filled her voice. "You parked under the security camera."

His eyes jerked up, moved to the window, and up to the camera's eye pointing down on the truck.

"Shit," he muttered.

Laughter bubbled from her lips as she pulled her shirt down, hiding the succulent, tempting little berries he was dying for.

"You're a bad boy," she accused, scrambling from his lap and trying to straighten her clothes and her hair. Laughter gleamed in her eyes and curved her luscious lips.

"Hell, you sound surprised." Dawg sighed as he shifted in his seat and tried to relieve the pressure of his jeans against his cock. That portion of his body was so engorged now it was painful.

"Never surprised." She shook her head with a soft laugh as she flipped down the visor, smoothed her makeup beneath her eyes, and fluffed the silk of her hair before checking her shirt.

After adjusting the neckline, she flashed him a teasing glance, then pushed her door open and jumped from the truck. Damn her. She knew what she was doing to him, Dawg thought, and he couldn't help but grin as he forced himself from the vehicle and hit the automatic lock on his key chain. The truck lights flashed as the small beep assured him it had locked.

"Come on, you little tease." Moving around the truck, his arm slid around her waist as they headed for the employees' entrance. "I'll lock us in the office and have my wicked way with you there.

"I don't think so. You have orders to finish, and you still haven't made up the list for the winter inventory yet. You need to get a jump on the larger stores and plan your displays."

He scowled down at her as they moved for the office steps.

"I don't do winter displays. They cost too much, and they're not effective."

"Only because you're the one doing them," she stated. "I've been watching your displays, Dawg. They aren't effective because you have no idea what women are looking for."

"I know what women want." He frowned down at her, wondering then if somehow he had been ineffective with those explosive orgasms he'd been giving her.

"What women want in a bed and what they're willing to buy in public are two different things." The laughter in her voice warmed him, made him grin. "Trust me. I've got you covered on this. We're going to have incredible winter displays. Just wait until you see the Santa Claus I'm thinking of bringing in. And I found some incredible wrought-iron arches at a steal. Very classy, and for the most part unavailable in this area. I want to buy the distributor's stock in whole, to make certain the larger stores don't get one up on us."

As he listened to her, he was tempted to shake his head.

She had plans, and he'd be damned if he disagreed with her. At the rate she was going, she would end up making his father roll in his grave at the success of it.

"I need you to check with Jim Bedsford and see what happened to the Connelly order, now that I think about it." She frowned as they entered the office and she moved to the desk. "I nearly forgot, with everything that's been going on. Layla had to reimburse him for a fourth of his order when it didn't arrive on the site. He's pretty upset over it."

Dawg took the inventory order and frowned down at it. He had worked damned hard to get Connelly to let Mackay's handle the supplies for the apartment complex he was building.

"Damn," he growled. "I'm going to have to work today."

Soft laughter and feminine warmth whispered around him then.

"You and me both. Now go take care of Bedsford. And if I were you, I'd seriously consider replacing him."

"With who?" Dawg grunted.

His gaze met hers. She was confident, certain.

"Layla's husband, Jamie. He has experience, and he spends half his time here with Layla anyway. Might as well put him to work."

And she was right, damn her.

He grunted noncommittally, knowing damned good and well he'd end up doing it.

"Stay out of trouble," he warned her before pressing a hard kiss to her lips and heading for the door. "And don't leave the store with anyone but me. You're not safe until Cranston has Johnny picked up. Promise me, Crista."

"Yes sir," she snapped teasingly. "Any other orders, sir?"

He turned at the door and lifted his brows. "Be naked when I return?"

"Only in your dreams." She rolled her eyes and waved one hand back at him. "Bye-bye, Dawg. Catch you at lunch."

He chuckled as he left the office, amazed now at the feelings running through him. He was still so damned hard his jeans were uncomfortable, but that knot of discontent, which had followed him all his life, was easing. Because of her.

Shaking his head, he moved quickly down the stairs,

threw Layla a wave, and made a mental note to talk to her about her husband before heading to the back of the store. Bedsford was obviously going to have to go; Dawg just wanted to find out first why he was sabotaging the supplies Mackay's Lumber was in charge of.

TWENTY-TWO

Summer displays were as important as winter and Christmas displays, but a hell of a lot harder without the time it took for preparation.

Crista spent the first several hours staring out the tinted windows that overlooked the floor of the store, her gaze narrowed as Layla worked at the desk behind her to get a count on the proper items they were going to need to create the design Crista wanted.

The front of the store was important. At the moment, it was all parking lot. There were no fenced areas for the summer displays and landscaping. Nothing for shoppers to get curious about as they drove in front of Mackay's to reach the large grocery store and outdoor strip mall housed farther up the road.

"Do we have the gazebo plans at least?" Crista asked Layla.

Dawg had ordered only a small amount of the gazebos, which were steady sellers through the past few years.

"We have several plans." Layla moved to the lateral files on the other side of the office. "I put them in here after the last gazebos shipped in. The supplier sends the plans or they'll build them for you. It would be incredibly cheaper if Dawg would pay a few of the younger workers to put in some extra hours to put them together."

She pulled a file free and laid the first plan out on the coffee table. "These are the ones that are selling best at the moment."

The smaller gazebos had a two-seat swing with a bench on the other side. Crista stared down at the design, pursing her lips thoughtfully. "We have the swings?"

"Plenty of those." Layla nodded. "And we could get the flowers you were talking about within three days. There's a local greenhouse owner I know who would make certain Mackay's has only the freshest blooms. They'll train the employees to care for them and check them every few days. What we don't sell, we don't pay for. Especially the perennials, flowering bushes, and trees, because they can be planted in the fall and sold to landscapers the next spring."

Crista made a few quick notes on the clipboard she carried, around the sketch she was making of the outdoor display she wanted.

"Are your boys working this summer?" she asked Layla.

Layla shook her head quickly. "They haven't applied for anything yet. They have summer classes at the college, so it would be hard for them to work most places right now."

"Could Mackay's hire them for evening work and weekends?" she asked. "We'll need someone to build the gazebos and to put the displays together. There're a few of the girls working the floor right now that I have in mind for the gardening section, but I'd like to get this taken care of first."

"That would work perfectly for them, Crista." Layla nodded.

"Let me find Dawg." Crista turned and looked out over the floor once again. "He was supposed to be talking to Bedsford about the Connelly order."

"I saw him in the lumberyard before you called me up here. They were loading the items missing on the inventory sheet. He called Connelly and got an agreement to hold off on buying the items elsewhere if Dawg would take care of the orders personally. I heard him arguing with Connelly on his cell phone," Layla admitted with a shy grin. "Dawg can be persuasive. I'd guess he'll go after Jim around closing instead. The lumberyard is pretty busy right now."

How many orders was Bedsford messing up in the mean-time, Crista wondered, a frown working at her brow at the thought of the other man.

She knew Jim Bedsford, not well, but she knew him.

Her heart jumped in her chest then, an odd memory flash-ing in her head. She had seen Johnny and Jim one night. It had been late, after she got off at the diner. Jim had been getting into Johnny's car, but she hadn't seen Johnny. Oh Lord, she had seen a woman. A woman with long hair and shadowed features. It had been too dark to see much, but it had felt odd, out of place, because she knew Johnny was gay. She thought he had loaned his car to a friend; he did that sometimes. She had borrowed it herself once.

It had been Johnny, dressed as her, and Bedsford had known it.

Jim was a bit taller than Johnny, broad, with a barrel chest and a perpetual scowl on his pitted face. He had been dis-charged from the service for medical reasons, she had heard, though there had been no specifics.

"I have to find Dawg," she whispered, her heart in her throat.

Layla looked back at her in surprise. "He should be fin-ished in the lumberyard by now. He's probably on the floor. Is something wrong?"

"I need to talk to him about the outside display so we can get started on it," she said. She also needed to talk to him about Bedsford and Johnny. "Could you stay up here and watch the phones while I'm gone?"

Layla nodded. "I have Crystal watching the floor right now. That won't be a problem."

"I'll be right back."

Crista left the office quickly and moved down the metal steps. Her gaze scanned the rows and aisles as she headed across the floor toward the end of the building where the lumber and building displays were arranged. Some of the stock was kept inside for small purchases, while the majority of it was kept in a covered hangar behind the store.

As she entered the lumber section, she paused, frowning

when she didn't see Dawg. Turning up one of the narrow aisles, she walked quickly toward the back of the store, then headed toward the other side when one of the stock boys mentioned seeing him in appliances.

Damn it, they needed a few walkie-talkies. She didn't have her cell phone on her, and right now she could have used a clue as to where the hell he was. She made a quick note on her clipboard to have him set up a system for the employees. It would also make helping customers much easier.

"Bradley." She stopped in appliances by one of the young stock boys loading a washing machine onto a metal roller cart. "Have you seen Mr. Mackay?"

"He just went back outside." Bradley nodded his shaggy head toward the employees' door that led to the side parking lot.

"Thanks, Bradley." Nodding quickly, she moved for the door, pushing it open and stepping outside as she shaded her eyes to stare around.

"Hello, Miss Jansen, can I help you?" Jim Bedsford stepped from between several delivery trucks, tossing a cigarette to the ground as he stared back at her with a heavy scowl.

"I was looking for Dawg." She gave him a cool smile, fear suddenly lashing inside her. "Perhaps he's inside."

"He's in the lumberyard." Jim moved closer. "He fired me, you know."

Crista froze as he blocked the way around the side of the building.

"I'll discuss it with him." She attempted to bluff her way back to the door.

"Miss Jansen, open that door, and I'll shoot you."

She turned back slowly, her eyes widening at the sight of the black barrel beneath the dark ball cap Bedsford was carrying in one hand.

She glanced up at the camera. There was no way to tell that the man was carrying a weapon.

"You're going to come with me, nice and easy like." He smiled coldly. "We need to talk."

"Dawg will know who I left with, Jim," she warned him. "Dawg will know."

"Don't try to run your mouth at me, bitch." His voice didn't raise or lower, it remained cold, vicious. "Just get in the fucking van and stop arguing with me before I have to kill you. I don't want to hurt you, but I'm not above it."

Crista stared around the parking lot desperately.

"If I have to kill you, then I'm going to have to kill Dawg, too," he pointed out in what she assumed was a reasonable tone. "It won't be hard. He's not the only Somerset boy who went through stealth training. Or the only one who can play assassin. Now, are you going to cooperate, or do I have to get pissed off?"

Dawg would miss her soon. Crista looked up at the camera desperately, her fists clenched by her sides as she moved out of the range of the blinking eye and realized that the monitor probably hadn't even picked up Bedsford. But he would know, she told herself. Dawg would know, and he would come for her.

"I don't want to hurt you." He opened the door to a small panel van and pushed her in before following her. "Get in the driver's seat. We'll drive out of here nice and easy."

"Why are you doing this?" Crista moved into the driver's seat and took the keys with a shaking hand. "I'm sure you could find a job somewhere else, Jim."

A rough laugh met her words. "Hell, you think this job means shit to me?" He sat on the floor behind the passenger seat, the gun held firmly in his hand and leveled at her. "Lady, I couldn't give a shit about this job except for the fact that it helped us keep an eye on Dawg. We needed to know what he was up to, so I worked here and kept up on things. Kept him busy where I could."

"We?" She pulled from the parking lot, praying someone had seen her, that someone would know who she had left with.

"Come on, you're not a stupid bitch," he clucked in amusement. "Johnny knew this morning that he'd been set up by Natches. Someone figured it out. He did a damned good impersonation of you until Dawg hooked up with you and was able to track your movements. We just needed a little more time, and we would have had the money while those nasty little terrorists would have believed it was you. Even those yahoos who helped steal the missiles didn't know who Johnny was. Or you, for that matter. Until the other day."

"He told them who I was?"

Bedsford laughed again. "Walked right into the detention center and flashed your ID and signed your name. They all know who you are now. I don't think Dawg's going to be able to keep you safe. The men who helped Johnny steal the missiles think you have them. The men who paid half down on a shipment they're never going to get think he's you." His smile was satisfied. "You're dead, no matter what."

He wasn't going to let her go. Of course, Crista had figured that one out already.

"So why not just shoot me now and get it over with?" Her hands clenched the steering wheel hard as she turned down the road leading to the highway.

She didn't believe in going easy. She had one chance, and it would be risky. At the end of the lane was a traffic signal. It was green right now, but if she timed it just right, she might have a chance to escape.

Her heart was racing, fear thundering in her head as she drew closer.

"You know, I won't mind blowing your head off if you try something crazy." The gun shifted in his hand, the barrel pointing up as she brought the van to a stop as the light turned red. "Wouldn't it hurt so much less to just go along with me and pray your boyfriend rescues you?"

He couldn't rescue her if he didn't know where she was or who had taken her. And he couldn't rescue her if she had a bullet in her head.

She glanced at the gun again, then up at the scowl on Jim's bulldog face.

"Dawg will kill you," she told him, knowing he would. But she would still be gone if she didn't do something. Fast.

Johnny's warning look earlier in the day had assured her that she had taken the wrong side. He would show no more mercy toward her than he had the transport driver whose truck he had hijacked.

"Dawg won't kill me if all he has to do is clear your sweet little name and I'm nowhere to be found," he grunted. "Look bitch, we just have to do one more thing. That's all. If you're missing when it goes down, and we fly out of here, then we're in the clear, no matter what you say. Your word against ours, plain and simple. And it won't matter anyway. Johnny's going with me to Nicaragua. I have some friends there. Some contacts."

"Are you crazy, Jim?" she asked as she pulled onto the highway, amazed at the man's gullibility. "Do you think Johnny did this just so he could escape to some damp jungle? He has no intentions of leaving Somerset with you or of letting me go."

"I don't really care what he does with you." There was a shrug in Jim's voice. "And he promised. We're going to take the money and set up in a nice little hacienda there. We have it all picked out."

Crista blinked in surprise, directed a look back at him, then jerked her eyes back to the road.

Bedsford was in love with Johnny? She could hear it in his voice. It softened, and the scowl was no longer on his face. His expression radiated with emotion, and his dark brown eyes gleamed with purpose.

"Johnny couldn't live without being close enough to his cousins to throw their failure in their faces," she whispered painfully, knowing she was driving herself to her own funeral.

"Turn at the next light," he ordered. "We're going to head out of town. I'll let you know when to turn again."

"We're not going to Johnny's?"

"Why would I do that?" Jim asked her as though surprised. "That would be like hanging a sign on his door. We're going to meet him somewhere else. That's all."

"Where he'll kill us both." She was certain of it. "He killed the driver of the transport truck for no reason, Bedsford. He's not going to let you live. Or me."

"Johnny loves me." The belief in his voice terrified Crista.

"Johnny loves the money his mother gives him, trying to steal more from his cousins, and convincing everyone how socially acceptable he is," she said. "He won't see that destroyed. And he won't allow either of us to live."

Her eyes scanned the road frantically. At each stoplight she searched for someone she knew, anyone who could help her. And no one met her eyes. Time was running out, and she knew it.

Jim chuckled at her assessment. "When I came back eight years ago, Johnny was a mess over his uncle's death and what Dawg had stolen from him. Chandler Mackay tried to do right by Johnny. He knew Johnny was smarter, better than his son was. And Johnny knew how much Chandler wanted to make certain he was rewarded for being the son Dawg wouldn't be. Dawg stole that inheritance, Miss Jansen. And I built Johnny back up. I helped him regain his confidence and his sense of place in the world. He loves me. And he will leave with me. What his mother or the Mackays have is nothing compared to what I can give him in Nicaragua."

"A country filled with war and death. With insurgents, rebellions, and terrorists?" Crista shook her head. "He will never leave Somerset for that, Jim. You know he won't."

"If you don't shut up, I'm going to blow your head off right here in the middle of town." Once again, his voice only became harder, darker. Vicious. There was no conscience there, no regret, and no second thoughts.

Crista inhaled roughly, then flinched at the sound of a cell phone. It wasn't hers. No, she couldn't be that lucky. Hers was back at the office.

"Hey, baby," Jim answered the call, his voice gentling. "I'm heading to the meeting point. Do you have everything ready?"

Crista gripped the steering wheel harder, knowing she couldn't go much farther. If she actually managed to let him get her out of town, then no one would ever know what happened to her.

She stared at the traffic around her, in front of her. There was one more stoplight. If she timed that one right and ran it—

A car pulled in front of her, and from the backseat, a hand waved. Crista focused, nearly whimpering in relief at the sight of Rowdy Mackay.

She didn't know who was driving, but Rowdy was in the backseat. He was holding up fingers. Six fingers. Pointed around her.

Six. Six people following them. She didn't dare nod, couldn't do anything to draw attention to herself. She checked the rearview mirror but didn't see Dawg. He would be there, though. If Rowdy was here, then Dawg was close.

Rowdy held up a piece of paper then.

"Do as he says!" The thick black wording glared back at her.

She lifted one finger from the steering wheel to indicate she understood.

"Don't worry, Johnny. I'm watching her," Jim assured him. "We'll be there soon, and everything can proceed as planned. Just make certain you're ready."

She glanced back at him. He kept his eyes trained on her, his scowl firmly in place.

She turned back. Rowdy was holding up another note.

"You're covered!"

She lifted her fingers to indicate that she understood. Then he turned around; the car changed lanes again and let the van pass them.

She was covered. She inhaled slowly. Deeply. Dawg wouldn't let anything happen to her now. She just had to stay calm.

"I love you, baby. Just stay cool. Another fifteen minutes, and we'll be there." Jim's rough voice softened, almost making Crista ill. And it had nothing to do with the obviously sexual relationship between him and Johnny. But how could a man love anyone that much and be a killer?

Jim shifted then, moving between the seats and glancing out the front window. He looked around with quiet satisfaction, checked the rearview mirror, then moved to the back of the van to look through the dark, tinted windows.

"Excellent," he grunted. "See, we got away free and clear, Crista. Dawg didn't even know when you left. I wonder if he's even realized that you're not at the store any longer."

"He'll know." He would have known within minutes.

Jim laughed. "He doesn't know shit. I made sure of it. He had such a mess to untangle in the lumberyard that he's probably still trying to figure it out. I planned this very carefully, you know."

Not well enough. Crista stared straight ahead and tried to concentrate on just breathing. Dawg was close; she could feel him. Everything would be okay. She repeated it to herself over and over again and prayed she was right.

Dawg kept the van in sight from the backseat of the bright red extended-cab pickup truck Cranston and Dane had been waiting in outside the front of the store.

He was sweating. He could feel the moisture rolling from his forehead and dampening his back. He had promised to keep her safe. He remembered that. As they drove to Johnny's, he had promised her that nothing would happen. They were just going to let him know they were onto him, make him mess up. Everything was going to be just fine.

He should have known better. God help him, he should have figured out a year ago that he couldn't tempt fate that damned far. He should have known Johnny had an accomplice. Someone close to Dawg. Someone who had somehow figured out he was working with the ATF.

That someone was Jim Bedsford. Ex-military with contacts that Dawg was certain extended into the law enforcement community. Jim had been involved with Special Forces and deep cover investigations during his time in the Army.

"Someone messed up on this one," he commented as though he weren't imagining drawing someone's blood for the mess-up. Particularly Cranston's.

"We have her covered, Dawg," Cranston assured him, not for the first time. "We have a tracker on Alex's vehicle as well as that purse we found in Grace's house. His tail verified he left the house by the back door dressed as Crista, and he's driving Alex's car. We won't lose him."

Surveillance video on the detention center had managed to identify the car Johnny had been using to visit his buddies. Alex's car was supposed to be locked in the unattached garage behind the house he and Crista had grown up in. Johnny had her house keys and the keys to that garage and to the car.

"Do you know how many different ways I'm going to kill you if you do, Cranston?" Dawg asked him softly.

Cranston cleared his throat uneasily. "I don't have a worry, Dawg. We have it covered."

"Grace just turned off the highway and headed up a hunters' road to the lake," Greta Dane reported. She pulled up a map on the laptop she held on her lap, the moving red dot indicating the car Johnny was driving.

"Natches, are you getting this?" Dawg asked over the speaker line set on his cell phone.

"I have it here, Dawg," Natches said softly. "He's heading toward the old Bridgeland hunting cabin. I'll circle around and get in place. Don't worry, Bro. I'll cover her."

Dawg heard the complete unemotional determination in Natches's voice and felt the tight knot of fear begin to uncoil in his belly. Natches's loyalty was unquestioned, as was his ability with the rifle Dawg knew he kept close by.

"I'm heading there," Dawg told him. "Don't take any chances, Natches. I don't care if Bedsford and Johnny both lose gray matter. Keep Crista safe for me."

"No fears, Bro."

Dawg knew that tone of voice. There was every chance in the world that Bedsford and Johnny would end up with a bullet in the head anyway.

"Natches, you follow fucking orders," Cranston snapped out furiously as he flicked Dawg an enraged glare in the rearview mirror. "We need those two alive."

The call disconnected.

"Damn it, Dawg," the special agent snarled. "If those two end up dead, I'll take it out of your hide."

"If those two end up dead, I won't lose a single night's sleep over it," Dawg growled in return. "Don't fuck with me, Cranston. You knew Bedsford was involved in this, and you didn't deign to tell any of us. And don't bother denying it."

It had taken Dawg a few minutes to put it together, and if he hadn't known Cranston as well as he did, he wouldn't have suspected it. But he did know Cranston. Throw a wild card in the mix, and he was killer-cold. Cranston wasn't cold. If he wasn't driving, he would be rubbing his hands together in glee.

"How did you figure out Bedsford was involved in this?"

Cranston cursed under his breath. "He's related to the dead transport driver, Private Dwayne Stockton. There were cell phone calls to Bedsford in the weeks before he was killed."

"And I didn't know this why?" Dawg had to force the words past his lips and his hand off his weapon.

"Because he was working for you, and I decided to wait before informing you of the fact."

Son of a bitch. "You thought I was involved."

"I didn't believe you were involved, but I had to be certain. By the time I was certain, Miss Jansen was involved, and I had to decide the best way to handle it. I handled it by watching your back and hers until I knew what was going on."

"The van is turning off," Dane said softly. "Natches has directed our men in front of him using an alternate route. Grace is in place, and Natches has him in sight."

"Turn right at the next road," Dawg directed them, hating the thought of losing sight of Crista in that damned van. "The next road will keep us parallel to him and put us in place to move on foot to the cabin."

The Bridgeland hunting cabin had more than one dirt track leading to it due to the four-wheelers often used to access it.

Dawg wiped his hand across his brow, his gaze locked on the van ahead of them until Cranston made the turn. The coil of fury and fear iced in his gut then.

Dawg pulled his handgun from the holster at his back and checked the clip. Replacing it, he pulled the extra clips from the supply Cranston had tossed in the back, checked them quickly, then loaded the bulletproof vest before pulling it on and strapping the sides in place.

God bless Layla Matcher's heart. If it hadn't been for her standing at the window and seeing Jim Bedsford forcing Crista into that van, then Dawg would have never found her.

Cranston had been watching for Johnny Grace in the main customer parking lot. It was evident that no one had expected Bedsford to move this fast or to do so without Johnny physically backing him.

"Bedsford had the contacts for the black market buyers," Cranston told him. "We found that out only in the past twenty-four hours. The Swedish mercenary making the buy finally made a deal with the federal prosecutor. He didn't have Bedsford's name, but he had enough information for us to ID him. He spent his time in the Army making contacts in the black market and setting up weapons deals."

"You should have been on the ball, Cranston." Dawg strapped a backup weapon to his ankle and stuffed several spare clips for it into another pocket of the vest. "You fucked up."

"Information was slow coming in." Cranston shook his head. "Our sources do have other things they're working on as well, you know."

"You fucked up. And if Crista gets hurt, then you've really fucked up. Because I'll kill you."

Dawg didn't let free the fury burning in a small corner of his mind. He kept it bottled, kept it contained. He couldn't afford it now, not when logic and clear thinking alone were going to get Crista through this.

His cell phone beeped.

"Give me the goods," he answered with the order to Natches.

"I'm positioned in one of the pines beside the cabin on the side Bedsford's van will have to use. Johnny's here in full Crista disguise. Hell, Dawg, he looks hot." There was murder in Natches's voice. "Want me to draw a little blood?"

"Hold tight. Cranston has a transmitter in that damned pocketbook Johnny's carrying as well as in the wig. I'll be in place before Bedsford gets there. We'll go in together."

"Here." Cranston tossed him an earbud. "We're close enough to use these. Tell Natches to put his in place now. Don't fuck with me, Dawg. This is a team play, not a vendetta."

"Use the earbud, Natches." Dawg grinned back at Cranston through the rearview mirror. The sight of that smile had the special agent's gaze flickering.

Attaching the communications device, Dawg activated it, then tested it quickly before disconnecting the phone. Cranston and Dane were both similarly wired as, Dawg assumed, the rest of the team was.

"Now, we're all here," Cranston spoke into the device.

"Now I can tell you I'm going to kick your ass personally when this is over, Cranston," Natches spoke through the ear receiver. "Didn't I warn you about pulling surprises on us, man?"

Cranston grunted. "Keep your finger off that trigger, Natches, and your eyes on Grace. Let's at least get a little evidence against these bastards before we start shooting. If you don't mind, that is?"

"And if I mind?"

TWENTY-THREE

Natches kept his sniper rifle trained on Johnny and his finger on the trigger. That finger twitched. He wanted to kill the bastard so damned bad it was all he could do to hold back. It ate at his gut with a power that nearly gave him indigestion.

Johnny Grace. He was a first cousin. He had been raised with them when he was younger, until he, Rowdy, and Dawg figured out that Johnny was more like Natches's father than the gentle, smiling father Johnny'd had.

Ralph Grace, before his death, had managed to keep his wife and his son in check. After his death, though, Nadine and Johnny had revealed the vicious, evil streak they possessed.

He caressed the trigger of his rifle as he trained his sights on Johnny's forehead. Fucking bastard. God, how he hated Johnny. It was a hatred that nearly rivaled the hatred he had for his own father, Dayle Mackay.

As he stared through the rifle sights, he didn't see the image Johnny was trying to impersonate, that of Dawg's lover, Crista Jansen. No, he saw Johnny. Just Johnny. His beady little eyes narrowed as he leaned against Alex's car, his arms crossed over his fake breasts as he watched the dirt road he expected Bedsford to use.

Natches knew he should have expected this. He should have known Cranston was hiding shit; it was what Cranston did best. And to be honest, he had suspected it; he just hadn't put two and two together fast enough.

Because he had been too damned busy holding back a more personal fury.

It was bad enough that Rowdy had to be so damned possessive over Kelly, but now Dawg had to go and do the same thing with Crista. That lack of connection was affecting him. He was beginning to feel disassociated, cold. That tight knot of bitter ice inside his soul that he had fought all his life was hardening now.

Rowdy and Dawg had grown up, and they had grown away, though he was certain they didn't see it that way. Since Rowdy had taken Kelly, Natches had tried to share time with Dawg and Rowdy rather than women. But hell, women took up time, and Kelly was as spoiled as any female ever had been by Rowdy.

Sometimes, Natches thought they lived in each other's pockets, and now Dawg and Crista were taking the same route. And Natches was left standing on the outside, watching, wondering, and regretting.

He had thought the sharing would continue. He had let himself care for Kelly, let her into his heart, believing that when Rowdy came home that he would be a part of the intimacy, only to find out that Rowdy had found a core of possessiveness somewhere.

And Dawg. Dawg was doing the same thing. No other man would touch Crista without finding himself wishing he had held back. And Dawg was a mean bastard when he was riled.

And this was why Natches hadn't connected Bedsford and Johnny. Because he was too busy adjusting to changes that he hadn't expected, too busy trying to find a way to keep the ice around his soul melted.

He wasn't succeeding. A testament to that fact had his finger aching to twitch just enough to put a bullet in the back of Johnny's head.

Johnny had instigated every beating, every humiliation, every vicious attack Dayle Mackay had ever made against Natches. He had carried rumors to his father, and in many cases, proof of Natches's supposed crimes.

Sharing his women. Drinking too young. The instances were too many to name and too dangerous to remember right now.

His shoulder ached like hell as he stood amid the thick branches of the pine tree, his rifle resting on one thickly needled tree branch as he bent to keep Johnny in sight.

The bullet that had taken him out of the Marines hadn't completely taken him out of the game. Once an assassin, always an assassin. Once a man deliberately set his sights on another man and pulled the trigger, then it was a part of him forever. He might walk away from it, but he could never escape it.

Natches hadn't wanted to walk away or to escape. He just hadn't had any other choice.

"Natches, we're moving into position." Dawg's voice came across the receiver in his ear. "Bedsford should be driving into the cabin yard any second."

Natches lifted his gaze from the gun sights and stared down the road.

"In sight." The van was pulling up the dirt track, bouncing over the ruts as the driver obviously took her time.

Crista was driving. Natches's gut clenched at the fear she must be feeling. She was depending on them to protect her, trusting Dawg and him to make certain nothing happened to her.

"Natches." Dawg said his name, nothing more, but he understood the message in it. The plea that Natches keep her safe, no matter the cost.

"I have her covered, Bro," he said quietly. "No fears."

"Natches, we need those two alive," Cranston repeated. "We need them all alive. Don't you pull any shit on me."

The corners of Natches's lips kicked up in amusement. It was a good thing he liked Cranston.

"Do your job; I'll do mine," he said softly. "Crista is priority. Period."

Cranston cursed, but Natches could have sworn he heard Dawg's breath of relief.

He'd die for Dawg and Rowdy. Without them, he wouldn't

have survived past his teens. He was irked at the direction their lives had taken; at times, he was damned pissed off over it. But he understood it. Rowdy especially. Rowdy had never known the darkness that Natches and Dawg had lived through. And even Dawg, who had known the pain but not the pure evil that Natches had experienced.

Kelly and Crista had healed Rowdy and Dawg. He couldn't blame the two women for not seeing the loneliness it had caused in Natches.

Loneliness doesn't kill, though. It aches, it taunts, but it doesn't kill. He could survive loneliness.

"Van in sight." Natches came to attention as the white panel van drove into the cabin's yard.

He wrapped the strap of his rifle around one hand, held it steady against the branch, and caressed the trigger with the other. He'd have to take Bedsford out first, then Johnny, if it came to killing.

He would protect Crista. Rowdy and Dawg had protected him, saved him. He could do no less for them now.

Crista pulled the van to a stop beside Alex's car and stared at the vintage '67 navy blue Camaro. She stared at the car and would have winced at the fury Alex was going to experience if he ever learned his baby made it out of the garage he kept it locked in.

He was going to explode all over Johnny Grace with a force that would strip the man's flesh from his bones and make him pray for forgiveness.

If Johnny managed to live past Dawg, that was.

"You know, Johnny just signed both your death warrants with that car, right?" she asked as Bedsford straightened behind her. "Alex will hunt you to hell and back."

"He'll have to find us first." The side panel door opened, and he turned back to her with a wave of the gun. "Come on, lady. Let's get this over with so we can get the hell out of your fine little county."

Crista moved stiffly from the driver's seat, her gaze on the gun in his hand before moving past it and stepping out into the dirt clearing to face Johnny.

She stared at him, her gaze going over the clothes he wore. One of her best dresses. The wig was a near-perfect match to her hair, and with the makeup he had used, his features were almost similar.

And he was leaning against the Camaro, a wide smile on his face as she watched him silently.

"You did good, baby," Johnny told Bedsford quietly as the other man moved to him.

Johnny lifted his face and gave Bedsford a quick kiss while keeping his eyes on Crista.

"Poor Crista." Johnny sighed as Bedsford moved away from him. "You should have kept your distance from Dawg. I could have helped you out a bit here if you had. Besides, torturing my cousin was one of the points of this game that I enjoyed the most."

"How sad," Crista whispered, meaning it. "You've spent your life coveting everything Dawg is and has rather than building your own life. Why?"

His eyes narrowed on her. "Because it should have been mine. Haven't you figured it out yet, Crista? I actually thought Dawg would have figured it out, but he was never smart enough to put two and two together."

She stared back at him, old gossip whipping through her mind as she traced his features, his build. He looked like his mother, nothing like his father, so it was impossible to tell.

He chuckled, a low, frightening sound. "You remember, don't you? After Ralph Grace died, the rumors began slithering through the county like snakes that refused to die. Mother was pregnant when she married Ralph. Unfortunately, Ralph wasn't the father, no matter how much he thought he was."

It was sickening.

Crista glanced away from him, her eyes closing momentarily at the thought of those old tales.

"Yes, Chandler Mackay was my father." He sounded girlishly pleased at relating that information. "I was actually born first, by a few days. Brenda Mackay, Dawg's mother, knew, of course, and used it to force our father to sign it all over to Dawg in his will. The stupid bitch, she should have taken her little bastard and left then rather than hang around and steal everything that should have been mine."

Crista felt her knees weaken at the fury in Johnny's voice.

Incest. Chandler Mackay, it had been rumored, had been sleeping with his sister for years before she married Ralph Grace, and then again, after the other man's death. There were those who swore that Chandler Mackay had had a hand in Grace's death himself.

She turned and looked at Bedsford then, watching as his gaze roamed around the area, eyes narrowed, as though searching for something.

"Your boyfriend here thinks you're going to run to Nicaragua with him, Johnny," she said, more to distract Bedsford than anything else. "I told him you would never leave Somerset or Dawg. What would be the point of all this if you couldn't torture him with it?"

A self-satisfied smile shaped Johnny's lips as Bedsford turned to him.

"Our plans may change now that I have you here." He shrugged his shoulders as though it didn't matter. "Why leave Somerset when, like you say, I can stay here and torture all parties involved?"

"So you definitely intend to kill me." She prayed Dawg was close. Surely if he was here by now, he would have done something.

"I really don't have a choice, sweetheart." He sighed, shaking his head in mock compassion.

"That wasn't the plan, Johnny." Bedsford stared at him in shock. "We can't stay around here now. There's no way the Mackays won't know we were involved."

"They won't know anything, Jim," he promised, reaching out to touch the scowl on the other man's face. "Settle down, lover. Everything will work out perfectly. You'll see."

Crista saw it coming, and she was certain Jim should have, most likely did. The hand holding the gun twitched as his scowl deepened, but Johnny's other hand came up too fast. The gun he held exploded. The bullet tore into Bedsford's chest, straight through his heart, and left him staring back at Johnny in shock.

He fell to his knees, his hands reaching out to Johnny as Johnny stepped back; then Bedsford toppled over to the ground.

Crista stared in shock, her eyes locked with Jim Beds-ford's surprised, agonized gaze as it slowly dimmed and grew cold.

"That was unfortunate." Johnny sighed.

Crista lifted her head, only then noticing that Johnny wore clear latex gloves over his hands.

"He loved you," she said, knowing it didn't matter. Nothing mattered to Johnny but destroying Dawg.

"Of course he loved me." Johnny rolled his eyes at the declaration. "He adored me. I worked hard to make certain he did. But I no longer need him. This way, I don't have to split the million dollars, and I don't have to leave Somerset for fear of him growing a conscience over his cousin's death. Jim was a bit of a whiner. He didn't like killing the boy."

"Dawg knows you're involved in this, Johnny. If you kill me, he won't need the law on his side. He'll take you apart. You know he will."

"A million dollars can buy a lot of protection. And Dawg and Natches aren't the only ones who know how to hide and fire a rifle, Crista," he told her with amused unconcern.

Johnny couldn't know the evidence the agents had on him; if he did, he wouldn't be so certain. All she had to do was be patient; Dawg would be there. Johnny wouldn't expect that. As far as he knew, no one would even consider suspecting him of impersonating her.

"And Alex? Do you think he won't take up where Dawg might fail? This isn't going to go over as easy as you think it will, Johnny."

He was silent for long moments. Moments that seemed to drag out, to stand still as the forest around them held its breath. Silence descended in the clearing as the smell of blood and death began to fill Crista's head.

She could feel herself shaking, shuddering.

Where was Dawg? Rowdy had promised he would be here, that they were watching her, following her. A chill of fear raced through her body, causing her to clench her teeth to keep them from chattering.

"I've had this planned for a long time, Crista." He sighed. "Though I hadn't intended to kill you. Only make certain you were arrested for my crimes." His smile was maniacal. "That would have destroyed Dawg. He's really in love with you, you know that? He nearly drank himself to death after you left eight years ago. Of course, he didn't remember the night you spent with him. And"—his smile became demonic—"he didn't know about your miscarriage either, did he? Does he know now?"

"He knows." Her throat was so tight she felt as though she were strangling. "What you don't understand, Johnny, is that he knows you were involved. The Homeland Security agents know it's you; Alex will know. You are not going to get away with this."

"No one has enough proof for anything." He waved her warning away. "No one can touch me, Crista. I made sure of it. When your bodies are found, it's going to look like you had a disagreement and killed each other. And of course, I'll give a statement that Jim confided his affair with you to me. Too many people are aware that we were at least friends. I have it all worked out, sweetheart." He moved then, sliding to the side as he waved the gun toward Alex's car. "Move on over here now."

Crista moved slowly, praying. Dawg had to be close by. She could feel him, feel eyes watching her, just as she was certain Jim had until she distracted him. Before Johnny killed him.

"There you go." Johnny smiled back at her as he bent and lifted Jim's gun from the ground. "Now, all I have to do is put a bullet in your heart, place the weapons appropriately, and drive out of here. It's all over now."

"Like hell!" Crista snarled. She wasn't going to make this easy for him.

Everything seemed to happen simultaneously then. Crista threw herself in front of Alex's car, hitting the ground as she heard a bullet ricochet off the metal. Then the forest seemed to come alive with gunfire.

She rolled to her back, watching as Johnny took the first bullet to his head, the second, third, and fourth to his chest. His body jerked violently as blood sprayed around him.

"Crista!" Dawg's voice screamed out her name. Then he was there, his arms coming around her, jerking her to the other side of the car, his hands running frantically over her.

"Are you okay? Crista, baby, answer me." She stared up at him, dazed, feeling the blood racing through her head, pounding into her brain as shock began to shudder through her.

"Oh God," she whispered, feeling the darkness edging around her. "I'm going to fucking faint."

His face swam in front of her vision as her lashes fluttered.

"You faint on me, and I swear to God I won't fuck you for a week," he snarled, his voice low, his expression violent. "Don't you dare, Crista Ann."

Won't fuck her for a week? Could she make it a week? Could she keep the darkness from spreading through her?

She smiled, feeling amusement thread through the darkness.

"It's okay. Week works." And she gave in to it.

There were no wounds. The only blood on her was what had splattered from Bedsford. She was dusty, her arms scraped from throwing herself to the ground, and tears tracked her face.

She was pale, but she was breathing.

Dawg clasped her to him, burying his face in her hair as he realized he was shuddering and tears were escaping from between his lashes as he rocked her against his chest.

She was alive. Dear God, she was alive, she was safe. She was safe, and nothing else mattered. He pulled her as close to his body as he could get her, feeling the silent sobs that racked his chest.

He had no idea how much he had loved her until he saw that gun leveling on her. Until he saw the moment that Johnny was actually going to pull the trigger. His world had narrowed down to one thing. To stopping it. No matter what it took. No matter how much blood Johnny shed or whether or not Cranston had his suspects.

Then the forest had exploded with gunfire.

"Dawg, man, is she okay?"

Alex? Dawg lifted his face from her hair and stared at the camouflage face paint, the fear in the other man's gray eyes, and the savage contours of his expression.

"What the fuck are you doing here?" Dawg snarled, his hand pressing Crista's head closer to his chest. "Where the hell were you when he was pointing the gun at her chest?"

Alex's smile was tight as he sat back on his heels and indicated the four other similarly painted and dressed men around him. "Recording this little event for the authorities," he stated. "Tyrell had point; he put one of the bullets in Grace's head. I suspect Natches can take credit for the other one. Mark." He waved his hand to the hard-eyed soldier at his side. "Crista stayed with him and Ty in Virginia. When you called the emergency number, it went through Mark. He pulled in some friends while I ditched a mission in Afghanistan. We pulled in here at midnight last night after Mark managed to get the information on the op here and we followed Johnny in."

"You moved fast." Dawg inhaled roughly, his hand pressed at Crista's back, feeling each breath.

"I had a feeling she was being pulled into something last time I talked to her." Alex sighed. "I had everything in place just in case."

"Everything but the emergency number," Dawg snapped. "Son of a bitch, Alex, don't you think she needed it?"

"If she had it, she wouldn't have gone to you," Alex told him then. "I wanted her where she needed to be."

"She didn't come to you, you stupid bastard." Dawg was enraged. "She nearly got her ass killed in a warehouse during the attack we made on the buyers and sellers of those stupid fucking weapons. Grace set her up, Alex. She almost died there."

Alex paled. "She didn't call you?"

"Not even on a fucking dare." Fury was pounding through him now. "You're a lucky bastard I managed to save her ass. Otherwise, I'd have to kill you now."

"Hell, I didn't know she was that damned stubborn." Alex rubbed his hand over his face, smearing the face paint he wore as he stared around the clearing. "I'll have to have a talk with her about that."

"The hell you will." Dawg gathered her closer as sirens wailed along the rough track leading into the cabin yard. "Tell me there's a fucking medic here somewhere?"

"Ty." Alex turned to one of the two men standing behind him. "Get your pack and check her out. Where's Cranston?"

Alex rose to his feet, his in-charge voice echoing through the area as Cranston cursed in the background.

Tyrell Grayson came down on his knees beside Crista, his fingers going to her neck, his expression concerned.

"She lived with you?" Dawg snarled. "Slept with you?"

Hard lips kicked up in a grin. "Mark and I babied the hell out of her," he said then. "See if you can do near as well."

Dawg's gaze sliced to Mark Lessing. Both men were dangerous, as dangerous as Alex and just as hard. There wasn't an ounce of softness in them.

"Thank you." He had to force the words past his clenched teeth. "For taking care of her."

Ty nodded sharply. "That's us. Protector of broken hearts. Take better care of her this time, or we're going to break your bones."

It wasn't a threat, it was a warning. An unneeded one at that.

"She's good." Ty finally nodded sharply. "She'll wake up with a headache, probably. I've never seen her faint, but I know tension gives her killer headaches. I'd be more comfortable if you'd let them transport her to the hospital and keep her overnight though, just to be sure."

Dawg nodded as Natches and Rowdy flanked him then.

"I see you don't need our help." Ty stood to his feet, staring down at Crista with the first flash of softness that Dawg had glimpsed in him. "She's a damned good woman, man. And she's grieved for you for far too long. See if you can't make up for that now. She deserves it." He nodded before giving Dawg a chance to say anything and turned away.

"My bullet hit Johnny's forehead at the same time someone else's did," Natches informed him. "Same place, same time. Those boys aren't slouches."

Alex's team was slowly disappearing into the forest as Alex kept Cranston busy.

"Alex recorded everything." Dawg stood, lifting Crista into his arms as the ambulance Cranston had had standing by pulled into the lane. "Cranston has what he needs. I have what I need."

Crista, resting against him, safe, unharmed. And hell yes, he would make damned sure he made up for those lost years. Just as soon as he had her checked out at the hospital and she was capable of taking his loving.

Wait a week as he threatened? There wasn't a chance in hell. The minute he could get inside her and assure himself she was still his, unharmed, safe and sound, the better. He wouldn't breathe easy until then. Hell, he didn't know if his heart was going to stop racing like a runaway horse until then.

"She did good," Natches murmured. "Made them talk. And when she realized Johnny was ready to shoot, she fought. She's strong, Dawg."

"Yeah. She is." He kissed the top of her head as the EMTs jerked the gurney from the back of the ambulance and another raced toward them. "And she's safe. That's all that counts."

TWENTY-FOUR

"Look, I'm just fine." Two days later, Crista paced the living room of the houseboat and glared at Dawg as he sat back on the couch. "I want to go back to work."

"Not yet." He was as uncompromising as he had been hours before when she tried to leave for the lumber store.

"I have to get those displays set, or it's going to be too late."

"Layla and her brood are taking care of it." He picked up his glass of sweet tea and drank from it casually as his green eyes stared at her from over the rim of the glass.

"I'm bored." She propped her hands on her hips and faced him, heating up at the way his gaze went over the shorts and loose T-shirt she wore. "I don't like being cooped up for no reason. I'm not a damned invalid."

But she could have been. Or worse.

Dawg set the glass carefully on the end table, forcing back the remembered horror of the day he nearly lost her.

"Dawg. Would you please put that glass on the coaster beside it," she bit out. "That is why I put it there."

He smiled blandly and placed the glass on the protective coaster before staring back at her.

He had noticed her hard nipples an hour before. The way she watched him expectantly, obviously more than ready to be touched.

He'd held back since bringing her home the day before. Despite his own arousal, his anticipation, and the need to take her, he had forced himself to control the need.

She had to come to him. He'd blackmailed her, more or less forced her into his bed, and despite the fact that he knew she loved him, he needed her to reach out for him.

"What do you intend to do today, then?" Her gaze flickered to his lap and his obvious arousal.

"Whatever you want to do. As long as it doesn't entail leaving the marina," he inserted as her lips parted in reply.

A frown creased her brow as her lips tightened.

She had no idea how little he wanted to share her with the curious employees and customers at that damned store. He didn't want anyone else around her right now. He wanted to stare at her, hear her voice as she spoke to him alone, and let himself believe she was safe.

He had nightmares now. He'd spent four years in the Marines, two of those years training as an assassin, and he'd brought no nightmares home with him. But now, demons chased him through his dreams. Demons intent on forcing him to relive the day he had nearly lost her. Forced him to face the horror of his life as Johnny's bullet pierced her chest.

He could handle the nightmares. He couldn't have lived through the reality of it.

"Stop looking at me like that." Her soft voice drew him back from the nightmares. "I'm fine."

She was still bruised. Her arms were still scraped. There was a scratch on her cheek. He stared back her, refusing to forget what he had nearly lost.

"Yes, you're fine." He nodded as he stretched his arms on the back of the couch and let his gaze linger over her body.

Hard nipples pressing against thin cotton. He wondered if her pussy was wet. Silken bare flesh glistening with feminine cream. The thought of it had his mouth watering.

"Your business is going to fail at this rate," she warned him, but he saw the softening of her body, the almost imperceptible shift of her thighs, her accelerated breathing.

"So?" He licked his lips at the thought of tasting her.

"Could I convince you to go in later?" The insinuation in her voice had his brows lifting as he met her gaze.

"I'm easy," he assured her. "If you have something to bargain with." He made certain his gaze let her know exactly how he liked bargaining.

Crista almost smiled at the look. She had known when she awoke in his arms, his erection prodding her rear, but Dawg was in an unusual mood. He wasn't intent on relieving his arousal. For some reason, he was making himself wait. As the morning progressed, she began to figure out why.

He wanted her as bad as she wanted him. But Dawg needed acceptance. He needed her to come to him. The past hour had been a battle for that as she pushed him, tested his resolve, and only became more aroused as he held back.

What would he do once that control slipped? Once the hunger had him by the throat, how much more intent would he become?

She didn't want slow, easy sex. She didn't want foreplay. She wanted affirmation. She wanted him hard and deep inside her, pounding into her pussy and marking her with his hunger.

She wanted Dawg wild. She wanted all that hunger and all that emotion washing over her like a tidal wave.

But he wasn't going to be pushed into taking it.

"Yes, I've heard you're easy." She nodded sagely, hiding her grin at the frown that snapped between his brows.

"Easy for you," he amended with a scowl.

"Really?" She lifted her brows in disbelief. "You're being very stubborn today."

"You're just not convincing me the right way." His lips twitched in amusement, though his gaze was intent and hot.

"Really?" She shifted, her fingers playing with the hem of her T-shirt as she stared back at him beneath her lashes. "What would it take to convince you, Dawg?"

He swallowed tightly as she eased the T-shirt higher. She wasn't wearing a bra. She hadn't bothered after her shower in the face of Dawg's stubborn refusal to go to the store.

His hands tightened on the back of the couch.

"Do you know what I used to dream, Dawg?" she whispered as her fingers played over her stomach.

"What?" His gaze was locked on those fingers, his own fingers caressing the back of the couch in reflex.

"I used to dream that you came to me. That you walked into the apartment I shared with Mark and Ty. They would be gone. You'd step into the door, take one look at me, and then you took me. Against the wall. My legs wrapped around your hips as you pounded into me."

She pulled the shirt over her head and tossed it to the floor before her hands moved to her shorts. She got as far as pushing the elastic band over her thighs before he moved.

His shirt ripped over his head and flew to the side. Before she could do more than breathe in roughly, he was on his knees in front of her, pulling her thighs apart and burying his lips between them.

"Fuck it," he snarled. "I'm a wimp. No control."

She would have gone to the floor if he wasn't holding her up. His tongue slid through the narrow slit of her pussy, licking as he moaned before his lips surrounded the hardened bud of her clit.

She wanted hard and hungry, and he was going to give it to her. She could feel it.

Her back met the wall before she realized he had maneuvered her the few steps to it. Her shorts were on the floor, and Dawg lifted her leg, laying it over his shoulder as his head dipped and his tongue drove inside her sex.

"Oh God!" Crista's head hit the wall as she shuddered at the feel of his tongue fucking inside her.

His lips moved, slid back to her clit, while his fingers took the place of his tongue, and she was melting around him.

"I have to fuck you," he muttered, licking around her clit, sipping at it, kissing it. "You're killing me. I can't wait a week."

"Don't wait a minute," she moaned, pulling at his shoulders. "Fuck me, Dawg. Now."

"Soon."

"Now."

He replaced her foot on the floor and rose to his feet, but his hands pressed to her shoulders.

"Suck my cock," he ordered roughly. "Let me watch you suck me."

Crista went eagerly to her knees, her hands surrounding the thick, hard flesh as she covered the head hungrily. She wasn't teasing. She was too desperate now, the heat rising hard and fast inside her, burning her alive with the need to feel him inside her.

She sucked at the engorged crest, her tongue flickering over it as her hands stroked the throbbing shaft. She loved having him in her mouth, feeling the hard throb of blood pounding through it, tasting the sharp saltiness of pre-cum on her tongue.

He was fucking her lips with shallow movements, his hands tangling in her hair, his head thrown back in pleasure. His thighs were rock hard, his abs flexing tight as the fingers of one hand curled around his balls.

"Fuck. That's good," he groaned. "You suck like a dream, Crista. So fucking good."

His voice was rasping, sending a thrill of sensation racing down her spine at the pleasure it contained.

Her tongue probed beneath the crest before curling over it, her mouth sucking him deeper as she stared up his broad chest.

Sweat beaded on the hair-spattered flesh, glistening on the teak skin and catching on the short curls. She mouthed his cock head, moaned on it, and then cried out in impending ecstasy as he pulled her to her feet.

"Against the wall," he bit out, his lips pulling back from his teeth as he stared back at her with fiery lust. "Oh, baby, I can take you against the wall."

One arm wrapped around her hips as he lifted her, the other easing one leg around his hip as her other leg followed on the opposite side.

A second later, Crista cried out sharply, pain and pleasure whipping through her at the fierce, hard thrust that sent him burrowing through the snug tissue of her pussy.

"God, yes!" His hands gripped her rear as he rocked against her, stroking her internally, sending cataclysms of sensation to attack her nerve endings. "You're so fucking tight, Crista. So hot and sweet."

"Do it again," she moaned, her hands gripping his shoulders, nails biting into his flesh as he pulled back. "Take me hard again."

He retreated, nearly sliding free of her grip before shafting inside her with a quick, forceful thrust.

"Oh God, Dawg. I love that," she cried out hoarsely.

"Love that, do you, sweetheart?" He retreated again, plunged inside her again, stroked the internal blaze higher until sweat soaked their bodies in an effort to regulate the body heat.

There was no regulating the hunger building sharp and fast inside them. Crista could feel her juices flowing between them in response to the pleasure. Dawg's cock was fierce, thick inside her, stroking once-hidden nerve endings and burning her with the liquid-hot lust building harder inside them.

"Want more?" His hands tightened on her rear, his fingers sliding inside the narrow cleft until they met the damp entrance there.

He stroked, he played. He let his fingers dip inside her as his cock pounded inside her pussy. Tingles of sharp heat, hard thrusts that sent shocking waves of sensation tearing through her womb.

It was too much. He began to thrust faster, harder inside her with deep, plunging strokes that sent waves of sensation, violent pleasure, and emotion clashing inside her.

"I love you." She couldn't hold the words back. "I love you. Always loved you. Dreamed . . ." Tears filled her eyes and fell to her cheeks. "Oh God, Dawg, I dreamed . . ."

"And I dreamed, Crista," he groaned, his lips moving to her shoulders, then her neck, as his hips thrust and surged, filling her with his cock in quick, hard strokes. "Dreamed of loving you. Holding you. Always loving you."

Emotion fueled pleasure and fueled lust. The conflagration that resulted had them both crying out. Crista's wails mixed with his harsh, male groans as ecstasy began to explode inside them, then around them.

She felt the hard, fierce jets of cum exploding inside her. He felt the tight, heated clasp of her pussy gripping him like a fiery fist, flexing around him and throwing him higher into his own release.

Long minutes later, they found themselves on the floor, breathing hard, their bodies still tangled together, arms wrapped tightly around each other.

"Leave me again, and I won't fuck you for a week," Dawg mumbled against her ear.

"Forget about fucking me again, and I'll shoot you myself." She gave him an unladylike snort, then smiled at the slow stiffening of his cock inside her.

"I didn't forget the first time," he whispered then. "I just didn't want to accept that I had been so damned stupid. You lived in my dreams, Crista. Every night you were away from me, you lived in my dreams. And in my soul."

She leaned back and stared at him, seeing the intensity in his eyes, the light green seeming to glow inside his dark face as the sensual fulfillment relaxed his features.

"No more dreams," she whispered. "Just this."

"Just this."

This being more than love, more than lust. It was the dream, the hidden wish, and the fulfillment of two hearts meeting, two souls merging.

"I love you," she whispered. "And I'm looking forward to many many naughty nights in your arms, Dawg."

"Many," he promised. "Many naughty nights in my heart."

There, in the center of the room where it had all begun eight years before, the future began. For Dawg and Crista.

Weeks Later

Natches listened to the sounds of the night. It was late summer. The lake was filled with those determined to take advantage of every second of the final days of summer.

Kids laughed, parents chided, teenagers dashed about the docks, and the sound of boats returning for the night filled the air with life.

And if he listened closely, really closely, he thought he could hear the sounds of pleasure coming from the boat beside his. He'd moved from his place beside the *Nauti Boy* after Kelly moved in with Rowdy. He'd parked the *Nauti Dreams* on the other side of Dawg's boat instead.

There was no place left to move to avoid the late-night whispers of passion and pleasure that sometimes flowed from the two boats.

He slouched farther in his chair and stared out over the lake from the upper deck of the boat and considered his options. There weren't a lot.

He was sure sick of bullets chasing him, though, sick of toting a sniper's rifle, and sick to damned death of the lovey-dovey kissy-faced shit going on around him. His two cousins and their women, monogamous and proud of it.

He finished his beer at the thought of that, then opened another. There wasn't much danger of getting drunk; he didn't keep the hard stuff on the boat, so that kinda canceled out becoming oblivious.

Hell, he could move into town. There was an apartment over the garage, and he was spending more time there anyway. Anything to get away from the monogamous bliss settling in on the back side of the Mackay docks.

He breathed out roughly. They weren't the hell-raising, high-living, hard-loving trio they used to be. The Mackay cousins were no more.

And that made for a very, very lonely night.

Look for Lora Leigh's
new Novel of the Breeds

Styx's Storm

Available now from Berkley Sensation!

The bar was hopping, with music pounding, drinks flowing smoothly and customers packing the bar area and dance floor. It was one of those country holes-in-the-wall that attracted both criminal elements and the upper class, and everything in between. It was one of those places Storme could slide into, and her scent would become masked by the dozens of sweating, lusty, alcohol-infused bodies that filled it.

The band was actually pretty good, the lead singers sultry when they needed to be, hard and filled with desperation when the song called for it.

The smell of cigarette smoke, booze, sweat and lust was so strong that it didn't take Breed senses to detect it, Storme Montague decided as she sat in the corner of the room and watched the customers milling through the large area. A human with any sense of smell could detect it.

From where she sat she could see the Breeds in the far corner as the crowds shifted and moved between them. There were four, and she knew all of them. Not personally, of course. Storme knew a lot of Breeds—she'd made it her business to learn who they were, especially when she caught them trailing her.

Navarro, no last name listed, a Wolf Breed with Asian heritage. He was tall, dusky skinned with the exotic slant of eyes and high, flat cheekbones. Black, brown and a hint of gray filled his hair, though the gray wasn't from age, it was from the gray wolf genetics he carried. He was dressed a bit more sophisticated than the three he was with. Black silk slacks, leather shoes and a white silk shirt matched with an expensive black leather jacket.

His hair was long, falling nearly to the middle of his back as his black eyes, narrowed and intense, surveyed the room.

Lawe Justice and Rule Breaker were Lion Breeds. Both men were extremely handsome, as all Breeds were, and rumored to be full brothers, perhaps even twins. Shoulder-length black hair was pulled to the napes of both men's necks while their powerful bodies were attired in jeans, boots, T-shirts and denim jackets.

It was the fourth one that seemed the odd Breed out. He sat back casually in his chair, one hand lying on the table, his fingers tapping to the music as he glanced at the dance floor and the women that sauntered around the table to attempt to draw the men's attention.

Blue eyes. Ocean blue. She could see those eyes each time she caught a glimpse of his face through the crowd. Long red hair flowed past his shoulders, coarse rather than soft, and was tied back at his nape as the others were, though it had the appearance that it was tamed only under protest.

Squared, strong features drew instant female attention, as did the exotic eyes that appeared to be lined with the faintest edge of kohl. High cheekbones, well-molded male lips, broad shoulders, a strong chest and impressive biceps. He was larger and broader than the other men and looked exactly like what he had been created to be. A Scots warrior. He would have looked at home in a kilt with a sword strapped to his waist.

Leather pants, heavy boots, white long-sleeved shirt and leather riding jacket was the perfect covering for him. It made him look harder, broader, more dangerous.

He was Styx Mackenzie, the one Breed she was seriously growing tired of playing games with. He had been on her ass for more than a year now, off and on, determined to track her down and force her to listen to the proposition the Breed community had for her.

She already knew the details. Protection in exchange for information.

She wanted to laugh at the thought. As though a Breed could ever protect her. They would be more inclined to tear her throat out if she displeased one of them.

A flash of memory, buried so deep that she rarely let herself remember it, had her eyes closing briefly as she fought it back.

Her brother's death. The Breed ripping out his throat, the sounds of James's last gurgled breath and her father's cry of fear and pain.

They should have gone with her. They should have escaped as well rather than staying behind to destroy the last of the files they had on whatever secret project they had been involved in. That information had been more important than their lives. More important than her life, because her father entrusted her with the care of it, despite the fact that he should have known the Council would know exactly who he would have given it to.

The Council scientists knew, and the Breeds knew, and she had been running from both for the past ten years.

She was tired of running, but there was a part of her that still refused to give up the information she had.

Glancing down at her hands, she watched as she twisted her mother's antique ring on her finger. The wedding band her father had given her mother had been in the Montague family for generations upon generations. The diamonds, sapphires and emeralds were family jewels, the blues and greens family colors. And Storme was now the last of the Montague line. There were no sons left to carry on the name and there would be no daughters left to wear the ring.

The ring had been intended for James's wife, a wife he never had because the danger of the job he had undertaken with his father had been too great.

Creating Breeds.

She glared across the room at the four Breeds. Monsters. Animals. She hated every damned one of them. As far as she was concerned there was no crime greater than that of creating such farcical replications of humans and trying to convince the world they deserved to move freely among them.

Hatred swirled inside her for the loss of her father, her brother, the loss of her childhood and the dreams she had had of freedom. Dreams that had never come to fruition because each time she thought she had found peace, Breeds had managed to find her.

It didn't matter if they were the few Breeds still aligned with the Council or those who proclaimed to desire nothing but peace and freedom. They were all killers. They all wanted her for a reason, for the information they thought she had.

As she glared across the room, his head turned. Blue eyes, radiating amusement and warmth, met hers and locked. For the space of no more than a second, Storme felt mesmerized, locked in a circle of hatred, anger, laughter and hunger.

She had rarely looked into a Breed's eyes. They were too intuitive, their senses too sharp for you to hide if they managed to look into your eyes. But this time, for that second as the crowd parted, he held her.

Then, like an erratic school of fish, dancing bodies separated them, flowed between them, breaking the contact but assuring Storme that she was hidden no longer.

She came out of the booth instantly, moving along the edge of the crowd at a near run as she moved toward the back entrance of the bar.

She had to get out of there. She had rushed inside to hide, only to be followed by the four bastards that had obviously been tailing her. She had thought, this close to Haven, the Wolf Breed Sanctuary, that maybe she could rest for a few days, stay hidden and figure out what to do next.

They were getting too close. Her hotel room had been ransacked the night before, and the only reason she hadn't been there was because she had slipped out for fast food and walked to a nearby restaurant rather than driving. Her car had been parked in the parking lot of the hotel, her belongings in her room destroyed, the car broken into.

There was no escape now. Until she acquired another vehicle, she was fucked. If she didn't get the damned Breeds off her ass, then she was fucked anyway.

A quick check behind her had her sighing in relief as she

pushed through the back entrance into the dimly lit back alley of the bar.

Aldon, Colorado, had grown over the past ten years after the Wolf Breeds had been granted the nearly three hundred thousand acres of land the government had once set aside as a wildlife preservation area. The grant had given the Wolf Breeds the land in reparation for the American government's part in their creation and torture for so many decades.

Storme didn't advocate torturing any creature, but she didn't advocate allowing them to run wild outside confined areas either.

Feeling for the weapon she carried beneath her jacket, Storme closed the door behind her and began moving quickly for the end of the alley.

Head down, the bill of the baseball cap she wore shading her face, she prayed the small amount of scent neutralizer she'd applied to her body would work its miracle and hide her from sensitive Breed noses for a bit longer.

She was running out of the formula used to hide from the Breeds that she tried to keep on hand for emergencies. The spray-on camouflage had saved her life more than once in past years, but lately she'd been forced to rely on it more and more. It was almost as though it wasn't working any longer.

"Well it's about time."

Storme drew up short, her head jerking up at the malicious tone as a dark figure stepped from the shadowed indent of a closed doorway at the edge of the building.

Coyote.

Stepping back she stared into the cruel dark eyes as the Coyote Breed was joined by a partner from the building on the other side of the alley.

She knew this Coyote. He'd been chasing her for the past four months. He seemed to be a bit more tenacious than most, or just more scared of whoever controlled him. It surprised her that he'd brought company though.

"Two against one. You boys like to hedge your bets, now don't you, Farce? So, are you Council or Haven Breeds?"

They had been doing that for a while, sending teams out rather than a lone Breed to capture her. Farce, another Breed with no last name, had shed more than his fair share of blood over the past six months as he followed her.

But the Breeds chasing her for the past ten years were known for that.

"Does it matter who sent us?" the first Breed asked, his tone rasping, rough with a cruel edge of intent.

Hell, she would have thought she could have figured out who his handlers were by now, but Farce was a bit more mysterious than most Breeds. There were no records of him in the Breed or Council databases she had managed to hack. Even her sources within the Council didn't seem to know who he was or who he worked for. Not that she trusted those sources, but it was the best she had to work with.

"Well, a girl likes to know the origins of the Breed courting her," she mocked. "It does make all the difference."

Between life and death in some cases.

She hadn't managed to truly upset Haven's Breeds yet. Of course, she hadn't been forced to kill one as far as she knew either. The Council bitches on the other hand were another story.

She slid her hand beneath her jacket, fingers curling over the butt of the precise, illegal laser blaster she carried there.

"Come on, bitch, let's not get into a firefight here," Farce suggested, though his tone was anything but conciliatory as he noticed the movement. "I don't think our bosses would like it near as much if we brought you in dead."

Which still didn't tell her which faction had sent them.

"Ten years and you still haven't given up." She shook her head in disbelief. "What will it take to make you understand that whatever you want, I simply don't have."

"You have something," the other Breed growled. "Or you'd already be dead."

That she didn't doubt in the slightest. Neither the Council nor the Bureau of Breed Affairs were known for their patience in acquiring whatever they wanted.

"Well, I guess we're just going to have to quarrel over this." She could feel the panic beginning to edge inside her now, the fear she had fought since the night her father and brother had been killed.

She gripped the butt of the weapon, her finger sliding over

the automatic trigger as her gaze moved quickly behind the Coyotes. She didn't want to hurt innocent bystanders, but she wasn't letting them take her. She didn't dare.

Life meant a lot to her, and freedom, as dangerous as it could be at times, was still a hell of a lot better than what was waiting for her in either Breed or Council control.

They both wanted something from her. The same thing— information they believed she held. Information her father had given her before he was killed.

She had sworn she would only give it to the person her father had promised would come for it. It was the only task he had ever trusted her with, the only vow he had asked her to make. He and her brother had died for her safety; she wouldn't betray them.

But she was so tired.

She was tired of having to fight to live, so tired of running.

Farce stepped closer.

"Please, let's not play this game," she whispered. "Tonight, one of us will end up dead, Farce. That's not what I want."

A hard, sardonic chuckle rasped from his throat as Storme felt resignation begin to fill her.

"Hell lads, what ye doin' cornerin' a pretty lass like this in the dark?" Mocking, smooth and sexy, the Scots brogue had the Coyotes facing her stilling even as Storme restrained the curse rising to her lips.

Storme turned, careful to keep both the Coyotes and the newcomer coming from behind her in the corner of her eye, and watched as Styx Mackenzie moved from the back entrance into the alley.

"Well, isn't this my lucky night?" she drawled.

"I was rather thinkin' the same thing, lass." He chuckled.

The weapon he carried loosely in the crook of his arm was big, heavy and lethal. The fully automatic laser rifle would put holes in a Breed that would leave nothing left to identify, let alone survive.

"You're making a mistake, Wolf," Farce growled, but she heard the defeat in his voice.

"Lad, anytime I'm rescuin' a pretty little thing from your clutches, then my time's not bein' wasted." Smooth as aged whisky, rough, filled with amusement, that brogue seemed to caress the senses despite the fact that there was nothing about Breeds that she considered the least bit caressive.

"Run along now puppies, and I'll pretend to be the nice Breed everyone thinks I am and let you live for another day."

Storme searched for a way to escape and came to the conclusion that she was stuck between a rock and a hard place in the most literal sense.

"This isn't over." Farce directed his comment to her.

Storme kept her mouth shut. The Wolf Breed standing so imposing and determined to her right seemed to have the bluff on the bastards to her left.

That meant the Coyotes were Council controlled. She knew Styx was a part of the Wolf Breed community Haven. Since he appeared less than friendly and certainly familiar with Farce, it answered the question of his handlers.

Farce snarled back at her, his canines gleaming in the dim light, before he and his partner slowly eased back, each man disappearing around the side of the building.

Running was an option now.

"Lass, they're just waitin' until you try to run," Styx warned her as he lowered the weapon before moving to the lethal black motorcycle she had only now realized was sitting in the shadows. "I can give ye a ride wherever you're goin', if you like."

She stared at him in confusion. This Breed had been tracking her for nearly as long as Farce had been, yet he acted as though he didn't know her.

She almost smiled.

"Ye know, the scent of your fear is being overshadowed by the vaguest scent of pure devilry." His smile flashed in the darkness. "Come on now, I've work to be doing tonight. Let's not waste our time here."

"And your work is?" She didn't budge.

He grunted at that. "Chasin' shadows, if you be askin' me."

"You're a Breed," she said, making certain she did nothing to deliberately deceive him. She was well aware that Breeds could clearly scent emotions, deceit and lies.

"No? How did you figure that one?" He laughed back at her as he pushed the weapon into a compartment at the side of the cycle's base before turning back to her. "Come now, don't leave me to worry about ye for the rest of the night. I've another woman to track down; then I'd like to head to my bed for a wee bit of a nap sometime before dawn."

"Lost a woman, did you?" She stepped closer. It was possible that he didn't know what she looked like, that the neutralizer she wore had hidden her scent enough that he had no idea who she was.

She couldn't imagine he would get this close to her and not jump her if he knew who she was, if he knew she was the shadow he was chasing.

"Let's say, there's a lass that enjoys playing hide-and-seek." He chuckled as he reached back and scratched his neck with the air of a man that found that confusing. "Some women enjoy games I've found."

"And you don't?"

"Only if it involves chocolate and sweet, heated flesh," he drawled with a quick, charming grin before straddling the motorcycle and turning back to her.

Patting the seat behind her, he watched her expectantly.

"And I'm supposed to trust you?" she asked.

"Beats the alternative, lass." He glanced back at the entrance to the alley. "You can ride out of here with me safe and sound or take your chances with Farce and his buddy, Max."

Max, interesting name for a Coyote Breed.

"They didn't seem like the type to take home to Mother," she commented as she took another step toward him.

"Hell, are any of us?" He chuckled. "Come on sweets, pony up and let's ride."

He had no idea who she was. Storme moved closer to the cycle, watching him warily as she felt a strange tingle of anticipation running through her.

"So you're searching for your shadow tonight then?" she asked as she did as he suggested and mounted the bike behind him.

"Perhaps." He shrugged. "I'm the new Breed here tonight, you might say. When I couldn't find the lost little waif on my own, they sent in reinforcements."

He didn't sound as though it bothered him.

"I thought Breeds could scent their prey a mile away," she

commented as the powerful motor began to throb beneath them.

"Here, lass." He handed her a helmet.

Pulling it on, she found the headgear was equipped with communication devices, evident by the short mic that rested close to her lips.

Following suit, he pulled on a larger, full-face helmet he had taken from the handlebars and strapped it on.

"You'd have to get a scent of your prey to track it first," he told her as he slid the powerful machine into gear and moved toward the entrance. "Hold on, we're gonna blast out, just in case."

Just in case Farce and Max were still waiting at the entrance.

He shot out of the exit as Storme gripped his waist and leaned in close to maintain her seat. The exit was exhilarating, filled with the throb of the cycle beneath her, the heat of the Breed in front of her, and the danger that could be waiting just outside the alley.

But it seemed Farce and Max had slunk back into whatever slum they were hiding in. They weren't waiting outside the exit, though she was certain they were watching from nearby, just to be certain Styx hadn't left her alone.

"Where you stayin' lass?" he asked through the comm link.

"The Lincoln Arms," she answered. It seemed she would be renting another hotel room for the night.

"You'll be easily found there if Farce and Max decide tonight's the night for havin' fun," he told her. "Ye'll need to check out and find another hotel."

"Suggestions?"

He was silent for several moments. "Hell, get a room at my hotel for the night. I'm not leavin till mornin', and knowin' Farce, he'll definitely be lookin' for ye tonight."

What an interesting invitation.

Could she be wrong? Was he simply more deceptive than most Breeds?

"I thought you were chasing shadows tonight?"

He chuckled again. "Join me for dinner and I'll let my friend continue the chase while I enjoy your fair company for an hour or so. It's not as though I've picked up the scent of her yet. I'll be of little use to them."

She had been successful. In the months this Breed had been tracking her, she was aware that he had never really gotten that close. He was always several steps behind her, there but not really a threat.

Maybe the neutralizer combined with her attempts to stay on the move had managed to put enough distance between them that she could remain hidden for just a little longer.

"So how 'bout that offer of dinner?" he asked. "The hotel I'm at has excellent room service."

She could rest. Maybe he would even be nice and get the room.

"The Lincoln was the cheapest accommodations I could find," she said regretfully. "I can't afford anything more expensive."

"Never fear, I've a suite. I know how to share."

She just bet he did.

"What about your friends?"

"They're not invited," he growled good-naturedly. "Let's say I know who to share with, and some treasures are like fine chocolate and meant to be enjoyed without company."

So his friends wouldn't be there.

"Are there strings attached?" She had no intention of becoming his playmate or his chocolate for the night.

"Only if you want them," he promised. "Come on lass, I'm the knight in scuffed and dented armor tonight, remember? Besides, some things a man doesn't force, if ye know what I mean."

She knew a bit about this Breed, and that seemed to be a philosophy he lived by. Of all the Breeds that had been sent for her, Styx was known more for his playfulness toward women than anything else.

At the moment, he was the safer bet though. No doubt Farce and his buddy would track her to the Lincoln before the night was over. They had tracked her to the last hotel she'd taken, and she'd lost the security of her vehicle, her clothing and several weapons.

She was hungry, tired, and just wanted a chance to rest for a few hours. A nice meal would be a hell of a bonus.

Styx Mackenzie was still a Breed. He killed, and it was rumored he killed with a smile. But the only hits she knew of him making were against Council soldiers, Breeds or scientists.

She wasn't naïve enough to think she knew all there was to know, or that this Breed wasn't as deceptive, bloodthirsty and capable of damned near anything. The simple truth was that he was her only chance of escaping a fate worse than him tonight.

Of course, could there be any fate worse than a Breed?

"Here we go, sweets." The motorcycle roared up to the entrance of the most exclusive hotel in the sprawling city.

"You're a Breed, why not stay at Haven? It's not far from here," she asked as she dismounted and pulled the helmet from her head.

"Lass, I told ye, I'm supposed to be workin'. If I were at Haven, then my boss would realize I'm more intent on the pretty lass some Coyote Breeds were harassing than the one I'm ta be lookin' for." He winked with a quick grin as he pulled the wicked black helmet from his own head and then he secured both pieces of headgear to the side of the motorcycle before tossing the keys to the valet. "Did you know we were followed?"

He placed his hand against the small of her back, forcing her forward rather than allowing her to turn and glance behind her as she would have done. As self-preservation urged her to do.

"They followed then?" The weariness was dragging at her.

The Coyotes Breeds chasing her had stayed hard on her ass for weeks, giving her very little time to sleep and no opportunities to find the odd jobs that had sustained that pesky desire she'd acquired for food.

"They followed, but we'll take care of it," he promised as he guided her through the elegant lobby to the elevators on the other side. "It would be interesting to hear how ye managed to acquire their attention though."

The edge of amusement in his voice assured her that he wasn't really suspicious . . . maybe.

"Same ole, same ole." She shrugged, thankful that certain Coyote Breeds had the same reputation that a member of a criminal family may acquire. "All you have to do is be in the wrong place at the wrong time."

"That's fairly accurate." There was a hint of a growl in his voice now and less of that Scottish brogue that she realized had managed to calm her some small amount.

That surprised her. Breeds had a tendency to make her incredibly nervous, and she never allowed herself this close to one.

"Here we are." The elevator came to a smooth stop on the top floor, the doors opening soundlessly to the secured eleventh floor. "I've a suite here. You can have a lovely meal with me. The chef in the kitchen is damned near a genius with food, and let's not discuss his abilities with chocolate." There was an edge of love in his voice.

That was right. This was the Breed known to love his chocolate. She'd heard rumors, jokes, and had even eavesdropped on a conversation between two other women several nights before regarding his penchant for women and chocolate together.

He was known to kill with an easy smile and a complete lack of mercy, then turn around and devour chocolate as though it were the nectar of the gods.

"Here we go." He opened the door to the suite and escorted her in as though he were no more than a good Samaritan, eager to please and store brownie points.

The suite was elegant, with soft cream carpeting, caramel leather furniture grouped in a seating area in front of a large television screen. To the side, an eight-place conference-and-dining table sat, and through double doors, she glimpsed a king-sized bed that looked airy and comfortable.

"There's another room through here." Styx opened another set of doors to reveal another bed that looked just as comfortable.

God, she would give her eye teeth to curl beneath the snowy white comforter and just sleep until she couldn't sleep another wink.

"Dinner menu is on the table," he told her as he strode to a wet bar behind the table. "What would ye like to drink, lass?"

Something strong enough to make her forget he was a Breed. That was what she wanted. Something that would loosen the knot of fear in her stomach and allow her to relax long enough to enjoy a few hours without the threat of Breeds hunting her.

Styx had no idea who she was. As far as he was concerned, she was just another woman he wouldn't mind fucking. The fact that he obviously had an ulterior motive for helping her should have pissed her off rather than intriguing her. Maybe she was just too damned tired to care?

Moving to the menu, she stared down at it for long moments, mouth watering, fighting to make a choice.

"Why don't I just order a sampler of the chef's favorite fare?" he suggested when she didn't answer.

"That sounds perfect." Clearing her throat, she looked around the opulent room once again. "Haven takes care of its Breeds while they're on a mission."

He chuckled at that. "Ah, lass, if only I could convince them to be so kind. No, the suite was in exchange for a fine hand of poker I played. The owner lost, I won. Unfortunately, he was a bit short on cash at the table, and I don't take IOUs. So we made a bit of an exchange."

"Must have been a hell of a hand," she commented.

"Lady luck was smilin' on me. Now, about that drink?"

From #1 *New York Times* Bestselling Author

LORA LEIGH

and National Bestselling Author

JACI BURTON

NAUTI AND WILD

Two all-new novellas of the games men and women play between chrome and hot leather.

Lora Leigh revisits her sultry Southern landscape with a story of a good girl gone bad. But she's not the only one going down that road . . .

Jaci Burton writes the story of a hot biker hired to keep an eye on the reckless daughter of a Nevada senator. She's hooked up with a rival biker gang— a dangerous move that makes the wild beauty more vulnerable than she imagined . . .

penguin.com

M698T0510

Also from
#1 *New York Times* bestselling author

·LORA LEIGH·

Styx's Storm

A NOVEL OF THE BREEDS

When Storme Montague's father and brother are killed
by the Breeds, her father's research is also destroyed—
except for a crucial data chip that both the Council and
the Breeds would kill to possess. Betrayed to the Council, she is rescued by Styx, a Wolf Breed who is different
from most other Breeds she has ever known. Storme
has something he wants too—but it's not a data chip.

There's never been a woman who bad boy Styx
couldn't seduce. But can the charmer of the Wolf Breeds
charm the enemy?